THE VOODOO KILLER

A GRIPPING SERIAL KILLER THRILLER WITH A SHOCKING TWIST

DI STEPHANIE BROADBENT SURREY HILLS CRIME THRILLERS

BOOK 1

JACK PROBYN

CLIFF EDGE PRESS

Copyright © 2025 Jack Probyn. All rights reserved.

The right of Jack Probyn to be identified as the authors of the Work had been asserted him in accordance with the Copyright, Designs and Patents Act 1988. Published by: Cliff Edge Press, Essex.

This is a work of fiction. Names, characters, places, and incidents either are the products of the author's imagination or are used fictitiously. Any resemblance to actual persons, living or dead, businesses, companies, events, or locales is entirely coincidental.

No part of this publication may be reproduced in any written, electronic, recording, or photocopying form without written permission of the author, Jack Probyn, or the publisher, Cliff Edge Press.

eBook ISBN: 978-1-80520-195-3
Paperback ISBN:978-1-80520-105-2

First Edition

Visit Jack Probyn's website at www.jackprobynbooks.com.

In loving memory of Grandpa — my mate.

ABOUT THE BOOK

She returned home to start again. Instead, she woke the darkness she thought she'd buried.

DI Stephanie Broadbent hasn't been back to her hometown in over twenty years. A fractured childhood and a past best forgotten kept her away. But the sudden loss of a colleague leaves her burned out and broken—and the quiet promise of the Surrey Hills, along with a chance to reconnect with her sister, proves too hard to resist.

Peace, however, is short-lived.

Before she's even settled in, a university student is found dead in her halls of residence after a night out. What first appears to be an open and shut case takes a darker turn when a voodoo doll is found near the body.

With old memories resurfacing and members of her new team keeping her at arm's length, Stephanie is forced to confront the ghosts of her past—while racing to stop a killer whose next move is already taking shape in thread and cloth.

CHAPTER
ONE

In her eighteen and a half years of life, Jenny Wilde had never drunk as much alcohol as she had the night before. The past few days had been wild and had lived up to expectations. Freshers' Week. The first week of university. The first week of her newfound freedom. The first week of the rest of her life. So far, she'd spent it consuming dangerous and excessive levels of alcohol. Each night had grown progressively worse: doing shots in the kitchen, drinking in Leo's room – he had the biggest room on their level – before heading out to the club, where she'd spent an obscene amount of her parents' money. Eventually, she and her new best friends had called it a night; later and later into the early hours of the morning as the week progressed.

She couldn't remember what time they'd got home, but that was the last thing she cared about when she woke up. Water. She needed water. Beautiful, underappreciated water.

As she rolled away from the wall and lifted herself up to her elbows, the room began to swim, and the remnants of the night's take-away chips with cheese threatened to make a guest appearance on her bedsheets. She froze, closed her eyes, and willed the vomit back into her stomach. Carefully, she reached for the two-litre bottle of Tesco water beside her bed, unscrewed the lid, held the bottle to her lips, composed herself, swallowed the burp that had just exploded in her mouth, and necked the water as if she'd spent a month in the desert.

It seemed to do the trick, and after checking the time on her phone – an earlier than usual 10:24 am – she swung her legs off the side of the bed, shoved her feet into her *Shrek* Crocs, and shuffled into the bathroom. She was staying in International House, one of the few halls of residence on campus that offered en suite rooms for students. Naturally, the luxury came at a price, but she wasn't the one footing the bill. Thanks, Bank of Mum and Dad.

As she switched off the light in the bathroom, she heard noise coming from the kitchen down the hall. Laughter. With a serious case of FOMO – the fear of missing out – she draped her dressing gown over her shoulders and shuffled into the kitchen. Her floor had five other bedrooms. Five other flatmates.

She found three of them in the kitchen: Leo, Hannah, and Kamal, huddled over the kitchen stove. As soon as the smell of bacon hit her senses, the nauseating sensation in her stomach disappeared. She was cured!

'Here she is,' Leo called out as she entered. He was tall, muscular, had short-cropped hair, and was easily the most handsome person she'd ever seen.

She smiled at the sight of him. 'Morning,' she said, moving slowly to the fridge, where she found her carton of orange juice. She filled herself a glass from her designated cupboard on the other side of the kitchen.

'Want some bacon?' Leo asked. 'You're just in time.'

'Do you have to ask?'

Leo chuckled, then turned his attention back to the food. A few moments later, it was ready. They sat in silence as they each devoured their breakfast. When she was finished, Jenny gulped the rest of her orange juice and set the glass on the table with a heavy *clunk*.

'How you lot feeling?' she asked.

'Absolutely knackered,' Kamal replied, with the soft smile he seemed to offer everyone, as if he were constantly afraid of rejection and always seeking adoration in some form.

'My head's never hurt like this before,' Hannah replied as she sipped water from her Stanley cup.

All eyes turned to Leo, just as he placed the last of his food in his mouth. 'I don't feel that bad, to be honest.'

'That's because your body's a temple and you live off a thousand different vitamins every hour,' Hannah retorted.

Leo replied with a nonchalant shrug. 'Maybe you should try it.'

'No, thanks. I like the stuff that's bad for me.'

'You won't when you're forty.'

Hannah rolled her eyes. They'd only known each other for five days, and already she'd developed a dislike for Leo and his vain, slightly obnoxious personality. Sure, he was good-looking. But what made him so unattractive was the fact he knew it and insisted on encouraging everyone to live the same healthy lifestyle as him.

'Do you remember much of last night?' Jenny asked. 'It's all a blur for me. I remember bits of being in Popworld, but after that…'

'I don't remember much. But I know *you* were a mess,' Kamal said.

'I felt it.'

'You could barely stand.'

'Did I…' The hangxiety began kicking in. 'Did I do anything?' Suddenly the smell of tobacco activated in her brain, and she could taste it in her mouth. Then she remembered standing in the smoking area, cigarette in hand, puffing away like she was used to thirty a day when she'd only ever tried three in her life. She turned to Leo. 'You gave me a cigarette.'

'Only to stop you begging,' he replied. 'You wouldn't leave me alone.'

If only for another reason.

'What time did we get back?' she asked.

'Three-ish.'

Evidence of their night out and eventual return was all over the kitchen: the empty bottles of spirits on the counter, the jumpers and cardigans that had been discarded at the last minute before the cab had arrived, and the half-empty kebab box with scraps of food left inside.

As she stared at the food, a blinding pain swelled in her head, and she dropped to the table.

'I'm never drinking again,' she declared.

'Third time you've said that this week,' Leo replied as he climbed out of his chair and dropped his plate into the sink, where it would no doubt sit for a week like the rest of their crockery.

'Has anyone heard from Claudia?' Kamal asked.

'She left earlier with that guy, didn't she?' Hannah replied.

'Think they left after I got that round of Jägerbombs,' Jenny said, unlocking her phone. 'Did anyone hear anything when they came back?'

Her flatmates shook their heads.

'You reckon he's still here?' Hannah's eyes widened at the prospect of them catching Claudia's one-night stand victim doing the walk of shame.

As she said it, the sound of a door opening and closing reached the kitchen. Jenny, closest to the doorway, leapt out of her chair and hurried into the hallway. She stopped as soon as she spotted Shun-Chow, the international student who spoke little English and had uttered a handful of words to them since their arrival.

'Morning, Shun-Chow,' she said.

'Hi,' he replied shyly, before bowing his head and scurrying away to his room with his Tesco bag of food shopping.

Curiosity getting the better of her, Jenny hurried down the corridor and stopped at Claudia's room. They lived opposite one another. Hanging beneath the number 2 on her door was her name spelled out with Taylor Swift stickers she'd bought from Amazon. Jenny knocked, but there was no response.

She knocked a second time.

A third.

When there was still no response, panic began to creep in. Claudia was always quick to open the door or call out if she was in the bathroom. But this time there was nothing.

Jenny grabbed the handle.

'What're you doing?' Hannah asked. 'Don't, you'll—'

But it was too late. Jenny depressed the handle and, little by little, snuck in. She'd been half-expecting Claudia to leap out of bed and stop her. Nothing.

Jenny pushed, inching farther and farther into the cold room. The window had been left open. Her shoes were by the door. Several outfit changes lay discarded over the back of her chair, her books and notebooks were scattered across her desk.

There, in the corner of the room, lying atop her duvet, was Claudia, eyes open, staring at the ceiling, arm dangling over the side of the bed, dead.

CHAPTER
TWO

Her toes pressed into the crook of a gnarled branch, the bark slick with morning dew but still solid beneath her weight. She paused, her legs taut with strain, scanning the canopy above for her next handhold. A thick branch jutted out a few feet above her head – smooth on one side, knotted on the other – and she reached up, fingers brushing the bark and clinging on.

She was a little over ten feet off the ground, wearing nothing but her running trainers, leggings, and a damp nylon running shirt. Hardly tree-climbing gear. Her water bottle, phone, and house keys were tucked beneath a mossy root at the base of the oak, out of sight from the footpath behind her. It had been years since she'd last climbed anything higher than a stepladder – not since she was a teenager – but the tree had called to her, towering above the others as if daring her. She'd stumbled across it on her morning run through Chantry Wood and decided to climb it. She had nowhere else to be that morning.

The tree stretched up and up, branches like a staircase, only visible if you squinted just right. A fall from the top would be brutal, but she trusted herself. Trusted her grip. Trusted her strength.

Twenty minutes passed. The wind picked up slightly, cooling the sweat that had gathered at her temples. She hauled herself over the final stretch, the branches narrowing, and flexing under her weight, and settled into the crook, legs dangling freely beneath her. From there, the woodland fell away below her like a green ocean. The distant fields of Surrey peeked between gaps in the trees, hedgerows cutting through them like scars. Her arms throbbed with effort, biceps tight and forearms ablaze, but she welcomed the ache. It meant she was still capable. Still in control.

Now came the tricky bit: the descent.

With no rope, no harness, and no one to spot her from below, she'd have to climb down the same way she had come. Only slower. She reached for the first branch, her heart thudding as the downward stretch began. Breathing in, slow and deep. Trust the tree. Trust her grip.

Just as she was about to place her foot in the final foothold, her phone began ringing. The sudden, panic-inducing sound startled her. Her foot slipped from the groove, and she fell to the ground, landing on her shoulder. Ignoring the pain, she reached for her phone.

Kimberley, her sister.

'Hey,' she said, perching on the edge of a nearby boulder. 'Is everything all right?'

'Everything's fine. I just wanted to say congratulations to my big sister and good luck on your first day.'

'It's not until this afternoon,' she replied bluntly.

'What sort of job starts in the afternoon?'

'The type that requires long hours and a monumental amount of physical and emotional toil.'

'Sounds like my job,' Kim joked.

'Almost. I'm going in this afternoon for a meet and greet.'

'You got a bag of sweets at the ready?'

'Why would I have done that?'

'Like in primary school. You know, when you have to bring in sweets for the rest of the class on your birthday.'

'I bet you love it being a teacher. Get to take all the leftovers home.'

'My waistline doesn't.'

A man walking a dog wandered past. He said good morning, and Stephanie replied in kind.

'Who was that?' Kim asked.

'A stranger.'

'Where are you?'

'Climbing.'

'Where?'

'In the Chantries.'

'Outside? Alone? Steph…' her sister said with the same unimpressed tone a parent uses to their child. 'That sounds dangerous. I thought the idea was to start your first day without any broken bones.'

Stephanie massaged her shoulder. 'I'm fine.'

The sound of children screaming in the background echoed through the microphone. 'I told Dad you were starting today,' Kim said. 'I've been talking about this day for months, Steph. Ever since I found out you were coming back.'

'Yeah? That's good.'

'He'd probably tell you he's proud of you if he could. Finally coming back home after all these years. Have you thought about when you're going to see him?'

Stephanie hesitated before replying, even though she knew she should answer immediately. 'I've been busy.'

Kim sighed. 'You won't be able to use that excuse for much longer, sis.'

That was what she was afraid of.

'Anyway, I've got to go. Break time's over. Enjoy the rest of your morning. Have fun this afternoon. And *stop* climbing before you break something!'

Stephanie gave one last look at the tree before hanging up, retrieving her things, and continuing her run.

She made it half a kilometre along her route before her music stopped and was replaced by her mobile ringing again.

This time it was from a number she didn't recognise.

'Hello,' she said cautiously.

'Hey, Steph, it's DCI McGowan. Sorry to disturb your morning. I know we weren't expecting you until this afternoon, but something's come up. We need you at the University of Surrey campus as soon as possible.'

CHAPTER
THREE

The University of Surrey campus was nestled just outside Guildford's town centre. Founded in 1966 after being granted a Royal Charter, it had built a solid reputation for engineering, health sciences, and even space research. The campus had a modern, laid-back vibe and had produced its fair share of notable figures over the years, from TV presenters to physicists and CEOs.

Stephanie pulled into the entrance, drove past the famous stainless-steel stag statue at the mouth of the campus, and slowed to a stop at a small roundabout. Dozens of police cars were parked along the side of the road that wound around the north of the campus. In the background loomed Guildford Cathedral, a towering structure that was the focal point of the town and could be seen from miles away on the A3. She switched off the engine, climbed out of the car, and took stock of her surroundings. It felt strange to be there after such a long time, like stepping into an old family home. The three years she'd spent there had been some of the best of her life, during which she'd studied English Literature before eventually moving to Essex and finding a career in the police.

However, the campus had changed significantly since her last visit. The buildings had become more modern, and the grass greener. The standard of teaching and resources had undoubtedly improved. Yet she still felt that scintillating buzz, that atmosphere that rippled through the pavement and the buildings, as if it were carried on the wind that swept past her.

But now that buzz had a dark tinge to it.

Steph draped her backpack over her shoulder and hurried towards the uniformed constable stationed beside the outer cordon.

'DI Broadbent,' she said. 'I'm with Surrey Police.'

'Who?' the constable responded.

'DI Broadbent. I've just started.'

The constable checked his log. 'I've never heard of you.'

'That's because I'm new.'

The constable eyed her up and down, concerned that a detective inspector was arriving at a crime scene dressed in leggings and a running top.

'Do you have ID?'

'Only my Essex Police ID.' With a sigh, she reached into her backpack, produced it, and showed it to him.

The constable wasn't impressed.

'What're you doing here?' he asked. 'You're a long way from Essex.'

'I'm transferring. I start tomorrow. But DCI McGowan called me in early, as I understand there's been a potential murder in one of these buildings. Do you reckon you can let me through?'

The constable considered his answer for too long. Rapidly running out of patience, she moved beside him and tried to duck beneath the cordon. He stepped in front of her and raised a hand in her face.

'I'm gonna have to get it approved,' he said. 'I can't just let anyone through.'

I'm not just anyone, she thought. I'm going to be the SIO on the bloody case!

'Fine,' she said with as much venom as a wasp trapped in a jar. 'Do what you have to do. While you're at it, can you find me someone from the Major Investigation Team? They'll be able to confirm who I am. Or better yet, I'll get McGowan on the phone and you can speak with him directly, if you'd like?'

The constable hovered for a moment before eventually scurrying away to the nearest uniformed officer. Steph watched with renewed annoyance, arms folded, as they conversed. The second constable then glanced at her, nodded, and disappeared farther along the street, becoming the second in a long line of Chinese whispers. The officer in charge of the cordon arrived a moment later.

'We're just finding someone from the Major Investigation Team for you,' he said, turning his attention back to the cordon, signalling that he was finished with her and that she could do nothing but wait.

She stood there for five minutes, constantly checking the time on her watch, folding her arms, and huffing now and then to let the constable know she was less than impressed.

She understood he had a job to do, but she was frustrated that he was doing it properly, and was eager to get in there, believing they couldn't afford to waste any more time.

Another five minutes passed before anyone who looked remotely senior arrived.

The man who approached her was dressed in a white paper forensics suit. His mop of hair spilled out of the suit, thick, dark. Tall, and of medium build, he slouched as he walked, as though his parents had never taught him how to stand properly. He introduced himself as Detective Sergeant Devon Lafferty, and he was less than pleased to see her.

'Who are you?' he asked bluntly.

'Stephanie Broadbent,' she replied, matching his tone. 'I'm your new DI.'

He furrowed his brow as though someone had just taken the last slice of pizza from him. 'What're you doing here? You're not due till tomorrow.'

Stephanie explained.

Devon surveyed her outfit. 'You can't enter a crime scene wearing that.'

'I'll be in a paper suit. What's the problem?'

Devon didn't appreciate her tone, but she took it upon herself to duck beneath the cordon tape and hurry towards the forensics van. She returned a few moments later, clad in white.

'Where are we going?' she asked.

'International House.'

Without needing to be told where it was, Steph started towards the building that, from above, was shaped like the letter "E". As they moved along the street, the area became quieter and quieter, almost reminiscent of a zombie film set, with the faces in the student accommodation room windows those of people protecting themselves from the next wave.

They arrived outside the entrance to block D a few minutes later. There, they signed in at the inner cordon, thanked the constable standing guard, and started to climb the stairs.

'Third floor,' Devon instructed as he overtook her. He wanted to be the first to arrive. To be the one in charge.

A knot began to form in Stephanie's stomach. It was the same knot that formed every time she approached a crime scene. The one that constricted movement. The one that made her mind run away with itself and forced her to imagine the victim before she'd even seen them.

On the third floor, the corridor was teeming with crime scene investigators examining the carpets and the walls, ducking in and out of the rooms. Several of them were bagging evidence while others took photographs of the building and corridor, the flashes blinding her as she headed towards the first room on the right. The building was painfully silent, save for the sound of paper suits shuffling about.

The victim's room was exactly as Stephanie had imagined it: colourful, vibrant, and full of life. Full of hopes, dreams, and expectations; hopes, dreams, and expectations that had been cut drastically short. On her immediate left was the en suite bathroom. In the far right corner was a desk and two shelves. On the far left, the bed. Perched on the bookshelf were the hallmarks you might expect from a student's room: bottles of vodka and other spirits waiting to be eagerly consumed; course books that would no doubt last longer than the alcohol, perhaps gradually collecting dust; and reminders of home. Photos of family and friends adorned the shelves and walls. From them, Stephanie saw a young, pretty, enthusiastic woman with a beautiful smile staring back at her. The body on the bed had lost that vibrancy, and worst of all, lost that smile.

Three other bodies, not including the victim, occupied the room. Devon pointed to the only other male and introduced him.

'This is Kenji. Crime scene manager.'

Kenji, a Japanese man with warm, pleasant eyes, turned to Stephanie and held out his hand.

'Pleasure to meet you.' His accent was barely discernible, almost non-existent.

'Likewise. Who do we have here?'

'Claudia Bellini. Eighteen years old. First-year student studying food science, nutrition, and dietetics.'

Stephanie glanced at the inches-thick textbooks on the shelf. The knot in her stomach tightened.

'She was found this morning by her housemates. Four of them entered, so naturally they've contaminated a lot of the scene. Nevertheless, we're bagging and photographing everything we can. We should have it completed by the end of the day.'

Stephanie nodded. 'When's the pathologist coming?'

'In an hour,' Devon answered sharply. 'I've already contacted them. I'll deal with them when they get here.'

Stephanie didn't appreciate his tone but chose not to rise to it. She glanced at the body.

The young woman – who, in Stephanie's mind, was practically a girl – was still dressed in her clothes from the night before. A short skirt with tights. A thin black crop top that covered her top half. She wore no bra. A silver necklace sparkled in the light. On her face, her make-up was perfect. So detailed, so expertly applied. And yet none of it indicated how she'd died.

Stephanie took a moment's quiet reflection before asking, 'Where are the people who found her?'

CHAPTER **FOUR**

Naturally, Claudia's flatmates were distraught and in desperate need of consolation. Three uniformed officers and a pair of paramedics had spent the last hour trying to do just that. By the time Stephanie and Devon found them in the campus garden, a small green space managed by the University's Garden Society, all four flatmates were sitting on a garden bench, sobbing into each other's arms.

'I'll handle this,' Devon said as they approached.

Stephanie stopped and held him back. 'No, you won't. I'm SIO.'

He scoffed. 'Not until tomorrow you're not. For now, this is *my* investigation, and I'll handle this. They're *my* key witnesses.'

'*Our* key witnesses,' she corrected. 'One team. One investigation.'

'Uh-huh,' Devon said snidely. With a tug of the arm, he pulled away from her and started towards the flatmates.

Two women. Two men. Though none of them looked old enough to be classed as that. They all looked as though they should be completing their GCSEs and considering what A-levels to take. The females sat on either side of one of the males, who had his arms around both of them, as if they were his for the week.

Just as Stephanie was about to introduce herself, Devon beat her to it. 'I just wanted to ask you some questions about what you saw,' he said before she could open her mouth.

'Of course, anything you need,' Leo answered with the confidence and arrogance of a high school jock, flashing a leery smirk at them. The girls on either side of him nodded as if they had guns to their heads. The other male at the end offered a polite nod in agreement.

'I want to start by asking about last night,' Devon began, but Stephanie cut him off.

'Where are you guys from?'

The students shared confused glances between themselves and Stephanie. They continued to sniffle and wipe away their tears.

'Bristol,' answered Leo, eventually.

'Manchester,' replied Olivia.

'Nottingham,' said Kamal.

'Peterborough,' added Hannah. 'And Claudia was from Birmingham.'

'Far and wide,' Stephanie responded. 'What are you all studying?'

Devon shot her a disapproving stare, which she and the rest of the group ignored.

Leo pointed to himself and Kamal. 'We're both doing economics, Olivia's doing Maths, and Hannah's doing…'

'Veterinary Medicine and Science,' Hannah finished.

'Nice,' Steph said, smiling at each of them. They responded in kind, relaxing a little and becoming more at ease in the presence of police officers. 'That's quite an array of courses. I remember when I came here, a long time ago now, to study English.'

'You studied *here*?' Olivia asked.

Steph nodded. 'Like I said, many years ago. But it was great. The place has changed a lot since then; it's got much bigger, and I don't remember there being as many student houses. I was surprised to see Casino is no longer in existence.'

Olivia tapped her hand on the table. 'Ugh! My mum was devastated when she found out. She used to go there *all the time* when she was younger. Said it was the best place on earth. I think it's where she met my dad…'

Stephanie chuckled. 'It had its moments. Where's *the* place to go nowadays?'

Devon made to interrupt, to bring the topic of discussion to a close, but Hannah made sure to cut him off. 'The students' union, Rubix,' she said, giving him a sideways glance before addressing

Stephanie. 'It's Freshers' so they've got loads of special gigs and acts planned.'

'Freshers' week? Already?' Stephanie said to herself. She remembered it fondly. The late nights. The alcohol. The new people. The new friends. The pure euphoria of being away from home, enjoying her newfound freedom. 'Is that where you went last night?'

'Last night?' Kamal said, panicked. The four students looked at one another, as if they were in trouble.

'From the stench of alcohol coming from all of you, at I assume you went out somewhere last night. Same with Claudia.'

A moment of solemnity swept through them and they looked down at the table, avoiding her gaze.

'We didn't go to Rubix.' The responsibility of answering the question naturally fell on the most confident of the lot. 'My girlfriend's brother owns one of the new clubs that's just opened in town – Red One. So we went there. He got us free entry and discounted drinks. None of us were up for going to the headphone disco at Rubix, so that's where we ended up.'

'Red One?' Stephanie repeated, making a mental note.

Leo nodded. 'He's a big *Star Wars* fan.'

'Can you remember what time you got there?' Devon asked, finally joining the conversation.

'It was about half eleven,' Olivia replied. 'We were having pre-drinks in the kitchen before we got an Uber over there.'

Devon confirmed their time of arrival with Leo's Uber receipt: 11:32 pm. 'How many of you went?'

'Five of us,' Kamal answered. 'Us four, and then Claudia.'

'What about the sixth person on your floor?' Stephanie asked.

'We offered, but he doesn't drink, and he doesn't speak very good English. He keeps to himself mostly.'

Steph made a mental note for someone to speak with their last flatmate, preferably after she'd met her new team.

'What can you tell us about last night?' Devon continued. 'More specifically, what happened with Claudia? How was she behaving? How much had she had to drink? Was she with anyone?'

'She was with some guy,' Olivia answered. Stephanie thought she noticed a hint of disdain in her voice, as if she were envious of Claudia's success. 'They were necking the entire night, pretty much as soon as we got there.'

'Did they know each other?' Devon asked.

Olivia shook her head. 'Don't think so. I think they just fancied each other straight off the bat. She was pretty drunk.'

'Did he buy her drinks?'

Olivia nodded. 'I kept an eye on her the entire night, and he bought her a couple. But I don't think he spiked her with anything.'

Stephanie hadn't seen any signs of sexual assault; Claudia's clothes were still on so she didn't think it likely. Besides, if there were drugs in her system, by the time the pathologist ran their tests, they would all have gone.

'What happened at the end of the night?' she asked. 'What time did you all leave?'

'*We* all left at the same time.' Leo checked his Uber app again. 'We got picked up at 2:46. Then we went to the chip shop on campus and got some food.'

'Where was Claudia?'

Answers escaped the group. They all not-so-surreptitiously looked at one another, deciding amongst themselves who would be the one to answer. In the end, Olivia, pushing her hair back behind her ears, said, 'She left early with the guy. She said they were coming back here.'

'What time was that?'

'I think they left about one-ish.' She pulled her phone from her bra and stared at the screen. 'I messaged her afterwards to let me know when she got home.'

'And did she?' Devon asked, his tone accusatory.

Olivia stared at the last text message between them for a long time. 'She said, "Don't knock when you come home" with a wink emoji.'

'What time was that?' Stephanie asked, jumping in before Devon could.

'One fifty-eight.'

'Nearly an hour later?'

'I guess.'

'It's not that long a walk, is it?' Devon asked.

'Depends how legless you are,' Stephanie replied. 'Besides, we don't know what they did on the way back. They could've stopped for food. One of them could've been chucking up. They could've been making out the entire way.'

Devon pretended he hadn't heard anything Stephanie had just said and turned his attention back to Claudia's flatmates.

'We need to know everything about this guy that she was with. What can you tell us about him?'

Twenty minutes later, they were done. Stephanie thanked them all for their time, offered her condolences, handed over her contact details, and suggested they get in touch if anything came to mind. After returning the students to the capable hands of the uniformed constables who had previously been catering to them, Stephanie started towards her car.

'Where are you going?' Devon asked as he stuck to her side.

'To the office.'

'Why?'

'So I can start this investigation.'

'I've already started it. Before you got here.'

'Uh-huh.'

She cut through a group of chatting CSIs and rounded the corner of a building before arriving at her car, moving about the section of the campus with the ease of someone who had been studying there for years. It all came flooding back to her.

As she placed a hand on the car door handle, Devon said, 'I'm coming with you.'

'Not in my car, you're not.'

CHAPTER
FIVE

DCI McGowan answered the call with a sigh. For a usually mild-mannered and fairly even-tempered individual, his initial reaction took Devon by surprise.

'Yes?'

'What's going on, guv?'

'What're you talking about?'

'Broadbent,' Devon replied as he climbed into the car and switched on the engine. 'Why has she come in and taken over this investigation?' He placed the phone on loudspeaker and dropped it onto the seat beside him. 'I thought I was handling this one.'

There was no response as Devon swung the car into a three-point turn and sped after Stephanie. For a moment, he thought the call had disconnected.

'I've given it to her,' McGowan answered calmly, as if he were speaking to a child. 'She'll be in charge eventually. It made sense for her to come in now.'

A thick stream of hot air exploded from Devon's nostrils and he drummed his fingers on the steering wheel as he approached a roundabout. After being cut off by some arsehole in a Tesla, his frustration increased dramatically.

'She can't just barge in like that. It isn't on.'

McGowan cleared his throat. 'DI Broadbent is a very senior and experienced detective. I can't imagine for one second she would have done anything intentionally to upset or offend you. She is brand new to this team, this area, and our way of working, and I would appreciate it if you gave her the consideration and respect she deserves.'

'If you knew she was coming today, why didn't you let me know?'

'You're right. I should have told you. While I'm at it, would you like me to inform you when I'm next going to the bathroom or when I've got my next doctor's appointment for my prostate check?'

That was the final word on the matter. Devon knew better than to push McGowan further. If he wanted to voice his opinions again, he would do it in person.

'Where are you?' McGowan asked as Devon overtook a car in the outside lane and sped up right behind another.

'On my way back. I'll be there in the next ten minutes.'

McGowan said nothing for a long time, preparing himself for what was about to come his way.

'Fine. We'll talk about it when you get here. Just don't drive like an idiot.'

'Wouldn't dream of it, sir,' he said, flashing his headlights and intimidating the car in front.

CHAPTER
SIX

DC Giles Swinger moved the computer mouse absentmindedly from one corner of the screen to the other, chewing on a piece of gum. Another quiet morning. Beside him was DC Olivia Willard, or "Wellard" as she was affectionately known. Not because she was a dog, but because she possessed the behaviour of one: loving, caring, and above all, loyal. Though, as far as she was aware, she'd been given the name because Willard was one vowel removed from the beloved *EastEnders* character, which also happened to be her favourite show.

They shared the same bank of desks, and in the past six months, since the office had last been reshuffled, they'd managed to accumulate a small mountain of mess between them. To the untrained eye, they were disorganised and always fumbling through sheets of paper for relevant information. But to those who knew them, they were methodical, diligent, and well-trained, so long as they were given treats for a job well done every now and then.

Olivia was in her mid-forties, and Giles considered her a mother figure in the office, the woman he could turn to for just about anything.

They all did.

Over the years, she'd been entrusted with so many secrets that Giles was certain she'd been forced to sign the Official Secrets Act at some point in her life. She knew everything, and so far she hadn't let him or anyone else down.

'I bit the bullet and *finally* watched *Made In Chelsea* last night,' she said, setting her can of Diet Coke on the table. It wasn't even midday, and already she'd gone through two cans of the stuff. She was addicted.

'And?' Giles said. 'What did you think?'

'That they're all a bunch of pompous arseholes. But I *will* admit, I got sucked in. And I hate myself for it.'

Giles smirked at her.

'You knew I would, didn't you? You knew my addictive personality would just suck me right in by my cankles.'

Shrugging, Giles responded, 'I have no idea what you're talking about. It's my only guilty pleasure, and now I *finally* have someone to talk about it with; someone who isn't my mum, anyway.' He turned around and gestured to the half-empty office, where the only sound was the monotonous clacking of typing and the low hum of the air conditioning unit in the ceiling.

Just as he finished, the main doors to the office swung open, and an attractive woman wearing a tight-fitting running outfit stormed in. Her dark brown hair was tied into a long ponytail, and her face looked as though she'd just completed a half marathon to get there. She was petite, barely visible over his computer monitor.

'Where might I find DCI McGowan's office?' she asked, an urgent, hurried tone in her voice.

Giles didn't answer. Instead, he stared into her dark brown eyes for a long while. In the end, he pointed to the other side of the room.

She thanked him and then raced over to McGowan's office. Giles and Olivia watched her go. Just as they turned to look at one another, DS Devon Lafferty barged through the door and stormed after her. A moment later, they both burst into the chief inspector's office.

Slowly, Wellard turned to Giles.

'Who's that?' she whispered. 'I've never seen her before.'

'I'm surprised you don't know. You're the office oracle.' Their attention remained transfixed on McGowan's office. 'If only we had cameras or microphones in there,' he said, 'we'd be able to hear everything.'

'This isn't an episode of your programme, Giles,' Wellard said. 'Though she's pretty enough to fit right in with that crowd.' The corners of her lips rose into a thin, wry grin. 'Is that why you panicked when you saw her? Were you put off by the pretty girl?'

Giles scowled at her. 'Shut up. No, I wasn't.'

She placed a mocking hand on his shoulder. 'All right, lover boy. Whatever you say. Maybe if you ask her nicely, she might watch an episode or two with you.'

CHAPTER
SEVEN

DCI Clive McGowan sat, an imposing figure, behind his small desk, one eye on his computer screen and the other on Devon and Stephanie before him. They looked like two naughty schoolchildren sent to the headteacher's office, though one appeared much happier to be there than the other.

The chief inspector's office was a small, square room. His desk, positioned slightly to the left, occupied centre stage. Natural light flooded in over his left shoulder through a narrow, floor-to-ceiling window, and beyond the glass was a picture-postcard view of the Surrey Hills, stretching into the distance, a tapestry of different shades of green melting into one.

Stephanie felt oddly soothed by the colours in her peripheral vision.

'Good morning, Detective Inspector,' DCI McGowan said, rising from his chair to shake her hand. 'Sorry to have you in under such circumstances.'

'Happy to be here,' she replied, releasing his grip. 'Nothing quite like jumping in at the deep end.'

McGowan, a man now on the other side of fifty yet looking twenty years younger, placed his palms on his desk and nodded towards Devon. 'I see you've already met one of your detective sergeants.'

Stephanie quickly flicked her gaze in Devon's direction but couldn't bring herself to look at him. 'We've exchanged a few words.'

'I trust he's made you feel welcome.'

Stephanie matched the knowing smile on McGowan's face and conveyed all she needed to with a look in her eyes.

'Has he told you about himself?'

Stephanie shook her head.

'I'll give you the brief intro, as he sometimes likes to belabour a point: Devon's been here for as long as I can remember – so long that I can't *actually* recall how long it's been – and he's been filling in as inspector for us while we've been waiting for you to arrive.' McGowan spoke calmly and deliberately. He flicked his head towards Devon. 'DI Broadbent has joined us from Essex Police. How many years' experience do you have?'

'Six in the role, fifteen in total,' Stephanie answered.

'A lot by any standard, so she knows what she's doing and how to get things done. She comes here with a strong pedigree, but I've been told – and from our brief discussions, I'm sure you won't mind me saying this, Stephanie – that she has none of the ego that often accompanies it. That's why she's here. And that's why she's going to succeed with Surrey Police. I think having an outsider will be good for the team and give you a small kick up the arse.'

Out of the corner of her eye, Stephanie saw Devon shift uncomfortably on his feet and scratch the back of his head.

'Yes, I get all that,' he said abruptly. 'And yes, it's very nice to meet you, Steph.'

'Stephanie,' she corrected, casting him a sideways glance. 'Not Steph, not Stephy, not even Steph-fanny like some of the kids used to call me in school. Only once you've earned my trust and respect will you be able to call me Steph.'

She wanted to set the record straight right off the bat, especially in front of the chief inspector, so if he tried anything funny, she wouldn't be the only one to call him out on it.

Devon nodded his understanding, though she sensed from his expression that he had no intention of using her proper name.

'What happens now, guv?' he asked. 'When the call came in this morning, you said I'd be in charge of the situation at the university.'

McGowan lowered himself into his seat, conserving his energy for the discussion. 'Plans change. You have to learn to be adaptable and overcome obstacles in this role, especially if you want to become an inspector one day.'

Stephanie picked up on Devon's sudden intake of breath.

'Besides, you knew about Stephanie's arrival. You knew the case would naturally fall to her. All I've done is bring it forward a few hours.'

Devon sighed heavily through his nostrils, filling the room with his disappointment.

'But—'

'Deal with it, Devon. Now, if you wouldn't mind, I want to have a word with our new inspector.'

Devon shifted his weight to leave, paused as if about to say something, then spun on the spot and left the office. The door closed more firmly than would be considered polite. As soon as he left, the pressure in the atmosphere dropped a few levels and McGowan let out a long, heavy sigh.

'Well... I see your reputation precedes you,' he said slowly. 'Good to see you've made a lasting first impression.'

Stephanie pulled a chair out from beneath his desk. 'Is he always like that?'

McGowan tilted his head from side to side. She got the impression that he was mild-mannered, highly intelligent, and very clever with his words. 'Only recently,' he answered.

Stephanie assumed he was referring to Devon's recent covering of her role and decided to leave it there.

'Looks like I have my work cut out for me, and I haven't even started yet,' she said.

'When you've been around as long as I have, you find that shouting rarely works. At least, not in the long run.'

'I was talking about the crime scene I've just come from.'

'So was I. If what I've heard is anything to go by, I don't think you'll have any issues here.'

That was what she was afraid of. This "reputation" he'd mentioned earlier. The one she didn't know she had. The one that suggested she was a brilliant detective, capable of solving the most confusing and heinous crimes. Like she was a female Sherlock Holmes.

She hoped he hadn't overstated her abilities.

The phone on McGowan's desk chimed. He glanced at the screen quickly before returning his attention to her. 'You're not the only one who's going to have some of those first-day nerves,' he said. 'There's another new starter. Detective constable, as green as they come. Twenty-six, fresh out of training. Her name is—'

He was interrupted by a knock on the door.

'Speak of the devil.'

McGowan beckoned the person in, and a moment later, a young woman popped her head around the door. Behind the nervous expression, Stephanie saw an attractive young woman with sea-blue eyes and striking eyebrows who looked younger than her years. If she hadn't known her age, Stephanie would have thought she was still in school.

'DCI McGowan?' she asked, her voice hesitant. 'Am I in the right place?'

'Welcome! Please, enter.' Clive climbed out of his seat and gestured eagerly for her to come in. He shook her hand, then gestured to Stephanie. 'Stephanie, this is Eve Hope. Eve, this is Stephanie Broadbent, your new inspector.'

Eve took Stephanie's hand, smiling awkwardly, revealing a dimple in her left cheek and a set of teeth that hadn't been tarnished by years of coffee drinking.

'Nice to meet you, Stephanie,' Eve said, perking up a little. 'Ma'am,' she corrected.

'Stephanie's fine.'

Behind Eve's shy nature, Stephanie thought she saw a more bubbly, outgoing person. It was only natural that she was nervous on her first day.

'Stephanie's joining us today as well,' DCI McGowan began. 'She's got a lot of experience, has been with the police for a very long time, and I'm sure she'll be a great mentor for you. You've arrived at the right time, as something came in this morning. Stephanie can bring you up to speed. Now, all that's left is for you to meet the rest of your team.' He rounded the side of his desk, shuffled past them in the tight space, and placed a hand on the door. 'Don't worry, they don't bite.'

CHAPTER
EIGHT

When they entered the main office, they found DS Lafferty standing in the centre of the room, addressing the team. He came to an abrupt stop as soon as he saw the chief inspector step out.

'Priming them already, are we, Sergeant?' Clive said jokingly, then gestured for the sergeant to return to his desk. Devon did so with the reluctance of a teenager being forced to stay downstairs instead of retreating to their room. 'Good morning, everyone. There are some new people I'd like you to meet.'

Without realising it, they manoeuvred to the front of the office. There, DCI McGowan began introducing them to the team. As he spoke, she surveyed the team in front of her, but she couldn't see any of them. Her mind had gone blank, their faces had become blurry, and McGowan's calm, soothing voice had faded into the background.

She was only vaguely aware that he'd finished speaking, thanks to the silence. Then she sensed their expectant stares looking up at her.

'Stephanie? Do you want to add anything?'

She swallowed deeply. Nausea suddenly washed over her, and she wished she was back in Essex, with her old team, in her safe space, where she knew everyone and everything.

Stephanie cleared her throat. 'I'm not very good with names, so you'll all have to bear with me on that front. It might take me a day or two, but there aren't that many of you, so I can't see it being too much of a problem. Other than that, nothing else to say other than I'm really looking forward to working with you all and getting to know you better.'

'Excellent,' McGowan said with a clap of his hands that pierced Stephanie's eardrums. 'Before I forget, your office is next to mine. One of the team can help you move in.'

With that, the chief inspector left and went back to his office. As soon as he closed his door, the nausea intensified, and a knot formed in her stomach, sending bile to her throat. Her safety net had gone. It was just her and her new team.

'Well…' she began, surveying the tapestry of faces in front of her, examining them each in turn. 'I appreciate your patience while I get myself up to speed with processes, where everything is, and who everyone is. The same goes for Eve. You'll have two people asking you questions, I'm sure. But in the meantime, while we get ourselves set up and familiar with everything, this morning, the body of a university student was discovered in her halls accommodation. Our victim is an IC1 female: Claudia Bellini, eighteen years old, originally from Birmingham, studying food science. We're still waiting for the crime scene images to come through. What I'd like is for someone to create a log on HOLMES. Who's in charge of…?'

A hand, belonging to a short woman with long, curly hair tied into a ponytail, shot up in the audience.

'Already done it, ma'am,' she said, her tone soft and soothing. Stephanie immediately felt a sense of calm and comfort from her. It helped that she had a warm smile to match. 'HOLMES log started, just waiting on your instruction on who needs to do what.'

'That's perfect,' she said. 'And your name is…?'

She placed a hand on her chest. 'Forgive me. I'm getting carried away with myself, as usual! Before you know it, I'll go back in my box and you won't hear from me again. I'm Olivia. Olivia Willard, detective constable, but you can call me Wellard. The rest of these lot do.'

A nickname. That was always a good start. It helped break the ice a little and gave a flavour of what the team's dynamic was like.

'Do we have an operation name yet?' Stephanie asked.

'Behind you,' came the coarse response from Devon to her left.

Fortunately, she noted his desk was on the other side of the room from her office.

Stephanie swivelled on the balls of her feet. Behind her, running across the entire length of the wall, was their major incident room. It was smaller than she'd been used to. Previously, with Essex Police, she'd enjoyed a separate room or space in the building where the team could collate their evidence and progress in the investigation. What stood in front of her, however, was a series of documents – photographs, printouts, handwritten notes – dangling from a row of corkboards and whiteboards. Immediately in front of her, scribbled in black dry-ink pen, was their operation name: Operation Lucifer. Beneath it was a blank space where, over the coming days, weeks, and months, they would collate their information. So far, the space had only been populated with the victim's name.

'I got Wellard to do it just now,' Devon added in what Stephanie thought was an unnecessary point-scoring exercise.

'Good work, Olivia,' Stephanie said. 'Thank you.'

Out of the corner of her eye, she saw Devon's smug expression flip upside down.

All right, Steph, she told herself. Time to take control. Time to show them what you've got.

She cleared her throat, grabbed a nearby pen, and moved towards the whiteboard with the confidence and composure of a schoolteacher conducting the same lesson for the hundredth time.

'Forensics are still at the crime scene. We'll need the photos through as soon as possible. I'd like someone to liaise with Kenji to find out when we can get them, along with the complete evidence list. First things first, however: this was someone's daughter. I would like our family liaison officer to track down the parents and notify them of their daughter's passing. Right now, I am treating this as a murder investigation. Who's our FLO?'

Another hand was raised. This time it was tentative, laden with caution. It belonged to DC Petal Baptiste, a West Indian woman in her forties. She wore a pair of thick glasses in front of a set of delicate, glowing eyes and her cheeks were slightly reddened with make-up that made her look like a Disney character. Stephanie felt an immediate motherly, comforting sense from her, traits that were ideal for her role.

'Pleasure to meet you,' Petal said. 'I'll get right on it.'

'Wait until you and I discuss our plan of action. I want to control what the parents know and don't know.'

Petal nodded almost tentatively, as if that were an unusual request.

'According to her flatmates,' Stephanie continued, 'Claudia spent her entire evening with someone at the club, Red One. The couple later decided to go back to hers at about one in the morning, a little over an hour and a half before her flatmates left the club and returned to their halls of residence. Firstly, we need to find out who she was with, and where that individual is now. He is potentially the last person to see her alive and is our top suspect.'

She pointed to two people at random in the room.

'Your name?' she asked the first.

'DC Giles Swinger,' he answered.

He was very handsome in an obvious sort of way, and he reminded her of Leo from the university. His hair was cropped short and gelled at the front. His jaw was angular, almost chiselled, and two red blotches were splashed on his cheeks above a patchy beard. For a moment, Stephanie thought it might have been out of embarrassment, but she realised she was wrong when she noticed his eyes flickering towards the equally attractive Eve Hope.

'Nice to meet you, Giles. I'd like you to visit Red One with...' She gestured to the woman sitting on the opposite bank of desks.

'DC Fiona Singleton, ma'am,' Fiona replied with the ebullience and excitement of someone who'd been wound up all night.

Stephanie was taken aback by Fiona's striking eyes. She was in her late thirties, and from her slim figure, looked as though she had the same fitness regime as Stephanie.

'I'd like you to join Giles and speak with the owner. See if you can ascertain who was working that night and find CCTV.'

'Sounds delicious,' Giles responded.

The unusual phrase took her aback. 'We will also need someone to liaise with the university.'

Another hand shot up, taking her by surprise. This one belonged to DS Noah Mackenzie, a man in his early fifties who raised the average

age of the team. He was dressed in unusual attire, with different-coloured neon socks being the first thing she noticed.

'I'd be happy to give them a call,' he said. His voice was deep yet possessed a controlled, reserved quality.

'I'd rather you paid them a visit in person. Find the right person to speak with and allay their fears somewhat. I suspect they'll be keen to send out a message to the students.'

He fired a finger gun in her direction. 'Aye, aye, captain. Whatever you say.'

Stephanie decided she was going to have a much easier life with one detective sergeant than the other. Just as the thought entered her mind, the other sergeant opened his mouth.

'And me?'

'I'd like you to manage the team while I'm gone,' she answered.

His face scrunched into a ball of frustration. 'Where are you going?'

'I need to get myself and Eve set up. Then I'm taking us to speak with the press before we attend the post-mortem. If I could ask that you summarise anything that happens in the interim for when I get back, that would be a great help.'

CHAPTER
NINE

The corner of the victim's bedroom containing the desk had been entrusted to CSI Matthew Morpurgo, while the rest of his colleagues were busy in the bathroom or making an awful din in the kitchen. They sounded like a bunch of baboons throwing plates, pots, and pans onto the floor, destroying any evidence.

Matthew, on the other hand, preferred to be more delicate with his processes. He liked to take his time and do a thorough job. That way, if there were ever any issues with evidence that had been missed or accidentally mishandled, nine times out of ten, he knew he was out of the firing line.

This crime scene was no different. He had been left alone in the bedroom for the past half an hour, perusing Claudia's possessions and looking into the window of her academic life through her textbooks and the notebook she'd started to scribble in to get a head start.

Matthew appreciated his job. It was cathartic, sobering, and by the end of it, he sometimes felt like he knew the victim better than their close family and friends ever had. Going through their belongings and peeling back the layers of their lives, he had an intimate view of their secrets, successes, struggles, and tribulations. He could peer behind the curtain and get to know the victim on a deeper, more profound level.

Claudia Bellini was no different. Like any teenager her age, she had her struggles, her difficulties. In another of her notebooks, one that had been wedged between a series of textbooks, he found a daily diary. In it, she had scribbled several entries from her first few days of Freshers'. Notes on how she'd been feeling. How she missed home already. How she could feel herself struggling with food. How it had only been a few days and she was already starting to lose control. The alcohol wasn't helping, but she felt she needed to drink to fit in with the rest of her flatmates. She thought they were all lovely, wonderful people whom she couldn't wait to live with for the rest of the year; except for Leo – she thought he was a bit of a creep, and she reckoned Hannah felt the same way.

Matthew was grateful her body had been bagged and removed from the crime scene. He wasn't sure how much he could have done with her lying behind him, her eyes staring lifelessly at the ceiling.

He had photographed each page of the diary, going back to the beginning, before bagging it up and placing it by the front door. So far, he'd managed to sift through over a dozen books, dusting for prints, checking for trace fibres, and photographing each page.

He turned his attention to the desk for a mental change. On it was Claudia's laptop, a wireless mouse and keyboard, a pen pot, and, bizarrely, a fully functioning microwave.

As Matthew crouched down, he winced in pain. His lower back had flared up again. He really should see the doctor about it, but he was afraid of what they might tell him; that they might confirm what he already sensed deep down.

Ignoring the pain with a few groans and grumbles, Matthew turned his attention to the microwave. First, he pulled out his dusting equipment, and with his fine brush, began rubbing the metallic compound onto the handle. A moment later, a fingerprint appeared. Matthew placed a strip on it and lifted the fingerprint.

Next, he photographed the front of the device before carefully opening it. As he did so, he noticed a Post-It note that had fallen beneath the device. He dragged it out and read it.

Open Me, it said.

But by that point, the door was already open.

He dropped the note as soon as he laid eyes upon what was inside.

There, sitting in the centre of the dish, was a dark brown voodoo doll. Two buttons sat perfectly in the places where its eyes should have been, and protruding from the centre of the doll's stomach was a brand-new kitchen knife that looked as though it hadn't been used.

Until then.

CHAPTER
TEN

Stephanie, Devon, Eve, and Noah hovered over DC Willard's computer. A photograph of the voodoo doll discovered at the crime scene occupied the entire screen. Stephanie felt uneasy looking at it. It seemed to be staring at her, calling her name. She had never been good with horror movies, or anything with an underlying threat of evil – she tried to avoid them at all costs – but despite how much she wanted to look away, she was unable to stop staring.

'This was discovered inside Claudia's microwave in her room,' Stephanie explained. 'The CSI who found it said that the knife became impaled in the doll *after* he'd opened the door.'

'Like a booby trap?' Eve asked.

Stephanie noticed the woman chewing on her fingernails and nodded. 'He found a note saying "Open Me" on the desk. It had fallen off and floated under the microwave.'

'The killer must have put it there,' Devon offered.

'She's at university. She's fairly intelligent. I can't imagine she would have needed an instruction to open the door every time she wanted to use it,' Stephanie retorted.

The comment elicited a deeply unimpressed glower from Devon, who folded his arms across his chest. Stephanie noticed Olivia Willard smirking up at her.

'Why would the killer have left that behind?' Eve asked.

'We don't *know* it was the killer,' Stephanie responded quickly, keen to interject before anyone else could. 'CSI lifted a print from the handle, and they're going to take the doll for examination, so if there are any matches, we'll find them. Besides, it could have been her flatmates or someone she knew playing a prank on her. We have no reason at this stage to unequivocally believe it was the killer. Yes, it makes sense for us to lead that way, but I don't want to make any assumptions until we know for certain.'

As she glanced up at the doll again, a lump swelled in her throat, and a bead of sweat formed at the nape of her neck. To combat her anxiety, she reached for her necklace and began tracing it around her neck. It had been her mother's, given to her when she passed away, and for Stephanie, it was more than just a comfort blanket. It was a memory, a lasting possession. She wore it everywhere and only ever removed it if absolutely necessary.

'I don't want us focusing too much time and effort on the doll for now. Our main priority is finding the man she went home with last night.'

She hoped she was more convincing than she felt.

The voodoo doll was bad news. As much as she didn't want to, she believed it could only mean one thing: that more victims were coming.

They had no idea when, or where, or who.

But one thing was certain.

If she didn't get a grip on her new team and the investigation, fast, they would find more of those dolls.

CHAPTER
ELEVEN

DC Fiona Singleton didn't know what to make of Stephanie. Her first impression was that she was understandably shy, nervous, and a little timid. But was she a good fit for the team? She wasn't sure. The team had worked together as a unit for the past four years – undisturbed and unperturbed – until their last detective inspector had moved on a few months before. That had been the only disruption the team had known. Over those years, they'd grown closer and built a strong bond with one another. They were cohesive and got the work done; Fiona hoped Stephanie wasn't going to come in and rock the boat. That didn't stop her from thinking she was attractive.

'What do you think of her?' Fiona asked as she jumped into the passenger seat.

'I think she's nice,' Giles replied, switching on the engine and looking in his rear-view mirror.

'Nice?'

'Yeah. Seems fairly outgoing. And she's pretty.'

That was something she agreed with him on.

'It will be interesting to see how Devon reacts to her,' she said.

'Eve?' Giles spun the steering wheel several times and pulled out of the car park.

'Eve? Is that who you're talking about? I was talking about Broadbent, idiot.'

'Oooohhhhh,' Giles said slowly as he pulled out at the junction and headed towards Guildford town centre.

She scoffed. 'Figures *you'd* be thinking about one thing.'

'Says you,' Giles retorted. 'I saw the way you were looking at her.'

Fiona rolled her shoulders to mask her discomfort. 'She carries herself well.'

'I think they'll both be good fits. They'll bring a different dynamic to the team. It's been getting a bit stale in there recently.'

They arrived at Red One a few minutes later. The small club was situated on the corner of a roundabout, wedged between a solicitor's office and, naturally, a kebab shop. To the untrained eye, it looked like a pebble-dashed house, were it not for the posters of the DJ acts and artists they had performing over the coming weekend. But to those in the know, it was a deep house nightclub filled with trippy strobe effects, smoke machines, and a narrow staircase leading to the toilets, designed to confuse and disorientate.

The only problem was finding a parking space.

Giles, however, didn't see it as an issue. He pulled up outside the kebab shop, bumped the kerb, and hopped out. The aroma of deep-fried food combined with a litany of herbs and spices quickly wafted up his nose and sent his stomach into a frenzy.

He suddenly fancied a side of chips. But he couldn't. He was trying to be good, trying to escape the hamster wheel of losing weight only to put it back on again after seeing how successful he'd been, only to become disgusted with himself before losing it again. Right now, he was in the losing phase and had seen significant progress. He was sticking to his fitness regime, eating mostly salads (and hating himself in the process), and had already shed a few kilograms.

Just a portion of cheesy chips... he thought, dreamily licking his lips. *Won't hurt anyone.*

The sound of a car horn blaring past them brought him out of his reverie and reminded him what he was there for. He followed Fiona to the front door. A stream of traffic trickled past them as they waited.

A moment later, a man in his early thirties, dressed in a tight-fitting black T-shirt and black jeans, appeared. His hair was receding, and he'd tried to compensate for the loss by growing a beard. Two dark bags hung under his eyes, as if he'd just woken up after only a few hours' sleep.

'James Daniels?' Fiona asked, flashing her warrant card at him. 'My colleague spoke to you on the phone?'

Daniels scanned the ID carefully. Without saying anything, he moved aside and let them in.

The nightclub's interior was cramped, almost claustrophobic. Two modest seating areas flanked a narrow bar, its shelves crammed with bottles of every colour and type. A pair of DJ decks dominated one side of the room. Above, a lattice of white strobe lights hung from the ceiling. In the clarity of daylight, the illusion was shattered. What had only a few hours before throbbed with energy now looked bare and exposed. The air was thick with the smell of stale alcohol, acrid display smoke, and the sour tang of regret, clinging to the scuffed furniture, the walls – everything. As if refusing to leave.

James Daniels stood in the centre of the space. Nerves plagued his expression, but he tried to mask them by folding his arms and leaning against a black column.

'My colleague explained to you why we're here?' Fiona asked.

'Yes.'

'Might there be somewhere we can sit? An office, perhaps?'

'Upstairs,' James said, then spun on the spot and disappeared around the corner, before taking them through a back door and up a narrow, winding staircase.

Upstairs, the corridor was only wide enough for single file. Perfect for them. Not so when you were drunk and in a rush for the toilet.

They entered James' office. Inside was a small desk and two black leather chairs. James and Fiona sat while Giles stood. Fiona reached into her pocket and produced a photo of Claudia Bellini that they'd taken from her social media profiles.

'How long have you had this place?' she asked.

'Three years. We've just entered our fourth. And we haven't had an incident since.'

'With the exception of last night,' Fiona said with a gentle nod.

'Right,' James replied, caught off guard. 'But the incident didn't happen here, not on the premises, did it?'

'Not as far as we understand it,' Fiona replied.

'So we've maintained our record. I want this to be a safe place for people to come, have a good time, and create memories. I don't want what happened last night to tarnish that reputation. And I don't believe in that "no such thing as bad publicity" bollocks. There is if people believe what they read and stop coming.'

Fiona played with the photograph in her hands, keeping the image out of sight. 'What can you tell us about last night?'

'Only what I was told on the phone and what I've seen online.'

'Were you working?'

'Always.'

'Anyone else?'

'Michaela, my bartender.'

'That's it?'

'We're a small bar. We don't need that many people to run it.'

Fiona passed the photograph of Claudia Bellini to James. 'Do you recognise her?'

James looked at the photo for a few seconds before shaking his head. 'Can't say I do. I've never been good with faces, and we get so many people coming in every night that unless they're regulars, I don't remember them.'

'She was here between eleven thirty and one-ish,' Fiona said. 'Came with some of her student flatmates.'

'We had a lot of students last night,' he said. 'Freshers' Week is one of our busiest weeks.'

'She spent the entire evening with someone. We wondered if you might be able to identify him for us?'

The question was rhetorical, and James knew it. He rubbed his arms thoughtfully. 'I don't recognise her, and I don't know anything about her being with someone. I was too busy behind the bar. But if you think I can help in any way, sure, let me know.'

Fiona pointed to the computer. 'You got CCTV?'

'You'd think,' he said, rubbing his arm more aggressively. 'But, no.'

'No?'

'Because we've never had an issue. Never had a need for it. We've never been robbed. We've never had any trouble. Our cups are plastic.

Nobody's ever been assaulted. People just want to get off their faces and have a good time. That's the type of crowd we attract here.'

'Drugs?' Fiona asked.

Giles was certain there would be evidence of that all over the toilets.

'We try to police it as much as we can, but what good would CCTV do?'

'You could catch them and ban them.'

A small snigger broke onto James' face. He looked between Fiona and Giles, almost bewildered. 'In today's struggling economy, seriously? Where this generation of kids are drinking and going out less and less... I'm not going to turn away the only business I'm getting. If I do that, this place won't be here, and I won't be here. Obviously, I'm not saying that I condone drug use, but I'm not about to cut off the blood supply to this place.'

Fiona took the photograph from James and slipped it into her coat pocket. Then she reached into her other pocket and produced a business card.

'We'd like to speak with Michaela as well. She might remember more. I'll need her contact details and address. Here are my details if either of you need them.'

James took the card tentatively before surveying it for a long moment.

'Would you like me to show you out?' he asked.

'Not before we get Michaela's contact information.'

CHAPTER
TWELVE

For the first few minutes of their journey, they drove in silence. Stephanie closely monitored her driving, keeping an eye on the dodgy clutch that had caused her grief for months. She wanted to make the right impression on Eve; that she was in control of the car, not the other way round. It was just one of her anxieties.

As they reached the end of the hill leading out of Mount Browne, Surrey Police headquarters, the sun crept through a break in the clouds.

'Lovely weather for your first day,' she said.

'I had a dream it was going to piss it down,' Eve replied. 'Then I woke up for a wee.'

Stephanie chuckled. 'How are you finding it?'

'Great so far,' Eve replied with an ebullient, almost childish smile. 'I was, like, a little nervous at first, but everyone's been lovely so far.'

Her face glowed with youthful, naïve optimism.

'Though I am a bit worried about this case,' she added. As Stephanie turned to her, she waved her hand apologetically. 'I'm excited as well. Like, don't get me wrong. I'm excited, really looking forward to it, but, like, nervous at the same time, y'know? It's my first one.'

Stephanie smirked. Eve's innocence and naïveté shone through in the way she spoke.

'I felt the same way on my first day,' Stephanie added. 'Minus the pissing myself.'

'Really?' Eve said as if she had just discovered fire.

'It was a long time ago now, back when I was just starting out in uniform. A guy had done a hit-and-run and broken into someone's house. I went in after him with one of my colleagues and stopped him.'

'Literally?'

'Literally.'

'Wow,' she said with genuine awe.

'I remember thinking it was the most stupid thing I could have done, but also the *only* thing I could have done. The adrenaline is what got me through.'

'That's so brave,' Eve replied. 'I never had anything like that happen to me when I was in uniform. It was mostly old people call-outs and dealing with minor traffic incidents.'

'All necessary parts of the role. What you see and experience there prepares you for the rest of your career.'

Eve began biting her fingers before brushing her hair behind her ear. 'You say that, but I never saw a dead body.'

'No?'

'I was only in uniform for literally twelve months before I got the transfer, and the worst I saw was someone from the other side of the room, not right up close, y'know what I mean?'

Stephanie nodded. 'We'll change that when we attend the post-mortem.'

Some of the youthful glow on Eve's face faded.

'You'll have the next couple of hours to prepare yourself. But you'll be fine. Like I said, the adrenaline will get you through it. And if we need to, we'll have a bucket ready.'

Eve chuckled uncomfortably as her attention fell on the dashboard in quiet discomfort. Thoughts of dead bodies quickly began to consume her.

In that moment, Stephanie felt an overprotective urge swell within her, one she hadn't felt in years. Ever since she and her sister had grown up and grown apart, it had been dormant, but it had never faded. Eve reminded her of her younger sister in many ways – her naïvety, her youthful innocence, her eagerness and drive, not to mention her mannerisms and the way she spoke – and Stephanie suddenly felt her big sister instincts kick in.

She wanted to simultaneously guide Eve, mould her, and shape her into a good, solid, well-rounded constable. But she also wanted to protect her, to shield her from the harsh realities and horrors the world had to offer.

A task at which, for the most part, she'd succeeded with her sister. At least when it came to the greatest evil the two of them had ever known.

CHAPTER
THIRTEEN

A large part of being a detective inspector, she'd quickly learned, was about being in control.

Not just having control of her team and what happened within the investigation but also having control over what occurred outside of it. Manipulating and pulling the strings from behind the steering wheel of her mind. Furthermore, if she was in control of the investigation, she was in control of herself. And vice versa. The two went hand in hand.

It was something she'd always done, something she'd been forced to learn as a child: the need to feel in control, not just of herself but of her sister too.

If she were in charge, she couldn't get hurt. Nor could her sister.

The same rules applied to a major investigation. If she was at the helm, everyone benefited, and having a strong handle on the flow of information that leaked to the public was a massive part of that. In Essex, she'd developed a close relationship with several journalists at the local newspapers. She controlled the messages and information that leaked to them, and in turn, they assisted her with any hurdles or speed bumps she might encounter.

It was a two-way relationship.

They arrived at the *Surrey Live* headquarters in Guildford twenty minutes later. The building was a large block that towered above the trees, standing like a red-brick sentinel on the edge of the River Wey. Once a Victorian warehouse, its façade rose five storeys high, its symmetry broken only by the faded white door marked "Private" and the jutting loading deck suspended on iron braces. Etched high into the brick was the old newspaper's name, The Surrey Advertiser.

Inside, pink lavender air freshener failed to mask the smell of rotting wood and the decades-old carpet.

As Stephanie and Eve climbed the steps to the second floor, they could hear furious typing on keyboards, and as they reached the open door, the sound intensified. To Stephanie's surprise, there were only four people in there creating the noise, their attention solely focused on their computer screens, and oblivious to their arrival.

Stephanie knocked.

The man closest to them swung round on his chair and approached them. Fast approaching sixty, he wore a suit that looked three sizes too big for him. Either he'd lost a lot of weight, or he no longer had anyone advising him on what size suit to buy.

'Can I help you?' he asked.

Stephanie introduced herself and Eve and asked to speak to the person in charge.

'That'll be me. Louis Brown.'

Stephanie took his hand. His grip was firmer than she'd expected.

'I'm the editor of *Surrey Live*,' he continued. 'Is there something I can help you with?'

'I just wanted to introduce myself,' she said. 'Get a sense of how you work and how we can collaborate.'

Louis's eyes darkened, along with the rest of the room, as a cloud swallowed the sunlight outside.

'Step into my office,' he said.

His "office" was a small coffee shop round the corner of the building. They ordered drinks at the counter and found a table by the window, surrounded by customers ordering lunch.

'They do a mean chicken and pesto grilled sandwich,' he said.

'We're not here to eat,' Stephanie replied. She had no appetite.

'How have you worked with Surrey Police and the Major Investigation Team in the past?'

Louis licked coffee from his lips. 'It's been a fairly standard way of working,' he explained. 'We've always been very grateful to the team for providing the information requested. I realise we're not the biggest fish in the pond, but we get a lot of local residents asking for information on issues in the area, and many people rely on us, especially when it concerns Surrey. Sometimes we have the information. Sometimes we don't. More often than not, we're unable to report anything because our reporters don't know about it, or by the time they get there, they're too late. And if they're too late, communication can prove tricky. We try our best not to undercut you guys or step on any of your toes.'

'Who have you been working with recently?'

Another sip. At this rate, he'd finish his drink before he started answering the question. 'Most recently Devon, since your predecessor left.'

That was what she feared. Back in Essex, she and her old DS, Caleb Morgan, had closely managed the relationship with the press, working together as a team. With Devon, however, she sensed that partnership would be one-sided at best, if not non-existent.

'I plan to work a little differently,' she said, straightening her back. 'For starters, I will be your main point of contact. I know it's slightly unorthodox, but I like to be in charge of the flow of information both ways. I see you and your team as a valuable asset, and from previous experience, I know that you can be a real game-changer in assisting investigations. What I envision is a two-way partnership. I will give you as much information as I can, preferably to you first. And in return, you will pass on any leads or guidance that might be relevant.' She knitted her fingers together in a metaphorical gesture. 'What do you think?'

Louis glanced between Stephanie and Eve. In his mind, it made sense. In fact, it was too good to be true. He'd never been approached like this in his twenty-year history at the publication. He took a moment to consider his response.

'While it sounds good in theory,' he said softly, 'we'll just have to wait and see how it plays out in reality.'

'No time like the present,' Stephanie began. 'I've got a story for you from the university. Got your pen and paper?'

CHAPTER
FOURTEEN

She had been careful to omit the most important element: the discovery of the voodoo doll at the crime scene. Sure, she wanted to get their relationship off to a good start, but she didn't want to reveal all the information just yet. Not when they didn't know what it signified.

Control. That was what her old chief inspector had said. Control the flow of information, and you'll have everyone at your feet, begging for more. The more they beg, the more they'll be willing to help.

Shortly after leaving the coffee shop, Stephanie received a phone call from someone claiming to work with the pathologist assigned to Claudia Bellini's body, confirming they were ready for her and Eve's visit.

The journey to Surrey University Hospital was fraught with lunchtime traffic, and after navigating several roundabouts and sets of traffic lights, they arrived five minutes late.

The mortuary was entombed in the lowest, loneliest part of the building, forgotten by sunlight, where the air hung heavy with antiseptic and sorrow. No windows. Just a stretch of grey corridors that swallowed sound and seemed to echo with the soft, persistent whispers of the dead.

Steph hated attending post-mortems. She'd seen her first dead body when she was nine years old – a moment branded into her bones. Since then, death had become a quiet, persistent companion. She knew its smell, its stillness, the unnatural hush it brought to a room. And yet, despite the years, despite the uniform and the badge, it had never got easier.

The dead disturbed her, not for what they were, but for what they could no longer be. Each one lay there unfinished, a life cut short mid-breath, mid-thought. A teenager with a slit throat who would never sit exams. A middle-aged man who had a heart attack and would never say sorry. A woman who still wore chipped nail polish, her toes peeking from beneath the sheet, who would never get to paint them again.

Underlying it all, sometimes, Steph found comfort there. In the silence. In the certainty. The dead couldn't hurt her. They couldn't shout or lie or raise their hands.

Unlike the living.

'You must be Steph,' a voice called from the other end of a long corridor.

'*Stephanie*,' she replied as she approached.

The voice belonged to Leanna Moore, the Home Office Pathologist. She had removed her splash guard and lowered her face mask to reveal thin lips framed by a narrow face. Beneath the paper suit, she wore a multi-coloured array of clothing. 'Pleasure to meet you. I'm sure we'll be getting to know one another from this point onwards. I presume you're here for the girl, and not the scintillating conversation?' she said.

'Both.'

Leanna's face broke into a smile. 'We're very accommodating down here. All our guests have a fantastic time.'

'I bet you haven't had any bad reviews yet,' Eve said as Leanna placed her hand on the heavy fireproof door.

As the door opened, colour drained from Eve's cheeks, and she froze. Leanna noticed the hesitation and stepped back into the corridor.

'First time?'

Eve nodded, staring blankly at the door.

'You get used to the smell. Eventually. It's like pub carpet at the end of the night, though I wouldn't recommend sticking your tongue out. Once you've seen one, you've seen them all.' Leanna placed a hand on the door again and turned to Stephanie. 'You good?'

'Me? I'm fine.'

'Good. Because I've only got one mop.'

The mortuary room was cold and clinical, the walls painted a shade of white that made everything look a little too clean. Stainless-steel worktops gleamed under the harsh strip lighting, and in the centre of the room, on a metal table, lay Claudia Bellini, naked. Underneath her clothes, Claudia was skinnier than Stephanie had realised. Her ribcage, collarbone, and pelvis protruded prominently beneath her pale skin. A faint bruise circled her throat like a tight necklace. Her arms lay by her side, fingernails painted a chipped sky blue.

A small bird etched onto the girl's wrist caught Stephanie's eye. She froze, her gaze locked on the wings outstretched mid-flight. Her mother had a similar tattoo; one Steph used to trace as a child. She reached for her mother's necklace and pinched it. Immediately, her rising heartbeat began to decrease.

The solemnity of the room was distorted by The Rolling Stones blasting through the speakers. Leanna moved to a workbench in the corner and lowered the volume before joining Eve and Stephanie at the door. Both detectives had changed into suits and donned face masks.

Leanna shuffled towards the body, then beckoned them over. Stephanie made the first move but then hesitated, waiting for Eve to follow. The rookie detective's movements were cautious and deliberate, like a lion cub approaching a carcass for the first time. Stephanie watched her closely, walking by her side every step of the way. She resisted the urge to grab her hand and squeeze it tightly.

Leanna observed them with quiet reflection as they approached.

Eve let out a small, sharp gasp as soon as she laid eyes on Claudia's face.

'It gets easier,' Stephanie whispered. 'Trust me. I like to pretend they're sleeping.'

Unable to tear her gaze from Claudia's body, Eve nodded slowly.

'Claudia Bellini,' Leanna began, moving the conversation along.

'Eighteen and a half years old. Brown hair, brown eyes. Fifty-eight kilograms. Hundred and sixty-eight centimetres.' She moved to the victim's head, pointing at her neck. 'Bruises and marks on the skin indicate she was strangled or suffocated.'

'That's the cause of death?'

A nod.

'Fingerprints? DNA?'

A shake of the head. 'It wasn't done with a pair of hands,' she said.

Stephanie released her mum's necklace. 'What was used to kill her?'

'Judging by her crushed windpipe, I'd say something stronger, bigger. A knee, perhaps.'

'Her killer knelt on her throat?' Eve asked. To Stephanie's surprise, she was holding up extremely well. She hadn't been sick. She hadn't fainted. She hadn't burst into tears, although, from the redness in her eyes, it was possibly only a matter of time. Perhaps it was the shock of it all. Perhaps she was too stunned, too taken aback to do anything other than keep her eyes fixated on Claudia Bellini's head.

'Yes, that would be my hypothesis. Something that would have almost crushed her windpipe and eventually suffocated her.'

'How long would he have been on top of her for?'

'With that pressure on her throat? Couple of minutes.'

Eve looked between Stephanie and Leanna. 'Wouldn't someone have heard her? Would she not have been screaming?'

Now it was Leanna's and Stephanie's turn to glance at one another, silently deciding who should answer.

'Sorry if I'm asking too many questions,' she said, her tone panicked and self-conscious.

'Don't apologise,' Stephanie responded. 'Questions are good. They're how you learn. And remember—'

'There's no such thing as a bad question,' Eve finished.

Stephanie smiled in response. That was exactly the sort of thing her sister would say.

'You're asking all the questions I had in mind, anyway. At this rate, I'll be out of a job and won't need to come down next time. But in answer to your question, you raise a valid point. However, at that time of night, the only person on their floor was Shun-Chow. I will make a note for someone to speak with him and find out if he heard anything. And, Leanna can back me up on this, but if the killer had their knee on Claudia's throat, the last thing she would have been able to do is make a sound.'

Leanna nodded.

Eve looked deeply dissatisfied with that response. 'She didn't put up a fight?'

'As far as I understand, she was incredibly drunk. She may have even been slipped something. She might have tried to defend herself, but in her state, it wouldn't have made much difference. If she had, Leanna would have found DNA under her fingernails.' Stephanie turned to the pathologist, offering her an expectant look with one eyebrow raised.

'Looks like I won't be in a job either, at this rate.' Leanna adjusted her face mask, pinching it against her nose as she moved towards Claudia's hands. 'I've swabbed, but underneath those blue nails, I couldn't find anything. The pillow smothering her face probably didn't help either. Her killer went full-on belt and braces. Knee to the throat, pillow to the face. She wouldn't have lasted long.'

There was something blunt, something starkly matter-of-fact about the statement that took Stephanie aback. She paused to imagine the scene: Claudia stumbling through the bedroom door, laughing, hanging around her lover's neck, hushing him as he made a sound. Then he threw her onto the bed, pinning her down with his knee, crushing her windpipe. Had she been conscious? Had she known what was happening? Had she thought it was part of a sex game to which she hadn't consented?

That particular train of thought prompted Stephanie's next question: 'Is there any sign of sexual assault?'

Beneath her mask, Leanna pursed her lips. 'Nothing at all. She came to me fully clothed, and she died fully clothed. No signs of vaginal or anal penetration. I've had a look, and her hymen is still intact.'

'She was a virgin?'

Leanna nodded.

'Is there anything else we should know?'

Leanna ran her eyes along the full length of Claudia's naked body.

'Not much more in relation to her cause of death; however, some things you might find interesting are that she was definitely drunk – I could smell it as soon as I opened her – but she hadn't been a heavy drinker before this.'

'Natural, given her young age and that she's just started university.'

'True. However, I did spot some damage that this young girl had done to her body.'

'Like what?'

Leanna moved towards Claudia's mouth and opened it, revealing a set of poorly maintained teeth. 'She was a vomiter,' she said.

'A vomiter?' Eve asked.

Stephanie closed her mouth almost involuntarily.

'The enamel of her teeth has been severely worn down from excessive vomiting. There are several tears on her oesophagus. Her kidneys are in a real state. I don't think she'd had a period in a few months, and her bones were slightly less dense than I'd expect from someone her age. I haven't tested them, but I'm certain her potassium and sodium levels would be shockingly low. If I had to say, she most likely had an eating disorder; one that she'd struggled with for many years. I would guess the last time she vomited was several hours before her death.'

Stephanie placed her hand on her mum's necklace again, and any hunger she felt disappeared. The urge to put a piece of chewing gum in her mouth returned, but she suppressed it by swallowing deeply.

'Thank you for that,' she said slowly. 'That's very helpful.'

Just as she was about to turn her attention away from the body on the table, Eve signalled that she wanted to say something.

'I hope you don't mind me saying this, but…' She scratched the top of her head. 'I'm a bit inspired by both of you.'

Stephanie and Leanna glanced at one another curiously. Neither had any idea what she was referring to.

'I think you're inspirational,' Eve continued. 'Women in high-ranking jobs. You're showing me that it can be done.'

Leanna scoffed. 'I look at dead people all day. There's nothing glamorous about that.'

'But it's important.'

Stephanie smiled warmly at her. She felt the same. That relentless drive to prove herself – to be better, sharper, tougher, career-driven – had never gone away. She'd poured herself into the job like concrete, letting it set around the cracks of who she used to be. Friendships had fallen away. She'd lost contact with her sister. Love, whatever shape it once took, had been left at the door years ago. But she'd kept climbing. Not for glory. Not even for herself. For moments like this. If she had to carry the bruises so people like Eve could rise without suffering, then so be it. It was worth it.

CHAPTER
FIFTEEN

Devon stubbed out the cigarette against the wall, the last drag of smoke still sharp in his lungs. He held it there for a moment, letting the toxins spread through his body, before slowly releasing it between pursed lips. The tobacco helped settle his nerves, calming the irritation coiled in his chest that flared every time he thought of Stephanie. She'd stormed in like she owned the case – an outsider who knew nothing about the area or the team – leading them in the wrong direction. She was too focused on the little pissant who'd gone home with the victim, but Devon knew that was the wrong avenue to take. Their attention should be solely on the doll discovered at the scene.

The incident room was quiet when he stepped back inside, half-lit by the grey wash of late afternoon. The bulk of the team were at their desks, silently working on the tasks Stephanie had given them: Giles, Olivia, Fiona, and Noah. The original members of the team. The people he trusted.

Devon clapped his hands once, sharp and deliberate, drawing the room's attention.

'Fiona, Giles, what are you working on?'

Giles opened and closed his mouth like a fish. He hated being put on the spot. 'I'm trying to reach out to the bartender at Red One.'

'Fiona?'

'Looking for CCTV of Claudia's walk home last night,' she answered, more clearly than her constable counterpart.

'Noah?'

The other sergeant pushed himself away from his desk and leaned back in his chair in his usual laid-back style. 'Typing up notes,' was all he offered.

Devon pointed to the back of the office. 'Wellard? Same question for you.'

'Managing HOLMES, sarge. I've been inputting stuff into this bastard system all morning, and I think something's messing with the Wi-Fi, because it's been a nightmare. I've had dial-up Internet faster than this.'

'Maybe it's the voodoo doll,' Giles commented.

Devon turned his attention to the incident board on the wall. His eyes narrowed in on the picture of the voodoo doll that had been pinned to it with a red marker. He hurried over to it and yanked it from the board.

'I've just spoken with DI Broadbent, and she says we need to change tack.' He prodded the photograph of the voodoo doll repeatedly. 'This is our main priority. We need to find out where this came from, who it belongs to, and what it means.'

'What about our other tasks?' Fiona asked.

Devon didn't appreciate the insinuation in her tone.

'You drop everything you're doing and do what I'm about to tell you: we need to find or bring in a local expert on voodoo. Failing that, Fiona, since you asked so nicely, I'm nominating you to do the research for me.'

Fiona's expression soured.

'Next, I want lab analysis of the doll and the fingerprint on the microwave sent away as a matter of urgency. The specialists need to expedite this as fast as they can. It doesn't matter how much it'll cost. Noah, can I leave that with you?'

Noah fired a finger gun in Devon's direction as he swung round in his chair.

'What about me, sarge?' Wellard asked, her forehead peeking over her computer monitor.

'Keep doing what you're doing. Let me know if your connection issues persist.'

Wellard slowly lowered her head to a natural position without responding.

'Why the sudden change in direction, Devon?' Fiona asked. This time she had the courtesy to raise her arm, which Devon greatly appreciated.

'I stressed the significance of the doll to Steph. She was already on the fence, and we agree that the knife in the doll could signify the method of killing that will be used on a potential second victim. If we're not careful, we might have a serial killer on our hands.'

A wave of solemnity rolled through the office.

'In other news, I did *also* float the idea of us going to the pub after we finish here. Get to know Eve and Steph a little better.'

'I thought she liked being called Stephanie,' Fiona commented. She had overheard one of the IT guys making that mistake while they'd been setting up the inspector's desk.

Devon waved the comment away as if it were a fly. 'Who's up for it?'

Nobody answered straight away.

'Sadly, DI Broadbent refused,' he said. 'She's got loads of unpacking still left to do. But I know Eve will be up for it.'

He hoped. He would have to ask her and do his best to convince her.

Eventually, after a few moments of silent persuasion, looking down at them with stern eyes, they all agreed.

CHAPTER
SIXTEEN

Perched along the River Wey, right in the centre of Guildford, The Weyside was typically teeming with people at all hours of the day: midweek lunchers, post-work drinkers, and everything in between. Ducks and geese meandered elegantly on the water, floating from side to side, moving aside to allow passage for the kayakers and riverboats through their home. It had been the team's regular haunt for the past five years, and they all knew the owner, Cindy, as though she were one of them.

They trickled in one by one, shrugging off coats and the day's weight in equal measure. Devon made a beeline for the bar, ready to order the usual round, and an extra gin and tonic for Eve. Giles flopped into the corner booth, Fiona and Noah nestled in beside him, while Eve positioned herself on the edge of the booth on the other side of Noah. Olivia dragged a chair over from a nearby table and dropped herself into it.

As soon as the drinks arrived – beers, lagers, gin and tonics, and a rogue cider for Noah – something in the group eased. For the next few hours, they were just normal people. They could forget about the horrors they'd witnessed. They'd left their demons at the door until they were forced to pick them up on the way home.

'Well,' Devon began, raising his pint glass in the air, 'on behalf of the team, I just wanted to offer a big welcome to DC Hope. I can see you're already fitting in well, and I suspect you'll flourish here with us. I'm really looking forward to working with you and seeing what you can do.'

A cheer echoed around the table. They lifted their glasses, clinked them together, and then took a unanimous, celebratory sip of their drinks.

Eve lowered her glass carefully to the table, a smile beaming on her face. In the short span of the few hours since she'd first entered the office, she had transformed from a shy, timid woman uncertain of herself into someone who looked as though she'd been there for years and was an integral part of the team.

'Thanks, sarge,' she began, flexing the dimple in her cheek. 'I literally wouldn't have been able to do it if it weren't for you lovely lot. I really appreciate everything you've done for me today. Like you've all been fantastic, and I'm super grateful to be with a team like you; you're literally miles better than the people I was previously working with. It's just a shame Stephanie couldn't be here.'

All eyes turned to Devon, eagerly awaiting his response. He hid behind his glass of Guinness. 'Maybe some other time,' he replied. Keen to move the conversation along, he turned to Eve. 'What are three interesting things we should know about you? What sort of thing would you share on a first date?'

Eve set her glass on the table. 'Chance would be a fine thing, for starters. How about we play two truths and a lie?'

'I *love* that game,' Olivia said eagerly.

'Go on then,' Devon replied. 'Eve first. Impress us.'

Eve considered for a moment, staring into her glass, deep in thought. 'Okay... I own eleven houseplants and they all have names; I've never broken a bone; and I can recite every word of *Mean Girls*.'

A contemplative hush fell on the table as they all internally calculated the lie among the truths.

'I believe the *Mean Girls* one, hands down,' Giles said, certain of himself. 'I'm sure my sister can do the same, and she's about your age.'

'I find it difficult to believe you've never broken a bone,' Noah said. 'Like, ever? I think I broke my ankle when I was ten.'

'Not everyone's a daredevil like you,' Olivia responded with a disapproving shake of her head. 'I think that's the most likely to be true.'

Eve nodded, confirming Olivia's suspicion. The table erupted in cheers.

'Go on then,' Giles said, 'what are your plants' names?'

Eve counted the names on her fingers. 'Terry, Jeremy, Sir Prickles, Malik, Dresden, Eric, Kevin, Moira, Rhubarb, Petal McGee, and Planty McPlanterson. Now it's your turn. What are your two truths and a lie?'

The rest of the team looked at one another sheepishly. Giles immediately brandished a finger at Devon, who was in the middle of licking his lips.

He cleared his throat. 'All right, you asked for it: I once got locked in a pub overnight; I have a tattoo of a penguin; and I can play the violin.'

'Violin.'

'Bollocks can you play the violin.'

'If you can play the violin, I'm Dave Grohl,' said Giles.

Devon confirmed that his lie was that he couldn't play the violin. He couldn't play any instrument, for that matter. He was as musical as a donkey in the middle of the Patagonian desert.

'I'm dying to know,' Eve said, leaning forward. 'Where's the tattoo?'

'Wanna see it?'

'So long as it isn't anywhere near your arse,' Noah jumped in.

Smirking, Devon climbed out of his seat, untucked his shirt, and lifted it to reveal a skiing penguin, complete with ski mask and scar, on his ribcage.

'Wow,' Eve said. 'That's brave. I've got one on my wrist and that hurt enough. What possessed you to do that, and what made you get it there, of all places?'

'Immaturity,' Devon replied as he returned to his seat, leaving his shirt untucked. 'I was eighteen, and I'm fairly sure it was a dare. I wanted to get rid of him for a long time, but now I've grown quite fond of him, and he's a good conversation starter. Though I try not to get naked all the time. Right, who's next? Noah?'

Reluctantly, Noah shared his version of the game. 'I was almost recruited into MI5. I once ran a marathon dressed as a banana. I've never drunk a cup of coffee in my life.'

The team's answer was unanimous: that he'd run the marathon as a banana, solely because he didn't have the physique for it. He was in his late forties, and his stomach protruded like a watermelon.

'Wrong,' he responded, grinning as if he'd just completed the marathon. 'I did that when I was in my twenties with a couple of mates. We thought it would be funny to take part in fancy dress. I came first out of a group of ten of us. I used to be quite fit back in the day.' He quickly lost focus as he began to reminisce about a time when his cardiovascular system was in much better shape. 'My lie was that I was almost recruited into MI5. Slight twist on the truth: I applied, but they never accepted me. Didn't even make it past the first stage of the selection process.'

'They probably saw you running a marathon in a banana costume and thought, "We can't trust this guy with government secrets. He'll slip up on the road somewhere…"' Giles said, laughing at his own joke. But when it didn't land as well as he'd hoped, he added, 'I made a joke? Get it? Banana peel… skidding… like on *Mario Kart*?'

Eve placed a consolatory hand on his forearm. 'We all understood,' she said. 'We just didn't find it funny.'

'Rude,' Giles retorted, taking a long swig of his beer.

'Your turn,' Devon said.

'Don't wanna play now.'

'Stop showing off,' Olivia snapped.

The team's motherly figure had spoken. It took Giles all of two minutes to work out his responses. 'I once went viral on TikTok. I can hold my breath for over four minutes. I've never been outside the UK.'

'Bollocks,' Devon said immediately, lifting his sleeve up to reveal a Tag Heuer watch. 'Prove it.'

'That defeats the point of the game.'

'If it's true, you have to prove it.'

'Fine,' Giles murmured with a shrug of his shoulders.

'I think it's the TikTok one,' Olivia answered. 'I follow you on TikTok and I've never seen you post.'

Her argument was enough to convince the rest of the team. Devon and Noah had no clue, while Eve knew not enough about him to make a decision with any conviction. Though she was thoroughly enjoying herself. She thought the game, along with the alcohol, was the perfect icebreaker, the perfect way to get to know her team better. It was just a shame that Stephanie wasn't there to join them.

'My lie is...' Giles drummed his fingers on the table, building suspense. 'I have left the UK before; a lad's holiday when I was eighteen.'

Devon raised his hand in the air. 'Hang on. So you're saying you've gone viral on TikTok *and* you can hold your breath for four minutes?'

Conviction oozed from the young constable as he nodded. 'I was involved in a TikTok that went viral on my mate's account, and—'

'That doesn't count!' Eve chimed in, feeling herself getting a little giddy from the alcohol currently circulating in her bloodstream. '*You* weren't the one going viral.'

Giles put his hand in her face jokingly. 'I'm counting it.'

Devon tapped his watch. 'Hold your breath. Prove it.'

Clicking his knuckles and the joints in his neck, Giles inhaled deeply several times before holding his breath. His cheeks puffed as wide as they could go. Devon started counting, keeping one eye on his watch and the other on Giles' chest. If the detective constable made the slightest movement or suggestion he was breathing illegally, he would spot it.

For the first two minutes, nothing. No sign of struggle, or that Giles was cheating.

But after another twenty seconds, Devon spotted the man's nostrils flare slightly. Just as he was about to call him out on it, Eve pinched the bridge of Giles' nose, and within a few seconds, he flinched and exploded into a gasp.

'What're you doing? Tryna kill me?'

'Cheat,' she said proudly, to a chorus of cheers. A handful of heads from other customers in the pub sent admonishing looks their way.

Last in the team to go was Olivia.

'All right. My turn,' she said, wiping a drop of her gin and tonic from the corner of her mouth.

The table leaned in.

'One: I met my husband at a Take That concert. Two: I gave birth to my son in the back of an Uber. Three: I make my own gin in the garage.'

There were a few murmurs.

'I believe the Take That one,' Giles said. 'I think you'd probably marry your *next* husband there as well.'

'Only if it was Gary Barlow.' She smiled, slow and satisfied. 'It's the gin. I can barely make toast without supervision, and I wouldn't even know where to begin with distilling my own. I've been down to the Silent Pool for a taste of theirs, but I could never do it myself. I'd probably end up drinking it all and getting pissed. As for the Uber… best tip that driver's ever had, I reckon.'

'I hope you gave him five stars after that…' Noah commented.

Laughter swept around the table. As it came to a gradual end, Devon finished the last of his drink, set it on the table, and climbed out of his chair.

'Right,' he said, clapping his hands. 'Who wants another?'

CHAPTER
SEVENTEEN

The microwave hummed in the cramped kitchen, whirring like a vacuum cleaner. Stephanie stood barefoot on the cold linoleum, arms folded tightly across her chest, surrounded by boxes stacked haphazardly, watching the tray rotate with dull anticipation. The air was thick with the smell of scorched plastic and artificial cheese.

Dinner: a lasagne that would no doubt be barely warm in the middle but scalding hot around the edges. If she could summon the courage to eat it.

As the food continued its journey to becoming something resembling a meal, her gaze drifted towards the bathroom. The door was ajar just enough to reveal the slim outline of the digital scales tucked beside the toilet. She didn't move at first. Just stared at them, pain welling in her clenched jaw.

Then she padded over on her toes, silently, as if doing so any louder would bring the building crashing down on her. The scales blinked to life as she manoeuvred around a box labelled *Bathroom?* in thick black marker and stepped on in silence. She stared at the number that appeared, then exhaled through her nose and waited for it to blink again.

It didn't change.

She stepped off, wordless, and returned to the microwave just as it pinged. The plastic film protecting the food had ballooned and split.

She peeled it back mechanically, releasing a plume of steam that scalded her face.

The lasagne sat heavily in her hands as she carried it to the sofa. She pushed aside a half-opened box marked *Books & Bits*, set the tray down on the coffee table, and sat.

But she didn't eat.

She just sat there, still and silent, watching the steam curl upwards and vanish into nothing.

Soon, the image of the television screen in front of her melted away and was replaced with the image of Claudia Bellini, resting on the mortuary table. The teenager had been thin. Thin in a way that made her look brittle. The way Stephanie looked and felt at times. She had noticed something wasn't right about Claudia the moment she approached the body in the morgue. The sharp collarbones, the pale ridges of ribs too visible beneath her skin. The same things she saw every time she looked in the mirror.

She'd spent years battling the same quiet war. One fought with silence. And *in* silence. The obsessive eating, the purging, the skipped meals, shying away from food.

For a while now, she'd been in control of it. She'd monitored her weight closely, kept an eye on her mental health. But since her colleague's death – since the day she blamed herself for losing one of the closest people in her life – she'd started to feel her control slip away, to feel herself slide back into old habits.

I won't do it.
I won't do it.
Don't *do it.*

Stephanie blinked hard and reached for her mother's necklace, and the images suddenly melted away. She stared at the lasagne. Still steaming. Still untouched. The smell of it made her stomach clench. Standing, she crossed to the window and pulled back the tired, half-hung curtain left by the previous tenant. Outside, streetlamps illuminated the sky a dull amber, and damp leaves clung to the pavement. A pair of headlights slowly crawled along the road before turning away into darkness.

She needed to get out. Movement. Breath.

Without another glance at the lasagne, she stepped into the

bedroom and changed into her running gear: leggings, long sleeves, and trainers that had seen too many miles and too few rests. No music, no phone, just her and the night.

She tied her laces with military precision. Tight, double-knotted.

Running was one of the few things in her life that provided her with rules: measurable pain, something she could control.

She locked the door behind her, the early autumn warmth still clinging to the last of summer's heat as she stepped outside. She started slow, letting the rhythm take over, feet hitting the pavement like a metronome, carrying her wherever they wanted.

CHAPTER
EIGHTEEN

Cold water streamed from the mouth of the tap. She reached for the soap, squirted it onto her palm, and began kneading it into her skin and beneath her fingernails. As she placed her hands beneath the hand dryer, the bathroom door opened, and in stepped Eve, bleary-eyed.

'Morning,' Stephanie said.

'Morning, ma'am,' Eve replied groggily.

The smell of alcohol leached from her pores and hung thick on her breath.

'Heavy one last night, was it?'

What colour was left in Eve's already washed-out face quickly disappeared. 'We were only supposed to stay for a couple.'

'That's what they all say. I suspect there will be a lot of sore heads this morning.'

Eve chuckled awkwardly, hovering in the doorframe.

'Where did you go?'

'The Weyside, down by the river.'

'I know it.'

'Did you get all your unpacking sorted?'

'My… unpacking?'

Eve's head tilted as her eyes narrowed. 'Devon, I mean DS Lafferty, said that you couldn't come because you still had loads of unpacking to do.'

Stephanie's mouth fell open. How best to approach this? Go along with it and save herself and Eve an awkward conversation? Or come clean and call out DS Lafferty for the snake he was quickly proving to be? There had been no invitation, no request for her to join them for their welcome drinks.

In the end, she decided it was better to save face.

'Yeah,' she said unconvincingly. 'Still got a mountain to climb, but most of it's pretty much done now.'

Eve's smile suggested she wasn't fully convinced. 'You'll still be finding boxes in six months' time when you think you've done it all.' She shuffled past Stephanie towards the nearest cubicle. 'My mum and dad had the same thing when they moved house. It was never-ending.'

The alarm on Stephanie's phone vibrated.

'I'll see you in the morning briefing,' she said.

'Already?' Eve replied from the cubicle. 'I need a wee!'

Steph didn't blame Eve for what had happened the night before; she was brand new to the team, eager to impress, eager to get to know everyone on a personal level, and she had been none the wiser. But that didn't stop Steph from feeling disheartened and disappointed by her decision to attend. Eve was her safety blanket, the bridge between her and the rest of her new team. If she lost touch with her, it would prove difficult to integrate herself. Sure, it had only been one night, it had only been one drinks gathering, but she didn't want to feel left behind before she'd even started.

By 9:01 am, DS Noah Mackenzie was the only one sitting by the incident room, legs crossed. He was about as laid-back as a surfboard.

Stephanie began pacing from side to side. Over the next two minutes, the rest of the team gradually began to appear from the kitchen, carrying coffee cups in their hands, deep in conversation, with the exception of Eve, who hurried in from the bathroom. The newest addition to the team was the only one to apologise for being late.

There was no sign of DS Lafferty.

On the outside, Stephanie was a picture postcard of calm. But on the inside, she was fuming. Nine am meant nine am. No exceptions. Back with her previous team in Essex, she had drilled them so hard to arrive at 8:55, sometimes even 8:50 and had never run into any issues. It helped that she had a willing detective sergeant, whom she'd admired and respected greatly, to ensure everyone toed the line.

She didn't want to rule with an iron fist. She didn't want to scream and shout to get her point across; more often than not, it had the opposite effect. Instead, she preferred to lead by example. She would never ask someone to do something that she wasn't prepared to do herself. To her, that was what leaders did. Instead of barking orders and creating disruption among the team, she wanted to manage them closely, intimately. She wanted to get to know them one by one on a personal level. Everyone worked differently, and she was keen to understand what made each person tick as she wanted to get the best out of her team. But if things didn't begin to change, then she would have to.

'Morning, everyone,' she began, resolute. 'I know there might be a couple of sore heads out there, but a deadline is a deadline. If I ask for you to be here at nine o'clock, I mean nine o'clock. We're at the beginning of a murder investigation, and we need total focus.'

Gentle murmurings rumbled through the team. She was sure she'd heard an apology in there somewhere.

'While we're waiting for Devon to arrive, I'd like to know how you all got on yesterday.' She pointed to Giles and Fiona. 'What happened at Red One?'

Fiona gave her a clear and concise update.

'Were you able to find any CCTV surveillance of Claudia walking home?'

Fiona shook her head.

'What about finding his identity?'

Another shake of the head. She looked at her coldly.

'I looked into the voodoo doll, ma'am,' she said, caution lacing her tone. 'I've got an expert coming in later today. I just need to confirm a time.'

Stephanie's mind went blank. 'Voodoo doll?'

'Lafferty said you wanted us to focus our efforts on finding out who the doll belonged to and how it was made,' Olivia "Wellard" Willard added.

Of course he did.

Devon had hijacked her investigation. He'd told the team to disregard her instructions and follow his own. He was taking control away from her investigation. She should have been livid with him. She should have called him out on it in front of the team. But every time she thought about Devon, she was reminded of her previous sergeant, Caleb. The last time she had given an instruction to him, he had come face to face with a killer and died. It was something she hadn't completely forgiven herself for, and something she suspected she never would.

She wasn't sure if she could tell him what to do. Not yet.

'Right,' she said after a long pause. 'Sorry, yes. Just forgot for a moment. And… and how did you get on?'

Just as Fiona was about to answer, the office door opened, and Devon fell in. He chucked his bag to the floor and rushed towards a seat at the back of the group. He apologised, but Stephanie sensed there was no authenticity behind it.

Somewhere in the office, a telephone rang. Olivia was the first to it. She leapt off her chair and lunged for the phone. She spoke efficiently into the handset, writing notes at the same time. When she hung up, she turned to Stephanie.

'Sorry to interrupt, ma'am, but the man Claudia Bellini was with on the night she died has just come forward and said he'd like to talk to us.'

CHAPTER
NINETEEN

Kieran Holt was a second-year sports science undergraduate who lived in Battersea Court, directly opposite the library, though he spent little time there. Instead, he spent most of his time at the gym or the sports park. He was a member of several sports societies: rugby, lacrosse, football, and American football, and he was part of a local running club. Possessing the boyish charm that came with playing those sports and standing over six foot tall with broad shoulders, he presented himself as confident, outgoing, and popular. However, as he showed Stephanie through to his room on the fourth floor of the Tate building, he shied away from his neighbours and lowered his University of Surrey Rugby Society hoodie over his face.

If Stephanie needed any further evidence of his athleticism and love for sports, it was evident in the mountain of gear she found in his room. Stephanie had chosen to speak with him in his accommodation: a place where he would feel calmer and more relaxed. His room smelled faintly of deodorant and aftershave. The single bed was unmade, and clothes – mostly jogging bottoms, T-shirts, and a pair of muddy rugby shorts – were scattered across the floor. A row of protein powders lined the windowsill like trophies, and a shaker bottle sat beside a half-eaten protein bar on his desk. A gym bag had been discarded by the leg of the desk, with a rugby ball, a tangled pile of resistance bands, and a weightlifting brace poking out of it. A towel was draped over the back of a chair, drying in the warmth emanating from the radiator. On the bedside table was a half-empty bottle of water and a copy of *Men's Health* featuring a smug, shirtless man on the cover.

It was a room that screamed energy and ambition. But beneath it all, Stephanie sensed an insecurity within Kieran: the chaos of a boy trying hard to look like a man.

'Make yourself comfortable,' he told her as he made a haphazard, last-minute attempt to tidy the place.

She wondered how many women he'd said that to before. 'Standing's fine.'

Kieran hovered awkwardly in the centre of his room, placing his hands in the pockets of his hoodie.

'What's sharing a bathroom with your flatmates like?' she asked.

He shrugged. 'Not as bad as you might think. It gets a bit awkward at times, but we all get on fine, so it's okay. Nobody's walked in on someone else yet...' He started to laugh, but the animation in his voice quickly faded.

'Must be a nightmare if you want to have people over,' she said.

'I... I wouldn't know.'

'Is that because you've always gone round to their place instead?'

Kieran's jaw twitched. 'I didn't the other night, if that's what you're referring to.'

'Tell me what happened,' she said, reaching into her pocket for her phone to make notes.

Kieran shoved his hood back, revealing a thick head of blond hair. 'I know how it looks,' he said, keeping his voice low. 'I bet you've heard from all her mates how we were all over each other and how we went home together. But I just wanted to clear my name. It's been eating me up inside.'

'Tell me what happened.'

The hood came back, as if it were his cloak, granting him the superpower of courage.

'We got talking in the queue to the club, all right? Red One. I'd been there a couple of times before. It's never really been my type of vibe, but my mates and I thought we'd go there for a change. There were four of us in total: lads from rugby.

'As soon as we got in the queue, I started talking to Claudia, ribbing her for having an Italian surname but no Italian blood. She said the only Italian thing about her is that she likes pasta, but then I said by that standard it made the entire world Italian.' His face flashed with the reminder of their conversation. 'When we got inside, I offered to buy her a drink. She was already pretty wasted by that point, but I needed another one just to keep me going.'

'Why?'

'Because… because she wasn't my usual type, you know. I… needed more alcohol to…'

'Ease the pain of getting with someone less attractive than yourself?' she finished.

Kieran's eyes fell to the ground in shame. He was too much of a coward to admit it.

'So you bought a couple of drinks. Then what?'

'We started getting off, dancing, chatting.'

'Did you slip her anything?'

Kieran's eyes widened with offence. 'No! Never. We just got drunker and drunker as the night went on.'

'What happened after?'

'I don't remember what time we left. It must have been about one-ish. But by that point, I was pretty waved. Not nearly as much as she was, though. She was clinging to my arm the entire way home.'

'You walked?'

'Past the station, down Walnut Tree Close.'

Stephanie remembered it well: the never-ending road that became even longer after a night out. Worse for the residents, no doubt.

'It took us forever,' he continued. 'We kept stopping for more kissing. She was telling me all the things she was going to do to me. And then, when we got to the bridge over the train tracks, she threw up everywhere. All over my trainers and jeans; absolutely ruined them.'

The smell and sensation of vomit invaded Stephanie's nose and throat. She grabbed for her mum's necklace again.

'Do you have them still?' she asked.

'The jeans are in the launderette, but the shoes weren't that bad. I gave them a bit of a clean.'

'I'm going to need them for evidence.'

'Will I get them back?'

'Potentially. What happened after she threw up?'

'She just panicked. Went absolutely berserk on me. Pushed me away and told me to leave her alone.'

'What did she do?'

'Ran back to her accommodation.'

'Did you chase after her?'

'I thought about it, but...' His Adam's apple convulsed as he swallowed deeply. 'But to be honest, I was a bit put off, so I went back to my room. I think she was embarrassed, more than anything. Can't blame her really. If I'd chucked up in front of a girl, I'd probably want to get rid of her as fast as possible.'

Stephanie nodded thoughtfully, then finished typing the notes on her phone.

'Do you believe me?' he asked, the desperation in his voice causing it to break.

'It's not a case of whether I believe you. It's whether we can prove what you say or whether *you* can prove it.'

Kieran reached for his mobile phone in his pocket and shoved it in Stephanie's face. On the screen was a handful of messages he'd sent to a group chat, explaining what had happened. The timestamps on the messages corroborated what he said, but that didn't absolve him of any guilt. If Claudia had been in the state everyone said she was, then she would have been oblivious to his sending those messages if he'd attempted to cover his tracks. No, the only thing that would exonerate him and remove him as a suspect in the investigation was a handful of eyewitness accounts and CCTV.

'Please,' he began. 'Please, you have to believe me. I didn't have anything to do with this. All I know is that she went through the library and then just disappeared. That's all I know. I didn't follow her; I didn't chase her. I would never do anything to hurt someone like that. You have to believe me.'

Even though she wasn't supposed to, Stephanie did.

She did believe him.

CHAPTER
TWENTY

Stephanie pulled the door closed behind her and Kieran. A forensics unit would soon come down to bag pieces of evidence for analysis.

As she turned to go, she nearly collided with a man rounding the corner.

'Deary me,' he said, stepping back. 'My apologies. Wasn't expecting you to be there.'

The man was tall, broad-shouldered, and well put together. Dressed in a pair of beige chinos, a matching Gant shirt, and suede leather ankle boots, he was a navy scarf away from completing the look of an English lecturer. However, the lanyard hanging around his neck that read "Martin Bell - Student Welfare" quickly put paid to that.

'Are you… are you with the police?' he asked Stephanie. A flash of surprise registered on his well-groomed face.

She nodded slowly. 'Detective Inspector Broadbent.'

'*Broadbent*? Perfect. I'm Martin Bell. Did Noah tell you to come here? I did wonder if anyone would be here on time. I know you're all very busy. I didn't want to put too much pressure on you.'

Stephanie studied his eyes. He hadn't blinked in over a minute. 'Pressure on us for what?'

'Noah didn't tell you? We agreed that it would be a good idea to have a chat with some of the students to allay any fears. They're…

they're understandably shaken. We've already sent out a note to the entire cohort notifying them of what's happened.'

'Yes, I helped put it together with Noah,' she lied.

'Perfect. You'll be best placed to give a talk in person then,' he said, brushing a cuff down. 'If it's not too much of a problem? Like I said, I know you're busy.'

Stephanie checked her watch. She was happy to help. It made sense for her, as the figurehead of the operation, to help allay the students' concerns.

She turned to Kieran, told him to wait there until a uniformed constable arrive to take him down to the station. The teenager nodded and lowered his hood over his eyes.

'Lead the way,' she told Martin.

'These kids live online so much nowadays,' Martin explained as they descended several flights of stairs. 'Everything they're reading or seeing is just adding to the uncertainty. It's all very different from our day, isn't it?'

Stephanie shot him an unimpressed stare.

'Sorry,' he said, holding the exit open for her. 'I didn't mean anything… I didn't mean…'

'I know what you meant,' she said as she skipped into a small forecourt. Outside, the smell of weed, which she'd vaguely noticed when she arrived, had now intensified. It was coming from an open window somewhere. She was sure it was against the rules, but that wasn't going to stop them. She doubted the increased police presence would have an effect either.

Martin led her down another flight of steps – had there always been this many? – towards the library; the entrance was a hive of activity. Knots of students huddled together in coats, bags draped over their shoulders. Each with their own identity, each with their own passions, their own past, their own history, their own future. Stephanie eyed them all with fondness.

Sometimes she wished she could go back to being a student. Reliving the freedom. Reliving her youth; enjoying what hadn't been destroyed of it, anyway.

A moment later, Martin pointed to the campus's amphitheatre. Seven rows of seats, shaped in a hexagon, surrounded the focal point. Behind it was an oasis of green amongst the beige and grey of the buildings and accommodation for other students to stand. Already, the area had become populated with over a hundred of them, cramped together. The gentle murmuring of panicked conversation echoed around the space.

As Stephanie followed Martin to the centre of the amphitheatre, he introduced her to two female members of the student welfare team. They shook her hand eagerly, thanking her repeatedly for being there.

'Happy to help,' she said, though the knot that was quickly forming in her stomach suggested otherwise. She had never quite been good at public speaking. Never really enjoyed it. She always found her nerves got the better of her and caused her to trip over her words. She never enjoyed addressing the younger generation, either. She was afraid they would judge her, whisper words of cruelty to their friends, like they had done so often during her childhood.

'Thank you for joining us here today,' Martin began, his voice echoing around the amphitheatre, clear and concise. 'The university has liaised with all your lecturers, and they are aware that many of you will have come this afternoon. As you will all be aware, a terrible incident occurred with one of your peers yesterday, and it is our duty to help you through this process. Whether you are grieving, whether you are afraid, whether you are worried; we are here to help. We've invited Detective Inspector Stephanie Broadbent along to answer any questions you may have. She is in charge of the investigation looking into Claudia's death. We were all very sad to hear the tragic news, and we will do everything we can to assist you. Stephanie...'

Martin took a step back and gestured for her to replace him.

Tentatively, she took a breath, squared her shoulders, and moved forward.

They're all naked, she told herself. Even the unattractive ones.

An overwhelming silence settled on the amphitheatre. For a moment, the world seemed to stop spinning.

'Thank you for the introduction, Martin,' she said, casting her gaze around the crowd. 'My name is Detective Inspector Stephanie Broadbent, and I am the senior investigating officer for Claudia Bellini's murder investigation. I'm not here to scare you, but I won't lie to you either. Yesterday morning, she was discovered in her accommodation after a night out. She was asphyxiated. We do not have all the answers, but we suspect someone followed her into her room and took her life.

'I know that may sound distressing to you, but it's important you know that we're working around the clock. We're doing everything we can to find the person responsible for this. But we need your help. If you saw something, even if you're not sure it matters, please come forward and tell us. If you feel unsafe, speak up. If you're scared, that's okay. We're here for that too.

'I've been doing this job a long time. Long enough to know how quickly fear spreads, how fast stories can twist. So here's the truth: it's not your job to solve this. It's ours. But it is your job to look out for each other. Keep your heads up. Trust your instincts. And please, please, please, please, don't walk home alone, no matter how close it feels. I hate to say it, but your life may depend on it. And if you do see something, please call the police. No matter how trivial or small it is. We can't do anything to help you if it's too late.'

Her final sentence seemed to echo longer. A wall of solemn, morose faces stared back at her. Whatever hushed murmurs or whispers she had expected didn't come. Nothing but a low thrum of silence.

'Does anyone have any questions?' the student welfare officer asked beside her.

A hand half rose in the front row. It belonged to a man who looked as though he'd just entered puberty. 'Was it someone from the university? Like... someone we know?' He spoke in a thick Scottish accent.

'We don't have all the answers yet, but we're looking into every possibility, including connections to the university. That's why your awareness matters. If you know something, even if it seems small, tell us. Anyone else?'

Nothing.

'If anyone does have any questions and isn't prepared to ask them here, then please reach out to your tutors, your lecturers, your friends, your welfare officers. There are plenty of people on hand who can help you. And we are working closely with the university to ensure every question and concern is answered. You won't be dismissed. You won't be ignored. Lastly, I would also like to add, rumours can do as much damage as the truth. I know you're all on social media, and I know you're all probably discussing it in your group chats, but please, don't spread stories unless you know they're fact. Let us do our job properly.'

As the students began to stir, Stephanie stepped back, a pang of guilt flaring inside her. They'd looked at her like she held all the answers, like she could somehow put a shield around them. But she couldn't. All she could do was arm them with the information they needed to protect themselves. It was up to them to make sure they heeded her words.

And it was up to her to make sure she caught the killer before they ever needed to.

Stephanie sank into the driver's seat, the door thunking shut. She didn't start the engine. Instead, she stared blankly at the dashboard, her eyes unfocused, and in the reflection on the plastic trim, the faces of the students reappeared. Wide-eyed. Frightened.

Then another face emerged. Softer. Older. Her mother's. Lying dead on the sofa, red marks around her throat. Stephanie blinked hard, but the image lingered. Her fingers moved instinctively to the thin silver chain at her neck, tracing it around her throat. It had always been too tight for her, constricting her airway slightly. But she kept it regardless, wearing it like a penance; the pain she felt was a daily reminder of her inactivity, of how she'd been too late to protect her mother from what had been inevitable. Her fingers dug into the chain, pressing it harder into her skin, as if the pain might somehow make up for the years of guilt. It never did.

As she put the keys into the ignition, her mobile vibrated.

'All right, Chief?' Noah began. 'Heard you gave a blinding speech just now.'

'Blinding's not the word I would use to describe it. What do you need?'

'A lead's just come through,' he explained. 'Claudia was a member of the rock-climbing society. Apparently she'd got a bit flirty with one of the other members on their union night on the first night of Freshers'. I'm heading there now to speak with the guy, if you want to join?'

CHAPTER
TWENTY-ONE

The Surrey Sports Park was a massive, multimillion-pound structure situated a twenty-minute walk from the campus. It contained an eight-lane, Olympic-sized swimming pool, several football pitches, squash courts, tennis courts, basketball courts, a modern state-of-the-art gym – also used by the Harlequins professional rugby team – and a forty-foot rock climbing facility.

With eighty different boulder problems of varying difficulty, there were challenges for all levels. Stephanie craned her neck skyward, admiring the height and impressiveness of the structure.

'Fancy yourself up there?' a voice called from behind her. Distant. Far off.

It wasn't until the figure stood in front of her that she realised he was talking to her. Lean and wiry, with forearms corded from years of climbing, he was light on his feet. A faded Surrey Sports Park T-shirt clung to his wiry frame, and on his feet, he wore a pair of professional, top-of-the-range climbing shoes. Just above his eyebrow was a faint scar, and his short dark hair was flecked with traces of chalk. A climbing belt around his waist jingled like wind chimes as he moved.

'I'd give it a go,' she said.

The man eyed her for a moment, taking in her cheap smart trousers and blouse. She wasn't dressed for the occasion, but that wasn't going to stop her. Keeping her attention focused on the top of the forty-foot wall, she stepped out of her shoes and removed her light jacket.

'I'm going to have to get you to sign some forms,' the man said.

She waved the comment away.

'No, really. It's for health and safety. I can't just let you go up.'

Stephanie sighed, began to slip her feet back into her shoes, then had a sudden change of heart. Ignoring the man beside her, she padded across the soft mat to the foot of the wall and placed her hand on the first boulder. She began climbing, her moves instinctive. She had free climbed so often that she saw the path in front of her, her next handhold or foothold illuminating like a light.

'Hey, you can't do that! You need to come down!'

But she wasn't listening. She was too focused, too entrenched in her next move.

There was nothing like free climbing. The risk-reward element was unparalleled. The risk was that she could fall and seriously injure herself; the reward was an ego boost, a silent pat on the back that she'd done it without support, without anyone else's help.

She'd been climbing for as long as she could remember. The thirty-foot oak tree in the garden to escape the shouting. The drainpipes up the side of the foster home to run away for the evening. It was an escape. A release. Just her and the brick. Her and the boulders.

Her, her hands, her feet.

If she made a wrong move, it was her fault. Nobody else's. She was in control.

'Stephanie,' Noah called from below. 'I'd appreciate it if you could come down, please. I'm not very good with blood!'

That seemed to trigger an alarm in her brain. That perhaps what she was doing, given the circumstances and the company she was currently with, was, in fact, a bad decision. Carefully, more carefully than she had the previous day, Stephanie climbed back down the wall, easing her foot into the precarious holds, steadying her breath, ignoring the searing pain in her forearms and lungs.

A few worrying moments later, she reached the bottom and jumped the last metre, landing softly on the padded surface. She glanced up at Noah. His eyes were wide with fear and disbelief. The staff member matched Noah's expression.

'You really shouldn't have done that,' he said.

'I know. But you did ask if I fancied myself.'

'That wasn't an invitation for you to climb it without any safety harnesses, though.'

'I think it was impressive,' Noah interjected. 'I mean, a little bit psychotic, but impressive all the same. At least you weren't afraid of heights as a child. You won't be seeing me up there.'

She quickly glanced up the wall, then back to Noah. 'Not even with support?'

'No chance.'

Chuckling awkwardly, the man jumped in. 'Sorry, guys… I don't know what just happened there, but what's going on here? Is there something I can help you with?'

Noah reached into his coat pocket and produced his warrant card. 'We were looking to speak with an Alec Donnelly, about—'

'That's me.' Panic flashed across Alec's face as he took a step back. 'What's this… what did I… what's going on here? Is this some sort of joke?'

'We were wondering if we could speak with you regarding your relationship with Claudia Bellini?'

It took a moment for the name to register on Alec's face.

'Claudia? Why?'

'You've heard the news about her, presumably?'

Alec nodded, eyes wide. 'She joined the society on the first day…' He spoke slowly, the cogs in his mind shutting down.

'And the two of you got overly friendly with one another the other night,' said Noah.

Now Alec's mouth opened, revealing a set of yellow, tobacco-stained teeth. 'I… I… You think that I had something to do with what happened to her?'

Stephanie became suddenly aware that they were having the conversation in the middle of the climbing centre, surrounded by groups of climbers who were gradually beginning to listen in.

'Is there somewhere more private we could be having this discussion?' she asked.

Alec looked as if she'd just spoken to him in French.

'More for your benefit than ours,' she added.

Eventually, he came to and led them into a small manager's office near the front desk. Noah shut the door behind them and said, 'Is it true the two of you became intimate the other night?'

'Intimate? Intimate? No, we didn't become intimate. It was just a kiss. A couple of times. And that was it. We were both pretty drunk. But nothing happened between us. Ask any of the other guys who were there. Ask Dean. Ask Varun. Ask any of them. They'll tell you nothing happened between us!'

His voice amplified in the small room.

'Why did nothing happen between the two of you?' Stephanie asked. 'Whose decision was it?'

'Eh?'

'Who decided not to pursue things?'

'We both did. We went out, got drunk, made out, and then moved on. It wasn't like there was anything serious between us. We'd just met. Besides, it would have been awkward if we'd slept together and the next day we had a social meet. I tried that in my first year and it didn't work out.'

'So she didn't turn you away?'

Alec shook his head as if his life depended on it. Then he raised both hands in surrender. 'Honestly, we was just at the pub in town, on a pub crawl. I was talking to some of the new guys, she was nearby, we caught each other looking, and then we just kissed. It was nothing more than ten, twenty seconds – *max*. After that, we both went our separate ways.'

'Have you spoken to her since?' Stephanie asked.

Alec shook his head. 'If I'm honest, I haven't really thought about her. It was just one of those things.'

'Well, if her text messages and conversations with her friends are anything to go by,' Noah began, 'she was definitely thinking about *you*.'

Alec let out a big sigh, laden with guilt.

'I'm sorry,' he said. 'I know what happened to her was a tragedy, and I still can't believe it. But I haven't spoken to her or thought about her since that night. I had nothing to do with it.'

'Is there anyone you can think of who might have wanted to hurt her?'

He didn't think for long. 'I honestly have no idea. Like I said, I'm sorry.'

Stephanie reached into her pocket and produced her business card. As she handed it across to Alec, she said, 'Keep your ear to the ground. I bet you get a lot of students coming through these doors. If you hear anything, whether it's someone mentioning her name or discussing what happened to her in any way, I want you to give me a call. Understood?'

Alec took the card from her and surveyed it. 'I'm sorry again.'

'It's fine,' she replied. 'You can make up for it by signing me up to be a member here. I assume you allow anyone to use the climbing walls?'

'So long as you've got the right equipment.'

Twenty minutes and several documents later, she was a fully-fledged member of the Surrey Sports Park.

'Shame they're not open late,' she said as they headed back to her car.

'Shame they haven't got a policy for keeping people with death wishes away,' Noah remarked. 'You almost gave me a heart attack back there.'

Stephanie chuckled. 'What? You've never lived life on the edge?'

Noah came to a stop beside his car and placed a hand on the handle. 'No, I have a mortgage. And no life insurance. I can't afford to live dangerously.'

'Either that, or it's because you're afraid of how much you might like it.'

He opened the car door. 'Chasing the bad guys from behind my desk in the comfort of the office is adventure enough for me.'

She gestured to the grey sky above their heads. 'This being the exception?'

Noah didn't respond. As he hopped into the driver's seat, he called, 'I spoke with the guys, and they're keen for round two at the pub tonight. It took some convincing, mind. So you can put your moving on hold for a couple of hours.'

'And if I say no?'

'Then you'll look like a right bitch. They're only coming out because you didn't last night.'

'Why would they do that?' she asked.

'Because they want to get to know you. They're not a bad bunch if you give them a chance. Oh, and because I already told them you'd said yes.' Noah fired a finger gun at her, smiling from ear to ear as he shut the door. 'See you back at the station, ma'am. Drive safely. It would be good to have you back in one piece.'

CHAPTER
TWENTY-TWO

The Weyside buzzed with the low murmur of chatter, the occasional burst of laughter rising above it, mostly from the long booth the team had taken in the corner of the room. Stephanie spotted them instantly. Not by sight, but by sound – the low rumble of Noah's deep, guttural laugh and Olivia's high-pitched cackle.

She hovered at the threshold for a moment. It should have felt comforting, ordinary. It had, eighty miles away in Essex, with her old team. But here, she still felt very much like an outsider, an alien. It didn't help that she felt the weight of the investigation pressing heavily behind her eyes. That Claudia Bellini's killer was still out there while they relaxed, while they drank, while they forgot about the horrors of the day. She didn't belong in this kind of ease. And yet, here she was – trying. Trying to smile. Trying to soften the lines that work and trauma had carved into her. She wanted to know these people. To trust them. Maybe even be one of them.

Before she could think about turning away, Noah caught her eye and waved her over with an exaggerated flourish. With a sigh and the faintest smirk, she made her way to the table, each step feeling more deliberate than it should.

Noah shifted to make room, patting the bench beside him with a grin. She slid in wordlessly, offering a polite nod to the others, her eyes lingering on Devon for a beat too long. He raised his pint in mock greeting, his smile sharp around the edges.

Eve leaned forward, her expression bright. 'You made it! I was starting to think you were a myth.'

Stephanie managed a smile. 'I figured I had a couple of hours to spare.'

'You're spoiling us,' Fiona remarked, sipping a glass of wine. 'Drink?'

Steph shook her head. 'Not tonight.'

'More unpacking to do?'

'Something like that.'

'You missed it last night,' Olivia said beside her, placing a hand on Stephanie's thin wrist. 'We were playing two truths and a lie. We're missing yours…'

Stephanie stared into the wooden table for a long moment. She knew where this was headed, and it wasn't a place she wanted to go just yet. But, just like her invitation, she had no choice but to play along.

'Two truths and a lie?'

'Don't make 'em boring,' Eve said.

'Not boring? All right. Let's see…'

Around the table, the others quietened, watching her with varying shades of interest. Eve was on the edge of her seat, Giles leaned in slightly, and Olivia offered a soft, encouraging smile. Even Devon looked up from his pint.

'Don't make it boring,' Stephanie repeated, more to herself than anyone else. Her first instinct was to deflect, but they would see right through it. 'I'm not very good at this.'

'None of us are. You're not getting out of it that easily.'

Stephanie exhaled, a slow, careful breath. 'All right. One: I love to paint and have over two hundred paintings at home. Two: I speak fluent Polish. And three: I once considered quitting the police the night before I found out I was going to be a sergeant.'

There was a beat of silence around the table as they absorbed Stephanie's words. Then Giles leaned in, squinting at her like she was a particularly tricky Sudoku puzzle.

'No offence,' he said slowly, 'but I can't picture you painting. Like, at all.'

Eve grinned. 'I'm with Giles. Though the Polish thing could be true. You've got that vibe, like you could unleash hell on someone in five languages and never break eye contact.'

'I think the lie is the quitting,' Noah said, surprisingly thoughtful. 'You don't strike me as the type who backs down. Ever.'

Stephanie raised an eyebrow, lips twitching at the corner. 'You sure about that?'

Noah didn't respond. Instead, he took a tentative sip of his drink.

Olivia placed her hand on Stephanie's arm again. 'I think it's the Polish one,' she said.

Stephanie pointed at Olivia. 'We have a winner,' she explained. 'I mean, I can swear a bit. There was a sergeant back in Essex called Tomek Bowen, and he was half-Polish, half-English. We were working together on a case, and we had an afternoon spare, so I just asked him to teach me some Polish. Naturally, he gave me all the curse words, which I still remember to this day.'

'That's the same as me,' Giles said. 'The only thing I remember from GCSE German is the naughty stuff, and it certainly wasn't my teacher who taught me.'

A ripple of laughter echoed around the table.

'Wait… two hundred paintings?' Eve asked, setting her drink on the table. 'Seriously?'

Stephanie shrugged. 'I don't like blank walls.'

Nor did she like what they reminded her of.

'What do you draw?'

'Anything. Nothing.'

'Can we see some of them?'

Steph shook her head. 'I doubt it.'

'Oh. Really? But still, that's, like, actual talent. Giles can barely microwave soup.'

'Oi!' Giles replied, mock-offended. 'I'll have you know I mastered the art of the Pot Noodle today.'

Stephanie smiled, despite herself.

Fiona tilted her head. 'Why'd you almost quit?'

'Excuse me?' Stephanie asked.

'Your third one. You said you almost quit the night before you made sergeant. *Almost.* Why?'

Stephanie didn't appreciate Fiona's accusatory tone. At that moment, she felt all eyes were watching her, burning holes into her flesh. She took a moment, her eyes fixed on the rim of Noah's beer glass, the noise of the pub suddenly distant.

Before responding, she took in a large gulp of air.

'Because I'd just come off an investigation that gutted me. I was working days and nights, barely sleeping, shutting people out. That night, after it had all finished, I realised I didn't recognise myself anymore. And I didn't know if the job was turning me into someone I couldn't live with… or just revealing who I already was. The next morning, I showed up anyway. I wasn't done.'

The table went quiet; not awkward, just thoughtful. And for the first time, Stephanie didn't feel like she was on the outside looking in. She was still figuring them out, and they were definitely still figuring her out, but something had shifted. She'd given away a little about herself and her story.

CHAPTER
TWENTY-THREE

The office at night was a different beast. Abandoned, desolate, stripped of its daytime urgency. It was silent, save for the hum of the server behind a closed door, the air conditioning someone had left on, and the faint buzzing of the overhead lights, casting long shadows across the scuffed linoleum floor. Desks sat deserted like little islands, paper trails abandoned mid-thought, coffee mugs frozen beside unfinished notes. The only activity came from the slow, mechanical blink of the photocopier on standby.

Stephanie stood in the doorway for a moment, keys still clutched in her hand, her breath shallow. It felt like walking into a church after hours – quiet, empty, full of ghosts. None of them friendly.

She moved carefully, her flat shoes echoing softly as she crossed the floor to her desk. She dumped her coat on the back of her chair and sank down, staring at the case notes on the surface. Her chest tightened. The investigation was stagnating, slipping through her fingers. It had only been twenty-four hours, but she was losing control of it. Devon's earlier antics hadn't impacted her at the time, but now that she was alone, now that she was alone with her thoughts, she realised how much disruption he'd caused. And yet she hadn't had the heart to confront him about it. What was wrong with her? Why was she so weak?

And the confession at the pub.

Why had she done that? She'd opened a window into her life, albeit minutely, and given them an insight into that version of herself. Now that the window was open, it would be much easier for them to climb in, take a look around, and leave with a souvenir.

If she wanted to get a handle on the investigation and her relationship with the team, she was going to have to shut it off. And deal with it the only way she knew how.

The silence clawed at her ears, scratching at her thoughts. She opened her laptop. Closed it again. Two minutes passed. Then five. Her stomach gnawed with its familiar, anxious hunger. She grabbed her phone, found the app she was looking for – downloading it again from the App Store after deleting it several weeks earlier – and then placed the order.

Twenty minutes later, a knock came at the door. Stephanie recognised the woman from around the building.

'I think this is for you...' she said, stepping into the room and setting the Domino's pizza box on the edge of Stephanie's desk.

Stephanie feigned a smile. 'Perfect, thanks. Want a slice?'

The woman placed a hand on her stomach almost instinctively. 'Me? No. I'm trying to be good. You enjoy it. Smells *delicious*.' She inhaled deeply as she left the office.

Stephanie stared at the pizza box for a moment, her hunger pangs intensifying. She grabbed the cardboard box and rested it on her keyboard. The smell sent her stomach into a frenzy. And then she devoured it. Slice after slice. Grease, salt, cheese, all melting together in her mouth. Until there was nothing left. Her stomach clenched with relief and regret in equal measure. It filled the hollow in her chest for all of five minutes.

Then came the wave of guilt. Thick. Acidic.

She moved automatically, quickly, like she had a hundred times before. Into the toilet, locking the door behind her. Fingers down her throat. Knees on the cold floor. The usual burn in her throat, the pressure behind her eyes, the shaking hands on the bowl afterwards. The relief that came wrapped in shame.

As the toilet flushed behind her, she staggered out of the cubicle and began washing her hands. She bent over to rinse her mouth, avoiding the mirror. Always avoiding the mirror. Always unable to face herself after what she'd done. Unable to confront her demons head-on.

Just as she was about to wash her hands, the stench of vomit thick in her nostrils and throat, the bathroom door opened.

Stephanie froze.

DC Olivia Willard stood there, one hand still on the handle. Her eyes flicked from Stephanie's pale face to the cubicle rapidly filling with water.

Stephanie remained hunched over the sink, panic-stricken.

Neither of them spoke for a long moment. Then Stephanie straightened up, wiping a stray drop of water from her chin.

'What are you doing here?' she asked, her voice hoarse and raw.

Olivia looked behind her, as if the answer was back in the hallway. 'I followed you here,' she said. 'After the pub. I saw something in your face. So I followed you. Thought about coming in for a long time. Then I remembered I needed something from my desk.'

'I see.'

'I didn't mean to...' Olivia continued. 'I didn't... I mean, I heard it, but—' She swallowed deeply. Then her face quickly filled with warmth, a silent understanding in her eyes. 'I won't ask, and I won't say anything,' she continued, her voice low despite the emptiness of the office. 'Just... just know that I'm here. If you ever want to... you know. *Not* be okay.'

Stephanie's throat tightened. She gave a stiff nod, eyes fixed somewhere over Olivia's shoulder. Something about the way Olivia spoke hit hard. There was no judgement. No performance.

'Get some sleep, ma'am,' Olivia said. 'We've got work to do in the morning.'

Then she walked away, leaving Stephanie in the silence, the ache in her chest somehow louder than before.

CHAPTER
TWENTY-FOUR

Juggling his stainless-steel coffee mug in one hand and his sketchbook in the other, Dr Ian Kettle wedged the door to the Ivy Arts Centre open with his leather satchel. The sound of eighties pop blasted through his Walkman headset. As he walked through the corridor, humming along to the synth pop of Depeche Mode, he caught sight of himself in the reflection. One of his better outfits: a deep purple corduroy blazer, a matching fedora, black braces attached to his waistband, and a pair of brogues that showcased every colour of the rainbow.

He was a man of style and class, renowned throughout campus for his eccentric dress sense. It was often said that he'd missed his calling by becoming an artist rather than a fashion designer, but he liked to blend the two, creating art with fashion and fashion with art. Both, in his mind, were universal forms of expression.

At this time in the morning, before the campus had awoken from its night of carnal, alcohol-fuelled desire, the Ivy Arts Centre was desolate and quiet. He loved it. It gave him time to think, time to breathe, and to focus on his latest piece.

His corner of the arts centre was situated at the back of the building, away from the performing arts facilities. Usually, the place was teeming with actors, choreographers, stage designers, and directors putting together the latest production, pouring their lives into their work.

The song changed to 'Sweet Dreams' by Eurythmics as he made his way through the corridors, moving deeper into the building. Eventually, he found what he was looking for: Room 3BA. Home to his latest masterpiece. It was in the centre of the room and available for all students to see. Artists. Actors. Performers. Anyone who took an interest. He often spent his early mornings there, adding to it, touching it up, and covering the previous day's mistakes. All before the working day began. He adored every moment of creation, and on days he was unable to fulfil his passion, he felt lost and bereft.

As he approached room 3BA, he noticed the door was ajar.

Odd.

The Art Society was always diligent about locking it up after their meetings.

He removed his headphones and cautiously approached, his shoes echoing along the hallway. He knocked gently on the door and pushed it open.

'Hello?' he began. 'Is anyone in there?'

No response.

What hit him first was the smell. Not paint or varnish or turpentine, but something sour and heavy that clung to the back of his throat.

Perhaps someone had spilled something and panicked, fleeing the room in embarrassment.

Or perhaps someone had broken in and vandalised his painting, defacing it with their mess.

He stepped inside.

He was wrong. So, so wrong.

A girl, wearing baggy jeans and a loose-fitting sweatshirt, lay sprawled across the floor, her blood pooled out beneath her like a grotesque shadow. One arm was thrown aside, fingers limp and stained crimson. Thick, rich red gashes stained her jumper and shirt. At first, he thought it was paint. Evidence of a cruel and sick joke.

But then a strip of bare skin across her belly button revealed a puncture wound below her abdomen.

Ian's coffee hit the floor with a dull splash, and his throat closed around a sound he hadn't made in years.

'No! Jesus Christ, no!'

His hoarse cry echoed along the endless corridor.

CHAPTER
TWENTY-FIVE

Visions of Olivia's awkward, unsettled, yet oddly warm and comforting face had kept her awake the entire night. Worse, she had been disturbed by the thoughts that accompanied it. What if she told the team? What if she called her out in front of everyone? What if she held it against her and used it as blackmail?

Her deepest, darkest, most embarrassing secret – something she'd struggled with almost her entire life and had been ashamed of for just as long – had been laid bare in front of someone she hardly knew.

She felt a sense of relief when she entered the office and didn't see Olivia at her desk. Before she had a chance to settle in, DCI McGowan emerged from his room.

'I thought I heard someone,' he said, with the kind of gentle smile that made most people feel safe. 'Got a min?'

Stephanie dropped her bag to the floor and followed him into his office. He closed the door behind her and moved round to the other side of his desk, his movements slow and methodical, as if he had all the time in the world. Perched on his desk, a ceramic mug emblazoned with the words "Keep Calm and Let the DCI Handle It" steamed furiously.

'You're here early,' he began.

'So are you.'

'I also hear you were burning the midnight oil.'

Stephanie's body flushed cold. She said nothing.

'I heard you were good,' he said, slowly lowering himself into his chair. 'Now I can see why.'

She let out a long, steady sigh of immense relief. He didn't know. Or, if he did, he wasn't choosing to bring it up.

'I just had some things I... I wanted to take care of,' she answered.

'I'm pleased to hear it. How's everything going?' He leaned back in his chair in anticipation.

Stephanie sat, her back straight, palms pressed together in her lap. 'Settling in, sir. It's been... full on. But the team seems capable.'

Clive studied her for a moment. 'Many of them are singing your praises. Any causes for concern?'

Devon, she thought instantly.

'This is a private space,' Clive said softly. 'What you say here won't go beyond these four walls. You have my word.'

Stephanie sniffed sharply. Her throat still ached from the previous night's purge. 'I'm struggling with Devon, in all honesty. I don't know what it is, but he seems to be hijacking some elements of the investigation.'

The chief inspector nodded thoughtfully. Stephanie began to play with her necklace.

'He gave the team a new set of tasks and instructions, pretending that I'd given them to him to pass on. I've worked with some arseholes in the past, sir. But he's proving to be the biggest yet.'

'Thank you for bringing this to my attention,' he replied with a soft, gentle sigh that was almost a whisper. 'Devon's having a few... personal issues. But that's no excuse to bring it into his work. Would you like me to have a word with him?'

She shook her head. 'Leave it with me. If I don't get a handle on it, then I'm happy for you to jump in.'

'Very well. How goes the unpacking?'

She scoffed. 'Slow.'

'Sounds about right. Shame about the timing. Have you got anyone helping?'

Steph shook her head. 'Just me, myself, and I.'

'What about your sister? From what you said, she was desperate to get you back here.'

'You haven't met her. She's a neat freak. Won't go anywhere near it until it's all done.'

'Smart woman,' he said after a beat. 'How are things coming along with the university? What progress has been made?'

Stephanie filled him in on the latest, about her visit to the campus and the sports park, how they were waiting on the analysis of the voodoo doll, and how they were still trying to identify the killer via the CCTV footage around campus.

'What's your gut telling you?' Clive asked.

'My gut?'

'I didn't bring you here for your people skills.'

Stephanie shifted into a more comfortable position and finally released the necklace. 'I think this is more than just a targeted attack. I think this is part of something worse. The voodoo doll... it disturbs me. I think we might have something bigger on our hands.'

'Like what?'

'A serial killer.'

The scoff that left his lips echoed around the room. 'A serial killer? In Guildford? I've heard of some fantastical things in my time, but... there's only been one murder.'

'Not if the knife in the voodoo doll suggests there are more to come.'

'But you don't know who, when, where, or why...'

She steeled her gaze. 'True, but we do know *how*.'

An unsettling pause fell over the desk, landing between them.

Before either of them spoke, Stephanie's phone rang in her pocket. Clive confirmed she could answer it.

'DI Broadbent,' she said.

'Hello? Inspector? Hi, it's Laurence from Control. I just wanted to make you aware that we're receiving several reports of an incident this morning at the University of Surrey campus.'

'At the university?' she asked, her eyes slowly meeting McGowan's.

'Yes. Reports indicate one of the students has been stabbed in a classroom.'

CHAPTER
TWENTY-SIX

By the time Stephanie arrived at the Ivy Arts Centre, feeling a powerful sense of déjà vu, Devon and Noah were already there, dressed in their forensic paper suits as she entered art room 3BA.

The space was larger than she'd expected. A circle of easels was situated in the centre of the room, resembling an artist's version of Stonehenge. On the outskirts, art supplies and equipment spilled from boxes, cupboards, and wardrobes. The first thing she noticed was the thick, cloying smell of paint in the air, and she was grateful for the face mask protecting her weakened throat from the fumes. On the left-hand wall was a half-finished sixty-inch by forty-inch canvas artwork, looking down on the room.

The body was in the far left corner, surrounded by two SOCOs who were busy taking close-up photographs of her face, wounds, and limbs. Stephanie thought there was something oddly artistic about the photos of her body, the way other photographs hung from the walls as inspiration, and how the killer had painted a savage and brutal image, using his victim as his canvas.

Many of the paintings and photographs around the room reminded her of her own: the scenery, the buildings, the obscure insights into the artists' lives and psyches, and the dark, forceful brushstrokes that bled onto the canvas. Hers were nowhere near as accomplished.

'What took you so long?' DS Lafferty asked as she approached.

THE VOODOO KILLER 103

'How did *you* get here so quickly?' she countered.

'I got the call from Control, just like you.'

'How? I asked to be the first port of call whenever something came in.'

He shrugged, nonchalant. 'I guess it was just force of habit,' he replied. 'We're all here now, so what's the problem?'

She chose not to respond, not to rise to it, letting her frustration fester deep inside her. She thought of Caleb, her old DS. He would never have done anything like that. Never overstepped the mark or interfered with her role as SIO.

She was beginning to think that giving him an instruction, with him suffering the same fate as Caleb had, might not be such a bad thing after all.

'You're here!'

The voice came from behind her. Leanna Moore, the pathologist, hurried in, walking quickly, and stopped beside Stephanie.

'Pleasure to see you again.' She gave a friendly nudge on the side of her arm. 'Glad I get to be here for this one, you know. Speeds up the process slightly.'

Leanna moved over to the body, nodding politely at the detective sergeants.

'I suppose you'll want to know how she was killed?'

'No,' Stephanie replied bluntly. 'I want to know if anyone's found another voodoo doll.'

Almost immediately after she asked the question, her eyes fell on a dark blue plastic container on the windowsill. Stencilled in pink paint on the side were the words, "Open Me." Stephanie made a beeline for the box and peered in.

The lid had already been removed. Inside, she saw another voodoo doll floating in a body of water. She reached her hand towards her neck.

'Who opened this?' She pointed at the doll, which looked up at her with its red eyes, moving silently across the water, haunting her, teasing her.

'I did.' There was a hint of pride and defiance in Devon's tone.

'Excuse me?'

'I opened it, ma'am. I noticed it as soon as I got here.'

She swallowed and took a deep breath. *Calm, calm, calm.*

'Who gave you permission to do that?'

'Nobody, ma'am. I noticed it and thought it would be good for the investigation.'

'Devon,' she snapped, still keeping her eyes firmly trained on the doll, which had now spun one-eighty. 'Are you in charge of this investigation? No. You knew I was coming; you could have waited for me. But you didn't. I am the only one who can open this. Do you understand me?'

No response.

She spun round and glowered at him.

'Do you understand me?'

Something flared in Devon's eyes as he nodded sullenly.

'And the rest of you,' she said, addressing Leanna and the CSIs in the room. 'If, God forbid, we come across any more of these boxes that say "Open Me," nobody, under any circumstances, is allowed to open them unless they have my explicit approval. Does you understand?'

Gentle murmurings of agreement rippled through the room.

Stephanie thanked them, then turned her attention back to the doll. The air in the room thickened, the weight of it pressing against her chest. She struggled to breathe as her mind pieced together what was in front of her. The body that lay on the floor had died exactly the way the last voodoo doll had foretold: a knife to the stomach.

Now there was no mistaking it.

They were dealing with a calculated, vicious killer. A killer who had a plan.

And if they didn't catch them, then soon, someone was going to drown.

CHAPTER
TWENTY-SEVEN

The team shuffled towards the incident room with a muted stiffness. Stephanie sensed an air of trepidation hanging thick in the room, exacerbated by the rumour mill beginning to percolate throughout the office. Word of the second voodoo doll had quickly spread, and by now everyone in the team was thinking about it, fearing the worst: that a potential serial killer had come to Guildford for the first time ever. Their quaint, pretty little town had now been tarnished, blemished, ruptured by one person's actions.

It was up to them to keep the citizens safe, and so far they were failing.

Much of this was unspoken, communicated in their eyes and expressions.

Still, Stephanie wanted to hammer home the point that if they didn't pull their fingers out, then more bodies would turn up.

She produced a printout of the victim's face and stuck it onto the corkboard next to Claudia Bellini's lifeless image. 'Paulina Potter,' she began. 'Nineteen years old. Second-year university student. Found dead inside the art room, stabbed to death.' She pointed to the photograph of the first voodoo doll. 'She was found killed in the way we were told she would be.' She affixed an image of the second doll in the body of water to the board. 'And this is how our next victim is going to die if we don't do anything about it.'

She paused to let that sink in. A mixture of horror and panic played on her team's faces. She glanced at them individually, lingering for a moment before moving on. However, she couldn't bring herself to look at Olivia. Not since the night before. Not since she found out...

'What do we have on Paulina Potter so far?' Stephanie asked.

'She was a food science student,' Fiona began.

'The same as Claudia?'

Fiona nodded. Stephanie drew a line between the two victims' names.

'She lives off campus,' Fiona continued.

'What was she doing in that room last night to get herself killed?'

It was Giles' turn to speak. 'She was attending one of the weekly Art Society meet-ups,' he explained, setting his cup of coffee on the floor. 'They meet every Tuesday to paint, draw, and show each other what they've been working on. The guy who found her, Dr Ian Kettle, was the one who put it together back in the day, but it's mostly run and managed by the students. Most of the time they keep the artwork for themselves; other times they sell it at craft fairs or stalls in the town centre.'

'This Dr Kettle bloke... is he a potential suspect?'

Giles shrugged unhelpfully. 'He seemed pretty distraught when I spoke with him.'

'Regardless, keep him in the back of your mind. What else did he have to say?'

'Not much.' He consulted his notes quickly. 'There are ten members in the society. They're all of varying talents. Some like to draw anime; some like to paint; some like to sketch faces. Every month they have a live drawing competition, but the first one this year is yet to happen.'

Stephanie didn't think any of that was important.

'Speak with the rest of the members of the society,' she instructed. 'Find out what they know and what they think about Paulina. Someone might have taken a dislike to her. Anything else?'

Eve tentatively raised a hand. 'I've tried checking her socials,' she began, 'and it appears Paulina was what you'd call TikTok famous.'

She said it in a way that suggested she didn't think Stephanie knew what TikTok was.

'What makes you say that?' Stephanie asked.

'She had just over half a million followers and tens of millions of views.'

'On what?'

'TikTok.'

'Yes, I know that. But what were her videos of?'

'Her art.' Eve produced her phone from her pocket, unlocked it, and began showing the team. 'She shows the before and after of her works. She did a load of things. Illustrations, charcoal drawings, scenery, buildings, scenes from movies, character art, hyper-realistic versions of portraits and people; she even got to share them with the people she'd drawn. From the looks of it, she was super talented.'

Stephanie looked on in awe at some of the videos that appeared on the screen. It was true: the young girl possessed an inordinate amount of talent that dwarfed anything Stephanie had. Her art had only ever been personal, a hobby, a cathartic escape from childhood. But seeing what this girl was putting out into the world made her feel inadequate.

You're worthless…

You'll never be anything in life…

'Very good,' Stephanie said as she passed the phone back. 'I want you to follow that up. See if anyone's been commenting on her posts, interacting with her, anyone from the university or anyone she might have come into contact with. And cross-reference it with Claudia Bellini's profiles and her diary as well.'

Stephanie turned her attention back to the board. The lights seemed to dim, with the exception of the one pointing at the voodoo doll floating in the water.

'Noah,' she began. 'How well do you know the area?'

'Lived here all my life, ma'am,' he replied.

'Good. I want you to call round to all the places that have a body of water – a swimming pool, lake, river – and get them to keep an eye out for any suspicious activity. If they've got any students working there, trying to earn a little bit of money to get them through university, then put them on a separate list. Our killer is going to target someone and drown them. We need to be ready for if that time comes.'

'We have to stop them before it gets to that point,' came a snide response from Devon. 'It sounds like you're writing off the next person already.'

She ignored him and turned to Olivia, though she was still unable to meet the woman's gaze. 'I'd like you to find connections between our two victims. Collate all the information from HOLMES and put it into victimology reports for me. There must be something linking Claudia Bellini and Paulina Potter. Look at their lecturers, any classmates they may have in common, any societies or groups they were part of… anyone they may have come into contact with recently. From there, we will need to build a list of potential victims and see if we can analyse who might be next. And *then* protect them before anything happens to them.'

The last sentence was spoken with venom and implicitly directed at Devon. The sergeant sensed it. He straightened his back and lifted his chin.

'And what do you want me to do?'

'I want you to take yourself to my office,' she said. 'You and I need to have a little word.'

CHAPTER
TWENTY-EIGHT

A heavy silence descended as soon as Devon shut the door with a soft click. No sound, no chatter from the main office. Not even the air conditioning unit had come alive. Still, silent.

Save for the deep drum of her heart beating in her ears.

She didn't speak. Didn't offer him a seat. Instead, she stood on the other side of the desk, arms folded, staring at him with intent. Devon lingered near the threshold, the tension between them crackling like static.

The room contained the bare essentials: two chairs, a desk, and a computer monitor with all the necessary accoutrements. In the little time she'd been there, she'd tried to make it her own, mark it with her presence: the wilting house plant on the edge of her desk; the tin of mint imperials; the half-opened bottle of hand moisturiser; the coffee mug that said "World's Okayest Boss". Aside from that, it was empty, her personal possessions capable of fitting in one small lightweight box. If she was kicked out at that moment, she would be gone within five minutes.

She wondered how quickly Devon could pack his things up.

'I think you and I need to have a chat,' she said bluntly.

Devon gave away nothing in his expression.

'Do we have an issue?' she asked.

Still nothing.

'I asked you a question, Devon.'

'No, ma'am,' he said as politely as a child forced to apologise. 'No issue at all.'

'Then why did you go behind my back?'

'When did I do that, ma'am?'

She sighed. She'd heard this act before. There was only so much playing dumb he could get away with before she called him out on it.

'The other day. You told the team I'd changed the plan. You gave out instructions under my name. What gave you that right?'

'The voodoo doll was a stronger lead. I made a call.'

'And what did you learn from your expert? Anything that's going to help us in this investigation?'

He shook his head. 'No, ma'am. Not yet.'

'You undermined me.' Her voice was steel. 'That won't happen again.'

He bowed his head, saying nothing. In that moment, she saw a flash of Caleb in the gesture. Her old sergeant had made the same movement, except it had always been under different, more amicable circumstances.

'And what happened earlier, at the crime scene? Why did you open the box before I got there?'

'I saw the box, and I opened it. I didn't think. I thought I was acting in the best interests of the investigation.'

Which roughly translated to: he believed he was acting in his own best interests.

'I'm SIO,' she intoned. 'I have complete autonomy over what happens.'

'We've never worked that way before,' he replied. 'I've always been given more control in investigations.'

She took a moment, inhaled, and steadied herself. 'That may have been the case with your previous inspector, but with me, you have to earn that privilege. It's not a right.'

Devon shifted uncomfortably at the comment. She sensed he didn't like the idea of having to work hard to get what he wanted, that he'd been so used to handouts and having control of certain aspects of an investigation that anything else seemed wrong and like a personal attack.

'I know it must be difficult for you adjusting to change, but I'm not the enemy,' she continued. 'I'm not a bad person. I've come here to help you, to help the chief inspector, to help the rest of the team.'

'Is that what you said to your last sergeant?'

The comment felt like a punch to the throat. She opened and closed her mouth, but nothing came out.

'Excuse me?'

'I had a look into your last case before you came here,' he began. 'That time you sent your sergeant off to his death.'

Stephanie's mind turned blank. Her knees began to falter. She grabbed for her necklace, but her body was so numb that she couldn't feel it.

'You have no right bringing that up,' she said, a crack in her voice. 'I live with that decision every day. You don't know the pain I've gone through over what happened to him, so don't talk about things you know nothing about. I will always fall on my sword for my team. Any mistakes they make, I make. Any time they mess up, it's because of me. And what happened to Caleb... nobody carries that burden or guilt heavier than I do. Now, if that will be all, I'd like you to leave my office, and I'd like you to go home for the rest of the day. We're done here.'

She watched him coldly as he turned his back on her and closed the door. As soon as it sealed shut, she let out a long, heavy sigh that deflated her entire body. Before she could think about Devon and his belligerent attitude towards her any further, her mobile rang.

Kimberley, her sister.

'Stephy-boo! How goes it?'

'Busy. What do you want?'

'You know what day it is?'

She opened her mouth to respond but then caught herself when she noticed the date on her computer. A lump formed in her throat.

'I can't...' she said.

'You can. You have to. Please, Steph. For me. And you can't get out of it. I'll know if you're lying to me.'

CHAPTER
TWENTY-NINE

The house smelled faintly of burnt toast, damp, mildew, and alcohol. Lots and lots of alcohol. In the kitchen, where she'd been offered a cup of tea, Fiona spotted several empty vodka bottles displayed on the surface like trophies; crumbs and stained surfaces alongside leftover food; unwashed plates and mugs piled high in the sink. This was a student house, all right. Years of neglect at the hands of careless teenagers had been exacerbated by a landlord who had even less respect for the house than its tenants.

The living room was much worse. Two lonely beige sofas, scarred by hundreds of scuffs, stains, and marks, faced a blank corner of the wall. The carpet, discoloured and frayed, looked as though it hadn't been changed in decades. In the space where a television should have been was a single IKEA dining table, large enough for two people. Beside it was a window that looked out upon a long, sprawling garden. They were only a few weeks into the tenancy, and already the garden had become overgrown. A tangled sprawl of long grass, low-hanging trees, and a weed-covered patio. At the far end, a sagging washing line swayed gently in the breeze.

'Would you like a seat?' Mya, a petite South Asian girl, asked. She wore sharp eyeliner and chipped nail polish. Her oversized jumper hung low over her shoulders, and her dark hair was tied into a ponytail.

'I think we should all take a seat,' Fiona replied as she moved to the nearest available space on the sofa. She immediately regretted it and felt sorry for the students who had to spend their time there.

A few moments later, the rest of the girls filtered into the living room. Four in total, each looking as if they'd just woken up.

'I'm sorry to disturb you this morning,' she began. 'I know you're all getting through Freshers' week, but there's something you need to know.'

Over the next few minutes, she explained what had happened to Paulina Potter. The girls' reactions were as expected. Tears flowed, and the windows almost cracked with the pitch of their wails. Fiona consoled each of them with an embrace and a comforting hand on the back before they eventually found solace in one another, huddling together in a group.

After they'd got over the initial shock, Fiona settled back on the sofa and smiled warmly at each of them. 'I know this is hard and a lot to take in right now; I appreciate that, and honestly, if I didn't have to have this conversation with you, I wouldn't. You're all in shock, and that's understandable. But right now, I have some questions I need to ask you so we can find the person who did this.'

'Was it the same person who killed that other girl on campus?' a girl named Georgia asked. Tall and willowy, her hair was dyed a messy strawberry-blonde, and she was dressed in mismatched pyjamas. She spoke animatedly with hand gestures.

'At the moment, we're treating the murders as unrelated,' Fiona said, so as not to frighten the girls into a panic.

'They must be,' Georgia continued. 'Why else would two people die on campus in the same week?'

'Like I said, for now, we're not treating them as connected. But that doesn't mean things won't change as our investigation progresses. That's why I'm here. You girls knew Paulina the best. You might be able to help us.'

Georgia's shoulders softened at the suggestion.

'How long have you all known each other?' Fiona asked, pulling out her notebook.

'Since first year,' Georgia replied, speaking for the rest of them. 'We all met in halls.'

'And you're living together now?'

They nodded.

'How's that been going?'

'Fine.'

'Who's got the biggest room?'

'Paulina,' Mya answered. 'Top floor. It was converted the other year. She helped organise everything, so we gave it to her as a thank you.'

'I'm sure she put it to good use.'

'It's perfect for her,' Lilly, a short, blonde girl with a nose piercing and thick-rimmed glasses, responded, fidgeting nervously with her fingers. 'You should see it. She's got paintings and drawings all over the place.'

'I'd love to,' Fiona said. 'Was she always creating?'

'Always. Even at, like, two in the morning sometimes. It was what she lived for. She even tried to teach us a couple of times, but none of us was any good.'

'I understand she was popular on TikTok?'

Georgia nodded. 'It was crazy. Some of the views she got were insane. She got her first brand deal last month.'

Fiona made a note. 'She must have been ecstatic.'

'She was, she really was,' Georgia continued. It was clear to everyone in the room that she wanted to be the one to talk. 'She put in so much effort and hard work. It was really great to see it pay off the way it did. I just... I just can't believe we've lost her.'

Fiona reached for a tissue and passed it to her.

'How did she seem in the past couple of days? Excited to be back?'

Georgia nodded, dabbing delicately at what make-up was left beneath her eye. 'She couldn't wait. I don't think... I don't think she particularly liked it at home. I think her parents were on her case about dropping the art, doing something that she could make money from. Guess that shut them up when the brand deal came through.'

'She wasn't *entirely* happy though...' Lucy began softly.

Fiona sensed that, of all the girls, Paulina was closest to Lucy – quiet, reserved Lucy.

'Why's that?'

'Over the summer, someone... someone had been messaging her on TikTok. A guy named Damien.'

'Ugh, Damien,' Georgia huffed, accompanied by an eye-roll.

'Did she get back with him?' Mya asked Lucy. 'She told me nothing happened with them.'

Lucy waited a moment before speaking, addressing Fiona. 'They met on a night out last year, a few months before we broke up for summer. He went over to her flat a couple of times, and she did the same. She didn't want anything serious from it. But he did. And...' She licked her lips, holding back tears. 'And over the summer, she told me he'd been messaging her nonstop, saying he couldn't wait to see her again, couldn't wait to hold her. He was being really creepy about it.'

'Did Paulina respond?'

Lucy nodded. 'Only a couple of times. Just to be polite. She realised she couldn't ghost him because she knew they'd bump into each other at some point.'

'How?'

'They were in the same running club.'

Another note. This time she had to go over her writing several times as the ink in her pen began to run out.

'Would you mind giving me his surname?'

'Veitch. Damien Veitch,' Lucy explained. 'I don't know what he looks like; I've never seen him. But I'm sure you can find him on the university courses somehow.'

Fiona finished making her final note. As she placed the cap on the end of her pen, she studied each girl, taking in their broken, beaten expressions. She wished she could hug them all, tell them that everything would be okay, that it was just a dream. But life wasn't that kind. Still, these girls needed positivity, a reminder of the good things about Paulina. They didn't need to sit there stewing, thinking about the way she'd died.

It was time for her to do what she was good at and inject some life into the room that had metaphorically seen two dead bodies in it.

'Right,' she said excitedly, bubbly, as she leapt off the sofa. 'Enough of that talk for today. Show me Paulina's room. I'd love to see some of her work in real life.'

CHAPTER
THIRTY

The time had finally come. The day she'd been dreading since her return. The day her sister Kimberley had incessantly reminded her about in phone call after phone call.

'Steph, don't forget it's Dad's birthday this week.'

'Steph, can you let me know if you're going to see Dad? I thought we could go together.'

'Steph, I've just heard from the home, and he's really looking forward to seeing us this weekend. They've got a party planned, and I told them we'd both be there.'

It was just her luck that her first day coincided with the same week as her dad's birthday. If she'd still been working in Essex, she would have had an excuse, a reason not to go, an eighty-mile distance justifying her absence for yet another year.

Now that wasn't the case. Now there were only a few miles separating her from seeing the man she wanted to spend as little time with as possible.

'He's had such a great birthday,' the male nurse, Wayne Lyons, began as they continued down the corridor towards her dad's room. 'We all sang 'Happy Birthday' in the common room. We had a lovely slice of lemon cake that Julie made for him. She's really good with cakes; she makes them for all our guests. Naturally, your dad had the most. I think he went up for two or three slices.'

'He did always have a sweet tooth.'

Wayne moved with a spring in his step and a joyous candour to his tone. To an outsider, he would have seemed enthusiastic about his job, someone who loved what they did. But for Stephanie, whose impression of him and the entire care home had been tarnished by her relationship with her father, he was just annoying.

She wanted to be as far away from there as possible.

'How's he been doing recently?' she asked.

'You know,' Wayne replied, 'he has his good days and he has his bad days, like we all do. Polly's your best person to speak to about that.'

Polly. She recognised the name. She was sure she'd heard it or seen it in some of the emails she'd glanced over when Kimberley organised the move into the home. That was as far as her relationship with the woman went.

Eventually, they came to a stop outside room thirteen. On the door, on a plastic nameplate, was the name Colin Broadbent.

A name she hadn't thought about for a long time. A name that made her feel sick.

Look at what you've done! This was all your fault!

Wayne gave a soft knock before gently opening the door. The room smelled faintly of antiseptic and urine, with a subtle hint of something sweeter: the lemon-scented air freshener in the room was fighting a losing battle. A single bed pressed into one corner immediately came into view. Beside it stood a sturdy oak nightstand cluttered with essentials: a water carafe, medication organiser, tissues, and a digital clock with oversized numbers. Photographs in mismatched frames crowded the chest of drawers. Images of Kimberley and her husband, Jason, at their wedding; a picture of Stephanie in her police uniform that she didn't remember having taken; a photograph of their mum, sitting on the beach, smiling up at the camera. Images of moments that now existed for Colin only in those captured memories.

The closet door was partially open, revealing carefully labelled clothing that Colin no longer remembered how to select appropriately.

Her dad was sitting in a worn armchair, staring at the television that played something cheerful at a low volume. Fortunately, he was only losing his mind, not his hearing.

The dementia had started a few years before. First, he'd begun showing signs of forgetfulness: asking the same questions, misplacing everyday items, repeating the same stories, calling people by the wrong names. Then came the confusion: not recognising the layout of his own house, getting lost on walks he'd done for years, struggling to follow simple conversations. The diagnosis had come soon after, but by then, the man she and Kimberley had known had already started to slip away.

He'd been in the home for six months, and already his mostly grey hair had thinned drastically, and his back was hunched in a way she didn't remember. He'd lost a lot of weight too. Skin that had once been taut now hung low on his cheeks, and the jeans that had once been snug around the waist rested loosely on his hips.

But there was still something about his face, his expression, his eyes that showed no signs of disappearing. The malevolence, the manipulation, the calculation. A history of evil etched into every pore of his face, every overgrown hair on his chin. He might have been fading – slowly, unrelentingly – but the man who had once made her life hell hadn't completely gone. He was still in there somewhere, beneath the blank, vacant stare he offered her as she entered. After a few seconds, recognition registered in his brain, and he slowly smiled up at her.

The same slow, curling smile that used to come just before he said and did something no parent should do. At the sight of it, she coiled one hand around the necklace and clenched the other in her pocket, pinching a piece of flesh on her thigh from within her trousers to abate the nausea.

'Stephy...' he said slowly, the leering grin widening and increasing in menace.

Shut up, you stupid bitch! Do you see what you've done!

'Hi, Dad,' she said, avoiding his gaze for as long as possible.

'*Well*,' Wayne said, overly cheerful. 'I see you've got a lot to catch up on. I'll leave you both to it. I'll be down in the office if you need me.'

He placed a hand on Stephanie's arm before leaving.

As the door shut, her chest tightened and her breathing became shallow. The air was being sucked out of the room. The walls were closing in on her. An overwhelming sense of dread and loss of control attacked her from all sides.

'How you doing, Stephy?'

She couldn't bring herself to answer. Killers, rapists, abductors; she'd come across them all. But none of them, none of them in her entire career, were as bad as the man opposite her.

'Happy birthday,' was all she could think to say, as she clutched the necklace so tightly it cut into her flesh.

'Is it my birthday? That's nice. Thank you for coming. Was there a party?'

She grimaced. 'Apparently.'

'Did you like it?'

'I couldn't make it. I had work.'

'Oh, yes. Where are you working now?'

'Here.'

She had nothing to say to him. Nothing in the twenty years since she'd last seen him that she wanted to discuss. He didn't deserve to know how well she and Kimberley were doing without him in their lives. How well they'd survived their childhood thanks to her sacrifices, her leadership, and how fast she'd been forced to grow up. Though she was sure her sister had filled him in on every detail of their lives.

'Where is Kimberley?' he asked, another grin slowly appearing on his face.

'She's come already.'

'Oh. That's nice.'

'And what about your mum?'

Stephanie clenched her jaw tight in frustration, clamping down on her cheek. Pain spread in her mouth, so powerful and intense that it distracted her from the bruise that was rapidly forming on her thigh.

Don't you dare talk about her. Don't you dare bring her up in front of me.

'Goodbye, Dad,' she said, already on the half-turn.

She couldn't stand to be there any longer. Couldn't stand to be in the same room as him any more than necessary. Her skin turned to gooseflesh as her body shuddered with discomfort, and a cacophony of emotions welled within her. Fury. Grief. Guilt.

Images of his leering smile were stained in her vision as she tore along the corridor. She needed to banish them. She needed to get him out of her head and out of her life.

She needed to be sick.

CHAPTER
THIRTY-ONE

Stephanie came to an abrupt halt by the exit. The door was alarmed and required a member of staff to open it. She tried repeatedly to do it herself, but it was no use.

'Someone's eager,' a woman with a limp said as she approached. 'They scared you away already, have they?'

'I've got to get back to work,' Stephanie replied.

The woman entered a PIN into a keypad and held the door open for her. Just as Stephanie was about to leave the building, the woman called her back and instructed her to sign out.

'Just in case of a fire,' she explained. 'I would say I don't make the rules, but sadly that's not true in this instance.'

As Stephanie scribbled the time of exit on the paper – precisely six minutes after she'd arrived – the woman leaned over and scanned the page.

'You're Kimberley's sister?'

'Yeah.'

The woman wiped her hand on her trousers. 'I'm Polly. Pleasure to finally put a face to the name.'

'Likewise,' Stephanie replied as she tentatively shook Polly's hand. She wanted to get out of there as quickly as possible.

'I've only ever dealt with your sister,' Polly explained.

'She's always been good with this type of stuff.'

'I understand you were away?'

Steph nodded. 'She seems to have managed all right without my support.'

'Kimberley said you'd moved to Guildford now?'

Stephanie confirmed she had with another nod.

'Does that mean we'll be seeing more of you? He's always asking after you.'

'You mean Kimberley?'

'No. *You.*' Polly pointed at her, as if placing blame on her. 'He's always mentioning your name, asking when you're going to visit. I think he really misses you.'

Steph forced a smile.

'He'd love it if you dropped by more often.'

What was this woman's game? Was she trying to guilt-trip her into seeing the man who'd ruined her life more frequently? Giving him her precious time while he ran out of his?

If only she knew…

'I have to get back to work,' Stephanie said sharply, indicating that there was no room for further discussion.

'Of course.' Polly extended her hand again. 'Well, it was a pleasure to meet you.'

As Stephanie took it reluctantly for a second time, an image of her dad resurfaced. This time he was half-naked, reeking of alcohol, lumbering up the stairs, going into her parents' bedroom, shutting the door in Stephanie's face before the noises and screams began.

And the bruises formed.

Shut up, you stupid fucking bitch!

Closing the heavy door behind her, Stephanie inhaled deeply. Great swathes of air flooded into her lungs, loosening the pressure in her body. She could breathe again. She could fly. She was free. Free from her father's constraints.

Just as she was about to enter the car, her mobile phone rang. She hoped it was a member of the team calling to give her an update on some of the tasks she'd assigned, and not the care home calling to say she'd forgotten something.

Instead, it was her sister.

'Stephmeister,' Kimberley shrieked down the phone. 'Have you been to see Dad yet?'

'I'm leaving now.'

'How was he?'

'Fine.'

'Did he remember you?'

'Yeah.'

'Told you he was always asking after you.'

'I thought you were just saying that so I would go.'

'Of course not. He misses you.'

'If you say so.'

'Don't be like that, Steph. He's all we've got left. And we don't know how much longer he's going to be around.'

Steph grunted.

'I really think you should make more of an effort now that you're down here.'

Another grunt, followed by a half-hearted response.

'Anyway,' Kimberley continued, 'enough about him. What are you doing this weekend?'

'I was going to get my mountain bike out and go for a ride.'

'Not anymore you're not,' Kimberley said. 'You're coming over for dinner with me and Jason.'

CHAPTER
THIRTY-TWO

Ever since she was younger, she had always struggled to switch off. The ever-present fear her father had instilled in her during childhood haunted her for the rest of her life. The crashes that would echo from the living room downstairs. The screams that came from the bedroom. The door that would creak open in the middle of the night…

Over the years, she had found several activities that helped her forget and process her trauma: painting, running, rock climbing, and jiujitsu.

One of the most recent additions was mountain biking. She loved the thrill of the climb and the rapid descent on the wet, uneven terrain. She relished the strain and torture it put on her body. She adored the adrenaline rush as she hurtled down a steep hill at thirty miles an hour, relying solely on her intuition and reaction times; an error of judgement and she'd be hurtling headfirst into a jagged rock or tree.

It was just her, the mountain bike, and the path. As with rock climbing, she was in control. If it went wrong, it was her fault. If she fell off, it was her fault.

If she tripped and broke her collarbone, she would have only herself to blame.

The past few days had flown by without incident. Namely, nobody else had ended up dead. During that time, the team had been working around the clock to uncover as much evidence as they could regarding who killed Claudia Bellini and Paulina Potter. They'd scoured both victims' social media channels, searching for connections, but had found nothing. They had trawled through Claudia Bellini's diary, but nothing had come of it. The only connections they had made were that both girls were part of the same running club and were on the same course, with the same lecturers and students.

What they lacked were any real, tangible pieces of evidence. At both crime scenes, there had been a dearth of it. Or, from a different point of view, there had been so much evidence, with so many different people coming in and out of Claudia's room and art room 3BA, that the forensics teams had been unable to discern anything concrete, with the exception of a fingerprint found on the microwave in Claudia Bellini's bedroom.

The key piece of evidence, however, lay with the CCTV footage found at the Ivy Arts Centre. Olivia had discovered the presumed killer entering the centre at the time of Paulina's death. A figure had snuck into the building, fully clothed and hooded, their features obscured, and had headed into art room 3BA. A short while later, they'd left.

The suspect was believed to be the student that Paulina's friends had notified Fiona about: Damien Veitch. He was the same height, same build, and from the photos they'd seen on his social media accounts, he was wearing a matching hoodie. Since then, several attempts had been made to track the youth down, and between them, Fiona, Giles, and Devon had visited his place of residence and attended some of his lectures in the hope of finding him there. But nothing. The man had vanished, disappeared entirely.

Stephanie was sure he would turn up eventually. But right then, all she could think about was the best route in front of her. The gradual, smoother decline? Or the steeper, bumpier one?

In the end, she chose the latter.

Overhead, clouds loomed heavy and low, casting St Martha's Hill in a steely grey. Her cheeks flushed with each breath as she stood at the top of the incline, one foot on the pedal, the other planted on the earth, heart hammering.

She shoved off.

The tyres spat earth and pebbles behind her as gravity took control.

She leaned forward, fingers feathering the brakes. They squealed like pigs, cutting through the silence of the woods. Trees blurred into dark green smudges on either side of her. Her heart surged. Her legs flexed. Her breathing was shallow, quick, and panicked.

For the first twenty metres, she was in control, manoeuvring the wheels through the path, over the roots and dips in the earth with care and precision. But a few metres later, something changed. She thought she saw a figure in the trees. A man resembling her father, watching her. In his hands, he held something that glistened.

Mum's necklace.

Behind him were two girls: Claudia Bellini and Paulina Potter. Their faces were pale, filled with the pleas they had directed at the hands of their killer.

Please let me go.
Don't do this!
Now they came to her.
Avenge us, Stephanie.

The apparition distracted her for a moment too long, and she missed the root that jutted across the path like a warning finger. Her front tyre struck it hard, jarring the handlebars sideways. For a moment, she hung in the air, weightless. Then the world flipped.

She was propelled through the air, her body hitting the ground with a sickening thud. Shoulder first, then ribs, then hip, expelling the air from her lungs.

The bike clattered down beside her, wheels spinning gently. She didn't move. Couldn't. A searing pain lanced up her side. Her vision blurred with tears. Whether from the impact or the sheer frustration, she didn't know. Above, through the canopy of trees, there was a break in the clouds, and a thin ray of sunlight beat down on the space where she had seen the figures. When she craned her neck to see them, she was relieved to find them gone.

CHAPTER
THIRTY-THREE

The pain in her shoulder and hip hadn't abated by the evening. She was still kneading her thumb into the side of her body when the front door flew open, and her sister greeted her. That evening, Kimberley was dressed in a smart black skirt with a black and white striped knitted cardigan. Her hair had been styled, and she'd applied a thin layer of make-up to a face that, Stephanie thought, had never needed it. Her sister was beautiful in every sense of the word.

Stephanie, by contrast, had always believed she was the ugly duckling of the duo. It was Kimberley who always received the attention from the boys at school. It was Kimberley who had the boyfriends in her twenties and thirties. Meanwhile, Stephanie was busy worrying about her, ensuring she was safe and sensible. She hadn't had the time, nor the inclination, to find love. Nor did she think she was entirely worthy of it. Perhaps that was why most suitors kept their distance as soon as they saw her attitude and expression.

Love, among other things, had never been high on her list of things to obtain. She had seen "love" before, and if what she'd experienced was anything to go by, it had put her off for life. As her parents' version of love was the only example she had, then she wanted nothing to do with it. Naturally, that made her cautious and wary of anybody who tried to interfere with and pursue her little sister.

'You're here!' Kimberley said, her voice echoing up and down the quaint residential street, where the houses were just shy of a million pounds and the cars on each of the driveways looked like something out of a James Bond movie.

'I can turn around if you want me to?'

'Don't be silly,' Kimberley said as she dragged Stephanie in by the arm.

She took off her shoes at the front door and surveyed the hallway. Kimberley and Jason's house was everything that hers wasn't: homely, well-decorated, modern; the type of place you'd move into in a heartbeat. It was clear they'd spent a lot of time, money, and effort making it look the way it did. Rather, *Kimberley* had spent a lot of time, money, and effort. She saw imprints of her sister's personality stitched into every fabric of the building, which was only accentuated as they moved into the kitchen: the Smeg fridge that she'd always talked about; the Aga she'd dreamed of having ever since she'd seen it in a catalogue in the foster home; the green panelling set against a dark blue backdrop that suited her personality. It was Jason's house – *officially*, anyway – but she had made it into a home.

On the counter, a series of pots and pans were bubbling, and the oven light beneath was on. The smell of food filled the room.

'Wine?'

Stephanie shook her head. 'I'm driving.'

'Rubbish,' Kim insisted. 'It's the weekend. You're off duty. And I'm making you have one, whether you like it or not.'

As Stephanie reached for her glass, she winced in pain.

'Are you hurt?' Kim asked, placing a concerned hand on her arm.

'It was just a biking accident.'

'You went biking alone? Again?'

Stephanie shrugged her sister's hand off. 'I always go alone.'

Kimberley ignored her and rushed to the freezer, where she found a bag of ice. Despite Stephanie's protests, Kimberley wrapped it in a kitchen towel and pressed it against her shoulder.

'You don't need to do this,' Stephanie replied. 'I'm capable of looking after myself.'

'It's my turn to return the favour. After all those years you spent looking after me.'

Stephanie chuckled. If only she knew the half of it. Holding the compress in one hand and the drink in the other, Stephanie asked, 'Where's Jason?'

'Upstairs. Just finishing off something for work. He'll be down in a minute.'

Stephanie took a sip of her drink and studied her sister as she busied herself in the kitchen. 'Is that what you wear to work?'

'This? What's wrong with it?'

'Just asking.'

Kim paused and glanced back at Stephanie's outfit. 'Is that what *you* wear to work?'

'It's all I own, so yes. Technically, I wear it everywhere.'

'You and I need to go shopping.'

'No, we don't.'

Stephanie hated shopping. Detested it. Couldn't think of anything she'd rather do less. She hated it so much she often thought she'd rather spend the night in the mortuary.

'It'll be good for you,' Kimberley continued, but Stephanie wasn't listening. 'How's the unpacking going?'

Stephanie took another sip. 'Still there. It's not going anywhere.'

'Do I need to come round and do it for you?'

'You look like you've got enough on your plate.'

That comment stopped Kim in her tracks. She froze in the middle of transporting a saucepan of boiling water to the sink. 'What do you mean?'

'You look tired,' Stephanie said sincerely. The playfulness of their earlier conversation had gone. Now she was using her big sister voice. 'Like something's been keeping you up.'

Kimberley shook her head. 'Work's just been full on.'

Stephanie didn't believe her. She knew her sister well enough to pick up on when she was lying. But before she could probe any further, the heavy clomp of footsteps rushing down the stairs disturbed her. A moment later, a tall, dark, and handsome man, dressed in a smart, tight-fitting shirt and chinos, appeared in the doorframe. Jason had come into Kim's life almost ten years before, and they'd been married for seven of those years. Stephanie remembered the first time she'd met him, at a coffee shop in the middle of Colchester, Essex, when Stephanie had forfeited her bedroom and slept on the couch over a long weekend. Stephanie had the same impression now as she had when she'd first met him: he was polite, charming, and knew all the right things to say. She had her suspicions – that was part and parcel of looking after her sister for as long as she had – but he seemed to make her sister happy. And as long as her sister was happy, she was happy too.

'Stephanie,' he said, embracing her. 'So good to see you.'

She winced as she pulled away. 'Likewise.'

'Sorry, I didn't mean to hurt you.'

'She hurt *herself*,' Kim jumped in. 'It's all self-inflicted. Don't feel sorry for her.'

A look of intrigue crept onto Jason's face. 'What did you do?'

'Fell off mountain biking.'

'And she went rock climbing on her own the other day,' Kimberley added. 'Alone, and *without* harnesses or support.'

'Quite the adrenaline junkie,' Jason responded, then placed a hand on her other shoulder. 'Well, you're looking good. It's been a long time overdue, and I'm sorry I was running late. Just had a couple of things to finish up.'

'On a weekend?'

'You know what it's like. The exciting life of trading never stops.'

'You're lucky he's here,' Kimberley noted. 'He was supposed to be in Japan for work, but the trip got cut short.'

Stephanie picked up a hint of accusation in her sister's tone that had gone unspoken for some time.

'I'm glad you could be here,' Stephanie said, keen to ease the rising tension in the room. She knew how these things started – had seen them first-hand – and she knew how they ended, too... She raised her hand to her mum's necklace and felt herself begin to calm.

'That looks a bit tight on you,' Kimberley noted. 'Haven't you thought about getting any links added to it?'

Stephanie shook her head.

'I think it looks fine,' Jason added, jumping to her defence.

'She's had it for as long as I can remember and still won't tell me where she got it from.'

'I told you, it was a gift from Mum.'

'I'm still annoyed I never got one.'

Before Stephanie could respond, the boiling water on the hob spilled over, sending plumes of steam into the air. Kimberley panicked and quickly cleaned up. Jason and Stephanie both offered a hand, but she sent them out of the kitchen and into the dining room, and they hurried in quietly, awkwardly.

Stephanie had never been good with small talk; forced conversation with people she didn't know very well. And Jason was no different.

'How's work?' he asked. 'How are you settling into the new environment and living back in Guildford again? Guess it must be like you never left.'

Except it hadn't. In some respects, everything felt the same as it had twenty years ago. In other respects, every part of the town, the area, and the people had changed. She didn't recognise anything anymore, and the longer she spent there, the more she felt like an outsider.

'Still early days,' she answered. 'But my new team are keeping me busy.'

'And that case I heard about on the news,' he said. 'With the students. You've got your work cut out for you already.'

Too busy to help around the house and spend time with your wife, but plenty of time to read about the local news, she thought.

'Nothing like being chucked in at the deep end,' she answered.

'Still, must be keeping you up at night.'

That, and the fear. And the paranoia. And the guilt. And the regret.

'Progress is slow, but I'm confident we can get there.'

Just as Jason was about to respond, the kitchen door opened, and Kimberley burst through, carrying several plates of steaming hot food. Jason and Stephanie skipped out of her way as she set the plates down onto the table. They offered another round of support, but again, she declined and ordered them to sit down. A few minutes later, a beautiful Sunday roast, complete with chicken, potatoes, vegetables, cauliflower cheese, and gravy, was sitting in front of them, wisps of steam rising gently into the air.

Kimberley tapped her spoon on her glass, commanding their attention. 'I just wanted to say, Steph, thank you for coming tonight. It's long overdue, but it's great to have you back. You don't know how happy I am, and how happy Dad is as well, to have my big sister back.' She raised her glass. 'To family,' she added.

'To family,' Stephanie replied, forcing the image of her dad to the back of her mind.

CHAPTER
THIRTY-FOUR

What had started as a pleasant, delightful evening had quickly been derailed by discussions about their father. About how great the care home was, how much support and love he was receiving there, how Stephanie needed to see him more frequently, and how she needed to reconnect with him and remind him of who she was before his memory faded entirely.

Throughout, Stephanie had nodded politely and played the role of the amiable sister, mostly for Jason's benefit, but also because she hadn't wanted to prolong the already painful conversation.

As a result, she left her sister's house feeling more stressed than when she'd arrived. To calm herself, she changed into her running gear and set off for a late-night run.

The aftertaste and burning sensation of vomit was thick in her mouth as she entered the university campus. Pools of light spilled from tall lampposts, stretching shadows across the empty path. The outlines of the academic buildings loomed against the night sky, their windows glowing like hollow eyes. Overhead, the clouds hung low and heavy, trapping the glow of sodium lights that turned the world a muted amber. The green spaces and concrete walkways that usually buzzed with students were deserted now, the benches empty, the air still. The place was oddly silent, a stark contrast to the usual buzz during the day. Stephanie's breath came in short, controlled bursts as she put one foot in front of the other. As she climbed a steep incline to reach the students' union, the sounds of conversation and laughter bled through the open windows of the accommodation: students socialising, getting ready for a night out, playing video games, living life with freedom, without boundaries.

At the top of the incline, she arrived at the amphitheatre. Flashes of her speech from the other day appeared in her mind but quickly disappeared as soon as she spotted a young woman casually descending the steps, a pair of earphones plugged into her ears.

Stephanie stopped at the bottom of the steps and flagged her down. The young woman came to a controlled stop and studied her carefully before removing one of her earphones.

'Yeah?' she snapped.

'What are you doing? It's midnight, and you're walking around on your own.'

'Sorry, who are you?' She had a thick East London accent.

'Haven't you seen the news about the two girls who died on campus? You need to look out for yourself. You shouldn't be walking around at this time of night, alone, and with headphones in. You need to be cautious. Anything could happen to you.'

The girl adjusted her bag strap on her shoulder. 'I could say the same to you. You're out 'ere on your own in the middle of the night.'

Stephanie raised her chin slightly. 'It's different. I'm a police officer. I can defend myself.'

'A police officer? You bin working on the case?'

She nodded.

'What... what you doing 'ere?'

'Running helps me think, helps me process.'

'You want summink else to think about?' the student asked.

'Go on...'

'I ain't 'eard too much 'bout it,' she began. 'Tried to keep my 'ead underground, 'n that. But what I 'ave 'eard, is that a lotta people saying one of them lecturers mighta done it, you know.'

Stephanie recalled what she'd said in that exact spot. That rumours were the death of truth.

'Thank you,' she said for the teenager's benefit. 'I'll bear that in mind. Where are you going?'

"Ome,' the girl replied.

'Where is that?'

'Kernel Court.' She pointed over Stephanie's shoulder. 'New accommodation that opened up a couple of years back after the uni kept getting oversubscribed.'

'Would you like me to accompany you?'

The young woman thought about it for a moment, then politely shook her head.

'I'll be all right,' she replied as she removed her headphones from her ears and placed them into her pocket.

Reluctantly, Stephanie let the girl go. She didn't want to intimidate or push her. Instead, she set off in the other direction and circled back, timing it so that she was able to see the girl just as she was heading off campus and onto the bridge leading to her accommodation.

Like a watchful protector, she kept an eye on the girl until she was safe.

The only problem was, she was just one student, and there were several thousand more just like her, and there wasn't enough of her to go around for all of them.

CHAPTER
THIRTY-FIVE

Stephanie was pleased to have woken up with no phone calls from Control the following morning. Even though she'd seen the girl enter her block of flats and close the door firmly behind her, there was still a part of her that feared she had suffered the same fate as Claudia Bellini. That someone had followed her in, snuck up to her bedroom, and ambushed her.

That feeling of insecurity and paranoia worsened as she entered DCI McGowan's office. Behind him, the blinds were drawn halfway, letting in soft, overcast morning light. He looked up at her, offering a nod that was both a greeting and an invitation. As she pulled out the chair, Stephanie tried to read his expression, but he gave nothing away. He was impeccably dressed in his police uniform, as usual, but that morning she noticed he was wearing a watch with a thin leather strap, one she hadn't seen before.

'Treat yourself over the weekend?' she asked, nodding at his wrist.

'This old thing? I've had it since I was a kid. They stopped making them and the parts for it about a decade ago. Now I'm afraid to wear it in case I damage it.'

Stephanie smirked. 'In case you knock it against your keyboard or get some pen ink on it, you mean?'

A thin smirk flashed across his mouth. The moment of levity was short lived.

'I trust you had a good day off over the weekend,' he said. 'A chance to rest, recharge, and so on. But now we need to kick things up a gear. I spent all day yesterday fielding calls from the West Midlands and Northumberland Police. Since the victims are from those areas, everyone who has ever come into contact with them has started ringing their local stations, asking questions and throwing names into the mix. Both chief constables are offering support, which I've turned down for now, but if things continue to escalate at this rate, then I'll have no choice but to bring others in.'

Stephanie said nothing. She simply held his gaze.

'There's also been a *lot* of coverage over the past couple of days,' he continued. 'It's been all over the *BBC*, *Daily Mail*, and the rest of it. I don't want to sound like a broken record – is that the right metaphor? Never mind, what I'm saying is, I agreed to have you join the team based on your pedigree. I was told you would get results. And so far all I'm seeing are two dead bodies, a load of noise, and not a whole lot of progress.'

I know! She wanted to scream in his face. *I know, all right! I know how bad it looks. I know how bad it makes me seem. I'm trying! Just give me more time!*

'Yes, I fully understand, sir,' she said softly. 'I'll speak with the team now and reiterate the urgency behind all of this.'

'Thank you,' he said as she rose from the chair. 'Like I said, I don't want to, but if things continue…'

'I understand.'

As Steph placed her hand on the door, he added, 'You have to realise that we've never had anything like this. And the more time goes on, I think you might be right, I think we might have something *big* on our hands. I'm just hoping we can deal with it before it reaches that stage. Inside, I'm panicking.'

She smirked. 'It's all right, sir. You're doing a much better job at hiding it than most of the people I've worked with in the past.'

CHAPTER
THIRTY-SIX

A few minutes later, the team assembled in the briefing room. Looking back at her were a mix of bleary-eyed, tired, Monday-morning-blues faces of people who didn't want to be there or hadn't slept enough over the weekend, alongside the energetic, vibrant faces of those who either had slept or were so full of caffeine that their bodies didn't notice. Fiona and Eve belonged to the latter category. They both looked full of life, and as if they wanted to be there. Eager. That emotion was evident on their faces as soon as they saw Stephanie approach. The cynic in her thought they were being over the top, trying to curry favour with her and instil confidence in her, as if she were a nervous co-worker giving a big presentation. The other part of her believed it was just part of their personalities. Everyone else, on the other hand, looked as though she had just told them to run a mile in thirty-degree heat. Everyone except Devon, who was quietly muttering to Noah at the back of the semi-circle, the hangover from their discussion still continuing.

'Devon,' she called out. 'You with us?'

'What? Oh, yeah. Sorry, ma'am.' He shuffled in his seat to face her.

'As you were.'

'Thanks,' she said, adding extra sarcasm so the rest of the team picked up on it. Turning to the incident board, she continued, 'We're now just under a week into Operation Lucifer, and I'd like to know where we are so we can best realign our priorities for the week ahead.'

Stephanie grabbed her cup of coffee from a nearby desk and took a sip. 'Devon, since you're so talkative this morning, let's hear what you've got for us.'

'Well…' he began, leaning back in his chair, hands clasped behind his head. 'I've been looking into the dolls, as I believe that's where our focus should lie. The two dolls left behind at the crime scenes are being examined. The results are due in a couple of weeks.'

'A couple of weeks? Why so long?'

'Because there's a backlog, like always.'

She let out a sight. 'We'll keep that on the backburner, if it's going to take that long. What are you examining for?'

'To see what they're made of and whether there's any trace evidence on them.'

'Why?'

'Because they might lead to the killer…?' he said as if it were obvious.

'What's the significance of what they're made of?'

He leaned forward slightly. He didn't appreciate her tone, nor the way she was speaking to him. It felt like an attack.

'The way I see it, someone's either bought them or made them by hand. If they've been bought somewhere, then we're in luck; there's nowhere in Guildford where you can buy that sort of thing, so all we have to do is find somewhere that sells them and see if they've sent any orders to Surrey recently. And *how many*.'

Stephanie didn't like that last sentence. How many? How many more victims would there be until the killer's rampage stopped? How many more victims until they eventually caught him?

The hairs on the back of her arms stood on end.

'If that doesn't work,' he continued, 'and it turns out they're handmade, then we might be able to find a local craft shop that sells the materials they're made from.'

'Let me get this straight. You want to search the vast ocean of the Internet in the hopes of finding somewhere that sells voodoo dolls? Or you want to search the country for a wool shop that sold the components to someone? Sounds like a big ask.'

'Country? Why the country?'

'Because this is a university. Students from all over the country, and the entire world, have come to study here. If our killer is a student, they could be from anywhere. I thought you would have realised that.'

Devon had nothing to say. Stephanie stifled a smug smirk as she addressed Giles and Eve. 'Where are we with the victims' friends, housemates, and classmates?'

The detectives glanced at one another, deciding who would be first to speak. Giles passed the mantle to Eve.

'We've conducted witness and character interviews with both Claudia's and Paulina's housemates. We've started speaking with *some* of their classmates; however, that's on our task list for this week,' she explained. 'Lotta people to get through, but I reckon we can do it, don't you, Giles?'

'Absolutely,' he said, his tone belying his word choice.

'It was brought to my attention that there's a rumour going round that we could potentially be looking at one of the lecturers,' Stephanie said. 'Now, I know I said I didn't want to focus on rumours, but it's something I've been thinking about, and it makes sense. They're trustworthy; they have access to all the places around campus, perhaps even more so than the students, and they may believe they can fly under the radar. So, I want you to focus on them. Make a list of all the lecturers both girls have ever had classes with and interview them. Again, if necessary. I'd suggest splitting the workload to get through it quicker, but find out where they were on both nights and what their connection is to the girls beyond their classes. Right now, a big concern of mine is motive. Why are they doing this? From what I understand, these girls were plain, simple, normal people. They didn't hurt anyone. But something suggests to me they were targeted for a specific reason. Why?' The question was rhetorical, but a few of the team shook their heads, unsure. 'Devon, you're our resident voodoo expert. Why is the killer leaving behind the dolls?'

A look of pride flashed across the sergeant's face as he adjusted himself in his seat. 'I had a video call with someone who knows a thing or two. A professor of religious anthropology at the university, actually. He said voodoo dolls aren't what Hollywood makes them out to be. They're not just about sticking pins into dolls to hurt people. They're actually spiritual tools used for healing, protection, and even communication with spirits or deities. What our killer's doing, telling us how the next person will die, is just hijacking the image, doing it for effect. It's got nothing to do with actual voodoo.'

Stephanie didn't know whether that helped or hindered.

'I guess that means our killer's not a religious person obsessed with the dolls; they're just using them to instil fear.' She inhaled sharply. 'Still, it doesn't tell us why…'

A moment of reflection descended on the room. Shortly after, a hand went up. It belonged to Fiona.

'What do you want us to do about the running club, ma'am?' the constable asked. 'Must admit, I wouldn't mind going down there on one of their runs. Might find the future Mrs Singleton down there.'

'Ew, they're all teenagers,' Giles retorted.

Fiona shook her head furiously. 'Nuh-uh. I'm told it's open to adults as well.'

'Perv,' Giles said jokingly. 'Always knew you were one to watch out for.'

'Nothing wrong with a bit of window shopping.'

'At least they'll be able to outrun you when you start chasing them with your tongue halfway out of your mouth.'

A ripple of laughter swept through the team. Stephanie found herself, much to her surprise, joining in. Then she quickly realised the moment was over.

'Olivia… Any update on CCTV?'

That morning, she was able to maintain eye contact for a few more seconds than before. There was a look of quiet knowing in the detective's face.

'I've continued to look through the footage on the night of Paulina's death. I've trawled through footage from the entirety of the campus, and there's nothing. I mean, there's not much to begin with. There aren't that many cameras, but for the ones we do have footage for… I can't see the killer entering the campus at all.'

On a section of the board, one of the team had placed a large map of the university campus. On it, two markers denoting the victims' crime scenes had been pinned in place, with the date and time on a note underneath.

'Both Paulina and Claudia were killed on the west side of the university,' Stephanie began. 'Presumably, our killer came in on either the main road that leads onto campus, past the Stag Hill statue, or via the cathedral to the south.'

'There's a footpath that leads to the sports park, Tesco, and loads of student housing,' Olivia added. 'By the Guildford School of Acting.'

'Any footage?'

Olivia shook her head.

'Okay, so let's suppose our killer came in this way… unnoticed, in the middle of the night.' She looked at the maps again, this time paying attention to the surrounding area. 'Where could he have gone? South, towards town? West, towards Manor Park and the hospital? Or north towards Stoughton?' She highlighted Western Road, which was situated north of the campus. 'Paulina Potter lived off campus but would have had to come along the pathway every day, especially on the night she died. Perhaps our killer knew her movements.' The cogs began to turn in her head. She closed her eyes, imagining the scene of Paulina's death. The girl had come onto campus with her painting equipment, ready for a night of expression and creativity. 'The killer had known where she'd be and at what time. He'd followed her and waited for her to be alone. If this were a random act, he could have killed anyone. He could have stabbed anyone to death. But Paulina… it had to be Paulina. And it had to be staged in such a way. Why…?'

She'd been speaking to herself, but Fiona answered her.

'Have we spoken to the guy who stalked her on TikTok?' she asked. 'He would have known where she'd be and when.'

Stephanie snapped her fingers.

'Good idea. But that doesn't explain Claudia…'

'Doesn't matter. There might be something between Damien and Claudia. We won't know until we speak to him.'

Stephanie turned to Olivia, hope leeching from her expression.

Olivia shook her head.

'Still can't get hold of him.'

'Noah, any luck with the university on that front?'

Another shake of the head. 'Nobody's heard from him, ma'am.

We've reached out to his flatmates. Tried knocking on his door. His lecturers haven't seen him. No one knows where he's gone.'

An idea occurred to her.

'Does he have a job?'

She glanced down at her notes. 'Someone mentioned he was a sales assistant at Tesco.'

CHAPTER
THIRTY-SEVEN

The car hummed along the road, tyres thrumming over the uneven surface. Accompanying her was Wellard, thumbing through her notebook. A sweet perfume rose from her clothes, fresh waves of the scent reaching Steph every time Olivia moved or shuffled in her seat. She was the constable who knew the most about their missing teenager, Damien Veitch, so it made sense to bring her along. The only problem was the silence between them, thick and heavy with the memories of the other night. As soon as they'd set foot in the car, Stephanie had felt uncomfortable, awkward. It was as if the words were on Olivia's lips. She tried to keep her attention fixed on the road ahead, but the noises in her head were increasing in volume.

'About the other night...' she started, her voice low, almost breaking.

'We don't have to talk about it.'

'I wanted to say thank you.'

Olivia turned her head slowly. 'You don't have to.'

'I do. You could've said something. But you didn't.'

'Like I said, your secret's safe with me. It's not my place; it's nothing to do with me. Unless you want to talk to me about it, that is.'

Stephanie said nothing, and they drove in silence for a few moments. As they pulled up to the traffic lights outside Red One, she said, 'You're the only person who knows, by the way.'

'Yeah?'

'Ever,' Stephanie added.

'That's some burden to carry.'

'I don't remember when it started,' she said as the lights changed to green. 'But it was a long time ago. I was young. Very young.'

'I'm sorry to hear that,' Olivia replied. There was no judgement in her voice.

'I guess I got so good at keeping it a secret from everyone that I never thought I'd get caught.'

'A problem shared is a problem halved.'

Except it didn't feel that way. If anything, it had been worse since Olivia had walked in on her. In Essex, she'd gone months, if not years, without purging. Sure, there'd been the odd slip-up when the stress of life, a murder investigation, and the pressures of the role got to her. But for the most part, she'd been in control of it, a part of her personality that she'd managed to suppress. She'd known it was still there – it would *always* be there; a demon lurking in the shadows – but she'd caged it, hidden it away, and she was in possession of the key. Only now… the cage was unlocked, and the demon was slowly coming out again.

'I just—' Stephanie faltered, then glanced over. 'I don't want you to think I'm less capable of doing my job because of it.'

Olivia closed her notebook, resting it gently on her lap. Her voice, when it came, was quiet but firm. 'Stephanie, if I thought for a second you couldn't do your job, I wouldn't be sitting in this car with you.'

Stephanie gave a tight nod, keeping her eyes on the road.

'You're a good detective,' Olivia continued. 'You're sharp, focused. You lead from the front. That doesn't disappear because you're carrying something.'

Stephanie swallowed hard.

'I've seen a lot of people in this job try to hide their issues,' Olivia said. 'They bottle it up, pretend it's not there. That's when it explodes. But you? You're still standing. That counts for something.'

Stephanie's jaw clenched. She could feel the emotion rising again, that strange blend of gratitude and shame. She felt unworthy of it.

'I don't want pity,' she muttered.

'It's not pity,' Olivia said. 'It's respect. But… just because you're strong doesn't mean you're unbreakable. Everyone has their breaking points. And I want you to know you can always reach out to me if you feel like that's going to happen.'

The car fell quiet again, but the silence was different.

A few beats later, Stephanie exhaled through her nose. 'Thanks, Wellard.'

'Anytime, sarge.'

And for the first time since that night, Stephanie could breathe, and she could look her constable in the eye without fear of judgement.

A fifteen-minute walk from campus, the Tesco Extra Superstore was the lifeblood for the sober, drunk, and high students who frequently inhabited it. Open twenty-four hours a day, it was always busy, densely populated with students who were usually hungover, half-awake, and skint, searching for frozen pizzas, instant noodles, late-night snacks to satisfy the munchies, and the cheapest beer or spirits.

As Stephanie swung the car around the roundabout and veered into the car park, she barely registered the zebra crossing ahead. By the time she saw movement, it was too late. A young man in a hoodie stepped out in front of her, his appearance sudden and shadowed in the dim early morning light. Upon impact, he thudded against the bonnet, rolled with a dull, fleshy thump, then collapsed to the tarmac in a crumpled heap. Stephanie slammed the brakes, her heart ricocheting in her chest, the car jolting to a halt.

'Oh my God, I just hit a kid!'

She switched off the engine, exploded out of the car, and rounded the bonnet. The figure was in the middle of picking himself up off the ground.

'What the fuck, man!'

Stephanie reached out to help him, but he threw her off.

'You hit me with your car!'

'I'm so sorry,' she said, overwhelmed with panic. 'I didn't see you. Are you okay?'

The kid climbed to his feet. He looked about nineteen, maybe younger, his face still carrying the soft edges of adolescence. Long black hair spilled from beneath the hood of his jumper, flopping across his forehead and half-covering one eye. His jeans were too big for him, cinched at the waist with a belt, and a battered rucksack hung from one shoulder.

'Think you fucked up my hip,' he said, then groaned loudly as he placed weight on the leg.

It was then, as he threw his head back, that Stephanie caught a glimpse of his face. She recognised him instantly from the photos Olivia had printed out and placed on the office board.

'Damien?'

Except it hadn't come from Stephanie. She turned to see Olivia half-stepping out of the car.

Damien Veitch froze. His dark eyes carefully studied Olivia. Then he turned to Stephanie. Recognition, combined with panic and fear, set in, and he bolted across a small, nearby playground. Stephanie didn't wait. Instinct kicked in, and she gave chase, her feet grateful for the familiar grassy surface. Damien veered off at an angle, heading to the main road that led to his Manor Park residence, limping slightly, one hand pressed against his hip. He wasn't fast, but he was desperate, adrenaline giving him bursts of speed that kept him just out of reach.

'Stop!' she shouted. 'Police!'

Damien didn't listen. He pushed harder, nearly tripping over his own feet as he clambered up a small incline that connected the park to the road. Stephanie gave a sudden burst and leapt onto his back, pushing him against the rear of a bus stop. Using as much of her weight as possible against him, she pinned him against the panel, her breath hot on the back of his neck.

'Damien,' she said, 'you're a hard man to find. I think it's time you and I had a little chat.'

CHAPTER
THIRTY-EIGHT

Damien Veitch had not stopped complaining about his injured hip since the moment he set foot in the interview room. Nor had he stopped threatening Stephanie with a massive lawsuit, something which, despite its absurdity, concerned her slightly. After all, she *had* hit him with her car. She *had* run him down at a blind zebra crossing. She *had* injured his hip. Maybe not to the extent he claimed if his sprint to evade her was anything to go by, but she still blamed herself for not noticing him around the bend, for being too distracted.

As a result, she had passed the interview on to Giles and Eve. The theory was that they had been interviewing witnesses and taking statements all morning and over the course of the weekend, so they should have been experts at it. In truth, they were. Secretly, Giles thought he and Eve made a good team. Not just in a professional sense, but in a romantic one too. A hopeless romantic, he fell in love with every attractive person he ever laid eyes on, which made it an absolute nightmare when interviewing certain witnesses and suspects. But with Eve, it was different. She was bubbly and outgoing, with a fantastic personality and sense of humour. To top it off, she was his type "on paper", as the contestants of his favourite reality show, *Love Island*, would say. They matched one another's energy, and he always found himself smiling as soon as she entered the room. Was it love? Too early to say. He'd known her for less than a week. But that didn't mean it couldn't be. The only problem was that they worked together, which created a potential minefield of issues down the line. In his ten-year career in the police force, he hadn't met anyone with a successful inter-work relationship. Sure, it happened, but he had nobody from whom he could draw experience, nobody he could call upon for advice.

Instead, he would have to venture down the path less travelled alone, with Wellard to pick up the pieces when it inevitably all went wrong.

Giles entered the interview room shortly after Eve, the trail of her perfume lingering in the air. There, they found the nineteen-year-old slouched in a chair, resting against the wall, one arm draped over the back of the chair, hood lowered over his eyes.

'Afternoon, Damien,' Giles began as he and Eve seated themselves opposite him. 'How's the hip?'

'Hurts like a bitch,' the student replied. 'I'm telling you, if you lot don't get me outta here soon, I'm suing.'

'There are just a few questions we'd like to ask before we do that, if you don't mind,' Giles continued.

'I *do* mind.'

Giles opened his mouth as if about to say something, hesitated, then said, 'Well, that's a shame, because we're going to ask them anyway.'

'Not doing it. Get me outta here, please.' Damien folded his arms and sank lower into the chair. If he went any deeper, he'd be almost horizontal and disappear beneath the table.

Eve pulled out her notebook and inspected it for a moment. 'Says here that you're a second-year student studying acting, is that right?'

Damien grunted.

'Is that what you're doing now? Are you putting on an act for us?'

Damien raised his head, scowling at her, visibly offended.

'I also understand you're from Exeter, is that right?'

'Yeah.' His attitude had dropped slightly, becoming less abrasive.

'How are you finding student life?'

'Fine.'

'And the course?'

'Also fine.'

'You haven't gone through the second-year doubts then?'

'What... what's that?'

'Where you decide to drop it all in your second year and consider joining the police force? No? Just me then,' Eve said, her tone far too pleasant.

Damien chuckled and rose slightly in his chair. In such a short space of time, she'd managed to disarm him and convince him to lower his defences. But the work wasn't done yet. There was still a long way to go before he was fully cooperating.

'Nah, I haven't gone through that yet,' he replied.

'Fingers crossed you don't. Sometimes I wish I'd stuck with it, the friends, the memories, the social side of it all. Don't get me wrong, I'd still have joined the police. Just at a different time in my life.' She glanced down at her notebook again. 'But if you haven't gone through the second-year doubts, then how come my colleagues and I were unable to find you in your flat or at your classes over the past couple of days?'

The sudden change in direction took Damien by surprise.

'*What*?'

'We visited your flat a couple of times, but you weren't there.'

'Why were you at my flat?'

'Why *weren't* you there?' she asked. 'We were getting a bit worried. For a second, we thought we'd have to call the police, but then we remembered we are the police. Good thing we didn't have to break down your door.'

'What're you talking about?' Damien asked, slowly rising in his seat, inch by inch.

'Where were you, Damien?' Giles asked, his tone more imposing.

'I was at a friend's.'

'For the whole weekend?'

A nod.

'Where?'

'In Stoughton. One of my mates from first year lives off campus.'

'What did you go there for?'

A shrug. The rough and abrasive exterior had started to crack, giving way to a softer, more respectful young man. 'I needed to get away,' he said.

'Get away from what?'

'From what I saw...'

'What did you see?'

Damien turned to face them, arms resting on the table, head down. 'You know what I saw,' he said. 'That's why I'm here, isn't it?'

Eve pulled out a photograph from her notebook and slid it across the desk. As soon as it came into view, Damien glanced at it, lifted his head, and pushed it back.

'Is that you?' she asked.

'You know it is.'

'What were you doing there, Damien?'

Before he could answer, he wiped the corner of his eye. 'I just wanted to see her,' he began. 'Surprise her. I didn't expect to see her like that...'

'What's your relationship with Paulina?'

'We're friends.'

'Nothing more?'

He shook his head.

'Though you'd like to be, wouldn't you?'

He raised his head a fraction, confused.

'We've been informed that you two had a little fling before the summer. Is that true?'

'It was just a kiss.'

'We've also been informed you became a bit obsessed with her from that point. Is that true?'

'*Obsessed?*'

'Commenting on her posts. Waiting outside her classes for her. Messaging her on TikTok.'

'I wasn't *obsessed*. I was just...' He broke down in tears, his body shuddering with each sob. 'I was just trying to talk to her, see if anything could happen between us.'

They let the young man sob for a few moments before Giles continued. 'What were you doing at the Ivy Arts Centre on Thursday night, Damien?'

Between short, sharp, hyperventilated gasps, he replied, 'I wanted to surprise her. She'd been ignoring me, so I thought I'd come and say hello, see what she was working on. But I didn't have anything to do with what happened to her. I found her like that. Honest!' When he looked them both in the eyes, his own were reddened and bloodshot, the thin film of liquid making them glisten beneath the artificial light. 'I didn't kill her. I didn't do it. You have to believe me.'

'What were you doing before you found her?' Eve asked.

'I was… in my flat, watching TV. Then I remembered what time it was and came out. I didn't think she'd still be there. I was running late…'

'So you walked in, found her, and then what?' Giles asked.

'I ran. I panicked. I… I knew you guys would come looking for me, thinking it was me, so I went to my mate's house where I spent the whole weekend stoned. I… I couldn't deal with it. I haven't stopped crying since. And as soon as the email from the university came out, I knew you'd be looking for me.'

Damien broke down into another flood of tears after he finished. Eve, taking it upon herself, left the room and returned with a box of tissues. He took them carefully, mumbling a "thank you" as he did so.

'It's the truth,' he said, sniffling. 'I promise you. I promise you I had absolutely nothing to do with what happened to Paulina.'

CHAPTER
THIRTY-NINE

Stephanie had been unable to process Eve's and Giles' update for long before she received a phone call. She glanced at the screen, thanked them for their time, and answered the call as soon as the door shut behind them.

'Louis,' she said, spinning round in her chair to face the window. 'Good to hear from you.'

'It's been on my mind for a while,' the editor of *Surrey Live* responded.

'Likewise. I've been meaning to call, but things have been getting in the way.'

'You said you wanted this to be a two-way partnership.' His tone dropped a couple of levels. 'But you haven't given me anything. No news, no updates. I'm seeing a lot of the nationals covering this more than we are.'

Outside, a large bird flew across the window. Below, in the field, several police officers were training police dogs on a variety of assault courses, the sound of their barking seeping through a crack in the windowpane.

'I assure you I've given them nothing,' she explained. 'You know what some of them are like. They'll cling to any little fact or rumour they can find. I've already told you everything there is to know. Two victims, two students, two young women who've been robbed of their lives.'

'I need more. I've got readers commenting and sending in emails asking for updates.'

Stephanie didn't doubt it. But in her experience, most of those emails were from readers sending in their condolences, not demanding more information.

'Listen,' she began, 'I'm going to level with you: we're currently interviewing former partners, housemates, classmates, and lecturers in connection with these deaths. We've not made any arrests, nor are we close to making any. Of course, we are still appealing for information from anyone who may know anything, so I'd be grateful for your continued support on that front.'

'It comes at a cost though, Stephanie.'

She sighed. 'No, it doesn't. You still get your ad revenue, just the same.' She placed the phone on the table and put it on speaker. 'Have you ever heard of trust, Louis?'

'It's earned,' he answered. 'And right now, you're not doing anything to earn it.'

'Likewise,' she replied. 'But, like I said the other day, we need each other. It might not be an immediate quid pro quo, but eventually, it will balance out. Things will work out for both of us at various points in the future.'

Louis grumbled down the phone. 'I have to write something new. Our team can't keep hashing out the same story. Engagement's dropped off a cliff.'

She inhaled deeply, releasing the breath slowly through her nose. 'I'm sorry, Louis. I haven't got anything for you. But at some point, you have to wonder what's more important, getting justice for the victims and finding the truth, or getting more clicks.'

An hour later, Stephanie was fighting two battles: the one in her stomach that told her she needed to eat and that she needed to eat fast, and the other involving a laptop charger that had become loose and threatened to switch off her laptop as soon as it fell out. The technological resources given to her on her first day had been less than adequate, but she hadn't wanted to complain. She could manage to work in the office without a laptop – if anything, it helped not having one – but she would need it fully functioning for any work she decided to take home with her in the evenings.

Before she could reach for the landline and call down to the IT team, a knock came on the door. A moment later, Noah popped his head round and immediately began surveying the bare walls of her office.

'Crikey, boss. I can see you've really made this place feel like home. Where did you get your eye for interior design?'

She leaned back in her chair, deadpan. 'Same place you got that haircut, I imagine.'

He fired a finger gun at her. 'Touché.' He stepped in and closed the door behind him. In his hand, he held two cups of coffee. 'It's giving "mortuary", "post-mortem", and "dead person" vibes.'

'On brand, then.'

Noah offered one of the takeaway coffee cups in his hand. 'Well, if we're leaning into bleak and soulless, I brought the matching accessories. Black, no sugar. Some might say it matches your sense of humour, but not me, ma'am.'

Stephanie took the cup, chuckling. 'You're lucky I'm too tired to throw this at your head.'

He flopped into the chair opposite, letting out a sigh. 'You're tired? I've got two kids under five, and one of them's teething. You ever tried interviewing a nineteen-year-old after three hours of sleep and a Peppa Pig song stuck in your head?'

She smiled. 'Sounds like a special kind of psychological torture.'

'Worse. At least murderers confess eventually.'

Stephanie sipped her coffee. 'What's up? You didn't come in here just to judge my feng shui or take the piss out of me.'

He set the coffee cup on the table, licking his lips. 'I just got off the phone with Martin Bell, the student welfare officer at Surrey Uni.'

'He seems a delightful man,' she said sarcastically.

'He's a *panicked* man, I know that much.'

'Why?'

'He says their office has been nonstop with requests and questions from students. He wondered if it wouldn't be too much trouble for someone, preferably yourself, to go down there and give another talk to the students.'

CHAPTER
FORTY

The welfare office was tucked away in the corner of a busy avenue on campus. Stephanie knocked twice before stepping inside. The air smelled faintly of stale coffee and lavender plug-ins. Sitting behind a cluttered desk was the university's student welfare officer she'd met before, Martin Bell. Since she'd last seen him, his hair had become neater, and his face glistened under the fluorescent light. His smile was immediate and wide, revealing a set of polished teeth. He gave the impression of calmness, but Stephanie sensed something else, a hidden panic in his eyes, like a duck scrabbling beneath the surface.

'Detective,' he exclaimed halfway across the office, his hand already outstretched. 'So good to see you again. And so good of you to come down on such short notice.' He gestured towards his desk at the far end of the room. 'I trust it wasn't too much trouble?'

'Never. Always happy to be the face of the organisation.'

Even though she hated every second of it.

They arrived at his desk. Martin gestured for her to sit, but she declined.

'Can I get you a drink?'

'I thought I was giving a talk to the students?'

'You are. But you're early. I thought I'd take care of you before then.'

Stephanie checked her watch, realised she had nowhere else to be, then pulled the chair out from in front of Martin's desk. 'I'll have a water, please.'

'Coming right up.'

Moments later, Martin returned with a plastic cup of water from a cooler in the office. The water was chilled, almost freezing, and numbed her teeth as she sipped it.

'How is everything going?' Martin asked as he lowered himself carefully into his office chair. There was a panicked, rushed quality to his voice now. 'With the investigation, I mean.'

She eyed him suspiciously. 'Slow, but steady. We'll get there.'

He nodded with mixed enthusiasm. 'Good... Good... It's been super busy here as well. I mean, nonstop. We've had so many students come forward, saying they've been feeling anxious and unsafe, that they're conscious of going out at night.'

'I'm pleased to hear it,' Stephanie said. Her tone remained even, but her gaze settled on the stack of colour-coded files by his elbow. 'Though not everyone's taking it seriously.'

'Oh?'

She explained the incident the other night involving the student at the amphitheatre.

'Kids these days...' he said. 'We do our best to look after them, but most of the time they think they know best.'

Martin's fingers fluttered over the folders anxiously. Stephanie watched him pick at a label in the top corner of one.

'What are the students reporting?' she asked. 'Any specifics? People, places, incidents they can point to?'

He swallowed. 'A couple claimed they've heard someone following them near the sports park late at night. But there's no pattern. Just heightened nerves, I think.'

'We'll need to see copies of those statements.'

Martin's smile flickered. 'Of course. I... I was going to send them over to Noah, but I've been swamped. Like I said, it's been so busy. We've had queues of people outside, asking questions we don't have the answers to. That's why you're here, to allay some of their fears and maybe answer some more questions.'

Stephanie nodded politely. Another check of the watch. Nearing the end of the working day. She had her first jiujitsu class that evening. She didn't want to miss it.

Martin cleared his throat, bringing her out of her reverie. 'We can head down now. The students should be filtering in.'

They made their way to the office exit. As Martin held the door open for her, he said, 'There's also one thing you should probably know: many students have mentioned the idea of leaving campus and going back home until this is all resolved. The vice chancellor has said that can't be allowed to happen under any circumstances.'

CHAPTER
FORTY-ONE

Stephanie didn't like the idea of keeping students at the university against their will, especially with a killer potentially roaming the campus. But she hadn't let her disagreement with the decision show on her face or in her speech. She reminded herself that she was a detective, not a decision-maker. Her job was to protect, investigate, and catch the person responsible. Still, the unease gnawed at her. As she looked out at the group of students gathered in the students' union, clutching their backpacks with wary eyes, she felt the weight of the investigation pressing down on her. What if the next victim was in that room? What if keeping them there was putting them directly in harm's way?

The thought lingered as she thanked them all for attending. There had been a Q&A session, where she fielded a handful of questions. On the way out, a handful of students approached her to ask the questions they were too shy to voice in public.

Just as she said goodbye to a young biology student, a man in his early forties approached. Tall, but narrow in build, as if his limbs had grown too quickly and never settled. His clothes were immaculate, and his face was well-groomed. His hair, a fading auburn, was clipped short, revealing a pale, freckled scalp beneath. He was an attractive man, probably a hit with the female students. But it was his hands that drew Stephanie's attention, long-fingered and restless, with nails bitten low.

'Detective...' His voice was calm, almost soft.

'You must be Tristan,' she said, shaking his hand.

'Tristan... How did you...?'

'I recognised your face from my colleagues' reports. I understand you taught both the girls during their undergraduate studies, and my colleagues have asked you a few questions about your interactions with them.'

The majority of the students' union had cleared out, but a few final clusters of students were still shuffling towards the exit.

Tristan glanced over his shoulder and lowered his voice. 'That's what I wanted to talk to you about.' Another glance. 'I hope you'll forgive me, but this hasn't been easy for me. I... I'm starting to get worried.'

'The killer seems to be targeting female students. I think you'll be fine.'

'It's not that,' he continued. 'It's about my job. Your colleagues... Eve, I think it was at first, and then Fiona after that... when they came to question me... they were threatening my job, my career, saying I was going to lose everything. I...' He tapped his left middle finger against his thumb, rapidly and rhythmically, as if counting out a beat only he could hear. 'I can't afford to lose my job.'

'Why would you lose your job?'

'Because...' He caught himself, tilting his head. Another glance over his shoulder. 'You're not aware?'

She gave nothing away in her expression.

Sighing heavily, he ran his long fingers through his immaculate hair. 'About the *incident*? With me and Paulina?'

Stephanie's interest was piqued. 'I haven't got to that part of the report. Care to elaborate?'

'It was a stupid mistake. It should never have happened. It was during my office open hours last year. Paulina had booked a slot to discuss an essay that was due, and... we got talking. About personal things. Her art. I mentioned I'd seen some of her TikTok videos; she offered to film one together. She got out of the chair and came to sit on my lap. I was taken aback; I didn't know what to do. Then she lunged at me, kissing me. I-I-I-I threw her off, but I did it so hard she fell over and hit her head on the chair. I tried to help her, but she ran out.'

Stephanie nodded slowly, her expression blank. 'And that's why you're worried?'

'That's not the worst part: she got it all on camera. It's been a horrible summer. I haven't been able to think about anything else. I was convinced she would use it to get me sacked.'

'Did she ever take it to the university?'

Tristan shook his head. 'No. Or if she did, nothing ever came of it. HR never contacted me. No formal complaint. I thought maybe she changed her mind or saw that it wasn't what she'd planned. But then…' He hesitated, the words catching on his tongue. 'This week, when she came back, she slid a sketch of me under my office door. And then, on the day she died, she came to my office.'

'Why?'

'She wanted to apologise. And then… then she tried again.'

'Why didn't you report it?'

'Because I was afraid,' he said quickly. 'Afraid that if I did, they'd assume the worst. You know how these things go. There's no way of explaining it that doesn't sound incriminating.' He laughed bitterly, wiping a hand down his face. 'I've been walking on eggshells ever since. Every time the department head calls a meeting, I think this is it. I'm finished.'

The tic had returned, faster now.

'Well, she's dead,' Stephanie replied bluntly. 'You've got nothing to worry about. Your job is secure.'

He wagged his skeletal finger in the air. 'That's where you're wrong. Now, after I told this to *you* guys, you probably think I killed her to shut her up.'

'Did you?'

Tristan's mouth opened and then closed again. His face twitched with a mixture of shock, offence, and indignation. 'No,' he said finally, his voice deeper this time. 'Of course, I didn't. But I know how it looks. A middle-aged lecturer and a twenty-something-year-old student, someone half my age, who suddenly winds up dead. It doesn't exactly scream innocence, does it?'

Stephanie didn't blink. 'You're right. It doesn't. Why are you telling me this?'

'Because I need you to believe me. I didn't touch her. After what happened between us on the day she died, I sent her out of my office, and I never saw her again. I don't want this whole thing to come down because of one mistake.'

Stephanie folded her arms. 'Then you've got nothing to worry about. Right?'

CHAPTER
FORTY-TWO

The mat felt cold beneath her as Stephanie lay on her back, catching her breath, the fluorescent lights overhead swimming in her vision. She winced as she pushed herself up onto her elbows, the pain in her hip and shoulder from her earlier fall flaring. She should have postponed her first jiujitsu lesson, but she was too eager. She'd already called ahead and signed all the waivers. She didn't want to miss out.

Stephanie had first discovered the sport by accident. A leaflet in a coffee shop in Essex had offered a free trial for beginners. After almost bailing, she quickly found herself falling in love with it. Falling in love with the physical release of her stress, resentment, and aggression. But it was more than that; it was the control, the precision, the way her petite size and strength mattered less than strategy. There, on the mat, it was just her and her opponent. Nothing else. No spiralling thoughts or memories calling for attention. No anxieties about whatever investigation she was working on or the voices inside her head. Just her bare feet, exposed hands, and the strength of every muscle in her body. Trying to survive.

If she got hurt, it was because she'd made a mistake.

Except when her opponent was a national champion and former Olympic hopeful.

Maya Corcoran was on her feet, hovering above her, offering a hand. Stephanie took it with a tight-lipped smile.

'Not bad,' Maya said, tightening her black belt. 'Getting better. But you're still leaving your left side wide open.'

Stephanie envied the girl in many respects. She was quick, agile, and deceptively strong. Worse, she hadn't even broken a sweat, and her thin layer of make-up was still perfectly intact. Meanwhile, Stephanie could feel the sweat dripping off her forehead and pooling at the small of her back.

'I'll remember that for next time.' Stephanie tightened her own belt. 'Hopefully by then the bruising will have gone down.'

Maya grinned, her youthful cheeks glistening beneath the light. 'Next time I'll try not to drop you on that hip again. You landed hard.'

'You never know, it might be the other way round.'

Chuckling, Maya said, 'Then you'll be the first.' Though there was no hint of arrogance in her tone. 'Most people I train with wouldn't come back after a throw like that.'

'Getting knocked down's the easy part,' Stephanie replied, wiping her brow with the sleeve of her gi. 'It's getting back up that counts.'

'How long have you been doing this?' Maya asked.

'About a year. Not long. You?'

'All my life. Someone from my school had a birthday party, and we were playing on the bouncy castle. One of the parents saw me flip someone over and said I'd be quite good. He got me into it.'

'Nice.'

'From there, I won a couple of tournaments and then competed at national level.'

Stephanie picked up a familiar accent. 'Where are you from?'

'Essex,' Maya replied. 'Chelmsford.'

'I know the area well.'

'Yeah?'

Stephanie nodded. 'I work with the police.'

'What pulled you away from the delightful streets of Chelmsford?'

'Work.'

Maya nodded thoughtfully, looking down at her feet. 'You been dealing with that case involving those two girls?'

Stephanie dropped her head.

Before either of them could continue, the class instructor clapped his hands, the sound reverberating around the small space. 'All right, everyone, that's a wrap. Good rolls tonight. Go home, ice your joints, drink water, and for the love of God, don't go out drinking right after this.'

There was a scattered laugh among the group, a few slaps on shoulders and bows as everyone began to peel away towards the edges of the room to retrieve their belongings. There were ten in total. Small enough to face every opponent at least once a session. Not so large that there wasn't enough space on the mats.

Stephanie and Maya moved to the corner of the room and began collecting their things.

'How are you getting home?' Stephanie asked, pulling her jacket over one arm.

'Walking.'

'Where are you based?'

'On campus. It's not far from here.'

'You're a student?' Stephanie asked, unable to keep the surprise out of her voice. 'I mean, I knew you were young, but—'

'Jiujitsu doesn't pay the bills,' Maya answered. 'Mum and Dad thought I'd better get a backup plan just in case.' She threw her bag over her shoulder.

They made their way towards the exit. Standing by the door was the instructor, Sam, whose wide frame almost filled it.

'Good work today, Stephanie,' he said, his muscles bursting through his gi. 'How did you find it?'

Stephanie gestured to Maya. 'So long as this one isn't here next week, I'll be all right.'

'And then I'll be out of business. We're lucky to have her. But you did well against her. I was watching you a couple of times. I can't say the same about everyone. You've got talent.'

'Or a concussion,' Stephanie muttered, rubbing her neck as they stepped into the cool night air.

Opposite them was the Friary Shopping Centre, looming behind the bus depot. Streetlights bathed the brick building in a dull, orange glow.

'You going to be all right getting home?' Stephanie asked. 'I'm more than happy to give you a lift.'

Maya smirked, then looked down at her black belt. 'I can look after myself. But if worse comes to worst,' she said, 'I can always take this off and start slapping them with it.'

CHAPTER
FORTY-THREE

Tom Singfield awoke with a start; the sharp jolt of something tugging at his hoodie. Blinking against the grey-blue haze of clouds above him, Tom squinted at the blur of feathers pecking at his chest.

'Oi! Get off!' he grunted, swiping at the magpie, which flapped indignantly and scurried off across the grass.

The pain in his body hit him next. The ache in his bones from an uncomfortable night's sleep on a wooden park bench. The dull throb in his head from the night's bad decisions. It was all worsened by the chill. His damp clothes, sodden with the moisture in the air and dew from the bench, clung to his back, leaching warmth from his body. He shuddered uncontrollably as he swung his legs off the bench and began checking his belongings, his spine clicking like a zip being undone.

Phone? Check.

Wallet? Check.

Keys? Still no. Otherwise, he would have spent the night in bed and not out in the freezing cold by the campus lake. Sleeping next to the large body of water on the east side of campus had seemed like a good idea at three thirty in the morning, but now, as a small gust of wind sent ripples across the edge of the water, he didn't think so.

Still, you learn by your mistakes.

Like not giving your flat keys to a complete stranger for a magic trick.
The bastard had well and truly made them disappear.

Slowly, Tom shuffled off the bench and stumbled forward, ready to start the long journey home. He just wanted to crawl into bed and forget the whole embarrassing night ever happened.

As he trudged towards the familiar outline of his block, he veered instinctively past the centre of the field, the shallow dip where the lake sat, mostly ornamental, with a small fountain feature that sometimes sputtered into life when someone remembered to switch it on.

He was halfway past when he slowed, frowned, and looked again.

There was something in the water.

At first, he thought it was rubbish. Maybe a black coat, dumped or thrown in by a student, tangled in the weeds. But as he stepped closer, the shape took on the weight of something real. Human.

It was a woman. Floating face down, dressed in a white martial arts suit, her arms spread out like wings, hair dark and fanned around her head like kelp. The gentle movement of the fountain nearby made her body rock almost rhythmically.

Tom's stomach twisted. The cold vanished in an instant, replaced by a nauseating jolt of adrenaline. He staggered back, shoes slipping in the wet grass, heart thudding.

'Shit,' he whispered, backing away. 'Shit, shit, shit.'

And then he turned and ran. Towards his flat, towards help, towards anyone who might know what on earth he was supposed to do next. Because what he'd seen on the woman's back had sent the fear of God into him.

A small box with a simple message on it: *Open Me.*

CHAPTER
FORTY-FOUR

The following morning, Stephanie felt like she'd been hit by a bus. Twice. Without any protective clothing on. And then beaten with hockey sticks.

The night's jiujitsu had taken it out of her more than she'd expected. Her muscles ached and throbbed with pain she didn't know was possible in places she hadn't realised it was possible to feel. She'd thought she was strong, well-trained, toned, but coming head to head against a national champion black belt quickly put things into perspective.

Carefully, able to move only an inch at a time, she swung her legs off the bed and shuffled to the toilet. For some reason, a pain swelled in her head, and she felt dizzy. Perhaps it was the untouched bottle of water on her bedside table, along with the full glass she'd been meaning to drink in the bathroom. She grabbed it and nursed it down her throat as she went to the toilet, sipping it carefully, not drinking too much so it didn't bloat her. A sickly smell lingered in the bathroom, reminding her that she needed to stock up on air fresheners. She wasn't expecting guests any time soon, but it was always a good idea to be prepared. Over the years, Stephanie had grown accustomed to the smell that followed her around everywhere; it was a reminder of the shame, of the guilt she felt. It was also a reminder of the way she looked, of the compliments she received from people who said she'd lost weight and was looking well.

She sat on the toilet for a few moments more, her thoughts drifting. Outside, through a small gap in the window, the sound of a high-pitched scream reached her, piercing the silence. For a second, she froze. Not because of the sound itself, but because of what it stirred up from inside her.

She was six again. Crouched behind the sofa. The thick static of the television humming behind her. The slam of a door. Her mum's voice, sharp with fear. Her dad's roar, followed by the sound of flesh striking flesh, and the scream that accompanied it.

And then the silence, which was quickly punctured by Kimberley screaming in her arms.

Holding her closely, tucked against her chest. Waiting. Praying the sound of footsteps didn't approach them both.

Stephanie clutched at her necklace, running it around her throat. Her pulse quickened, and her eyes became glazed over. The sound of children shouting to one another brought her out of her trance. She flushed the toilet, stood, and washed her hands slowly, watching the water swirl and run over her fingers.

When she was finished, she shuffled down the stairs. The pain in her muscles was still there, but her brain failed to register it. At the bottom of the steps, paintings, half-finished and abandoned, leaned against the skirting board. She usually painted every day, before and after work, but since Paulina Potter's death, she hadn't been able to look at her brushes. Every stroke, every line would have only served as a reminder of the TikTok star's death.

The rest of the house was in as fragile a state as her mind. Her jiujitsu gi lay crumpled by the radiator where she'd dumped it the night before. The bin in the kitchen was overflowing, plastic containers threatening to topple. Dirty laundry snaked out from the living room in small islands of clothing: odd socks, a pair of jogging bottoms, her once-white work shirt smudged with foundation.

It was chaos.

Then came a knock on the door.

She froze. The sound was light, tentative, but loud enough to cut through the pounding noise in her head. She tightened her dressing gown around her and padded to the door, pulling it open without checking the peephole.

On the other side stood a wiry man in his late seventies with grey hair, glasses too big for his narrow face, and a cardigan that had seen better decades. Her next-door neighbour. She'd seen him around and had been meaning to introduce herself.

'Good morning,' he said softly. 'Sorry to disturb you. I wasn't sure if you'd be home, but it's good to finally meet you. Thought I'd introduce myself and welcome you to the street. Jimmy, Jimmy Walgrave.' He extended his liver-spotted hand.

'Stephanie. Stephanie Broadbent.'

'Very "James Bond",' he said with a smile. 'How are you finding the area?'

'Quiet. Quieter than I'm used to.'

'Where have you moved from?'

'Essex. But I was born and raised here.'

'Ah. Us Guildfordians always find a way to come back to the nest,' he said. 'It was the same with my son and his wife. But I suspect it might have had something to do with needing a grandfather to babysit at a moment's notice.'

That explained the screaming outside the window.

'I apologise if they made a bit of a racket earlier. They're hyper as anything, and I'm not used to having that much energy bouncing off the walls.'

Stephanie blinked hard. 'It's okay, really. I didn't even notice.'

'You sure?' He peered past her shoulder at the cluttered hallway. 'I remember the struggles of moving. It's never-ending.'

She glanced back and observed the boxes on the floor. 'It's been a long week. But I'll get there eventually.'

'Well, if you need a hand with it, just let me know,' he said, his voice softening even more. 'I would offer my services, but my back isn't what it used to be. However, I can always get my son down, and he can help.'

Stephanie smirked, saying nothing.

'Anyway,' he said, stepping backwards. 'You know where to find me. Oh, and before I forget, it's black bin collection today. In case you've got anything that you need to get rid of.'

Stephanie said a polite thank you, then waved him goodbye. As she closed the door behind her, she inhaled deeply, observing the mess in front of her. She wasn't ready for such a monumental task. Not yet.

Upstairs, her mobile began vibrating on the bedside table. She sprinted up the stairs as fast as her fatigued muscles and bones would allow and answered the call.

It was Devon.

'Morning,' she said.

He was blunt, to the point. No airs and graces.

'You'll need to get yourself down to campus again. We've got another one.'

CHAPTER
FORTY-FIVE

I can look after myself.
 Maya Corcoran's words echoed in her head.
But if worse comes to worst, I can always take this off and start slapping them with it.

The girl's jiujitsu belt was missing, and for a moment, Stephanie wondered whether she'd tried. Whether Maya had been given an opportunity to remove it and whip her killer with it.

But even if she had, her attempts at self-defence had, ultimately, been unsuccessful. Her lifeless body lay there in the water, face submerged, her gi floating about her waist, making her look like a fallen angel. A handful of police divers, dressed in full gear with breathing apparatus and wetsuits, were in the lake, carefully moving her towards the edge. Stephanie watched, numbed and vacant, as they pushed her nearer.

The entire field had been cordoned off, with dozens of uniformed officers holding back the horde of students. This was the first time the killer had left a victim out in the open for all to see. The crowd's hushed, tense chatter spilled down the hill, drowning out the sound of the water fountain a few feet away.

A small army of crime scene investigators moved about the field. Their task of forensically examining the entire area would take all day. But first, they needed to remove the body, and

Stephanie had told them that no work was to begin until her arrival.

She wanted to be the one to open the box.

She wanted to be the one to find out how the next victim would be killed.

After anxious, painful minutes of waiting, Maya's body was finally removed from the water. The box was placed to one side, and she was rolled onto her back. The water, filled with algae and dirt, had been unkind to her pale, bluish face. The silt and filth had blackened her cheeks and her glassy eyes. Weeds had become tangled in her matted hair, and a small twig had lodged itself up her nose.

Stephanie's hip throbbed with pain again. Punishment, no doubt, for her handling of the investigation. But the pain she felt right now wasn't enough. She needed to feel more.

And she would.

Soon.

Her phone began to ring. She glanced at the caller ID: Louis Brown. How did he know about it already? Someone from the team? Devon? She rejected the call, her thumb pressing the red button a little harder than necessary, then put her phone on Airplane mode. That way, nobody could get hold of her.

'Ma'am,' Giles said softly from behind, as she pocketed the device. 'Leanna's here.'

Pulling her gloves tighter, Stephanie turned around to see the pathologist heading towards the crime scene, hurrying the final few feet as if it were the first time she'd run in years.

'Don't make me do that again,' she said as she stopped beside the body.

'Do what?'

'Make me run like that.'

'I didn't make you do anything.'

'Yes, you did.' She waved her finger in Stephanie's face. 'With that look you gave me. I don't like the feeling of being rushed.'

'It's in your head,' Stephanie snapped.

Leanna's eyes widened with surprise.

'Shall we?' Stephanie said, her mood worsening by the second.

The pathologist crouched to her haunches and began surveying

Maya's body. 'She's dead, all right. Unless she walked across that water?'

Stephanie shook her head, remaining silent and observant.

'There are no immediate signs of trauma,' Leanna continued. 'But I'd say she was drowned.'

As the voodoo doll had foretold.

'How was she overpowered?' Stephanie asked. 'She was strong. Freakishly strong.'

'How do you know, ma'am?' Giles asked.

'I sparred with her last night. She was a national jiujitsu champion.'

Giles sucked in a lungful of air sharply. 'Perhaps she was either taken by surprise or hit round the back of the head.'

'She wouldn't have been able to defend herself if her face was submerged underwater,' Leanna added.

Stephanie didn't want to believe it. She wanted to believe that Maya had defended herself, that she'd kicked her attacker's arse, and that it wasn't until he'd changed the rules of the game and hit her around the face with a weapon that she'd finally succumbed to his advances. And paid the ultimate price for it.

'How long?'

Leanna rocked her head from side to side, thinking. 'Tricky. The water's preserved her, but if you saw her last night, and she's still wearing her gear, then I assume it was soon after you were with her.'

Stephanie reached for her mum's necklace but failed to find it beneath the forensic gloves and suit.

If only she'd given Maya a lift. *Forced* her to get in the car with her. Perhaps she'd still be with them. Perhaps she wouldn't have become her third victim.

'Anything else?' she asked, her voice breaking.

'Not for now. More to come when I look at her properly.'

Stephanie closed her eyes and inhaled deeply. When she opened them, she shuffled around the length of Maya's body and moved towards the box.

'Boss?' Giles asked.

She didn't respond.

'Boss? Do you want me to do that? It might not be safe.'

'It's fine. I can do it.'

Stephanie crouched down, resting her knees on the wet, dewy grass. She stared at the note, OPEN ME, that had been written in black permanent marker.

Do as you're fucking told, you silly little girl!
Don't you ever disobey me again, you stupid bitch!

Her breath caught as she peeled the note from the lid, careful not to disturb any potential prints. She passed it to a nearby CSI, who delicately placed it inside an evidence bag.

Next, Stephanie turned her attention to the plastic lid. As she eased it open, the box released a faint click.

A spark flared.

In an instant, the doll that sat inside – the same one she'd seen twice before with its button eyes and stitched torso – ignited. Flames bloomed in its chest, licking up the thread and curling the fabric black. Stephanie flinched back, shielding her face with her forearm as the heat surged outward in a short, violent burst. The doll writhed in the fire, its button eyes bubbling and popping, the stitches splitting open to reveal blackened stuffing that smouldered like incense.

By the time she'd recovered, the doll had been reduced to ash and molten plastic in the bottom of the box, the stench of accelerant lingering in the air.

Behind her, someone swore under their breath.

Stephanie didn't move, just stared at the charred remains of the box.

'I don't believe it,' she whispered. 'He's going to burn someone to death.'

CHAPTER
FORTY-SIX

She didn't look at the menu for long. In the end, it all tasted the same and wound up in the same place.

'Giant doner kebab with extra cheesy chips, please,' she said, tapping her debit card impatiently on the counter.

'No problem, miss,' came the shop owner's response as he entered the order into the system.

As she tapped her card, the man began preparing her food. He tossed a tray of chips into a vat of cooking oil and started slicing the meat into a tray. Immediately, the smell of grilled meat and onions assaulted her senses, rapidly filling her mind.

The aches and pains from the night before had all but disappeared, replaced with fear, grief, and guilt. The investigation was beginning to slip away from her. Already, in less than a week, three people had died; three people who relied on her and her team to protect them. It was like trying to hold onto a bar of soap; every thread of the investigation was slipping through her fingers.

She couldn't shut off Maya's voice in her head. She couldn't silence the thoughts that plagued her.

Come here! Come here when I'm talking to you! Don't make me do it!

She reached for her mum's necklace. Mercifully, now out of the forensic suit and in her breathable clothing, she felt it. But it did nothing this time to quiet the noise, silence the thoughts, or erase the images of the burning doll.

There was only one way to do that.

A few moments later, the kebab shop owner handed her a hot, heavy plastic bag. She mumbled a quick thanks, then fled, bursting into the daylight. She lowered her head and kept her gaze down as she jumped into the car parked outside Red One nightclub.

Inside the car, she tore open the foil with shaking hands and began eating as if someone was going to steal it from her. She ate quickly, mechanically, barely chewing. The taste hardly registered in her mouth or brain, just the sensation of spicy, fatty food sliding down her throat with every swallow.

She pulled her phone from her pocket, saw that it was still on Airplane mode, then tossed it onto the passenger seat. Her team was probably trying to contact her, to find out where she'd rushed off to. But they could wait. The world could wait.

This was her moment of control before she lost it again.

CHAPTER
FORTY-SEVEN

Her head hung over the toilet bowl, a thin strand of saliva dangling from the corner of her mouth, the acrid taste of bile lingering on her tongue, her throat burning from the effort, her fingers covered in mess.

She forced herself to look into the bowl, a reminder of how it had all started: a punishment for eating all the food in the house, sneaking into the fridge, and enjoying the last of Dad's snacks so there was nothing left.

What makes you so special you can eat everything in the house while nobody else gets any? You fat little girl!

And then the beatings would start. Not to her. At least, not at first.

Mum. Always targeted at Mum.

She gets this from you. She's just like you, a selfish, greedy little piggy. An ungrateful little bitch.

Followed by a punch, a smack, pulling her mum's hair and throwing her to the ground.

I know what the two of you are saying about me. This is my house. My rules.

Stephanie spat into the water. The image of abuse disappeared amidst the ripples, and she pushed herself away from the bowl, sitting back on her heels. She wiped her mouth with the back of her hand. The pain in her body had returned, worse this time, thanks to the dull ache in her ribs and the empty, hollow feeling in her stomach. She stayed there for a moment longer, staring into the porcelain, thinking how much she wished she could have changed, about how different her life could have been.

When she first returned to Guildford three weeks earlier, everything had been under control. The bulimia had become manageable, only rearing its ugly head in extreme circumstances.

Until now.

When the murders of two young women were her fault because she hadn't acted fast enough, just as when her mother had died.

Control.

Back then, she'd had something to control: Kimberley. Making sure she and her sister hid in the wardrobe, singing together, pretending they were playing a game, drawing with their crayons under the torchlight she'd smuggled in. She had protected her little sister; controlled what she'd seen, heard, experienced.

Protected her.

But since they'd grown up and grown apart, she'd substituted her sister for her victims; she was in charge of protecting them.

Until now.

She flushed the toilet and climbed to her feet, her body shaking as she pulled herself up to the sink. Next, she grabbed the digital scales wedged down the side of the toilet and stepped onto them. Some strength returned to her body; she was lighter by a few pounds. As she returned it to its hiding spot, she avoided her reflection in the mirror. She couldn't look at herself; staring into the toilet bowl was punishment enough.

A quick mint or a piece of chewing gum to rid her mouth of the guilt and shame, and she was good to go.

She ambled out of the bathroom, clinging to her necklace. As she started down the stairs and entered the kitchen, she was transported to her parents' house almost thirty years before. It was dark, nearly midnight. The television was playing in the background. She had just snuck out of the bedroom for something to eat: an apple, some leftovers from dinner in the bin. She was starving, she'd never known hunger pangs like them, but it wasn't for her. It was for Kimberley. Her sister had been crying nonstop, begging for food.

Stephanie tiptoed into the kitchen and made for the fridge. As she opened it, a noise came from the living room. She froze. A moment later, her mum appeared, speaking hurriedly and in whispers.

'You should be sleeping,' she hissed.

'Food.'

'I know, sweetheart.' Her mum moved to the cupboard on the other side, opened a cabinet, and pulled out an unopened packet of crisps. The packaging rustled so much it almost gave them away. 'Take them,' she said. 'But be quick. And don't stop running.'

Her mum's words of advice had done little to stop her dad from catching them both. They'd done little to stop the beatings. That night, Stephanie had been separated from Kimberley and forced to sleep in the bathroom, where the pain had been so great, the desire for food so immense, that she'd nibbled on the toilet roll that hung by her head. It hadn't taken long for it to come back up again.

For a long while, she stood in her hallway, staring into her kitchen. The fridge poked out from behind the doorway, and she felt a flash of hunger explode in her stomach. A moment later, a figure appeared: old, malnourished, a pair of jeans hanging loosely around his waist, but it wasn't enough to distract from the malevolence and evil that swirled in his eyes.

'Get out of my house and get out of my head!' she yelled, pounding her temple with the heel of her hand.

She needed to get out of the house. Away from there, away from everyone.

Then her eyes fell on the mountain bike pressed against the wall of the corridor, mud and clumps of grass hanging from it.

CHAPTER
FORTY-EIGHT

The wind stung her face, tugging at her jacket and whipping her hair against her forehead. Each turn, each climb, each jolt over root and rock helped chip away at the fog in her head. Her muscles burned, her lungs heaved, but it was a welcome distraction, a welcome break from the endless symphony of pain and self-loathing.

Her journey had taken her through Chantry Wood, an ancient semi-natural woodland and meadow contained within two hundred acres, before arriving at Shalford, a short distance from Guildford town centre. From there, she'd cycled along the road, doing her best to keep up with the traffic, heading towards The Mount Cemetery. After an unforgiving incline, which had almost exhausted the muscles in her legs, she reached the cemetery from the south, dismounting her bike beside the Booker Tower. Built in 1839 by order of the town's mayor, Charles Booker, the octagonal structure had originally served as a place of remembrance for his two sons before later becoming a site for astronomical observation. The towering brick structure stood at the foot of the cemetery, acting as a gatekeeper. Leaving her bike resting against the iron fence, Stephanie traipsed into the cemetery, her breath shallow, her legs trembling.

Though it wasn't due to the climb.

The Mount Cemetery was home to many famous names, including Lewis Carroll, with several of the oldest burials dating back to the nineteenth century. But that wasn't why she was there. To her, there was someone more important than all those who came before and after.

It was the place her mum was buried. A place she hadn't visited since her last extended stay in Guildford.

The cemetery stretched out before her in quiet solemnity. The trees cast long-fingered shadows over the footpath around the perimeter. Beyond, she could see the sprawl of rooftops and Guildford Cathedral caught amongst the low-hanging clouds.

Her trainers crunched softly over the gravel path as she made her way up the incline, past the newer graves with pristine marble and artificial flowers, and past the ones with dates too close together to be fair. Her throat tightened, and she grabbed her necklace as her mother's grave came into view. Moss and lichen had claimed the headstone for their own, and the corners had eroded over the years.

Stephanie lowered herself to the damp grass and sat cross-legged at the base of the headstone. She glanced down at the grass and began playing with it as if she were a schoolchild in the playground.

'Hi, Mum,' she said, picking at a clump of moss. 'It's… Sorry it's been a while. I've been busy with work. I know it's no excuse…'

A handful of leaves were picked up by the wind and blew across the grass, catching her attention out of the corner of her eye.

'But the good news is I'm back now. Working with Surrey Police. Kim's happy, as you'd probably expect. I saw her the other day. She's looking well. Really well, in fact. It looks like she's got it together.' She dropped the moss. A smile carefully made its way onto her face. 'Guess she turned out all right, given everything. At least one of us did. I'll never forget the sacrifice you made for her – the sacrifice you made for *us*. I'm happy for her. She's got a great job, a lovely house, and a loving husband. But… but she's still in contact with Dad. I know it's a difficult one to manage. I've tried. But…' She inhaled deeply, held the breath in her lungs for a few seconds, then let it all flow out. 'Enough about him. The less I think about him, the better. How are you doing? Lots to catch up on, I'm sure. I… I know you've been watching over me. I've felt it, even when I've done things I'm not proud of.' She sniffed hard, wiping a tear from the corner of her eye. 'I miss you, Mum. And I'm still sorry. I'll forever be sorry…'

'Don't be sorry.'

The voice took her by surprise and sent a chill down her spine as her stomach clenched. At first, she thought it was her mum talking to her from beyond the grave, but when she heard footsteps, she realised she was wrong. A man, tall and slender, with bright grey hair and a pair of thin-framed glasses, wearing a checked shirt tucked into jeans, carefully approached, his arms behind his back.

'Don't be sorry,' he repeated. 'It's never a good idea to be sorry. Instead, be grateful. Grateful for the memories, grateful for the mistakes, grateful for the lessons.'

He came closer. Stephanie felt an immediate calm around him, so much so that she didn't mind his interruption.

'People think cemeteries are for endings,' he continued, his eyes drifting over the row of headstones, 'but really, they're a place for beginnings. The conversations we couldn't start or finish when they were still alive.'

Stephanie nodded. A lump had formed in her throat, holding her words hostage.

He gestured to the headstone. 'Your mum?'

Another nod.

'I've got my whole family buried here. Parents, brother. My wife.'

'I imagine you've got your place plotted out already,' Stephanie replied.

'Nope, not me.' He burst into a short cackle of laughter and displayed a cheeky grin, revealing a set of perfectly symmetrical teeth. 'You won't find me rotting away in here. Nope, I'd rather be burnt to a crisp, thanks. Either that or at sea.'

'Really?'

'Yeah. Just to piss off the family. Got it all figured out. I'll hop on one of my motorbikes and just drive straight into the water. That way nobody can come and tell me what they really thought of me!'

For the first time in what felt like an eternity, Stephanie laughed. An explosion that burst from her lips and rolled over the headstones. It took her by surprise. She hadn't felt the emotion in a while. And it had come from talking about mortality, of all things. The type of thing she spent all day, every day dealing with.

'I'm Dave, by the way,' he said, holding out his hand.

'Stephanie. I like your shirt.'

'This thing? My grandson bought it for me in Florida. He's my favourite.' His voice swelled with pride.

'Sounds like a nice guy.'

'He's my mate. So long as he works hard and stays out of trouble, he'll be all right.'

'A lesson for us all.'

Dave smirked, then hovered for a moment longer.

'It was nice to meet you, Stephanie,' he said as he started towards the exit, ambling along with his hands behind his back. 'Look after yourself.'

CHAPTER
FORTY-NINE

Nearly an hour later, she returned to the office. Washed, cleaned, refreshed.

As she entered the room, she noticed the silence. It was empty, save for Eve and Fiona, who were sitting beside one another, quietly whispering. Stephanie couldn't hear what was being said, but she sensed the conversation revolved around her. Even if it didn't, the anxiety in her mind convinced her it did.

'Oh my God, you're alive!' Eve leapt out of her chair and hurried over to her, as though she were a missing dog that had just returned after weeks away. 'Where did you go? Where have you been?'

Fiona joined them at the door before Stephanie could respond.

'We were worried about you for a minute there,' Fiona said.

'For a *minute*? Speak for yourself. I thought something bad had happened to you.' The youthful innocence and naïvety in Eve's face filled Stephanie with guilt.

It was the same expression her sister had given her growing up whenever Stephanie had received a beating or been forced to watch her dad inflict pain on her mum. When she'd opened the door to the bedroom, her sister had met her with the same wide-eyed, relieved gaze. She was helping Mummy and Daddy build something, she'd said. Helping them fix something. She'd been forced to lie to her sister then, to pretend that she was fine and that everything would be okay.

But she couldn't bring herself to lie to Eve.

'I needed to get away,' she said. 'I just needed to clear my head.'

'Where did you go?' Fiona asked.

'Home. And then out on my bike. I just… needed to process things.'

Fiona nodded thoughtfully. There was no judgement in her expression. In fact, Stephanie thought she noticed compassion. 'I know how you feel,' she said. 'It's a lot to take in. I can't begin to imagine what it's like for you – both of you, actually. You're brand new here. Everything's unfamiliar. You don't know us that well. Steph, you've got the added stress of moving in and dealing with all the anxiety that can throw at you. I get it…'

Steph didn't know what to say.

'I used to do something similar back when I was first starting out,' she continued.

'What do you mean?'

'Taking off. I used to just disappear when things got too heavy for me. At work, at home. I was a mess. A couple of times, I just left home and didn't come back for several hours. Sometimes I was gone the whole night. I was… broken's not the right word for it… but I wasn't in a good way for a long time. Then something just clicked, and I sorted myself out. I guess I just got used to it really. I became numb, desensitised to what we do, and I got a handle on whatever was going on inside my head.'

This was a side to Fiona that Steph hadn't seen coming. She'd opened herself up, made herself vulnerable by sharing such intimate and personal information. Stephanie admired her greatly for that. Eve, on the other hand, looked as if she'd just been told she had six weeks to live.

'Does that mean I'm going to go through something similar?'

Fiona placed a hand on the detective's upper arm. 'Probably. But you've got two strong, experienced women who can help you through it. We know when the bad times are here, and we know when they're coming. We also know when the good times are just around the corner. There aren't many of them, mind, but that's what makes them so much more beautiful when they come. When months, maybe *years* of hard work eventually pay off and you get the result you wanted.'

That seemed to allay some of Eve's fears. However, the residual look of angst on her face suggested there was still plenty more lurking beneath the surface.

Steph gestured to the empty office. 'What have I missed?'

Fiona glanced over her shoulder. 'You'll be pleased to know Devon's appointed himself in charge while you were gone.'

Of course he has, she thought.

'Giles is still at the crime scene, I believe,' Fiona continued. 'Either that or he's at the post-mortem. Noah's at the university, dealing with the chancellor, trying to discuss what to do next. And Wellard's speaking with the victim's housemates, and uniform are handling house-to-house.'

Stephanie responded with a nod. Of course, Devon had taken it upon himself to hand out roles and responsibilities to the rest of the team in her absence. Within a matter of minutes, he had taken control of the operation, ensuring he stamped his mark on it.

'What are you both doing here?' Steph asked.

'Waiting,' Eve answered.

'What for?'

'Instructions,' Fiona said. 'He wants us on standby in case anything comes in that we need to deal with. Between you and me, ma'am, I don't think he trusts us as much as the others.'

Stephanie pondered that for a moment. Was Devon picking and choosing favourites based on who she'd spent the most time with, or who he thought she was closest to? She didn't know much about the man, but she didn't think it was outside the realm of possibility.

Before she could respond, the sound of a cough echoed from inside the chief inspector's office.

'That reminds me,' Fiona said quickly. 'McGowan asked to see you when you returned.'

Steph glanced at the plaque on the man's door. 'Thanks for letting me know.'

CHAPTER
FIFTY

She waited for what felt like an age, shifting her weight from one foot to the other, head low, unable to look at her colleagues who were undoubtedly watching with eager anticipation. Eventually, the call came from inside, and she opened the door. Sitting behind his desk, removing a set of glasses from his nose, was DCI Clive McGowan.

'Ah, detective, you're here. Please, take a seat.'

There was no malice in the way he spoke. No aggression, no disappointment. It was neutral, calm. Yet Stephanie sensed the conversation would be anything but. She carefully pulled out the chair, as if worried it was a trick, then lowered herself into it, keeping her knees pressed together and placing her hands in her lap.

'It seems you've got some explaining to do,' McGowan said, his voice still calm and measured. 'From what I heard, you just left the crime scene without explaining where you were going, what you were doing, and how long you would be gone.'

'I can explain.'

'I was hoping you could.' He placed his hands on the desk, knitting his fingers together.

Stephanie inhaled, then let the air out slowly before beginning. 'It all got a bit too much for me. I was with Maya, the victim, last night. We were at a jiujitsu class. I offered to give her a lift home, and seeing her like that… it got to me. So I went for a bike ride. I needed to clear my head, forget about her for a minute, and ended up at my mum's grave. I just needed someone to talk things through with. It was the only way I could deal with it.'

McGowan absorbed what he'd heard.

'You abandoned your team,' he said. 'Eve was beside herself. She thought something *serious* had happened to you. And I must admit, so did I.'

She lowered her head. 'I know. I'm sorry.'

'If you're not suitable for the job, then—'

'Don't finish that sentence,' Stephanie interrupted. 'I implore you. I am still the right person for this job. You brought me in for a reason.'

'Yes, because I was told you got results. Because you were tenacious. Because you thought differently from the rest of your peers. Because you see things other people don't. And yet, so far, you've given me reason to believe that isn't true. That it's all been a lie.'

Stephanie opened her mouth, but nothing came out.

'I understand you've got some issues from wherever – I'm not interested in knowing about those – but you can't let them spill into your work, Steph. These people depend on you for leadership and guidance. How can you give them that if you're not even there?'

She nodded. 'You're right, I failed them.'

A shrug. 'Not yet. You've still got time to make up for it.'

'I get to keep my job?'

A hint of a smile. 'For now. It wouldn't be fair of me to get rid of you so soon without offering you any support.'

'What do you mean?'

'Assistance. Do you need any? Like I told you the other day, several chief constables and superintendents from neighbouring forces have reached out to see if we need any assistance. So far I've turned all of it down, as I didn't believe it was what you wanted. But if that's changed, then you just need to let me know…'

She understood, and she appreciated the offer of support, but she didn't want it. She was stubborn. And she believed in her abilities to get the job done, to get justice for the victims.

Even if it broke her.

'You can tell them we're fine,' she answered resolutely.

McGowan studied her for a long beat, his eyes searching her face for something – doubt, fear, the faintest sign that she was bluffing – but all he found was the fire he'd been warned about when he agreed to bring her in. That she was stubborn, unconventional, and relentless.

He gave a small nod, half in acknowledgement, half in resignation. 'All right. But understand this, Stephanie. Next time we have this conversation I won't be so lenient and understanding. And I won't be asking; I will take the necessary steps to give this investigation the resources it needs. If something like this happens again, I won't be able to defend you. You're more aware than most about the pressures of this job, and the decisions I will have to make if my hand is forced.'

She swallowed hard, her throat dry then forced herself to meet his gaze.

'I understand.'

McGowan leaned forward, resting his forearms on the desk. 'You've still got a team out there, Stephanie. Might I remind you to use them?'

'I think Devon's taken charge of that. From what I understand, he's already behaving as though I've been removed from the team for good.'

Clive chewed on his left cheek. 'Well, you'd better remind everyone who's boss, and how things work around here. If memory serves me correctly, you once said you'd fall on your sword for your team; that any mistakes they make, you make.'

She nodded.

'You still stand by that?'

Another nod.

'Then it seems like you've got some mistakes to rectify. And not just your own.'

CHAPTER
FIFTY-ONE

The sound of house music exploded from the gym as soon as she opened the door. The second assault on her senses came with the stench of cleaning chemicals. Usually, the smell would have set alarm bells ringing – that Sam, the owner, had been trying to cover up something from the night before – but because she had been there, because she had seen what had happened and witnessed first-hand how sweaty some of her opponents had been, she disregarded it instantly.

It didn't, however, make it any easier to stomach.

The six-foot-two former bouncer was skipping furiously at the back of the room. He noticed Stephanie and Eve as soon as they entered. Stephanie had brought the young constable with her as a way to apologise and heed DCI McGowan's words of wisdom. She carried a tablet, ready for diligent note-taking.

'Stephanie!' Sam called, dropping the rope to the floor and skipping across the mat. Despite his size and weight, he moved lightly, with the deftness of someone who knew how to control almost every aspect of their body. 'How are you feeling after last night?'

'Sore,' she said, then turned to Eve. 'Eve, this is Sam. Sam, this is Eve.'

'Nice to meet you,' Sam replied, wiping a drop of sweat from his forehead. 'She convinced you to sign up or something?'

'Not quite,' Eve replied.

'We're here about Maya,' Stephanie added.

'Maya? What about her?'

Before Stephanie could answer, he moved to the lockers on the other side of the room and switched off the music. A pregnant silence settled on the room as he slowly returned, seemingly losing his light-footedness.

'Please,' he said. 'Tell me what happened to Maya. Is she okay?'

'We're with the police,' Stephanie answered. 'I'm a detective inspector with Surrey Police, and Eve is a detective constable. Last night, Maya was killed on campus. We're trying—'

'Killed?' His voice broke. He reached for the wall for support. 'Maya? Are you sure it's her?'

Stephanie nodded.

'No... Surely not. How did she... how did she die?'

'Drowned. We're trying to ascertain her movements last night. Obviously, we were both here, but I wondered if you saw or heard anything unusual when she left?'

Sam shook his head. His eyes widened, and his gaze fell onto the mats in the centre of the room.

'What did you do after the session finished?' she asked.

'You think I did this?'

'Routine,' she answered. 'You and I were some of the last people to see her alive. I have to ask these questions.'

Sam wiped another bead of sweat from his forehead, though Stephanie sensed it was for a different reason than the exercise. 'About last night...'

'Go on.'

'I know how it's going to look. And I know how it's going to sound. But I'm raising this now, so you don't think anything happened between the two of us, because it didn't.'

'Tell me,' Stephanie intoned.

Folding his arms across his chest, he said, 'After you all left, I stayed behind for about half an hour, maybe longer. I was tidying the place up, same as I do after every session. When I left, I drove through town and saw Maya standing outside the cinema. So I pulled over and offered her a lift.'

Stephanie felt her breath hitch slightly in her throat. Eve, standing beside her, had already begun typing rapidly into her tablet.

'Did she accept?'

Sam hesitated, rubbing the back of his neck. 'Yeah. She looked surprised to see me there.'

'Why was she waiting there?'

'Well, she wasn't *waiting*. She was on the way home. She said she'd stopped for a Nando's on the way back after the session. I just happened to catch up with her.'

'Then what?'

Stephanie was oblivious to her surroundings, to the sound of Eve tapping on the screen, the cars driving past the window, the smell of chemicals that clung to the back of her throat.

'She gave me her address and I dropped her off.'

'Where? Where did you drop her off?' Her tone became more forceful, laced with a hint of desperation. Images of her and Maya battling together on the mats began to flash in the back of her mind, followed by the graphic visuals of her lying face down in the water.

'I dropped her off at the bottom of campus. By the bridge. She said it was fine, and that she could walk the rest of the way.'

'What time was this?'

Sam shrugged. 'It could have been about nine. Maybe later.'

'I need you to be specific, Sam. It's important.'

'About nine, quarter past nine.'

'Sure?'

'Yes. As sure as I can be.'

Stephanie glanced at Eve, who was busy making notes. She saw the times on the screen and was pleased the detective had noted everything.

'What was the campus like?' she continued.

'What do you mean?'

'Was it busy? Quiet? Was there a massive party going on in the street?'

'Quiet,' he said. 'Except for this group of hockey students coming down the road. They went off campus just as I pulled up at the bollard.'

'Then what happened?'

'I… I said goodbye, left her to it, and then that was it.'

'Did you see which way she went?'

Sam shook his head.

'Were you followed?'

'What?'

'*Followed*, Sam. Were you followed? Someone in a car perhaps? Or on foot? Did you notice anything strange at all?'

The man didn't dwell on it for too long. 'I honestly wasn't looking. And, to be honest, I wouldn't even know what to look out for.'

'Where did you go after you left Maya?'

'Home.'

'Which is where?'

'Worplesdon.'

'What's your registration number?'

Sam gave it to her.

Stephanie turned to Eve. 'Make a note for someone to check that on CCTV and ANPR.'

'You think I had something to do with this?' Sam asked, sounding almost offended.

'No. But I need to make sure you didn't. And I need to make sure nobody else thinks you did either. It's called ruling you out. And I hope for your sake, we can.'

Stephanie thanked him for his time and then gestured for Eve to take down his contact information. Next, they headed towards the exit.

As Eve held the door open, he asked, 'Will I need to close the gym?' His voice was laden with fear.

'No, Sam. That won't be necessary.'

'Will I see you next week for another session?'

She thought of Maya. Of the girl's smile, of the way they'd briefly bonded.

'No,' she said solemnly. 'I don't think you will.'

CHAPTER
FIFTY-TWO

Stephanie didn't know what time it was when she got home that evening. All she knew was that it was dark, she was tired, and the hunger pangs in her stomach hadn't abated since that morning. The rest of the afternoon had distracted her from eating or drinking anything substantial, apart from occasional sugary, heavily processed snacks from the vending machine. The team, upon their gradual return to the office, had celebrated her presence as if she'd returned from the dead. For Noah and Giles, those had been their exact words. To her surprise, they had taken it well. For the most part, they hadn't been bitter about her disappearance; they hadn't felt aggrieved, taken offence, or even taken it personally. With the exception of Devon, who'd said nothing on the matter, they had all been grateful that she was okay, safe, and feeling better. She had thought about pulling Devon aside again to lambast him for taking control of her investigation, but she couldn't find him; he was avoiding her at all costs. Every time she left her office, he got out of his chair and went down to the smoking area. Every time she entered the kitchen for a coffee, he pretended to receive a phone call.

He was behaving like a coward, but she had bigger things to worry about, like ringing through to Maya Corcoran's local police force and asking them to deliver the death message to her parents. By the afternoon, news of her death had broken, but it wasn't until Maya's parents had been notified of her passing that her name had been shared publicly with *Surrey Live*. Since then, the station had been inundated with phone calls from the community expressing their concern and support. A mixed bag. Their patience and sense of security was rapidly running out and the level of rancour towards Stephanie and her team was growing. Three teenage girls were dead within the space of a week, and they didn't even have a potential suspect. They had no tangible leads. There had been no further DNA or fingerprint evidence found at any of the crime scenes, and what little they did have was still being analysed and would not come through for another week or two. There had been no CCTV footage of the attacks on campus. All they had was a grainy image of a man in a hood, which had turned out to be Damien Veitch.

They were running out of options, and Stephanie would be lying if she said she felt confident about getting a result soon. She thought the start of World War Three might happen sooner.

The mess in the house did nothing to improve her mood. Chaos ran amok both inside her house and inside her mind, but she was too upset and demoralised to do anything about it. She'd heard that some people liked to clean when they were upset, but she could think of nothing worse. So she climbed over the myriad boxes, clothes, shoes, and toolbox in the hallway to get to the kitchen. When she opened the fridge and found nothing inside, she let out a long, heavy sigh.

She needed food. Something quick, something easy. Something she could put in the oven or microwave and forget about.

Releasing all the breath from her body, she closed the fridge and headed towards the front door, closing it with a forceful shove that echoed up and down the street, no doubt notifying her neighbour that she was there.

Outside, the night sky stretched wide and cloudless, save for the light from a plane that cut through the canvas. Lurking alongside the moonlight were several pinpricks of light, millions of miles away, struggling to break through. There was still that late-summer warmth in the air, so she decided to make the short journey to the local supermarket on foot.

She made it to the end of the driveway before she was summoned.

Her neighbour, Jimmy, threw his door open and leapt onto the patio, waving after her.

'I'm sorry to disturb you,' he said, suddenly lowering his tone when he heard it bounce around the houses. 'Are you in a hurry?'

'Not particularly,' she said, ignoring the growling in her stomach.

Jimmy pulled the door to, leaving a thin blade of light to cut through the grass, then hurried over, pulling his thin jumper tighter against his body. His head darted up and down the street as he came to a stop beside her.

'Sorry for all the cloak and dagger, but I don't want the whole street to hear,' he whispered. 'But I thought you should know. It's probably nothing. Probably me being a bit paranoid, and I don't want you to think I'm a nosy neighbour or anything, but—'

'What is it, Jimmy?' she insisted, the hunger pangs now shortening her fuse considerably.

'Earlier, there was a man,' he began, his voice a whisper. 'I thought you'd come home early, and I was going to help you with your bin.'

She cast a quick glance towards the black bin that was still where the refuse collectors had left it.

'But then I saw him looking through your letterbox, so I stopped to ask if he needed anything.'

'Who was he?'

'I don't know,' Jimmy replied. 'He didn't say.'

'What did he want?'

'He said he was looking for you.'

Stephanie paused for a moment. A scintilla of concern began to flare inside her. 'What did he look like?'

'Medium height, black hair. I wasn't paying much attention.'

Devon, she thought.

'When did this happen?'

Jimmy scratched the back of his head. 'Must have been about lunchtime, early afternoon.'

Nodding, she replied, 'It was probably just one of my colleagues,' she answered. 'There was a period they were trying to get hold of me.'

'Right. Well, if you're sure?'

She wasn't, but there wasn't anything she could do about it now.

'If they come by again, would you let me know?'

Jimmy confirmed he would, then Stephanie shared her mobile number with him.

'Thanks for keeping an eye out,' she added.

'Quite all right,' Jimmy replied. 'We have quite a good neighbourhood watch thing going on round here, just without the name. Now, I think I'll go to bed. The grandkids have absolutely knackered me out.'

The local supermarket had still been open when she arrived. Just. Five minutes from closing. As she rummaged through what remained of the shelves, she felt the staff's imperious stares wishing her unwell. What resulted was a last-minute snatch at a microwaveable lasagne with an expiry date that ran out in three hours.

As expected, it had been bland, tasteless, and soulless. But it had filled a gap.

She spent the rest of the evening staring mindlessly at the television, watching as the images flickered across the screen without taking any of it in.

When she finally felt herself beginning to get tired, it was nearly midnight. The entire neighbourhood was quiet. Fortunately, the sound of screaming children had also disappeared. As she switched off the living room light, she thought of the man who'd come looking for her.

Had it been Devon? And why? The latter concerned her the most. Why would he, out of the entire team, have come looking for her? Had he been hit on the head? Or was he just trying to make amends, to prove that he wasn't such an arsehole?

She struggled with that thought as she climbed the stairs and headed to her room. She always looked forward to getting into her bed at the end of the day, especially her teddy bear duvet cover that felt like she was cuddling the real thing. She used it all year round, even in sweltering summer heat. It reminded her of the blanket she and Kimberley had clung to in the wardrobe or when they'd hidden under the bed. It made her feel safe, protected. As she climbed into bed, she added to that layer of protection by reaching for her teddy bear and holding him against her chest.

The small cuddly toy, which she'd called Bart after her favourite character from *The Simpsons*, was small and threadbare in places, with one eye and leg slightly looser than the other, hasty repair jobs from years ago that had somehow held. Its fur, once a pale honey colour, had dulled with age into something tea-stained. But Stephanie didn't care. Bart was still with her. Bart still existed.

A gift from her mother, given to her on her fourth birthday, she had taken it everywhere. Dragged it along the road as they walked to the park. Smudged it with crayons when she'd played at nursery. Like the blanket, it had been by her side through every storm, clutched in her arms during late-night arguments downstairs, gripped tight beneath the sheets while she tried to block out the shouting and banging. It had soaked up tears she was too afraid to cry in front of anyone else.

It wasn't just a toy. It was a witness. The one thing that had never hurt her, never lied to her, never left.

As she curled around it, slowly drifting off to sleep, the world outside was still full of killers, violence, and pain, but in that moment, with Bart tucked under her chin and her duvet pulled tight to her chest, it was the closest she ever felt to believing she was safe.

CHAPTER
FIFTY-THREE

A light buzzed and flickered overhead, casting a pale wash over the tired faces of the team that had begun to assemble one by one. Stephanie stood at the front of the incident room, arms crossed, shoulders squared, trying to look steadier than she felt. A half-drunk cup of coffee steamed beside her on the desk, untouched for the past two minutes. She'd been in early, too early, and she was on her third already.

In that time, she'd read through the team's daily reports, scrutinising them for follow-up questions and lines of enquiry. To her surprise, they were all detailed and thorough, including Devon's, which she'd expected to contain half the work the others had.

Stephanie waited for the low murmur of voices to die down, then cleared her throat. 'Thank you for coming in early,' she began. 'I appreciate it's not nice, especially with the weather so bleak outside.'

Last night's perfectly clear skies had long abandoned them and been replaced by dark, moody clouds that carried an onslaught of rain.

'Hopefully it's not a reflection of things to come,' she continued. 'Now, I know we half-covered it yesterday, but I wanted to just bring it up again. My absence. It was nothing other than a panic attack. I'd spent the evening with Maya Corcoran, and seeing her like that had more of an impact on me than I thought. So I just had to escape for a bit, clear my head. I apologise for going off the grid. Devon, thank you for leading the team in my brief absence.'

The sergeant looked visibly shocked at the comment, so much so that he couldn't think of what to say.

'It's all right, ma'am,' Olivia said sweetly. 'We all have our bad days. You don't need to justify yourself or say anything else on the matter.'

Stephanie breathed a heavy sigh of relief. She'd put herself out there. She'd made herself vulnerable. She'd opened up to the team. And they'd respected it.

Case closed.

'I've gone through your reports from yesterday and want to discuss next steps with you,' Stephanie began. She gestured to DS Mackenzie. 'Noah, the university cannot force the students to stay. I don't give a damn if they think it'll hurt their reputation or they'll lose out on a load of money. This entire thing is about protecting the students, and if they want to leave, then they should be allowed to leave without any fear of repercussion. They're *adults*. It's about time the university started treating them like it.'

Noah nodded. 'Understood, ma'am. I'll have another word with the chancellor and see about putting in some safeguarding measures for the students. Curfew, that sort of thing. I'll also see if we can get a patrol going somehow.'

Stephanie thanked him, then turned her attention to Olivia. 'Wellard, did any of Maya's friends or housemates you spoke with yesterday give you any cause for concern?'

Olivia shook her head.

'Had any of them heard from her before she was killed?'

Another shake of the head. 'Only to say that she was on her way home.'

Stephanie turned to the board behind her. Underneath a picture of Maya Corcoran, Stephanie had pieced together a timeline of events. With her whiteboard marker, she pointed to the first timestamp. 'As far as I've been able to make out, she was dropped off on campus at nine fifteen. She lived on Twyford Court on the other side of campus, which is a couple of minutes' walk. Any update on CCTV showing her walking through the site?'

Giles took this one. 'I had a look yesterday, and we can see her walking past the Duke of Kent building at precisely 9:17 pm. From there she takes a detour through the field, and she doesn't emerge.'

'So we can assume her time of death is shortly thereafter,' Stephanie said, circling a 9:30 pm timestamp on the board. 'Is there any CCTV of cars coming through, or other people on campus entering the field at that time?'

A shake of the head.

'Could the killer have been waiting for her?' Eve asked.

'Possibly,' Giles answered. 'But by the university's own admission, there are blind spots on campus. Not everything is covered by security cameras, as we've already seen. *Especially* the field.'

Stephanie nodded, deep in thought. 'I think the killer either knew she was going to be there or followed her home. As with Claudia Bellini and Paulina Potter, I think Maya was targeted.'

'What about someone from the jiujitsu class?' Eve asked, holding a hand to her lip as if she'd spoken out of turn. 'I know we spoke with the instructor, but shouldn't we speak with the people who attended the session?'

'No harm in it,' Steph responded. 'But they would have to know the other two victims, so I'm not hopeful. Don't spend too much time on it.'

'Yes, ma'am.'

The conversation entered a natural lull and Stephanie used the silence to sip from her lukewarm coffee. It was bitter and stale, but it gave her something to do with her hands. She placed the cup down and stared at the timeline again, narrowing her eyes at the space between 9:17 and 9:30 pm.

'The timings are key,' she said. 'All the girls have been killed in the evening. Yes, the killer's used the cover of darkness. But I think there's more to it than that. There's a strong element of preparation here. This is someone who's spent a lot of time planning these killings. Fiona, what are the next steps with Tristan Penrose, Claudia's and Paulina's lecturer?'

'He doesn't have anything to do with Maya Corcoran,' Fiona answered briefly. 'She's a history student, which is about as far removed as you can get from what the other girls do.'

'Is he still a suspect?'

Fiona was taken aback by the question. 'I… I don't know, ma'am.'

'What about in your experience? Do you think he's still a suspect, or should we be focusing our attention on someone else like Damien Veitch?'

It didn't take long for Fiona to come up with an answer. 'Neither suspect has had anything to do with Maya Corcoran. There's nothing I can make out so far that connects all three victims to either of those two suspects.'

'So…?' Steph placed her hands on her hips.

'So… what?'

'What's your verdict?'

'I don't think they're suspects, no. But I don't think we should discount them entirely.'

'Very well. That's settled.' Stephanie turned to Devon. 'DS Lafferty, as you've made it your area of expertise, how are we getting on with the dolls?'

Devon snorted heavily and wiped the underside of his nose before responding. 'Nothing's come through from forensics yet. I've briefly searched online for doll suppliers, and nobody's come back to me yet, so I don't know where they've been sourced from.'

'Good work,' she said. 'Keep at it. Right now, the only thing connecting all three of these victims is these dolls. And… you all know what happened to the one at Maya's crime scene. I won't be able to live with myself if *that* happens to someone on campus. Noah, speak with the university and get them to send out an email or communication to the students, reminding them to stay in the light, stay indoors in the evening, and if they have to go out at night, to make sure they're in pairs. I've tried twice and it's made no difference.'

Noah shot her one of his trademark finger guns. 'Will do, boss.'

'Anything else?'

A hand shot up, belonging to Olivia. 'Not sure if it's anything, but while I was on campus yesterday, I heard talk of some of the students planning a vigil for the girls at the lake where Maya was found.'

'That's touching, but I don't think it helps our investigation.' Stephanie quickly glanced at the board, looking at each of the victims' faces before continuing. 'A lot of this is academic until we find out *why* the killer is targeting these girls,' Steph continued. 'If we can work that out, we can narrow down the who.'

'Actually, ma'am, I think that's the wrong way to look at it.'

Of course, the comment had come from Devon. She slowly turned to face him.

'Why's that, sergeant?'

'Because I think I've found something that connects them all.'

'Care to share it with the rest of the class?'

'They were all part of the same running group,' he said. 'I've got a meeting with the head of the society this morning, actually.'

'Thanks for the invite,' she said sarcastically. 'I'd love to join you.'

CHAPTER
FIFTY-FOUR

The first few minutes of the car journey had been filled with silence, save for the *whooshing* sounds of cars speeding past them on the other side of the road. During that time, Stephanie had thought about the best way to approach her conversation with Devon. She saw three options.

One, the simplest: say nothing at all. She was used to awkward silences and keeping her mouth shut for as long as necessary, so it wouldn't be difficult.

Two: launch a verbal tirade at him, letting him know what she really thought about him and his behaviour. If it had been Caleb, her old sergeant, she would have chosen this option and gone in guns blazing, giving him the tough love he responded well to. But Devon wasn't Caleb. And Caleb wasn't Devon. If she was going to make any inroads with her new DS, she would have to try something different. Pander to him slightly. Massage his ego as much as her tolerance would allow.

And so she chose option three: kill him with kindness.

'Thanks for managing the team while I was AWOL yesterday,' she said, placing her hands in her lap.

Devon glanced at her from the driver's seat. She noticed a hint of surprise in his expression. 'That's all right.' His tone was incredulous, as if he didn't believe a word she was saying.

'I couldn't have done it without you,' she continued. 'That's what a sergeant is for. I appreciate it.'

'Erm…'

'McGowan wasn't happy,' she added. 'But I'm used to dealing with chief inspectors and all their hormone imbalances. I swear some of them are worse than teenage girls at times.'

Devon didn't know whether to laugh or agree. He gave a short nod, his eyes fixed on the road. 'He's just doing his job. As was I. It's not like the place would fall apart without you.'

Stephanie resisted the urge to respond with a cutting remark. She was sticking to option three, for now. 'Good to know. Maybe I'll do it more often. Take a couple of days off next time.'

He didn't see the funny side of that and they drove in silence for a few beats.

'You all right now?' Devon asked suddenly. The question was clipped and awkward, as if he wasn't sure he should have voiced it.

Stephanie stared ahead, her reflection faint in the windscreen. 'I've never been all right,' she said. 'But I've learned to live with it. What about you? Do you ever have your moments?'

He pointed at his chest. 'Me?'

'You're the only other one here.'

'Weaknesses? Not that I can think of.'

'They don't define you,' she said. 'It's okay to have them, Devon. Everyone does. It's how we overcome them that shows who we really are.'

He returned his attention to the road, changing to a lower gear. He said nothing.

'Tell me about yourself,' she said.

'What do you mean?'

'Who are you, Devon? I'm not going anywhere for the foreseeable future. You can't get rid of me that easily. So I might as well get to know you a little better. I've already made some progress with the rest of the team.'

'And I'm last on your list?'

She shrugged. 'It's not like you've made it easy for me.'

He glanced at her, caught the glimmer of sarcasm, and almost smiled himself. Almost. 'There's not much to tell, to be honest.'

'Nothing at all? You just exist? One-dimensional?'

A shrug of the shoulders. 'Pretty much.'

The car bumped slightly as they hit a pothole in the road. He shifted gears again, the engine humming beneath them.

That hadn't gone as well as she'd hoped. She hadn't expected him to give her his memoir, but she had expected a little more. It was clear he was still wearing his armour, and it would take a considerable amount of time to find her way through.

They drove on in silence for a few more minutes, though it settled differently this time. There was no awkwardness clinging to it, no sense of animosity between them. Both sides of the army had called a temporary armistice, and progress was being made.

'How did you find my address?' she asked suddenly, as they passed the Stag Hill statue on their way onto campus.

'I did what?'

'When you came to my house yesterday?'

'I don't know what you're talking about.'

She slowly turned to face him. 'My neighbour said someone matching your description came to my house, looking for me. I figured it was you.'

Devon pulled the car into the car park on the north side of campus and eased the car into the nearest available space. 'Nope. Nothing to do with me,' he said as he killed the engine. 'Sorry.'

CHAPTER
FIFTY-FIVE

All thoughts of her relationship with Devon vanished the moment they stepped into the university's library atrium. The place pulsed with life, the beating heart of the campus. Clusters of students swarmed across the entrance, drifting in every direction like currents in a restless tide. To the right, students clutching snacks and energy drinks spilled out of a small supermarket, most with ear buds in, faces lit by the glow of their phones. To the left, the campus bookshop displayed a modest collection of coursebooks alongside shelves stacked with University of Surrey hoodies, mugs, and lanyards. Everywhere she looked were students wearing official hoodies and jumpers. Students of all shapes and sizes, all ages and demographics, moving from one place to the next. A kaleidoscope of cultures, races, and ethnicities. Immediately, she felt invisible there, anonymity wrapping around her like one of the jumpers. She was just another student looking to find a spot in the library to further her education.

The cloak of anonymity didn't last long. It was swept away the moment she saw a row of folding tables lining the wall opposite the entrance. Students stood behind them, handing out flyers with mechanical efficiency. The tables were plastered with homemade signs: *Remembering Claudia. Remembering Paulina. Remembering Maya.* Tealights flickered in jam jars. Printed portraits of the deceased smiled from posters taped to display boards, their eyes following her with quiet accusation. One table offered information about self-defence classes and safe walk-home schemes. Another advertised a vigil scheduled for that week.

Stephanie found her legs moving towards the tables.

A girl with purple hair stepped in front of Stephanie. 'I recognise you! You're the police person looking into the girls' deaths. Why haven't you found who's responsible yet?'

Just as Stephanie was about to respond, another student piped up. 'Students are dying! Nobody feels safe on campus anymore.'

Another said, 'You lot haven't got a clue. You couldn't find your bollocks if they slapped you in the face.'

Stephanie's eyes searched for the offender, but their face was quickly lost among the sea of students. Soon, the crowd began shouting questions at her, harassing her, throwing their arms in the air in disgust. Stephanie did her best to calm them, but the feeling of claustrophobia quickly suffocated her.

She was used to tight spaces, hiding in the wardrobe or under the bed for hours on end, a place of escape. But this was a total assault on her senses.

The noise. The proximity of those around her.

Images of her dad storming into her room, yanking her out of bed, and screaming in her face before raising his fist flashed in front of her.

The walls began to spin. The faces of her tormentors began to melt and blur together.

Until eventually, darkness suffocated the light from the room, and she collapsed to the floor.

When she awoke, she was blinded by harsh artificial light, worsening the pain in her head. She tried to move, but her muscles were weak.

'You all right down there?' Devon asked, placing a hand on her shoulder.

As she looked up to see him standing over her, another image appeared, this time of her dad, standing naked in the bedroom.

She flinched at his touch and tried to climb out of the chair.

'Where am I?'

'First aid room,' a soft, gentle voice answered. It belonged to a woman in her fifties. She reached out a hand and placed it on Stephanie's wrist, instantly calming her.

'My name's Jules. I work in the shop, but fortunately for you, I'm one of the only members of staff who's first aid trained. You gave everyone quite a scare back there.'

'What happened?'

'You fainted.' Jules held out a chocolate bar. A Kinder Bueno. 'Eat. You need sugar.'

Stephanie dismissed it. 'We need to finish the job we came to do.'

She started to get out of the chair, but Devon held her down. 'You need to collect yourself before you do any more damage.'

Too late for that.

As she looked up at him again, she was unable to shake the image in her brain. For some reason, under the sharp lighting, he reminded her of her father. Something in the eyes. Something lingering in the expression.

Discomfort plagued her body, and she shoved him away, climbing out of the chair. She snatched the snack from Jules and said, 'Come on. We don't have time to waste.'

After several moments spent bickering, Stephanie eventually convinced both Devon and Jules that she was fine to continue, though she could only leave if she finished the chocolate bar.

Playing with the wrapper in her fingers, guilt beginning to settle in, she opened the door and stepped into the library's atrium. Immediately, she was accosted by a tall, gangly man – at least six foot five – with arms freakishly longer than his torso. He was at least a foot taller than Steph, with hard cheekbones and a jawline that looked as though it had been chiselled from stone. Had she not been almost double his age, she would have found him attractive.

'Excuse me,' he said, his voice deep with a thin Bristolian tinge. 'Are you with the police?'

'I don't wear this suit for the fun of it,' Devon replied snidely, then held out his hand. 'You must be Elliot?'

The man with the long arms nodded and shook Devon's hand.

Stephanie was so busy trying to take in the sheer size of him that she didn't notice his hand in her face.

'You the runner?' she asked, licking a piece of chocolate from her lips.

'People usually assume basketball because… well, you know. But, yes. I'm the president of the running society. I had a room booked upstairs and was waiting for you. But then I heard about what happened and came straight down. Shall we?'

Devon gestured for the man to lead the way. Stephanie's legs felt a little unsteady as she climbed the steps towards the library on the first floor, but she refused help from both men, insisting that she could manage. It hadn't quite dawned on her what had happened. At least, not yet. She had fainted in front of her sergeant. She had fainted in front of a hundred university students. What must Devon have thought of her? First, she went AWOL. And now this? Three words came to mind: unreliable, unstable, unfit. The type of words that got whispered behind computer monitors or in corridors. The type that made their way into performance reviews. She had lost control of herself, and soon she would no doubt lose control of the team.

She needed to get it together.

At the top of the steps, they came to a series of turnstiles. Elliot slipped through with his library card; Stephanie and Devon were granted access by the member of staff. The atmosphere up there was calmer, muted. The hubbub of conversation and laughter downstairs didn't exist, as if they'd passed through an invisible barrier on the way in.

Elliot led them into a private room that was used for group meetings. The room was modern, with a table in the centre and a flatscreen television affixed to one the wall. The rest of the walls were floor-to-ceiling windows. Exposed, open. Nothing and nowhere to hide.

'Elliot,' Stephanie began, slumping heavily into a chair. 'Has my colleague explained why we're here?'

A nod.

'I think we should begin by discussing the running society. What is it?'

'It's what you'd expect. It's a group of thirty of us, all running enthusiasts. We include everyone, ranging from first-year students all the way up to post-grads. We've even got some alumni in there, people who recently left the university but haven't left the sport.'

'When do you meet?'

'Every Sunday. We cater to all experiences and levels, and we typically do runs between five and fifteen kilometres before heading to the coffee shop or sometimes the pub.'

'And you're the organiser?'

A nod. 'There's not much to it, to be honest. I just look after the WhatsApp group and tell people where they need to be and when they need to be there. Everyone gets there on time, so I seem to be doing something right.'

Stephanie turned to Devon, who was sitting on the other side of the table. He picked up on the cue and began addressing Elliot directly.

'Is it true that Claudia Bellini, Paulina Potter, and Maya Corcoran were all members of your running club?'

Elliot knitted his fingers together and looked down at them, tucking his chin deep into his chest. It was like he was in the middle of a job interview. 'Yes, it's true. Though I only saw Claudia once, on the Sunday just gone. She said it was one of the first societies she wanted to join.' A smile crept onto his face. 'She was quite the runner as well, actually. Had all the gear and managed to keep up with a couple of the long-distance guys too.'

'Did anyone take an interest in her?' Devon asked. 'Or any of the girls, for that matter?'

Elliot slowly tilted his head towards the sergeant. 'What are you suggesting?'

'Answer the question, please,' Stephanie stepped in.

'I didn't pick up on anything. But there are only five men in the group, if that's what you're insinuating.'

'Including yourself?' Stephanie asked.

He nodded gently.

'Any of them post-grads?'

Another nod. 'One is.'

Stephanie shared a glance with Devon. 'We're going to need the names of all the men in the running group, please.'

CHAPTER
FIFTY-SIX

Stephanie was perched on the edge of the sofa, her eyes fixed on the empty space outside the bay window. Any moment now, her sister would arrive, and she needed to ensure that, under no circumstances, Kimberley came in. The place was a mess, and she was in no mood for a discussion (translation: argument) about it. Her mind had been too focused on the investigation to care, and over the past few days, the number of boxes, clothes, piles of rubbish, and general mess had accrued, taking up more and more space in the little room she had.

The investigation had reached a standstill. Following her and Devon's interview with Elliot, the head of the running society, she had instructed the team to speak with the male members whose names they'd been given. From them, only one member had emerged as a potential suspect, solely because he was the only one without a solid alibi for Paulina Potter's murder, and the team had been left to corroborate his version of events. Since then, while their workload had increased, the inflow of serious leads had all but stopped.

Thoughts of the investigation and the girls had plagued Stephanie's every waking moment and distracted her so much that she'd forgotten what day it was. In truth, she'd always known – deep down, anyway. But perhaps it was her subconscious making her forget, forcing her to choose to forget the day she'd struggled to come to terms with for more than thirty years.

She involuntarily wrapped her fingers around the necklace. A moment later, as if summoned, an oversized 4x4 skidded to a stop in the driveway.

Steph quickly grabbed her things and left the house.

'Why do you need a car this big?' she asked Kimberley as she climbed six feet into the passenger seat. 'You don't have kids. You don't have any pets. Why?'

'Good to see you too, sis.'

They kissed each other on the cheek, then Steph buckled herself in.

'It was Jason's choice.'

'Because everyone else has got one? You suit the Surrey lifestyle well. Everyone seems to have massive cars round here, and it's always women driving them.'

Kim pulled away without looking. The car lurched to the side, and Stephanie grabbed onto the 'oh-shit' handle for support.

'Someone woke up on the wrong side of the bed today,' Kim retorted.

'Can you blame me?'

Kim glanced sideways at Stephanie, placing a hand on her thigh. 'No, I guess I can't. How have you been?'

Stephanie turned her attention to the houses that blurred as they passed. That morning, the sky was a gunmetal grey, and there was a pressure in the air, as if it were closing in on them the nearer they got.

'Fine,' she lied.

'Work?'

'Busy. You?'

'Same. Same with Jason too. I haven't seen much of him this past week. He's been up and down from London at all hours of the night. Gone out for a couple of drinks with the team as well.'

Let's hope that's all it is.

'He's living the life,' Steph replied, not wanting to worry her sister.

'You haven't been on any more dangerous bike rides or gone rock climbing on your own again? Or any midnight runs?'

Stephanie confirmed she hadn't. In truth, she hadn't been able to think about any of those things – running, rock climbing, or even painting – because doing so would only serve as a painful reminder of the students who'd lost their lives.

Kim slammed on her brakes, sending Stephanie plummeting forward in her seat. Were it not for the seatbelt keeping her in place, she would have collided face first with the windscreen. Kimberley swore repeatedly at the driver, giving him the finger as he tore past.

'You'd think he'd see you coming round that blind corner,' Stephanie commented sarcastically.

'Arsehole drivers. The roads are full of them.'

Stephanie leaned across the centre of the car and glanced at the dash. 'Especially when you're going five miles an hour over the speed limit.' She gripped the edge of her seat in panic. 'I've been on extensive driver training courses; I've driven over a hundred and twenty miles an hour; I've swerved through traffic on an A-road; and yet I've never felt more scared for my life than I have in the past five minutes.'

Her sister waved the comment away. 'Behave.'

'Are your classes like this? Absolute chaos.'

'Shut up.'

'Don't think I won't write you up for dangerous driving just because you're my sister.'

Ahead, a green light was about to change to amber. Kimberley slammed her foot on the accelerator, lurching the car forward.

'I'd like to get there alive, thanks,' Steph said.

Less than five minutes later, after praying for her life every second of the way, they arrived at the cemetery. Kim slowed the car to a crawl, pulling up beside a moss-covered wall. The graveyard was nearly empty, save for an old man tending a headstone with a watering can and a pair of gardening gloves. Stephanie recognised him from the other day.

Dave.

As she leapt out of the car, she was immediately hit by the scent of damp earth and cut grass. The clouds had thickened above, closing in further, and the wind carried a chill that raised goosebumps along her arms.

Kim opened the boot and pulled out a small bouquet of daisies.

'You bought flowers?'

'I do every year.'

The thought hadn't even entered her mind. Now she felt upstaged.

They walked together in silence, weaving through the crooked headstones and patches of wildflowers, until they came to their mother's grave.

Stephanie had never commemorated the anniversary of her death. She'd never found the courage to. She always busied herself with work. The reminder was too painful.

Thirty years to the day since she'd witnessed her mother's death.

Thirty years to the day since she'd just watched and done nothing about it.

Thirty years to the day since her and her sister's lives had changed forever.

Steph felt her body flush cold. Out of the corner of her eye, she saw Dave on his knees amongst the grass, his head turning towards her. She grabbed for the necklace again.

Hi, Mum.

Kim knelt to arrange the flowers and clear the headstone, while Stephanie stood motionless. She didn't cry. Couldn't. Wouldn't. Not in front of Kimberley. She'd never cried in front of her sister. It had always been the other way round. She'd needed to stay strong, tough, resilient. She hadn't been able to show that anything was wrong.

That was part of the pact she'd made with herself at ten years old – be strong, be quiet, carry on.

They stood there for a long while. Just the wind in the trees, the rustle of leaves, the occasional song from a bird.

'Do you ever wonder what she'd think of us?' Kim asked suddenly.

Stephanie stared at the headstone and nodded.

'Do you think she'd be proud of us?'

Another nod. 'A detective and a schoolteacher,' she said softly. 'We're both helping others in different ways when nobody wanted to help us. I think she'd be proud. Because we've survived.'

Stephanie looked out over the graves, the tops of the houses in the distance, the heavy sky above.

In more ways than one, she thought.

. . .

Stephanie climbed back into the car with a heaviness in her chest. She shut the door softly, then sat motionless, staring straight ahead through the windscreen. A moment later, Kim hopped in beside her and started the engine, the low rumble filling the silence between them.

'Ready?'

'When you are.'

Stephanie leaned her head against the window as the car pulled away, her breath misting the glass. She thought of their mum: of her laugh (on the infrequent occasions she heard it); of how beautiful she was; of how open and honest she was; of how she always put others before herself. A memory flitted through her mind: her mum painting the kitchen cabinets yellow one summer, saying she wanted sunshine even on rainy days. It had earned her a beating, and Stephanie too, but she hadn't cared. It had all been worth it just to see the smile on her face.

As they reached the junction at the end of the lane, Kim turned the car right instead of left, as Stephanie had been expecting.

She sat up slightly. 'Where are we going?'

Kim didn't answer. Nor did her sister look at her.

'*Kimberley*.'

'Just a quick stop.'

'A stop?' Stephanie repeated, her voice hardening. '*Where?*'

'We're going to see Dad.'

Stephanie blinked. Once. Twice. As if the words hadn't landed properly. 'No, we're not.'

'I spend this day with both of them, Steph. Mum and Dad. Every year.'

Stephanie's breath caught. Her hands clenched in her lap.

'You didn't tell me.'

'Because I knew you'd react like this. He isn't going to be around forever, Steph. I don't know how long he's got, and I want to spend as much time with him as possible. We owe him. Both of us. Without him, we would never have found who did that to Mum.'

Steph closed her eyes and inhaled sharply. She controlled her breathing because right then it was the only thing she could control.

'Turn this car around.'

'It's too late. It'll be fine. *You'll* be fine.'

'Kimberley. Turn this car around. Now.'

Kimberley did nothing. She kept the car on the road, heading towards the care home, cruising along the winding roads, as knots tightened in Stephanie's stomach. The thought of seeing him, of looking into the eyes of the man who had shaped so much of her trauma, made her want to open the car door and roll onto the A3.

Kim reached across and placed a hand on her thigh. 'Please, Steph. Do this for me. It's important.'

Steph began to hyperventilate. Her pulse was bursting through her neck. Her palms were covered in a thin layer of sweat, and she disconnected from her own body, as if her legs were moving against her will.

In fact, the entire visit was against her will.

This time, she hadn't needed a nurse to show her where to go. Kimberley led her down the quiet corridor, nodding politely to staff as they passed. Stephanie followed a few paces behind. Her chest was tight, her lungs shrinking. In the distance, the sound of the television in the common room echoed.

A visiting couple emerged from the room next door to their dad's. Kimberley greeted them, exchanging pleasantries as if they were best friends. Stephanie hovered awkwardly behind her sister, her breathing growing faster and shallower.

The walls closed in as they moved towards their dad's room. Her heart thudded against her ribs. She couldn't get enough air.

Kimberley was the first to enter. Stephanie just stood there, on the threshold, as her sister moved towards their father, slumped in his high-backed chair by the window, a blanket draped over his legs, his attention solely focused on the television in front of him. His eyes were glazed, unfocused.

Stephanie swallowed hard.

'All right, Dad?' Kim began. 'It's me.'

Colin Broadbent paid Kimberley no attention. But as soon as Stephanie crossed the threshold, his gaze began to turn, slowly, towards her.

'You,' he croaked, his voice hoarse. 'You're…' He blinked. 'You're… Stephy.'

'That's Stephanie, yes,' Kimberley jumped in when Steph was too choked up to answer.

Kim perched on the side of Colin's armchair, wrapping her arm around him. 'She's come to say hi. We both have. Do you know what day it is today, Dad?'

Obviously, there was no response. Colin's gaze didn't leave Stephanie.

'It's the anniversary of Mum's death. Can you believe it's been thirty years already? Where has the time gone? We've just been to see her grave, and it looks really beautiful. We laid some lovely flowers and said a few words for her, didn't we, Steph?'

Stephanie grunted, staring at a stain on the carpet.

'I think she's proud of us up there, Dad. Watching over all of us, protecting us. You, me, Steph… and in about six months' time, your granddaughter.'

Stephanie snapped her head towards her sister. 'What did you just say?'

Kim lowered her hand to her stomach. 'I'm pregnant.'

'Since when?'

'About three months ago. We didn't want to say anything until we had the all-clear from the doctor, and—'

Stephanie leapt across the room and embraced her sister. 'That's such fabulous news!' she exclaimed. 'Why didn't you tell me sooner?'

'We didn't want to stress you. After all the moving, work… it didn't seem like the right time. But today, it just…'

Colin slowly lifted his gaze towards Kim. 'A baby…?'

'Yes,' Kim replied. 'You're going to be a grandfather, Dad. Due in March.' She rubbed her stomach again. 'I can't wait for you to meet her.'

A potent mix of emotions overwhelmed Stephanie. The walls seemed to close in, and she struggled to breathe. 'I need some air,' she said, turning away and heading out of the room.

She took a right turn and found herself down a random corridor. How could she get lost in a care home? Then she remembered the place was like a prison for the elderly.

Mercifully, she found the entrance and caught a staff member. After what felt like forever, she was finally released. Outside, she gasped in bucketloads of oxygen, and soon after, the light-headedness disappeared. Standing a few metres away were two members of staff enjoying a cigarette. The smell gently wafted over. Despite her other vices, she had never taken up smoking.

In that moment, she thought she might need one.

'How's he getting on?' Wayne, the male nurse she'd met previously, asked her. His eyes were wide behind his glasses, and he had a new tattoo on his forearm.

'Fine,' she replied, placing her hands on her hips.

'He was asking about you the other day,' Wayne continued, taking a thick drag of his cigarette. 'Said he saw you on the news.'

She said nothing, just offered a polite smile and wished he would stop talking to her.

As if by divine intervention, her mobile buzzed in her pocket. She answered the call before he could say anything else.

'Fiona, is everything all right?'

'What are you doing right now, SB?'

'I'm somewhere I wish I wasn't. Why?'

'Perfect. Grab your bags, bring your ID, and get yourself down to The King's Head. Eve and I are bored, and we want you to join us for a drink. We've got a table booked from seven o'clock.'

CHAPTER
FIFTY-SEVEN

The pub was loud, warm, and crowded, a jarring contrast to the sterile silence of the care home just hours before. Stephanie stood awkwardly by the bar for a moment, her coat still half on, unsure if she had made the right decision in coming. But then she spotted Eve and Fiona tucked into a booth near the back, waving her over with half-drunk gin and tonics.

She ordered a drink at the bar, then crossed the room, weaving between tables and dodging a man carrying three pints as if he'd done it before.

'There she is,' Eve grinned, nudging a glass toward the empty seat. 'SB! I was starting to think you'd bottled it.'

'I nearly did,' Stephanie admitted, sliding in beside them. She set her drink on the table and shrugged out of her coat. 'But right now, I need this more than anything.'

Fiona tilted her head, studying her. 'Rough day?'

'Yes and no.' Steph took her first sip of the drink. The alcohol exploded in her mouth. 'I went to see my mum's grave with my sister, then visited my dad in the care home, and then found out my sister's pregnant with her first child. So it's been all sorts of emotions.'

Eve and Fiona looked at one another. In the space of a few sentences, Steph had shared more about her personal life than in the whole of the week she'd been there.

Fiona raised her glass. 'Well, here's to everyone: your sister and her baby, your dad and his health, and your—'

'Not my dad,' Stephanie replied, already taking a sip.

'No?'

'We didn't get on.'

'All right. Your sister, her baby, and your mum…'

'Cheers to that,' Steph said, as they clinked glasses. She took a massive gulp, almost finishing the drink in one go, then set her glass on the table. 'You didn't fancy inviting the rest of the team?'

Fiona licked her lips, shaking her head. 'We just wanted a quiet one, civilised. Just us girls.'

'Wellard?'

'Looking after the kids. One's got football practice and the other's got piano. Poor woman. They consume every moment of her life outside of work. And sometimes in it, as well.'

Steph glanced between Eve and Fiona. 'This is nice. Thanks for inviting me.'

'We only did it because you're the boss,' Fiona joked. 'Maybe we should do this monthly.'

Her suggestion was met with silence as neither Eve nor Stephanie were particularly receptive to the idea of a monthly meet-up, to the exclusion of the rest of the team. Stephanie didn't like the thought of cliques forming. There was already too much disarray and turmoil among them at the moment; that was the last thing they needed.

'How are you getting on with your landlord?' Fiona asked Eve as she finished the last of her drink.

Eve rolled her eyes and let out a deep sigh. 'I swear to God, if I have to call him one more time, I'll literally lose it. Last time I spoke to him, he called me sweetheart! If he doesn't fix the leak in my boiler soon, I'll have to show him how sweet I really am. He won't know what's hit him. Either that, or I'll get my mum down. She can just stare at him until the plumbing fixes itself.'

Stephanie laughed, a soft, surprised sound. 'Your mum sounds terrifying.'

'She's five foot nothing and full of rage. She grew up in South London with four brothers and no time for nonsense.'

Fiona grinned. 'That explains it. My mum's as sweet as they come.

Honestly, there isn't anything I wouldn't do for that—' She caught herself, eyes wide. 'Steph, I'm so sorry. I didn't think. Your mum…'

Steph waved a hand, dismissing the comment. 'It's fine.'

'I was being insensitive. I'm sorry.'

'It's fine, Fiona. Honestly. She died when I was very young. I've had a long time to come to terms with it.'

'Still, I feel like an idiot.'

'You're not. It's just one of those days. Besides, it's nice. I don't often get to talk about her.'

There was a pause as they each nursed their drinks. Steph played with her necklace. She could feel the alcohol swimming to her head already. 'She gave me this, actually,' she began. 'Before she died.'

'It's lovely,' Fiona replied, leaning in to look at it.

'She also gave me a teddy bear.'

'What happened to it?'

'I've still got him. I sleep with him every night. He was one of the first things I took out of a box when I moved in.'

'What's his name?'

'Bart.'

'Like the character?'

She nodded. 'Don't mock. He's very distinguished.'

Eve's eyes lit up. 'Yes! I knew you had a soft side. I've got this old hoodie from uni that I still wear every time I feel down.'

It was Fiona's turn. She rested her chin on her hand. 'I used to have a shoebox full of notes under my bed. Things I'd overheard people say. Strangers. My parents. Teachers. I thought I was going to be a writer. Then I realised I didn't want to create mysteries. I wanted to solve them.'

'That's kind of beautiful,' Eve said. 'And like vaguely creepy.'

'Thank you,' Fiona replied, deadpan.

Stephanie looked between the two of them and felt, for the first time in a while, like she was part of something again.

'You two are weird,' she said, raising her glass.

'Takes one to know one, SB!' Eve replied.

They clinked glasses again. This time, the smile on Stephanie's face lingered just a little longer.

CHAPTER
FIFTY-EIGHT

Brakes squeaked as she skidded to a halt. Priya swung her leg off the bike and removed her helmet. 'That was insane,' she gasped. Her hair was stuck to her forehead, and a smear of mud traced one cheek. 'I forgot how much I missed this.'

'We should've done it sooner,' said Tamzin, hopping off her bike and stretching. Her legs were shaking. 'We're making this a weekly thing. No excuses.'

'Agreed,' Megan added, brushing a pine needle from her sleeve. 'Even if I can't sit down tomorrow.'

They laughed again, wheeling their bikes towards the nearby rack. But the moment they reached it, Megan stopped short.

'They're all full.'

Priya blinked. 'Seriously?'

She surveyed the rack closest to their halls of residence. It was completely occupied. Dozens of bikes, including those available for hire from the town centre, filled the spaces.

'We'll have to find somewhere else to leave them,' Megan said as she climbed onto her bike.

'You can,' Priya replied. 'I can't be arsed. I'm just gonna leave mine in my car. It's easier.'

Megan looked uneasy. 'You sure? We could double up. Chain two together.'

Priya shook her head. 'Nah. It'll only take me a sec. You two go, I'll catch you up later.'

They split up, heading in separate directions. While Megan and Tamzin went up the hill towards the students' union, Priya took the long route around the outskirts of the campus, passing the lake, towards the car park on the north side. Usually, the car park – and the entire campus, for that matter – was heaving with cars, with students and lecturers vying for the limited spaces. But now, in the middle of the morning, it was completely empty. She had heard the rumours about students leaving and heading back home, but she hadn't expected so many to follow through with it. Maybe that was why the bike racks were full, she thought.

Gravel crunched beneath Priya's tyres as she coasted towards her silver Polo, parked under a lamppost. She stopped, unclipped her helmet, and reached into her pocket for her keys.

The car unlocked easily, and then she began the laborious process of manoeuvring the bike into the vehicle. First, she had to lower the back seats, which required finessing a tricky mechanism until it gave way. Then she had to remove all the clutter in the boot – the screen washer fluid, her brother's football, and a stack of tinned food her mum had given her for emergencies – before she could think about loading the bike in. The car was from the early two thousands, had over a hundred thousand miles on the clock, and was often a pain in the arse to drive. But it was her little pain in the arse. Reliable, resilient. Her first car, and it had helped her transport everything from Hastings to the university. She wouldn't have changed anything about it.

Priya was still on the first step, tickling the mechanism beneath the seat, when something cracked against her skull.

Her vision went white and her knees buckled.

Another blow landed, harder this time, and she dropped to the tarmac with a thud.

Hands grabbed her. She tried to scream, but the air had been knocked clean out of her. She felt herself being dragged, her limbs heavy and useless. The back door of her car was flung open, and she was shoved inside, the door slamming shut behind her.

She clawed at the handle, but it wouldn't budge. She was locked in.

Then she smelt it. A sharp, bitter odour. Petrol.

Her vision was still fogged, her head pounding, blood running into one eye.

The sound of liquid sloshing. A footstep. Then another.

She screamed. Pounded on the windows. Tried to kick the door.

A flick – the unmistakable sound of a lighter. Then fire.

It bloomed in an instant, a flash of orange against the window, and then heat.

She shrieked, thrashing her arms, her skin already blistering from the searing air. The last thing she saw was the silhouette of someone walking away. Calm. Unhurried. As the flames devoured everything around her.

CHAPTER
FIFTY-NINE

Stephanie hadn't moved for five minutes; hadn't been able to pull her eyes away from the sight in front of her for even longer.

Her head still pounded from the effects of the previous night's drinking. But right then, a different pain was swelling in her skull. Everything was closing in on her. Images of the doll found at Maya Corcoran's crime scene flashed in her mind: the initial spark, the immediate combustion, the charred remains of the doll.

The crime scene in front of her was the same. Cordons stretched across the entire length of the car park, staff and student cars untouched, blue lights illuminating them and the surrounding trees. The remains of the vehicle sat blackened and crumpled. The fire crew were still dousing the ground, a low hiss rising from the soaked concrete. The unmistakable stench of burnt rubber, charred plastic and accelerant clung to the back of her throat.

The destruction was so extensive that Stephanie couldn't even decipher the make or model of the car. It was nothing but a blackened heap on the ground.

And yet, the metal box that had been placed a few feet from the boot remained perfectly intact.

Bile rose in her throat, a combination of the alcohol and the thought of another victim. She didn't want to open it. She didn't know if she could.

The fourth victim in less than two weeks.

What stories lay with this one? What hopes, dreams and aspirations had been stolen from her? And *why*? Why had her life been taken from her? Why had the killer chosen her specifically?

And then the world went dark. She was six years old again, sitting on the sofa, trying to watch TV while her mum tended to a screaming Kimberley in the kitchen. Dad was on the other side of the room, playing with his lighter, bored, drinking, pretending to keep himself busy. It didn't take him long to run out of matches to burn; he stumbled over, grabbed her by the arm and clung to it tightly. No matter how much she tried to move and defend herself, he wouldn't let go. He was far stronger than her physically. But not mentally. He would never beat her mentally.

'Give me your thumb,' he said.

'I don't want to!'

The next time, he didn't ask. Digging his thumb into her pressure point, he pried her thumb free and ignited the flame. She always remembered the sound it made: the click, followed by the explosive smell of fluid.

'Let's see who can scream louder,' he said as he moved the flame towards her thumb. 'You or your little bitch of a sister.'

Within two seconds, her thumb began to burn above the tip of the flame. She yanked and pulled, but it was no use. He was still too strong for her.

Yet she kept quiet. Despite the agonising pain, she kept her lips sealed and screamed internally until her insides ached. She would not give him the satisfaction of crying at all.

Mercifully, he got bored after a few more seconds and dropped her hand onto the arm of the sofa. Stephanie wasted no time in rushing to the bathroom and plunging it under the cold tap.

Her fingers ran over the scarred patch on her thumb as someone called her name.

Giles.

'Ma'am,' he said cautiously, stepping beside her. 'The fire crew have finished. The car is ready for us to approach.'

She was only half-listening. 'Do we know the victim's name?'

'Eye-witnesses have said the car belonged to a Priya Chadha. A first-year student studying biomechanics.'

'Reliable?'

'They're her housemates, ma'am.'

'Do you know how she ended up like this?'

Giles removed his face mask and scratched his nose. 'They went mountain biking through the Chantries this morning while it was quiet. Three of them. They didn't have any classes or anything else to do. When they got back, they couldn't find any spaces in the bike rack by their halls of residence, so Megan and Tamzin, the people she was with, went searching for one elsewhere on campus, and Priya came to put hers in the car.'

Stephanie surveyed the wreckage. Among the mass of melted metal, she saw what looked like wheel spokes.

'Who found her?'

'Her housemates, ma'am. They came looking for her after they got back.'

'Did they see anyone fleeing? Anyone following her when she left for the car park?'

Giles replaced his mask over his mouth. 'No, ma'am. They didn't see anything. They both noted that the campus was really quiet, as if the place had been deserted overnight, and they would have noticed someone following her or running away. But they didn't see anybody.'

Stephanie inhaled deeply, closing her eyes. How was the killer getting away with it? For the previous murders, he must have been travelling on foot; otherwise, they would have caught him on CCTV and ANPR exiting the campus. But if he was on foot now, where could he go?

And then the answer came to her: the sound of a train trundling along the tracks on the other side of the car park, hidden behind a long row of trees that ran along the north side of the campus. Either the killer was fleeing through there somehow, cutting through the fences and jumping over the tracks, or he was hugging the perimeter of the campus, keeping out of sight of cameras. Either he was a student or lecturer who knew the lay of the land, or someone who had spent a considerable amount of time analysing its weaknesses, scoping out the perfect hiding spots.

'Is that what I think it is, ma'am?' Giles asked, pulling her from her reverie. He gestured half-heartedly to the box on the ground.

'I'm afraid so,' she answered. 'Where's Devon?'

Giles quickly glanced behind them. 'Not sure, ma'am.'

'Everyone else is here but he isn't?'

'Do you want me to find him?'

'I was going to get him to open the box for me. He's such an expert.'

Giles made a move to leave, but Stephanie held him back.

'Can you do it for me, Giles?' she asked softly. 'I don't think I can take another one right now.'

Let's see who can scream louder.

Giles hesitated. 'Ma'am… I…'

You or your little bitch of a sister.

'Find someone in the team who *is* willing.'

Without a second thought, Giles spun on the spot and started towards the crowd. A moment later, he was replaced by Eve.

'Do you feel as bad as you look?' Stephanie asked, referring to the young constable's tired, washed-out expression behind her mask.

'We only had a couple,' Eve replied. 'You needed me?'

'The box.'

Stephanie didn't need to tell her what to do. She didn't need to explain why. It was a necessary task, one she was too weak to deal with herself.

Fear crept onto Eve's face as the challenge of what was being asked of her dawned on her. She controlled her breathing for several moments before starting off. Stephanie held onto her necklace as she watched.

The constable moved slowly, cautiously, as if she were approaching a bomb. Her heart was in her mouth, and her fingers began to sweat beneath her gloves. As the box grew nearer, so too did her dread of what lay inside.

Eve came to a stop. Held her breath. Crouched down.

The metal box was made from steel and was warm to the touch. Her fingers traced the edge until she found the opening clasp. Then, on the count of three, she opened it carefully on its longest edge, the hinges screaming in protest.

There, dangling from the top of the lid, was another doll, a hangman's noose wrapped around its neck. The doll swung from side to side as she opened the lid, and it eventually came to a stop, resting against the metal, a pair of soulless button eyes staring back at her.

CHAPTER
SIXTY

An hour later, Stephanie found herself in the amphitheatre again. Except this time, the crowd of petrified students had been replaced by a small cohort of journalists and camera operators. The press conference had been called by DCI McGowan without her authorisation, yet, as the face of the investigation, she was expected to attend, even though she had prepared nothing and didn't know what she was going to say.

The podium before her had been borrowed from one of the lecture theatres, and over a dozen microphones dangled haphazardly from it, like a cluster of metal vipers hissing at her. The headache hadn't abated, and the smell of burnt rubber still clung to her clothes despite her having stepped out of the forensic suit and sprayed herself with perfume.

Behind her was a row of university officials, including Martin Bell, the welfare officer, and uniformed officers flanked her, solemn-faced and silent. Giles lingered at the edge of the row while the rest of the team tended to the crime scene. Elsewhere, the campus remained eerily silent, as if all the students had disappeared. There was no buzz, no hubbub rippling through the avenues and buildings.

Stephanie adjusted the mic slightly and cleared her throat.

'Good afternoon,' she began. 'My name is Detective Inspector

Stephanie Broadbent from Surrey Police. This morning, we received several reports of a car that had been set on fire. The emergency services arrived shortly after to extinguish the blaze, and it was then that we were alerted to the fact that someone had been inside the vehicle during the incident. Sadly, the victim lost their life in the blaze. We are now treating this as a murder investigation and will not be releasing the victim's name to the public until we have notified the family.'

Her eyes flickered towards Louis Brown's face amongst the crowd.

'We will, of course, be in touch with the family and will offer them our full support. What has happened today is nothing short of a tragedy, and we will do everything we can to find the person responsible. We are currently pursuing several active lines of enquiry and are working closely with the fire investigation team, forensics, and university security. This is not the first time tragedy has come to this campus, and we are doing our best to ensure this does not happen again.'

She paused briefly to catch her breath. An image of the doll, dangling by a thin piece of string, appeared in her mind, momentarily inhibiting her.

'We… We…' She lost her train of thought and grasped her necklace, as if that would summon it. 'We know that this is not an isolated incident and that there are similarities between each of the victims. As such, we are treating these incidents as connected and are looking for links between each of the victims.'

Another flash of the doll.

And the one before.

And the one before.

'We are treating this as part of a pattern; whoever is responsible has left behind a doll at each crime scene. We understand the fear and anxiety this has caused, especially within the student body, and I want to reassure the community that we are doing everything possible to protect you and bring the person responsible to justice. We ask anyone who may have seen or heard anything suspicious on campus in the past week to please report it to the hotline we have set up. At this stage in our investigation, there is no piece of evidence or suggestion too small. That'll be all for now. Thank you.'

Stephanie could feel her pulse thudding behind her temples, and pain flaring between her ears. It wasn't until she turned from the cameras that she realised what she'd said: that she'd given away their most important clue to the press.

CHAPTER
SIXTY-ONE

Stephanie pushed open the door to DCI McGowan's office without waiting for permission. He glanced up at her, peering over his reading glasses, his brow creased with concerned surprise as if she'd interrupted him. He stopped what he was doing and leaned back in his chair. The muscles in his jaw flexed, suggesting this would be more than a conversation.

'Thanks for coming on such short notice,' he said.

There was no gesture for her to sit down, but she took it upon herself anyway. She slipped into the seat and folded her arms across her chest, in no mood for a fight. But if that's what he wanted, that was what he would get.

'Talk to me,' he began. 'What's happened this morning?'

'Which bit? The body that had been burned alive in a car, or the press conference you blindsided me with?'

His eyes narrowed. He grabbed a pen from the table and started poking it into the desk. Hard. Stephanie wondered if he wished she were the desk.

'We will discuss the matter of the press conference shortly. First, I want to know what happened with the latest victim.'

Stephanie took a deep breath. 'We suspect her name is Priya Chadha. Eighteen years old. First-year student studying biomechanics. She and her friends had returned from a trip to the Chantries, and

Priya had gone to her car alone to put her bike in it. I suspect she was attacked and then set alight inside the car.'

'Where was the body found?'

Steph recalled the images of the fire examiner opening the back door of the car and the charred body that lay within, scrunched into a foetal position, her skin shrunken and black.

'In the back seat,' she answered, a lump forming in her throat.

'So unless she climbed into the back of her own car and set herself on fire, I would say that someone did this to her. Correct?'

She didn't appreciate his tone.

'Yes,' she answered.

'And that someone is the same serial killer we've been looking for these past two weeks. Correct?'

'Yes.'

'Assuming this is the same killer, was another doll left behind?'

'Yes.'

'And how will the next victim die?'

'They'll…' She sniffed hard. 'They'll be hung, sir.'

'Right. That now makes four victims in the space of two weeks, Steph. With a fifth to follow very soon, I'm sure. This has gone on far too long. Too many lives have been lost, and not enough action has been taken. I'm going to bring in a forensic psychologist to help build a profile of this killer.'

'Sir—'

He cut her off with a raised hand.

'I am also bringing in several members of staff from neighbouring counties who have offered their support.'

'Sir, that won't be—'

'We will have to work out the logistics, but there will be a lot of people in the office in the coming days.'

'Sir, please. I can—'

'Many of them will be constables, whom you can—'

'Listen to me!'

The explosion left her mouth before she'd had a chance to stop it. The words echoed around the room before escaping through the half-open window. After that, silence fell, as if she had destroyed all other noise. McGowan's face was one of shock and apoplexy.

'Sir, I'm sorry for that,' she said, panicked. 'But you need to listen to me. None of this is necessary. Everything is under control. I—'

'That is the first and last time you will raise your voice at me like that, Detective,' he said, his voice level and eerily calm. 'I understand you're stressed, tensions are high, and sometimes the lid can boil, so I am excusing that little outburst, but that is a perfect example of where things are not in control, Stephanie. You do not have control over yourself, let alone this investigation. You have to understand, none of this is to slight you or tarnish your name or reputation. I am doing this for the good of the investigation. Your team *and you* will benefit from the weight that the new staff will be able to lift from your shoulders. I get the impression that, like our victims, you are all drowning, getting set on fire, or suffocating from the weight of this investigation. My decision is final.'

'Sir…' Her voice was barely a whisper.

'You were warned. I said the next time we had this discussion, I would not be so understanding.'

Steph choked back the lump in her throat.

'Now, tell me what happened during the press conference,' he started.

She lowered her gaze and began playing with her fingernails in her lap, picking at them until it began to hurt.

'That was an oversight,' she answered. 'I… I wasn't thinking clearly. I should never have told them about the dolls. I just… I wasn't thinking properly. The press conference… it caught me by surprise. And the body… I'd just seen it, so it was still fresh in my mind.'

She ran her fingers over the scarred flesh on her thumb absent-mindedly.

'I apologise,' she added.

For a long while, he didn't respond. He just looked at her with a combination of pity and surprise on his face.

'I thought you'd seen it…' he said.

'Seen what?'

'Last night, on *Surrey Live*'s website and social media channels, they announced the news about the dolls being found at the crime scenes.'

Stephanie's eyes widened. 'They did *what*?'

'Naturally, it's caused quite a stir online. A lot of people are calling the killer "The Voodoo Killer", which I'm sure will catch on… Are you sure this wasn't your doing?'

She was too stunned to shake her head. 'Someone must have leaked it.'

And she knew exactly who'd been responsible.

Clive took a moment to assess her. 'I think you should take a breather,' he told her. 'Get yourself out of here. Clear your head. Go for a walk. Come back when you're ready.'

Absentmindedly, her mind half in the room with McGowan while the other half was imagining what she would say and do to DS Lafferty when she saw him, she lifted herself out of the chair.

A thought occurred to her.

'Am I still SIO?' she asked.

'Yes. You are still my SIO. Because you deserve to be. But your reputation will only carry you so far. I don't want you to give me a reason to change the situation.'

CHAPTER
SIXTY-TWO

'Where is he?'

Eve looked up from her desk suddenly, panic flashing in her eyes.

'Who?'

'Devon? Where is he?'

Just as Eve was about to respond, the sergeant entered through the main doors. As soon as she spotted him, she charged towards him and pointed to her office.

'We need to have a word,' she hissed, her tone brooking no argument.

'What about?' Devon responded with an air of defiance she abhorred.

'You'll find out when we get in there.'

With that, Devon dropped his keys onto his desk and made for her office. Stephanie followed close behind, breathing down his neck.

The door was half open when she began her tirade, unable to control herself.

'What's this I hear about you leaking information to the press? Who do you think you are? That's not your decision to make.'

'I did what I had to do.'

She scoffed. 'So you don't deny it?'

He placed his hands in his pockets and lifted his shoulders.

'What gave you the right?' she asked.

'You weren't here,' he said bluntly. 'You'd gone AWOL, so I took matters into my own hands. Like I said, I did what I had to do.'

'They published the article last night. You weren't in control of the operation then,' she replied, her mind processing the information at a thousand miles an hour.

'It's nothing to do with me how long it takes Louis and his team to publish an article.' His continued defiance filled her with rage. She could barely bring herself to look at him.

'From now on, you are to have nothing to do with Louis or anyone else at *Surrey Live*. Or anyone else in the media, for that matter. Any time someone tries to reach out to you, I want to know about it.'

He raised his hands in surrender. 'Of course, ma'am. Your wish is my command.'

'Now get out of my office before you do any more damage to this investigation.'

But she feared the damage was already done.

Stephanie stormed out of her office and headed straight for the exit, keeping her head down and avoiding her team's gaze. She sensed them all watching her, judging her. But she couldn't bring herself to look at them. She couldn't handle their questions or face the aftermath. Not only had Devon undermined her by leaking information to the press, but McGowan was about to do the same by sidelining her and bringing in extra help. Sure, she was still SIO – that was what he said – but for how long? How long would McGowan give her before he reached the end of his tether and pulled the rug from under her feet?

Outside, birds cawed and the guttural barks of training dogs rolled across the fields in the distance. But she didn't hear them over the noise in her head. As she emerged from the building, a static buzz crawled across her skin, from her fingertips to the back of her neck. Her palms were slick with sweat. Her skin felt tight – too tight. Her heart began to pound in her chest, and then her lungs shrank to the size of fists. Despite being in the open, battered by a cool breeze, she struggled to breathe, as if she had just entered a vacuum.

Crossing the car park, her vision began to tunnel, and the dark corners of her mind crept in. She hurried as fast as her legs would allow, scuffing across the tarmac and gravel, panting and gasping for breath.

Eventually, she swung the car door open and leapt in, slamming the door shut. In one large gulp, she filled her lungs with stale air, air that contained a hint of fast food. Within seconds of being inside the confines of the car, her breathing returned to normal and the panic attack abated; she was back in her wardrobe again, hiding. Safe.

Except this time, there was no teddy bear to cling to for support. No emotional support to help her get through the episode.

She would have to change that.

Her eyes fell onto the kebab wrapper in the passenger footwell. All that remained was the paper, laden with grease and leftover onions and lettuce, and the sickly aroma in the car.

Shoving the keys into the ignition, she put the gear into reverse and swung out of the car park. Mercifully, the drive to the kebab shop was short, and by the time she arrived, her breathing had returned to some semblance of normality. At least, normal enough not to raise suspicion.

She parked the car on the double yellow lines outside the outlet, heedless of the cars honking behind her, and rushed into the building. Immediately, the smell slapped her across the face, and she felt strength return to her body.

She was beginning to feel normal again.

'Good afternoon,' the owner said. 'What can I get for you, boss lady? Same as last time?'

Stephanie was stunned. 'You remember my order?'

'Of course. I remember thinking: a little lady your size, there's no way she can eat that much food. And then I watched you scoff it down in your car. I thought, she's got some serious appetite on her, you know.'

A pang of regret and embarrassment ignited in her. Usually, she kept her bingeing a secret, out of sight. But last time, she hadn't considered that. She hadn't thought about the cars driving past or the kebab shop owner watching her from behind his counter.

What was happening to her? She was losing control of herself.

Stephanie suddenly felt ashamed.

She lowered her head and started out of the shop.

'Where are you going, miss?'

'Changed my mind. I'm not hungry.'

As she set foot on the pavement, a man collided with her. She staggered slightly; he was broad and thickset, dressed in black jeans and a tight polo shirt that strained over a gym-hardened chest. His aftershave hit her first, followed by the glint of a gold chain resting against his throat.

'Oh my God, I'm so sorry,' he said. 'I didn't mean to.'

'It would be weird if you did.'

The man smirked, lifting one corner of his mouth, then stepped into the kebab shop. As Stephanie turned away from him, he called back.

'Do I know you from somewhere?'

You probably saw me stuffing my face with food in the car the other day as well, did you? she thought.

'You're the copper that's working on the uni case?'

She didn't answer.

'I recognise you from the press conference thing this morning. A couple of your guys came round the other day to ask me questions about the girl that got killed in her flat.'

She studied his features. 'You're the owner of Red One?'

He raised his hands in surrender. 'Guilty as charged. But that's all I'm guilty of before you think I'm confessing to anything.'

She found herself laughing involuntarily. She didn't know why.

'Name's James Daniels. My sister's boyfriend was with the girl that came here,' he continued. 'He's pretty shaken up about it. I think all of them are. Must be tough for them to deal with. But not nearly as tough as it is for you, I imagine.'

'You can say that again.'

'You guys making any headway?'

'Not nearly as much as we would like.'

He shrugged, as if the outcome of the investigation made no difference to him. 'I'm sure you'll get there. You seem like you've got your head screwed on; you come to the best kebab shop in town.' James turned to the owner. 'Isn't that right, boss?'

'Yes, boss!' the owner replied, pointing at James as he threw a tea towel over his shoulder.

'I tell you, it's dangerous being right next door to this place. The smell gets me every time.'

'You look good for it,' Stephanie replied, observing the man's lower half. For the first time in a long time, the thought of being intimate with a man entered her head. And in that instant, the man in question was James.

He smirked, as if picking up on it. Now it was his turn to eyeball her. 'You don't look too bad yourself,' he said.

She left him. As she climbed into her car, she glanced in the rearview mirror and was surprised to see the small grin still on her face.

CHAPTER
SIXTY-THREE

Stephanie pulled into the narrow drive, headlights sweeping across the neighbouring hedges before cutting out as she turned off the engine. Her house sat in darkness, save for the soft glow of the streetlamp outside. She killed the engine and sat for a moment, her forehead against the steering wheel, eyes shut. The ache behind her temples throbbed in time with her pulse.

As she climbed out of the car, her neighbour, Jimmy, emerged from his front door, holding a green recycling bag.

'You're home late,' he said, as he opened his recycling bin and dropped the bag in. 'Long day?'

'That's one word for it.'

'Fancy a cuppa? I've just put the kettle on.'

She glanced at her watch. It wasn't late by any means, but right now she wasn't in the mood to speak to or see anyone. Usually, in this state, she would go out for a late-night run, paint some more, or cycle, but the thought of doing any of those activities reminded her of Paulina, Claudia, and Priya. Right now, all she wanted to do was stay indoors, alone. She could control what happened within the confines of her four walls.

'Not tonight,' she replied. 'Maybe another time.'

'Of course,' he said, offering her a sympathetic smile; one that suggested he understood completely.

'You'll be pleased to know that you haven't had any strange men asking after you this evening.'

'I must have scared them off,' she said as she removed her keys from her bag.

'Maybe I did that for you.'

Jimmy opened his front door. Stephanie did the same.

Just as she was about to say goodbye, he called out, 'Oh, and don't forget to put your green bins out tonight.'

'Again? It's never-ending.'

She slammed the car boot shut, the sound echoing up and down the street. Stephanie paused, listening to the stillness of the night. Overhead, a thin sheet of clouds had rolled in, covering the stars from view. In the distance, she thought she heard a fox screaming. Either that or it was enjoying a night of courtship with a friend.

Carrying a crate of folders in her arms, she started towards the house. Inside, she made for the living room, where she'd cleared a small space on the floor in front of the sofa. Dropping the box to the floor, she lowered herself to the carpet and sat cross-legged.

The house was quiet. No television. No music. No radio. Not even the sound of Jimmy moving about or getting ready for bed next door.

Silence.

She reached for the folder at the top of the pile and set it in front of her. Over the next few minutes, she removed each file and displayed them on the carpet. The folders contained notes from the team, interview reports and witness statements, photographs of the victims, post-mortem reports – all the evidence she and the team had gathered so far in the investigation. And somewhere within it, she hoped, was the answer to it all. The answer to the identity of the killer. Lurking amongst the information. Hiding amidst the mass of letters and images.

The team had worked tirelessly over the past couple of weeks, and the culmination of it all was right in front of her.

They had done their job. And now it was time for her to do hers. To do what she did best: see the connections, find the clues that weren't there, and get results.

It was what had got her this far in her career. It was what had earned her the reputation McGowan insisted on reminding her of.

She wasn't special by any means. There was no particular talent that enabled her to find things others didn't. There was no part of her brain that others didn't have that she could tap into to find a name.

The only advantage she had over her peers was her history, her background. Growing up with evil had enabled her to see it, to treat it like a friend. She saw things perhaps others didn't. She spotted patterns and trends.

At least, that was the hope.

CHAPTER
SIXTY-FOUR

The next morning, Stephanie overslept. She had been deep in the throes of sleep and not heard her alarm. To make matters worse, her phone hadn't charged and was below twenty per cent when she left the house.

It was eight o'clock as she entered the station, over an hour later than she would have liked, and already the place was a hive of activity, filled with people she didn't know or recognise. All the remaining desk spaces had been occupied, with strangers perched on the ends of the banks, hunched over laptops or reading notes. Overnight, the office's capacity had increased fivefold. She searched for her team, for a familiar face, but was unable to find one.

Before she started towards her office on the other side of the room, she was accosted by a woman with thick, curly hair, wearing a black and white striped top with a black jumper draped over her shoulders. She looked like the type of person who had a second home in the South of France and enjoyed the sunset with a glass of wine from her small vineyard in the back garden. Stephanie was not expecting her to sound like she'd just come from a Guy Ritchie movie.

'All right?' the woman asked, extending her hand. 'Are you Detective Inspector Broadbent?'

'Who are you?' Stephanie asked, more forcefully than intended.

'Jordyn Snow. Forensic psychologist.'

Stephanie surveyed her intently. 'What are you doing here?'

'DCI McGowan asked me to come down as soon as possible. I arrived last night.'

Stephanie didn't care. She wanted the woman gone. 'Who are all these people? Are they with you?'

'I think they're from different forces. I asked a couple of people where I might find things, and most of them didn't have a clue.'

'Well, it's kind of you to come all this way, wherever you're from, but you shouldn't have been asked. We're not in need of your services.'

Stephanie made for her office but froze as soon as she saw McGowan emerge from his office. The chief inspector headed straight for her.

'I see you two have met,' he started. 'Jordyn's been brushing up on the case files all night. She's like a supercomputer, the amount she's absorbed!'

Stephanie said nothing. *Why don't you let her run the investigation then?*

She felt the rug move beneath her…

Slipping…

Slipping…

'We've also had support from Kent and Hampshire Police arrive. I believe they're all staying in the Holiday Inn by the sports park, so they're as close to the university as you could possibly ask for.'

What was she supposed to do with that information? Thank him? She didn't think so.

'You're here later than usual,' McGowan added.

'I know,' she replied bluntly.

She didn't need to add any more; he picked up on the intonation and offered her a nod.

'But you're just in time. You were the last to arrive. Now we can begin the meeting.'

'What meeting?'

McGowan pointed at Jordyn. 'The one where our forensic psychologist tells us who we're looking for.'

. . .

The entire incident room, which had spilled into the neighbouring kitchen and corridor, fell silent as Jordyn began speaking. Stephanie hovered behind her, arms folded across her chest, standing beside the whiteboards while all eyes were focused on the forensic psychologist.

'I spent all day and night yesterday familiarising myself with the investigation so far. I understand that there are some new faces here, so a lot of what I'm talking about might not make any sense to you yet, but I hope that by the end of it, it will.

'Usually, when I'm asked to advise on murder investigations like this, I like to look at the victims: similarities, connections, reasons *why* the killer has chosen them. From what I've been able to gather, these are all very different individuals. They are from all over the country. They all have different backgrounds and different upbringings. Some are from the same classes and belong to the same societies, but they are all living in different parts of the campus. The one thing that does connect them, however, is their gender. They are all women of roughly similar ages. And so I believe this is a man who despises women. He is exerting power and control over them in the worst way imaginable.

'The dolls that he leaves behind at the crime scenes are testament to that fact also. They are also an element of control. He is controlling the investigation with them, and he is communicating his next method of murder before it's even begun. As such, that requires a high level of planning. So this is someone who will have had plenty of time to plan these murders. Plenty of time to select his victims. Plenty of time to monitor their movements and lay the groundwork in many respects.'

'That doesn't apply to Claudia Bellini, our first victim,' Steph interrupted. 'He was in the right place at the right time with her. She would have spent the night with the boy at the club if she hadn't thrown up and rushed home on her own. The more I think about it, the more I suspect it was a chance meeting. Same with Priya; he got lucky that she couldn't find space on a bike rack and went to her car instead. He was in the right place at the right time. He saw his opportunity and he took it. Just as with Maya.'

Jordyn rotated her neck a few degrees, glancing at Stephanie out of the corner of her eye. 'He knew what he was doing with all those murders. He knew Maya Corcoran would walk across the field. He knew Paulina Potter would be in the art studio. He knew Priya would be in the car park.'

'How can you be so sure?'

'Because of the dolls!' Jordyn rotated to face Stephanie. 'With each kill, he has been transporting the box containing the doll with him. If he didn't know precisely what he was going to do, why else would he have carried it with him?'

Stephanie didn't have a response to that. She folded her arms tighter against her chest and rested against the whiteboard.

Jordyn turned to address the rest of the room.

'As I was saying, this killer is highly intelligent and highly prepared. It is also someone who blends in very well with his surroundings. For him to lay the groundwork, he would have to be on campus, I'm sure. Therefore, I do not think it is someone who teaches these students, as they do not have the time. My best guess would be that you are looking at a student of some description. A post-graduate or potentially a mature student. Someone older than the common cohort, but someone who also fits in. Perhaps they have a young face. In terms of build and size, I think he would need to be a big man or someone who is physically strong.'

'He hit Maya Corcoran round the back of the head,' Stephanie interrupted. 'The post-mortem found evidence of blunt force trauma to the back left side of her skull. Claudia Bellini was paralytic when he found her; she wouldn't have put up a fight. And Paulina Potter was five foot two and skinny as anything. Plus, she was stabbed, so I doubt she would have done much to defend herself against someone wielding a blade. As for Priya Chadha, it's my guess she was also hit round the back of the head. All these girls are small and slight. They weigh next to nothing.'

Jordyn gave her another side-eye glance. Stephanie could read the words on the tip of the woman's tongue: 'A bit like yourself, then.'

'In terms of the timings of the attacks,' Jordyn continued, ignoring Stephanie, 'they have all happened in quick succession. Very quick, in fact. Which also suggests to me that the killer is working on a timeline, perhaps a schedule. As such, I think your next victim, the one who is to be hanged if the latest doll is anything to go by, will be killed *soon*. Now, from what I understand, you are running quite low on leads, and therefore I do not think usual methods will apply if you are to catch him.'

'What do you suggest?'

'You will need people on the campus,' Jordyn answered, facing the crowd as if the question had come from one of them. 'Perhaps even send someone undercover. Someone to melt into the faces of the campus.'

'Why would we do that if you suspect the killer's already selected their next victim?' Stephanie replied.

Jordyn hesitated for a long time. 'This is just my advice. You do not have to listen to it if you do not wish. All I'm saying is, you might benefit from sending in someone who looks like a student' – Jordyn pointed Eve out in the crowd – 'someone like her, who looks young and looks like she'd fit right in. Get them to go to the same places as the victims, attend the same society meetings. See if they spot anyone acting suspiciously.'

'There's a vigil happening this evening,' DC Olivia Willard called. 'It's open to students and members of the public to pay their respects to the victims.'

Jordyn shrugged. 'That's as good a place to start as any.'

'No,' Steph said, stepping forward. 'I do not want anyone going undercover. It's too dangerous; the risk is too high. We'll have several uniformed members there to protect the students attending, and that will be enough. If some of you wish to pay your respects, then that's fine, but our time is better spent trying to find this killer. He's going to hang someone on campus. He will not do that during the middle of a vigil when the place is full of people.'

CHAPTER
SIXTY-FIVE

The knock on her door was quiet, despite the person on the other side.

A moment later, Devon peered around the door.

'Got a minute?' he asked.

'What do you want?'

'A chat.'

'Come to apologise?'

Devon ignored the question and stepped into the room, closing the door carefully behind him. He approached her desk before saying anything. 'I think you should reconsider.'

'About *what*?'

'Attending the vigil.'

'By all means, attend on your own time.'

'I meant as a team. For work.'

She closed her eyes and shook her head. 'We are not sending anyone undercover or as bait. Last time I sent anyone anywhere remotely dangerous, it didn't end well.'

'Ma'am,' Devon continued, folding his arms across his chest, 'I don't want to say it, but I have a feeling the killer could be there.'

'What makes you so sure?' She raised an eyebrow and tilted her head at him.

'Detective's intuition.'

'I didn't know you were a DI...' she said mockingly. Devon didn't find it amusing. 'Even if he is there, what do you expect us to do? Walk around shining a torch in people's faces until someone looks suspicious?'

'We could observe, profile. Pick up on behaviour.'

'We have no idea what this person looks like. Our every move will be watched by people with mobile phones and possibly the media, if they're attending, which they likely will be, thanks to you. Even if the killer were there, or if he were there to do anything to anyone, he wouldn't risk it. There would be too many people around. He's taken all his other victims in isolation, with nobody around to hear or see a thing.'

Devon opened his mouth to respond, but Stephanie cut him off.

'Not to mention we'll have a uniformed police presence there. He'd be stupid to try something. And this guy's not stupid.'

Devon pointed at her. 'Exactly. We'll be there, which makes me think something is even more likely to happen.'

'Why?'

'Think about it. Since Claudia, he's killed three students right under our noses, without leaving a single shred of evidence. The bastard's even told us how he's going to kill the next victim, and we've done nothing about it.'

'You don't need to remind me,' she said.

'If I were him, I'd use it as a chance to show off in a different kind of way, to take a victim right in front of us.'

There was a long pause between them. Stephanie rubbed her thumb over the inside of her wrist, thinking. She let out a long, slow breath through her nose, pondering, turning the decision over in her mind.

In the end, she shook her head.

'No. We're not doing it.'

The thin smile that had been on Devon's face faded. 'Ma'am—'

'I said no.' Her tone sharpened. 'We are not turning a vigil into a manhunt. Not with cameras everywhere. Not with the university and press breathing down our necks. And not while I'm still responsible for keeping you all safe. I said no, and my decision is final.'

Devon stood there a moment longer, his jaw working as if he wanted to argue. But in the end, he gave a short nod.

'Understood, ma'am. Of course, ma'am.'

He turned and started towards the door. As he opened it, she called him back. 'And, Devon, if you undermine me again, I will not be so lenient with you.'

He replied with a smile that suggested he didn't believe her. 'Understood, ma'am,' he said, then left, the door slowly closing behind him.

Devon walked across the incident room and slid into the chair beside Eve. The young constable glanced up at him, fixing her posture instantly.

'And?' she asked hopefully. Their conversation was quiet beneath the general hubbub of the office.

Devon gave a quick nod, not quite meeting her eye. 'How would you like to pretend to be a student for an evening?'

'She gave the green light?'

Another nod. 'Said it was a good idea after all.'

Eve's brows rose. 'I'm surprised.'

'I told her we'd keep it low-key. Just a quiet presence. Eyes open. She agreed, on the condition we keep it clean and don't engage unless absolutely necessary.'

Eve looked uncertain, tapping her pen against her notepad. 'She was dead set against it before.'

Devon offered a nonchalant shrug. 'This investigation needs an injection of instincts as much as it does procedure.'

'Is it just the two of us?'

'Giles, as well. We don't want to make it too obvious.'

Eve nodded slowly, staring at him a moment longer. 'All right. If she's signed it off, then I'm in.'

'Fantastic.' He knocked on the desk a couple of times. 'I'll see you tonight.'

CHAPTER
SIXTY-SIX

Martin Bell had shaved what little remained of his beard since she last saw him. As he entered the quiet, intimate meeting room inside the student welfare centre, he set a cup of water on the desk in front of her, beside a small box of tissues. She caught a whiff of tobacco on his breath.

'Thanks,' she said, eyeing him intently as he dropped into the seat opposite.

'It should be me thanking you for coming on such short notice.'

'You said it was urgent.'

'Right.' He hesitated, then leaned forward, elbows on the edge of the desk. 'It's about Tristan Penrose.'

'The food science lecturer?'

Martin nodded. 'I know you spoke to him already. And I know what he told you. But... there's something else you need to know.'

She stared at him, waiting for him to continue. 'I saw him last night. We caught up on campus, and we got talking. He... I think he's lied to you, Detective. Lied to all of you.'

She tried to keep her voice level, not giving away any excitement. 'How so?'

'From what I gather, he told you that Paulina was the first person to make a move during their little intimate moment in his office. Is that right?'

She didn't respond.

'Well, I have it on good authority that it was the other way around. Tristan made the first move on Paulina during one of his designated office hours. She came in to discuss her coursework, and then he made a pass at her. Said he'd been thinking about her. Couldn't get her out of his mind. Watched her on TikTok and thought she was stunning. He even said that he would leave his wife for her.'

Stephanie absorbed what she was hearing. Outside the room, a door slammed shut.

'Who told you this? I don't imagine he did.'

'*Paulina*,' Martin answered. 'At the end of last year, she came to see me and explained everything. She didn't name him at the time, but it's only now that I've been able to put two and two together, you see?' The corners of his mouth lifted into a leering grin. 'She was concerned about what to do. Said she felt uncomfortable and was worried about starting her second year with him. But she also said she'd entertained feelings for him.'

'Did anything advance between them?'

He shrugged. 'Potentially. I don't think it had when Paulina came to me. But that doesn't mean to say it didn't happen afterwards, over the summer, for example.'

Stephanie leaned forward slightly. 'What changed? Why would he lie to us?'

'Because, and he told me *this* last night, Paulina threatened to go public about it. I don't know what happened, but something changed, and at the start of this academic year, she threatened to go public.'

'What did he do?'

'Begged her to stop,' Martin answered with a knowing look. 'Maybe he took it one step further.'

The comment hung heavy in the air. She considered the weight of it with a soft nod.

'Does he know she came to see you at the end of last academic year?'

Martin shook his head. 'And he told Paulina it would be the end of him if anyone else found out. I got the impression that he would do whatever he had to in order to keep his job, his marriage, and his life intact. He was someone with a lot to lose.'

. . .

After she had finished explaining it to him, DC Giles Swinger looked like he'd just been given a maths exam to complete.

'Did you get all of that?' she asked, knitting her fingers together.

'I think so, ma'am,' he responded. He glanced down at his notes. 'Tristan Penrose. Suspected relations with a student. Big suspect.'

'That's one way of explaining it, yes. I'd like you to reach out to him and find out what the truth is. I would also advise speaking with her friends and housemates first. See if there's anything they know about the incident.'

Giles nodded. 'Friends. Roommates. Got it. Delicious.'

'And take Eve or Fiona with you. Split the workload.'

'You don't want me to give it to any of these new guys from over the border?'

She shook her head vehemently. 'We've managed just fine without them,' she said. 'Let's show them we can continue to manage while they're here.'

Giles' lips formed a wry grin as he scribbled something down in his notebook.

'Any other questions?' Stephanie asked.

He paused a moment. 'Forgive me if this sounds dense, ma'am, but what's this got to do with the other victims? Claudia, Maya, Priya... He wasn't trying it on with them as well, was he?'

Stephanie scratched the side of her face. 'You tell me, Detective. What do *you* think?'

Giles' face contorted deep in thought, tapping the tip of his pen against his notebook. The silence stretched, but Stephanie didn't interrupt. She could see the cogs slowly grinding in his brain. His lips parted slightly then closed again. Another few seconds passed before his eyes suddenly lit with realisation.

'The running club,' he said quietly. 'They were all part of the same running club. So they'd all have known each other through that.'

'Even Maya?'

'I'm told she went a couple of times then stopped. There, the girls could've talked. Maybe Paulina confided in one of them. Or all of them. Maybe someone else in the club overheard. If they knew what he'd done… and if he thought they were going to expose him…'

He trailed off, the implication hanging heavy in the air.

Stephanie sat back, folding her arms. 'That's your line of enquiry.'

Giles nodded, his earlier confusion gone, replaced by a steely focus. 'Yes, ma'am. I'll get on it.' He started towards the door but then caught himself and turned round. 'But if he is responsible, then why would he leave the dolls behind, ma'am? Why not just kill them without them?'

'I don't have the answer to that question yet, Giles. Hopefully, we'll know soon enough.'

CHAPTER
SIXTY-SEVEN

The television was playing, but she wasn't paying any attention to it. Her mind was elsewhere. Thinking about the investigation. About the forensic psychologist who had muscled her way into Stephanie's investigation. About Devon and the vigil. Whether she'd been right to deny it.

Before she could think about it any further, the doorbell rang, yanking her out of her reverie. She glanced at the time on her phone: 7:41 pm. She wasn't expecting anyone. Not that night.

I bet it's Jimmy, she thought, lifting herself off the sofa. How many more bloody bin collections are there this week?

Stephanie padded barefoot out of the living room, navigating the mess in the hallway to the front door. When she opened it, she found her sister standing there, phone in hand, face tight with fury and on the brink of tears.

'Kim, what are you doing here?'

'We had an argument. Big one.'

'Right.'

'I just needed to get away. Some place to clear my head.' Kim brushed past her and dropped her bag in the hallway with a thud. She stopped as soon as she noticed the mess on the floor. 'Christ, Steph.'

Stephanie's eyes followed her sister's.

'I know you've been busy but…'

'It's been a rough week,' Steph answered. 'Time…'

'I can see that. But this isn't normal. Have you always lived like this?'

Steph opened her mouth to respond, but nothing came out.

'Are you all right?' Kim asked. 'Like, genuinely?'

'Tell me about your argument with Jason.'

Kim grunted. 'Ugh. I just had to get out of there before I punched him in the throat. But we're not talking about me right now. We're talking about *you*. Why didn't you ask for help sooner?'

Steph felt ashamed at the sight of the mess. She couldn't look at it for too long, nor could she meet her sister's gaze. 'I'm fine. I told you – *time*.'

Kim paused, then gave a soft, sceptical scoff. 'You'd tell me if it was more than that, right?'

Stephanie managed a small, tight smile. 'Of course.'

The expression on Kim's face suggested she didn't believe it. At least, not entirely. She rolled up the sleeves of her shirt and said, 'Where are your bin bags? We're cleaning.'

'Now?'

'I need something to take my mind off my husband for a few hours.'

'Where is he?'

Kim shot her sister a look. 'Where else? About to go overseas for work. Or get on a late-night train to some other part of the country, for all I know. He's been called out again, so that means I have another night on my own.'

Steph looked at her sister for a moment. The thought of cleaning, of tidying up her month-old mess, filled her with as much dread as the investigation did. But now she had nobody to hide behind, nowhere to run. Kim was the sort of person who did whatever she set her mind to, and in the mood she was in, Stephanie feared nothing was going to stop her.

CHAPTER
SIXTY-EIGHT

Dozens of students surrounded her, shoulder to shoulder in the field, their faces illuminated by battery-powered candles and mobile phone torches. The sound of the water feature in the lake was drowned out by the murmur of conversation throughout the crowd. A slight chill hung in the air, and thin cloud cover had descended above, masking the stars from view.

A makeshift memorial had been assembled by the lake. Bouquets of flowers – roses, lilies, hand-picked wildflowers – packed in jam jars sat beneath photos of each of the victims. A speaker had just finished saying a few words, his voice breaking towards the end. A wave of applause rippled through the crowd. It was busier than Eve had expected. Over five hundred people had turned out to pay their respects. Students. Members of the public. Kids.

Eve stood in the middle of the crowd, quietly scanning the faces nearby, searching for something suspicious or untoward. She took a moment to herself, praying for the victims. She wasn't religious in any sense of the word, but she could feel herself getting caught up in it. She finished as her phone began ringing.

Devon.

'Yes?' she answered.

'See anything?'

She surveyed the teenage faces beside her. 'Nothing yet.'

'I'm hearing there are meant to be fireworks. Not sure if the university has approved it. So long as you don't mind loud noises.'

She chuckled. 'I've been to a few bonfire nights in my time.'

Devon told her to remain vigilant, then hung up.

Five minutes later, a handful of students left the crowd and hurried to a small section of grass where a box of fireworks was situated. Eve watched as they removed the fireworks from the crate and set them into the ground. She was no expert, but she didn't think they looked safe.

After a few moments, one of the students ignited the end of a firework. A hush of anticipation fell on the crowd as they waited.

Then – *ssssppp!* The firework ignited and shot off from its perch in the ground. But instead of flying upwards, the force of the combustion buckled the stand and sent the firework directly into the crowd, firing like a missile.

Before Eve or any of the students could react, the firework exploded, sending a shower of sparks raining down on dozens of shrieking students. Someone screamed. Another stumbled backwards and fell, taking two others down with them. Then another firework went off – this time launching horizontally into the lake, where it hissed and sparked before vanishing beneath the surface.

Panic erupted.

The murmur of conversation turned into a flood of shouts, cries, and the stampede of feet tearing through the damp grass. Mobile phone torches swung wildly in the dark, flashing over terrified faces. The vigil dissolved into pure chaos.

Eve got caught up in it all. She turned from the fireworks, where a couple of students were foolishly trying to stamp them out, and ran, swept up in the crowd that dispersed towards the safety of the nearby buildings. More fireworks started popping from the box, one after the other in rapid succession, misfiring in every direction.

Eve dove out of the way as a purple streamer shot past her, crackling as it skimmed the edge of someone's coat. As she neared the road, someone barged into her back and sent her sprawling forward. She landed hard on the grass. She tried to pick herself up from the ground, but a mass of feet and legs trampled over her, kicking her into the earth.

For a few painful, panicked moments, she lay there in the grass until she felt a pair of hands grabbing her and lifting her to her feet. By the time they came to a stop at the edge of the grass, they'd reached the outskirts of the campus and were hidden behind student accommodation.

Eve was doubled over, trying to catch her breath. She was disorientated, bruised, and sore, with no idea where she was or what had happened.

As she looked up to see the person who'd rescued her, he said, 'Fancy seeing you here, Eve.'

And then, before she could respond, he lifted his hand and plunged her entire world into darkness.

His ankle throbbed with each movement. He couldn't move and was forced to remain still while hordes of students and adults sprinted past him, escaping the chaos.

He reached into his pocket and pulled out his mobile. The phone rang repeatedly, but there was no answer. Another ring. Still nothing.

On the third attempt, the call was cut off. After that, nothing. Engaged. As if the phone had been switched off.

Giles didn't know what to do. The place was bedlam. Screams and cries pierced the air. Fortunately, however, the fireworks had stopped, and the last of the pinwheels had finished exploding and covering the grass in multi-coloured sparkles.

He navigated his address book until he found the office number. A few moments later, the call connected.

'DC Willard speaking,' came the soothing response down the line.

'Wellard, it's me. There's been an incident. Some fireworks have gone off during the vigil; this place is bedlam. I... I've tried to get hold of Eve and Devon, but they're not answering their phones. I've knackered my foot, so I can't move. Can you send help?'

CHAPTER
SIXTY-NINE

Stephanie had quickly realised her life would be easier if she put up less of a fight and allowed Kimberley to clean the house alone. Her interruptions only prolonged the process. So, she sat curled in the corner of the sofa, legs pressed against her chest, an untouched mug of tea cooling on the arm of the chair beside her. The television continued to murmur in the background – some reality TV show flickering across the screen – but she wasn't watching.

She was too busy feeling sorry for herself, wondering where it had all gone wrong and how she could have let her standards slip so much.

Wondering how she'd lost control of everything so rapidly.

Her team. The investigation. Herself.

Giles' earlier attempts to speak with Tristan Penrose, the lecturer, had proved unsuccessful. He had been unable to find the man at work or at his home. Consequently, he had spent the rest of the afternoon speaking with Paulina's friends, who had been unable to confirm the extent of Paulina and Tristan's relationship.

From the kitchen came the steady scrape and clatter of her sister cleaning, sounding as if she was trying to dismantle the toaster with a butter knife.

Her stomach growled at her, and she rested her head on her knees.

Another day without a proper meal. Another day where her dehydrated and tired mind hadn't been thinking or functioning properly.

'Steph, do you want to keep this?' Kimberley called from the kitchen.

Just as Stephanie crawled off the sofa to have a look, her mobile rang on the coffee table. She glanced at the screen and saw it was Giles.

'Mr Swinger,' she said. 'You're working late.'

'Ma'am,' he said, panicked and short of breath, as if he'd been running. 'Something's happened.'

'What?'

'Eve. Devon. We're at the vigil—'

'*What?*'

'Everything was going fine. And then the fireworks started, but it went wrong. The crowd went crazy. And now... now I can't get hold of them. I've tried their mobiles about twenty times, and nothing's getting through. I'm worried something might have happened to them.'

'*Steph*? Do you want this?'

She paid no attention to her sister, instead hurrying towards the cabinet on the other side of the room and grabbing her keys.

'Where are you now?' she asked Giles.

'The uni.'

'Okay. I'll come down. Stay exactly where you are.'

'Yes, ma'am. I couldn't move even if I wanted to.'

CHAPTER
SEVENTY

Stephanie leapt out of the car before the engine had finished winding down. The street was teeming, with knots of people huddled together on the side of the road. Some were crying, while others laughed, seeing the funny side of a box full of fireworks exploding in all directions. Except they didn't know what was really going on. They didn't know what had really happened.

What Stephanie *hoped* hadn't taken place.

She found Giles by the Rik Medlik building on the north side of campus. He was limping, placing all his weight on one foot. His head swivelled left and right as he scanned the faces around him.

As he caught sight of Stephanie, he waved and started hobbling towards her.

'You got here quick,' he began.

'You're injured,' she snapped, feeling like an overprotective mother. 'Stay still. You're only going to make it worse. What have you done?'

'Rolled my ankle,' he said dismissively. 'I've done worse in my career. It'll be fine. Just needs a bit of ice.'

He tried to place some weight on the damaged ankle and winced as pain flared up his leg.

'Don't try to be a hero.' Steph placed her hands on her hips, surveying her surroundings. From her viewpoint, she could see the water feature and the lake, but in the darkness, visibility was poor. She was, however, able to make out a group of people huddled around a mass of crates in the distance. 'What the hell happened here?'

'I don't know,' he began. 'We were in the crowd. A couple of people said a few words, others placed flowers by the pictures, and some lit candles. And then they started the fireworks. That's when it all went wrong. I just remember hearing this massive *bang*, like a gun had gone off.'

'The fireworks?'

Nodding, he replied, 'Straight into the crowd.'

'Any injuries?'

'I would imagine so.'

'We need paramedics down here.'

'Already on it,' he replied. 'I called the office to let them know, then called for ERT to come and assess the situation. I'm sure there are a couple of burn victims out there somewhere.'

That explained why people were crying. And not just over the shock of it all.

'Who else were you here with?'

'Devon and Eve, ma'am.'

'*Just* those two?'

A nod.

'Have you managed to get in contact with them yet?'

'I've tried calling both their numbers, but neither of them is answering. Do you think they could be helping people?'

I hope so.

Though the intuition, the knot that was rapidly forming in her stomach, told her otherwise.

She pulled her phone out of her pocket and began dialling Eve's number. 'You try Devon. Don't stop until you get through.'

For five minutes, they stood in the same spot, trying multiple times to get through to their colleagues. After the sixth minute, they stopped. Neither had picked up the calls. Both went straight to voicemail.

'You don't think something's happened to them, do you?'

'I don't think they're ignoring us.'

Giles ran his fingers through his thick hair. 'Oh God. I knew this was a bad idea!'

Stephanie said nothing. She just looked out at the cellophane on the bouquets of flowers, shimmering in the breeze. She would have *that* particular discussion later.

'Sorry,' Giles said suddenly.

'What for?'

'We weren't supposed to be here, were we?'

'That depends. Were you here in a professional or personal capacity?'

'Professional.'

'Then, no. You absolutely were not supposed to be here. Who said you were?'

Just as Giles opened his mouth, Steph cut him off. 'Actually, don't answer that. I know the answer already.'

Over an hour later, they returned to the station. A team of paramedics had arrived and quickly administered first aid to the burn victims. Fortunately, there had only been a few, and none of their injuries warranted a trip to the nearby hospital. During that time, Stephanie and Giles had continued trying to contact Devon and Eve, to no avail. And so they'd called it a night and left for the station.

Stephanie had expected it to be quiet – it was just after nine o'clock – and was surprised to see so many people moving about, darting from one side to the other. There was a buzz in the building, but also a current of fear hidden beneath it. Stephanie didn't want to accept that something had gone wrong. At least not yet. That would come later. Perhaps in the morning, if they were still unable to contact either detective.

She wanted to remain calm and level-headed. Not instil panic and dread into the rest of the team. Even though internally, her mind was beginning to do somersaults.

Stephanie clapped her hands together, bringing the entire room to a complete stop. All heads turned towards her.

'Evening, all, I am surprised to see so many of you still here. For that, I thank you. We are having an issue with contacting two members of our team: DS Devon Lafferty and DC Eve Hope. I would be grateful if someone could visit their houses, just to see if they might have turned up there. For context, they were caught up in an incident at the vigil that took place this evening. I would also appreciate it if a handful of you, along with some uniformed support, could station yourselves at the university, just in case they turn up.'

At once, a handful of faces she didn't recognise stood up and nominated themselves. With DS Noah Mackenzie's help, they instructed the volunteers where to go and whom to look for.

After they'd left, Noah pulled her aside.

'You don't think something's happened to them, do you?'

Steph allayed the man's fear by saying, 'I'm sure everything's fine. Now, if you'll excuse me, I have to make sure Giles is all right.'

She left Noah in the incident room and found Giles in the kitchen, rooting through the communal fridge for a bag of ice.

'What're you doing?' she asked.

'Where's Wellard when you need her? She'd have a bag of peas or something in her handbag. She's good like that.'

'You'll never find ice in the fridge, you dolt.' Stephanie moved Giles aside and began searching the drawers of the freezer. Inside was a handful of loose ice creams, covered in frost, that looked as though they'd been there for years. But, much to her surprise, she found a bag of ice. She pulled it out, wrapped it in a tea towel, and slammed it against Giles' ankle. The man yelped in pain, the sound spilling out into the main office.

'Sorry, did that hurt? That's what you get for blindly following whatever DS Lafferty tells you.'

Then, almost as if by magic, Devon appeared at the door. He was panicked, out of breath, and his hair was windswept, like he'd just run from the university.

'Devon,' she hissed, dropping the bag of ice to the floor. 'You've got some explaining to do. Where have you been?'

'The—'

'What happened? Where's Eve?'

Devon shuffled sheepishly into the kitchen. 'I… I don't know. I've tried to contact her. But I have absolutely no idea.'

'You took her and Giles out against my will, against my instruction, and now look what's happened. Who do you think you are?'

She kept her voice low so as not to make a scene. Giles stood awkwardly in the corner of the room, unable to bring himself to look at either of them for fear of being caught in the crossfire.

'Ma'am,' Devon started.

Before Steph could cut him off, DCI McGowan appeared behind DS Lafferty. He was dressed in plain clothes and looked as though he'd just been woken from a nap.

'Lafferty, Broadbent. My office. Now!'

All noise from the outside was sucked out of the room as Devon closed the door. DCI McGowan was already in his seat, but he made no offer for them to sit. Devon and Stephanie stood beside one another, hands behind their backs, like they were in the headteacher's office at school.

'It seems we have an issue…'

'Yes, sir,' Stephanie said.

'Who would like to explain to me what happened?'

Neither chose to speak first. Eventually, Stephanie bit the bullet.

'Earlier this morning, Devon approached me and asked if we should send some of the team down to the vigil that took place this evening on campus. It was his belief that we might be able to catch the killer, or at least stop something from happening. I agreed and said that it was a good idea, and between us, we decided to send Devon, Eve, and Giles along. In hindsight, we should have sent more; however, there was going to be a small, uniformed presence there as well.

'Now, from what I understand, the firework display went wrong, and some of them ended up firing directly into the crowd. From there, everyone panicked and split up. As a result, Giles twisted his ankle, and the team got split up.'

McGowan played with a pen in his fingers. He looked up at Devon. 'That right, sergeant?'

Devon glanced at Stephanie, but she chose not to look at him. Whatever came out of his mouth was his choice.

'Yes…' he said, his voice breaking. 'Yes, that's right.'

'The issue we have now, however, is that we're unable to find Eve,' Steph continued. 'We've tried to call her repeatedly, but she's not answering her phone. I've sent some of the county officers to her home, but I don't think she would have ended up there.'

'What do you mean? She's gone missing?'

'Potentially, sir.'

'Devon? Care to elaborate?'

DS Lafferty scratched the back of his head. 'I wouldn't like to assume. But it is strange. I spoke to her moments before the fireworks took place, and she seemed fine, and everything was under control. And then after that… nothing. She just disappeared.'

McGowan inhaled deeply, held it, then released the air from his lungs. 'How could this have been allowed to happen? What security measures did you have in place? What precautions did you take to stop something like this from happening?'

'We—'

'Not you, Broadbent. You've done enough answering for this evening. I want Devon to answer this one.'

Devon's mouth opened and closed repeatedly. 'We didn't have anything, sir. We… we wanted it to be under the radar. We didn't want anybody to know we were there.'

'And yet one of our team appears to have gone missing. I dare say, if anything has happened to her, I will hold you accountable.'

Stephanie took a step forward. 'This is on me, sir,' she said firmly. 'Devon hasn't done anything wrong or made any mistakes here. And if he has, if there are any oversights, then they're all on me. I'm the detective inspector. The buck stops with me. If anything happens to Eve, then it's… all… on… me.'

CHAPTER
SEVENTY-ONE

The woods were quiet that morning. Still, breathless. The sun was only beginning to thread gold through the trees. The earth beneath Roy Lavender's feet was damp, evidence of yet another rainy night he'd slept through while Caroline hadn't. Either that had kept her awake, or it had been his snoring again.

Classic.

Rory adjusted the leash around his wrist, giving it a quick tug.

'Come on, Ruby,' he muttered.

Ruby, his spaniel, suddenly darted ahead, her nose low to the mossy ground, tail wagging as she began sniffing through the undergrowth. They'd walked this path in Chantry Wood every morning for the past five years, ever since he'd retired. It was one of their favourites. At this time in the morning, it was always quiet, save for the odd marathon trainer or random dog walker. But usually, on a good day, they had the whole place to themselves. They could hear the wind whistling through the trees and the birds beginning to sing. The woods came alive in the morning, breathing, talking to him. He often talked back. But for some reason, that morning he didn't feel like it.

He sensed a presence there. Ominous, forbidding. As if he were being watched.

'Ruby, come on, girl.'

He gave another pull on her lead and led her down a different path. They came to a small incline. Ruby stopped beside an overturned tree and began sniffing.

Sniffing, sniffing, more sniffing.

Stop, start. Stop. Start.

Different from the brisk pace they were accustomed to.

As they ventured deeper into the woods, the uneasy sensation grew. Rory checked over his shoulder now and then, his senses heightening at the faintest sound. Ruby, meanwhile, was completely oblivious. She was devouring the smells, sights, and sounds.

Until she caught a scent that took her off their new path and onto a narrow thoroughfare. She darted towards a tree and began pawing at something beneath a fallen branch, barking at it to move. She tugged and tugged on Rory's arm, almost pulling him over.

But he paid her little heed. His attention was focused on something directly in front of him.

Something from a nightmare, a horror film. Not the sort of thing you'd find in Guildford.

A body, hanging from a thick, twisted oak branch overhead.

A woman, suspended high.

Her head lolled forward. Her long, dark hair shifted with the wind. She was dressed in dark clothes – black jeans, boots, a fitted coat – and her arms were bound tightly to her sides; She'd been hoisted with almost mechanical precision. Like someone had taken their time.

A shaft of early sunlight pierced the canopy, striking her pale, lifeless face.

Rory's throat closed. For a moment, he couldn't breathe. He took a stumbling step back, steadying himself against a nearby tree, and stared up in horror. The woman looked so young. Late twenties, maybe early thirties. Dark hair pulled back from her face. She could have been someone's daughter. Someone's friend.

Someone's colleague.

'Oh Jesus,' he whispered.

He fumbled for his phone, hands shaking so violently he nearly dropped it. It took three attempts to unlock the screen. He managed to dial 999 and held the phone to his ear.

'There's… there's a body,' he rasped. "In the woods. A woman. Hanging from a tree. Chantry Wood."

The operator began asking questions – name, location, is the victim breathing – but Rory couldn't stop staring.

There was something chilling in the way she'd been hoisted, like a dreamcatcher blowing in the breeze.

Ruby let out another low whine and pressed herself into Rory's leg, tail tucked between her legs.

'She's dead,' he said quietly. 'God help us, she's been murdered.'

CHAPTER
SEVENTY-TWO

Morning, and there was still no sign of Eve. No word, no contact. Help from the neighbouring counties had visited her house in Guildford and been stationed there the entire time, yet there had been no sign of her. She hadn't called. She hadn't communicated with anyone. They had traced her phone and soon realised it was switched off. To make matters worse, nobody on the campus had seen her either. They had been there until the early hours of the morning, asking passersby and students if they knew anything or if they'd seen someone matching her description. But by that point, most of the students had gone to bed, and there were far too many rooms and buildings for them to conduct door-to-door enquiries.

Stephanie, along with most of the office, had stayed overnight, burning the midnight oil. DCI McGowan had tried to send her home, but she had refused. Snatches of sleep had found their way into her office, but for the most part, she'd stared at her phone, willing it to ring, even though she knew it might never do so. Meanwhile, her sister was tucked up in Stephanie's bed. Kimberley had messaged to say that she'd finished cleaning late and was too tired to head home, not to mention the couple of glasses of wine she'd drunk.

The thin light of the new day crept through gaps in the French blinds, reminding her it was time to move. She hadn't left her office for hours. She hadn't eaten for longer.

Coffee.

That was the answer. That would fill her up, satiate the hunger pangs, prolong the inevitable. It was an added bonus that it would wake her up.

As she opened the door, a phone rang somewhere in the office. She paid it little heed as she moved sluggishly to the kitchen. She filled the kettle, switched it on, readied her instant granules and made the drink robotically. When she was finished, she shuffled back towards her office.

Her hand was on the door handle when a voice called from behind her.

It came from Fiona, who had arrived at some point in the night.

'Ma'am…' There was a catch in her voice. Strained.

Stephanie raised her head and looked across the office with bleary eyes.

'Someone found a body hanging in the Chantries. Two of the guys from here have gone down to have a look.' Her pause was filled with dread. A lump was already beginning to form in Stephanie's throat.

'It's Eve. They've confirmed it.'

The first thing to be destroyed in the carnage was the coffee mug. It clattered against the wall, shattering into a dozen pieces as a waterfall of dark brown liquid cascaded. Next was her chair: overturned and kicked with as much force as her body could muster. It was shortly followed by the rest of her office. A potent combination of rage, fury, revenge and guilt swelled within her.

Thoughts of her and Eve at the pub the other night, at the mortuary, in the car together, flashed through her mind as she took her frustration out on the few inanimate objects she had in her office. Then she screamed. Hard. Almost as hard as she had when she'd discovered her mum on the sofa, cold, staring at the ceiling.

A moment later, her office door opened. Fiona and Devon spilled in. Fiona was the first to manhandle her, grabbing her by the shoulders and pulling her away from the next potential victim of her outburst before turning her around and embracing her, holding on and not letting go.

Stephanie wriggled and writhed – she put up as good a fight as she could manage – but in her weakened state, Fiona was too powerful for her. Not to mention the woman was surprisingly strong. In the end, Stephanie relented and allowed herself to give in to Fiona, to let herself be taken in by someone she'd only known for a handful of weeks.

Together, they both sobbed.

As Stephanie pulled away, she spotted Devon, standing in the doorway. She brandished a finger at him. '*You. You* did this. If you hadn't disobeyed my orders, then she wouldn't have gone to the vigil, and she would still be here.' Her voice was a deep, almost demonic growl.

'I can—'

'I want you out of my sight. I don't want you in my office. Get out!'

Devon wasted no time in hurrying away. He left the door open behind him, and Stephanie followed him out. She began addressing the room.

'Noah, where are you?'

The man rose from behind his desk.

'Noah, I want you to go down to the Chantries. I want someone from our team to confirm that the victim is, in fact, Eve. And if that's the case, I want every last person in this building working on the case to find this bastard. He's taken one of our own. He's not allowed to take any more.'

CHAPTER
SEVENTY-THREE

The carpet of leaves squished underfoot, sodden and damp. A soft breeze brushed his ankles, gently flapping the tails of his coat against his leg. Despite the numerous figures moving about the woods – uniformed officers setting up the inner and outer cordons, and crime scene investigators erecting a tent in the middle of the path – there was a hush in the woods. An enclosed silence, as if a giant dome had been placed around them.

Noah walked slowly, treading carefully across the place markers on the ground. He kept his head low, staring at the rocks and tree roots until the very last moment, when he was forced to look up and see her.

Eve.

Hanging with unnatural stillness, a silhouette against the backdrop of trees, her face blue and bloated, eyes closed, head tilted to one side, hair matted against her skin.

Poor girl.

It didn't seem real. She was young, so fresh in her career, and yet it had all been taken from her. Even though he'd only known her a couple of weeks, he'd grown quite fond of her. The daughter he'd never had. Kind, polite, and always willing to share the biscuits she brought in, kidding himself he was doing her a favour by stopping her from eating them all herself. She was energetic, bubbly, and still possessed the eagerness and drive of youth, the drive that hadn't been ground out of her by months of hard work with nothing to show for it.

Noah swallowed the lump in his throat and stepped closer.

'What the hell did they do to you?' he muttered, barely above a whisper.

Slowly, a handful of crime scene investigators began lowering her body from the branch, gradually releasing a portion of the rope at a time. Noah was unable to watch her descend to the earth like a fallen angel. He turned away and waited until he heard the dull thud of her body.

But as his eyes fell on a nearby tree, he spotted something odd. Something out of place.

Black. Rectangular. The size of a shoebox.

At once, he knew what it was.

Noah hurried towards it, summoning help from a nearby CSI photographer, and crouched beside it.

'Photograph everything that happens,' he instructed. 'Understood?'

The CSI nodded and readied his camera.

Noah turned his attention to the box. As he pulled it out, he said, 'I don't hear the shutter going off. Photograph *every* step, remember?'

As soon as he heard the sound of the camera working, he set the box on the ground. Holding his breath, he carefully opened the clasp on the front and lifted the lid gently.

Inside, nestled in the centre of the box, was another voodoo doll.

Hand-stitched. Tiny eyes of mismatched buttons.

Across the doll's throat, a knife had cut away at the fabric, revealing the fluff inside that spilled out of the gash like flowing blood. Noah had half-expected a contraption to slice the doll's neck, but it just sat there, staring back at him.

He stared down at it, unable to tear his gaze away, a cold shiver sweeping across his body.

Then he regained his composure and carefully shut the lid, turning towards the CSI. He placed a hand in front of the lens and lowered the camera, as if saving the doll the embarrassment of being photographed.

Another doll.
Another victim.
Another method of murder.
But still no idea who it would happen to.

CHAPTER
SEVENTY-FOUR

Stephanie stared at the brass knocker shaped like a fox's head. The house was modern – red brick, ivy crawling along the guttering and up the side of the building – with a neat little garden out front that someone clearly cared for.

She raised a hand and knocked.

On the drive down, she had thought about how she would approach the conversation and what she would say. As she stood there waiting, she still had no idea.

A moment later, the front door opened, revealing a five-foot-two woman who looked as formidable as Eve had described. Karen Hope was dressed in a pair of jeans and a light pink jumper that hugged her skin and muscles tightly.

'Mrs Hope?' Stephanie began.

'Yes…' There was reticence in Karen's voice.

'My name is DI Stephanie Broadbent. I'm your daughter's boss. May I come in? There is something I need to tell you.'

They skipped the pleasantries, and there was no offer of tea or coffee as they made their way into the living room. Family photos lined the walls: Eve as a toddler, Eve with braces, Eve as an adult, flanked by her parents, beaming at the camera.

'Is your husband around?'

'He's at work. I'm working from home. What is it? What's this about? Has something happened to Eve?'

Stephanie swallowed, her voice more brittle than she'd expected. 'I'm… I'm so sorry. Last night, your daughter attended the vigil at the university, and there was an incident.'

'An incident?' Karen's voice broke halfway through the sentence.

'This morning, her body was found in Chantry Wood. She was hanged by the same person we believe is killing these students.'

Karen Hope inhaled sharply and covered her mouth with her hand. 'She's dead? Are you telling me my baby girl is dead?'

Before Stephanie could respond, Karen burst into tears. She wailed, threw her head into her hands, and began sobbing uncontrollably. Stephanie made for the bathroom and returned with toilet paper, but when she handed it to Karen, the woman swatted the roll away.

'How could this have happened? How could you have let this happen?'

Stephanie said nothing as she returned to her seat.

'What was she doing at the vigil? Whose idea was it to send her? Was it yours?'

Stephanie froze. Even if she wanted to speak, she couldn't.

'What were you thinking? Did you know she was at risk? Did you know something was going to happen to her?'

Stephanie decided not to correct her. She chose to take it all, to absorb the mother's entire fury. It was the least she deserved for not having caught the killer sooner. If she had, neither of them would be in this position. Despite having had nothing to do with the decision to send Eve to the vigil, Stephanie felt the blame lay with her.

'I can't believe this! My beautiful baby girl – dead! How? How did this happen to her? You sent her to her death. You know that, right? What made you think it was a good idea? You let her go to that vigil.' Each word dripped with venom.

Stephanie lowered her gaze. 'I wasn't good enough.'

Silence.

Karen Hope stared at her for a long time. 'You think that makes it better? Owning up? Coming here in your nice coat and your nice hair, thinking that buys you some kind of grace?'

Stephanie shook her head slowly. 'No. It doesn't.'

'You can't bring her back.'

'I know.'

'I hope you find whoever did this. But it won't change what *you* let happen.'

You're just a silly, spoilt, little bitch, Stephy! Look what happened to your mum because of you. This is all your fault. Everything!

Stephanie nodded once. 'I know that too.'

Suddenly, the tears stopped, and Karen's expression turned hard. 'I don't want to see your face anymore. You can show yourself out.'

Stephanie didn't need to be told twice. She rose, hovered for a moment, thought about saying something, but then decided against it. There was nothing she could say that would make the situation better. So she took herself to the front door and stepped outside, letting the cold wind bite at her face. It was the least she deserved.

Back in the car, she sat motionless for ten minutes before turning the key.

Instead of heading back to the station, she made a pit stop at her favourite fast-food establishment.

CHAPTER
SEVENTY-FIVE

Her mouth tasted sour, the acrid aftermath of vomit still burning the back of her throat despite the several pieces of chewing gum she'd shoved into her mouth. She hurried across the car park and made her way to the incident room. The office was filled with the low hum of chatter, and the sound of keyboards clicking and mice clacking provided a beat to the soundtrack. It all stopped as soon as she arrived.

'I want everyone in the MIR space in two minutes.'

The command in her voice cut through the silence. Chairs scraped back at once. Keyboards ceased clicking. DC Olivia Willard was halfway through a can of Coke, and gulped the rest quickly. Giles climbed out of his chair and hobbled towards the space, holding onto Wellard for support.

Within moments, everyone had gathered, and she waded through the mass of bodies to reach the head of the room. As she came to a stop, she looked out at the sea of grief in front of her. A tapestry of shocked, anguished faces stared blankly at the notebooks and laptops on their laps.

All of them looked to her for guidance, support, the next steps.

Before she spoke, a wave of nausea hit her, and she felt lightheaded. The corners of her vision flickered black, then returned to normal in an instant. She closed her eyes, and when she opened them again, the room had tilted slightly off-axis. Stephanie clutched her necklace, which eased the nausea slightly.

'This morning, a member of our team was found dead in Chantry Wood. This follows an incident at the vigil that took place last night at the University of Surrey campus. I want everyone who was at that vigil questioned and interviewed. Our killer was there, hiding in plain sight. He must have taken Eve then. Someone must have seen it. He would not have been able to move her against her will without being spotted or heard. I don't care how many people are required or how long it takes; get as many people down to the campus as possible.'

She paused to catch her breath and blink away the nausea again.

'I suggest we also increase the number of uniformed officers positioned on campus at all times. Have them set up more regular patrols so they can deter the killer. We know his next method, thanks to Noah: he's going to slit someone's throat. We need to ensure that doesn't happen under any circumstances.

'Yesterday, I caught up with Martin Bell, the student welfare officer, and he raised some concerns about Tristan Penrose. Giles, I want you to continue looking into this. See if you can find him today.'

'I would, ma'am, but I fear I'm not going to be much use with my foot.'

She glanced down at the man's ankle and let out a heavy sigh. 'Fine. Noah, Devon, I want you on that instead.'

'Yes, ma'am.'

'He's been lying to us, and I want to know why. Eve was one of the team who spoke with him originally, so if he is getting revenge on the people who know his secret, then Fiona... I fear you may be next. For that reason, I want you to stay here and ensure you're with someone at all times.'

'You think *I* might be the killer's next target?'

'Let's hope not.'

As she turned her attention to the rest of the office, her vision swam and the room tilted.

She blinked and swallowed hard. The taste of acid surged again, hot and punishing. Her heart hammered against her ribs. She gripped the back of a chair.

Fiona frowned. 'Boss?'

Stephanie opened her mouth to speak, but the next second, the floor seemed to give out.

The whiteboard blurred. The hum of the lights and computers grew louder. Her knees buckled.

Darkness.

She collapsed sideways, hitting the floor with a thud that echoed around the room.

The purging, the pressure, Eve, the guilt, the responsibility; all of it had caught up with her.

And now her team, already shattered from Eve's death, was watching their detective inspector fall apart before their eyes.

CHAPTER
SEVENTY-SIX

Giles put on a brave face as he entered the interview room, ignoring the pain that flared up his leg. Sitting in the corner of the room, resting against the wall, was Tristan Penrose. After several phone calls and attempts to find him on campus, he and a member of Kent Police, with the help of a university staff member, had located the lecturer in his office, responding to emails. For a moment, Giles considered conducting the interview where the man felt comfortable, but then he remembered what Stephanie had said. If this was the killer, if the man in front of him had brutally murdered five girls, including Eve, then he wanted him to be as uncomfortable as possible.

As he hobbled towards the desk, he tried to force the images of Eve's body dangling in the woods to the back of his mind.

Eve. Beautiful, perfect Eve. Her face caught in a freeze frame of innocence and beauty. She didn't deserve to die. None of the victims did.

Giles glowered at Tristan as he pulled out the chair and sat down. After the recording machine finished its beep, he began.

'Tristan Penrose, you have been brought in under suspicion of the murders of Claudia Bellini, Paulina Potter, Maya Corcoran, Priya Chadha, and Eve Hope. You do not have to say anything, but—'

'It wasn't me!' the man exclaimed, swinging round on his chair. 'Please. I had nothing to do with this. You have to believe me.'

Giles finished telling the man the rest of his rights, then opened a folder in front of him. 'I would like to begin with your relationship with Paulina Potter.'

'We've been over this. I told you: she wanted to start something, and I said no. She took it to heart, and I was worried she might twist it. But nothing ever happened between us.'

Giles lifted an eyebrow. 'You sure?'

'Yes! A hundred per cent.'

'It's come to our attention that something *did* happen between you two. A meeting in your office. According to reports, you made a pass at Paulina, and then continued to harass her, message her, and ask for more throughout the rest of the summer.'

Tristan opened and closed his mouth like a fish.

'You were worried about her going to the university, you were worried about losing your job, your wife, your home, so you started to threaten her.'

'No…' Tristan's voice was weak, almost a whisper. Broken.

'Did you kill her, Tristan? Did you find out she'd told her friends at the running club, so you killed them too?'

Tristan's eyes widened with fear. He began shaking his head profusely. 'No,' he said. 'None of it's true. It's all lies. You've got it wrong.'

Giles set the document on the table and folded his arms. Leaning back in his chair, he said, 'Why don't you tell me the truth then? What happened between you and Paulina Potter?'

Tristan bounced his knee up and down repeatedly, so fast and hard that it banged against the table. He was panicked, frightened, and his expression was one of someone trying to think of something quickly.

'Yes, all right. Yes. *Some* of what you said is true. Something did happen between me and Paulina. Last year, in my office. But it was a mistake. I realised that after it had happened. I spent all summer freaking out about it, wondering if she would go to the university and grass me up. I wondered if I would have a job to go back to. But I had nothing to do with what happened to her. I promise you. I was at home the night she died. I was at home the nights all the girls died. Their deaths have been tragic, but I had nothing to do with any of them. I'm not a killer; I wouldn't even hurt a fly. I could never do that. I haven't got a bad bone in me.'

'Your wife might have something to say about that,' Giles retorted, leaning forward in his seat. 'Tell me, what do you know about Eve Hope?'

'Who?'

'My colleague. The one who came to see you at your house the other day.'

Tristan's brow furrowed with confusion. 'What about her?'

'She was found dead this morning in Chantry Wood.'

'Oh my God. I'm so sorry to hear that.'

'What were you doing last night?'

'I was playing football. Seven-a-side at the Surrey Sports Park, and I stayed for drinks after.'

Giles bristled with discomfort. That wasn't the answer he'd been expecting.

'You weren't at the vigil?'

Tristan shook his head. 'No. I didn't want to go because I knew how it might have looked. I was at the sports park until about ten o'clock before I went home.' His face lit up with joy as realisation began to sink in. 'I have about a dozen people who can corroborate that. As sorry as I am to hear about your colleague's death, I had nothing to do with it. I was nowhere near the campus or Chantries at all last night.'

For a long moment, Giles said nothing, just mulling over what the lecturer had said. Thinking about Eve.

Then Tristan cleared his throat. 'Can I make a suggestion?'

Giles gestured for the man to continue.

'I don't know how you know the truth about me and Paulina, but if I had to guess, my best guess would be Martin Bell, the student welfare officer. I don't know why, but I get the impression he might have said something about me, presumably because Paulina went to see him about our relationship. But I think he might know more than he's letting on. He's not innocent in all of this. If Paulina did go to see him, then something may have happened between them, and now he's covering his tracks.'

'What evidence do you have to support this?'

Tristan threw his hands in the air in defeat. 'None whatsoever. But what I do know for a fact is that Martin was present at the vigil last night. And I bet he might know something about what happened to your colleague.'

CHAPTER
SEVENTY-SEVEN

Stephanie awoke to the sound of movement around her, the hushed shuffling of two people trying their best to be quiet and not disturb her. When she opened her eyes, she saw Fiona and Olivia standing over her.

She was in a hospital bed, hooked up to an IV drip.

Both women looked down at her with warm, sympathetic faces. Stephanie suddenly felt very self-conscious. She shifted in her bed, attempting to move onto her elbows, but Fiona held her down.

'Easy,' she said. 'You've just woken up.'

'What happened?'

Pain flared in Stephanie's head as she stared into the fluorescent light above.

'You fainted,' Wellard replied.

'I did?'

And then she remembered. The office. The faces. The floor rushing up to meet her.

'When was the last time you ate?' Fiona asked. 'Doctor said you were massively dehydrated and malnourished. He made it seem like the last time you ate was when we went to the pub the other night and had some peanuts.'

Steph didn't answer. Her eyes fell on Olivia, who avoided her gaze.

'You have to look after yourself,' Fiona continued. 'You can't run this team if you continue like this.'

Stephanie glanced between Fiona and Olivia, bouncing between them like they were playing in a tennis match. Eventually, she stopped at Olivia and glowered at the older woman.

'You told her?'

'I had to,' Olivia replied sheepishly.

'And I'm glad she did,' Fiona interjected. 'Don't be angry at her. I forced her, twisted her arm until she told me. I'm pretty good at getting information like that. I knew something was wrong from the way Wellard reacted.' She placed a hand on Stephanie's arm. 'You should have said something.'

Stephanie closed her eyes, shame sweeping through her like a tide.

'Does anyone else know?'

'Just us three,' Olivia responded.

'And it'll stay that way,' Fiona added. 'Our little secret.'

Stephanie looked at her, really looked, and saw not pity in her eyes, but loyalty. Concern. The kind that came from someone who cared deeply about the people she worked with.

'How long have you been doing it for?' Fiona asked.

'Ever since I can remember. It goes way back.'

'Has it ever been this bad?'

Stephanie's gaze fell onto her lap. She shook her head.

An image of her dad appeared. Holding an apple and throwing it onto the floor. Calling her a "fat little piggy" as she was forced to scavenge the scraps.

'I'll get a handle on it,' she said at last. 'After this is all done. I'll deal with it. I promise.'

Fiona snorted loudly. 'If you don't, I'm dragging you to therapy myself. You're too valuable for us to lose. Besides, I need to see you kick Devon's arse into gear.'

Stephanie smirked. 'The investigation…'

Olivia placed a comforting hand on her shoulder. 'Don't worry. It's all under control. Giles is with Tristan now. We should hear the outcome of that soon.'

'And Devon…?'

'What about him?'

'Where is he?'

'At the office. Why?'

'No reason…' she said softly.

'The doctor said you should probably rest,' Olivia began. 'I'm inclined to agree with her. As is McGowan. He said he doesn't want you near the incident room until you feel better. So I'll drop you off whenever you're ready.'

Stephanie said nothing, continuing to stare into the bedsheets.

For the first time in her life, people had found a way through her armour; her secret was out, and yet, contrary to what she'd convinced herself, they accepted her.

Maybe, just maybe, this was the start of saving herself.

CHAPTER
SEVENTY-EIGHT

Steph had heard nothing from her sister all day. Nothing to indicate that she'd gone home. Nothing to suggest that she'd made amends with her husband. So, when she opened the front door – wearily, and with more effort than usual – she expected to see her sister in the house, presumably still cleaning and tidying up after her.

Instead, all she found was a stack of boxes in the hallway, and the faint, lingering smell of bleach. Beside the front door was a row of black and green bin bags, ready for her to take out.

'Kim?' Steph called as she moved about the house.

She peered into the kitchen, downstairs bathroom, and living room. Nothing.

Odd.

'Kim?' she called again. When there was no response, Stephanie climbed the stairs and checked the upstairs level. There was still no sign of her.

Stephanie tried her mobile. Nothing.

Panic began to sink in quickly as she hurried down the stairs and knocked on her next-door neighbour's door. The wait was painfully long. Eventually, Jimmy opened the door and smiled brightly at her, the pale orange light behind him creating a warm glow around his head.

'Sorry to disturb you,' she said, panic in her voice. 'But you wouldn't have happened to see where my sister went, would you?'

'Your sister?'

Jimmy stepped out of the house and glanced towards Stephanie's front door, as if Kimberley had been standing there the entire time and Stephanie hadn't noticed.

'Similar height to me, except she's got blonde hair. We look alike but at the same time we don't,' Stephanie added.

'There was a man,' he said. 'Now that I think about it. He got out, knocked on the front door, and then she came out with him.'

'Did you see the man?'

Jimmy shook his head.

'Did she… did she go *willingly*? Did it look like she was being forced at all?'

This time he shrugged his shoulders. 'Looked fairly amicable to me. I think she had her bags with her.'

'What time was this?'

'About midday or so.'

'Did you see where they went?'

He shook his head. 'They went past the bushes outside my window.'

She paused for a moment. Had Jason returned home from work, driven over, and taken her back? Had they kissed and made up? Or was something darker at play?

She had never wanted to voice it, never wanted to put it out into the world, but at the back of Stephanie's mind was the nagging feeling that Jason, the man she'd only met a handful of times, had been having an affair, using his extended periods away for work as an excuse, a chance to fulfil his other commitments.

But then another thought entered her mind: perhaps he'd been controlling Kimberly, manipulating her in some way. His arrival earlier that afternoon was just another example of it. That her sister had, just like their mother all those years ago, found herself trapped in an abusive relationship.

She didn't like to think poorly of her brother-in-law, especially when she didn't have any evidence. But the maternal instinct in her, the *big sister* instinct, was sounding alarm bells. Stephanie cast her mind back to the night before. How had Kimberley seemed when she'd knocked on the door? Angry, full of frustration, sure. But had there been an undertone of something else? A cry for help that she hadn't picked up on because her mind had been too frazzled and distracted?

She didn't know, but in her current weakened mental state, nothing was making much sense.

In the end, she thanked Jimmy for his time, apologised again for disturbing him, and then shuffled towards the end of the driveway. She couldn't see her sister's car anywhere.

Inside, she tried Kimberley's mobile again.

'Hey, Kim, it's me. Just checking to see if you're all right? I was expecting you to still be here when I got home, but you're not. Unless you've gone out for some food, in which case I'll probably see you in a bit. Call me when you get this, please.'

She pocketed the phone and shuffled into the living room, finally taking in the amount of work and effort Kim had put in the night before. The space was spotless. The detritus had been tidied away. The empty boxes that had lain there for a week had been broken down and thrown into bin bags. She could see the floor again. The television and surrounding cabinet had been dusted and polished, as had the coffee table. Kim must have spent hours on it. Stephanie wouldn't be surprised if she'd spent the night in her bed, passed out.

However, one thing Kimberley had left untouched was Stephanie's case notes folder, resting on the coffee table. As soon as she saw it, Stephanie thought of Eve. Of her death. Of how the killer was still out there, toying with her.

Had he already slit the next victim's throat? She couldn't bear to think about it.

From the start, he'd been one step ahead. He'd meticulously chosen his victims, planning them in advance. How many more would there be before it was over? Would he ever stop?

Stephanie dropped herself onto the sofa and stared at her blurry reflection in the television screen. In the black space, the whiteboard from the incident room began to appear, filling with the names and faces of the victims. She thought about each of them in turn, placing herself at each of the crime scenes, tracing their steps, looking for clues or things she might have missed the first time round.

In her tired mind, she drew blanks on each.

They knew everything about the girls – what they studied, their movements, who they spoke to, what they did for fun – and yet there was nothing to connect them all to one another.

And now Eve…

Her death had thrown a spanner in the works. Previously, the killer's modus operandi had been to target university students. But now he'd chosen a police officer. And Stephanie believed the killer knew who Eve was and had targeted her for a reason. The only question that remained was: Why? How did she fit into all of this?

And then a name popped into her head: Devon.

She wasn't sure if it was because she disliked the man or if she had just cause, but there was something suspicious about him. The way he'd tried to control the investigation from the start. The way he'd manhandled the box at Paulina Potter's crime scene; had he done that on purpose so that his prints would naturally be ruled out? Or had he set the box there in the first place and was just trying to cover his tracks? Why hadn't he been present at Priya Chadha's crime scene? He'd been the only one missing. And Eve… Several hours had passed before he eventually returned to the station following her disappearance. Had he taken her from the campus and strung her up to the branch in that time?

Stephanie stretched, yawning loudly. She was tired and hungry. But she had neither the time nor patience to cook and eat, so she decided to go to bed.

Upstairs, she headed straight into her bedroom and collapsed onto the mattress, face first, letting the comfort of her duvet envelop her. It was worlds away from the discomfort she'd experienced in the hospital only a couple of hours before.

A few moments later, a sickly taste formed in her mouth, reminding her to brush her teeth. As she pushed herself off the mattress, something caught her eye.

Bart was missing. Her beloved teddy bear.

'That bitch,' Steph said.

Kimberley must have taken it when she left. Her sister had always wanted it growing up. She had begged for it and questioned why she didn't have one. But Stephanie had never given it to her. She had never allowed it to pass into someone else's care. So Kimberley had finally seen her opportunity and taken it.

Stephanie was reaching for her phone when the doorbell sounded downstairs. The sudden, jarring noise took her by surprise.

'You better give him right back,' she whispered as she clambered off the bed and headed downstairs.

She threw open the front door. Standing on the other side, a long black coat draped over him and silhouetted against the streetlight behind him, was Devon. For a moment, she thought she was looking into the eyes of the killer, that he had come to claim her as his next victim. But there was something about his face that suggested no animosity, no evil desire to attack and kill her. Instead, his cheeks were flushed and his eyes bloodshot. If she didn't know any better, she would say he'd been crying.

'Devon,' she said. 'What are you doing here?'

'I heard you were home from the hospital. I just wanted to come by and see if you were okay.'

She loosened her grip on the door. 'I've felt better. But I'll be okay.'

He stood there awkwardly, his eyes focused on the doormat by his feet. 'Could I come in? I've got something I want to talk to you about.'

Without thinking, she stepped aside and let him through. He shrugged off his coat and folded it under his arms. As he stepped out of his shoes, Stephanie took the coat from him and draped it over the banister, then led him into the living room.

'I would say excuse the mess, but my sister cleaned, and she's done a better job than I ever could. Do you want a drink?'

He shook his head. 'I won't be staying long.' He rounded the sofa and politely perched himself on the edge of it. 'I think I've got some explaining to do,' he began once Stephanie was sitting next to him. 'About everything.'

She said nothing, just pressed her legs tighter against her chest.

'I'm sorry,' he said. 'I'm sorry for being a complete arsehole. You didn't deserve to be treated the way I did. You're new to the team, and you should have been treated with warmth and grace. Instead, I acted like a child. That was wrong. I… I shouldn't have done that, and

I feel guilty about my behaviour. Ashamed, even. Not that this excuses it in any way, but I feel like you should know, I'm currently going through a messy divorce, and I'm fighting for custody of my child. I—'

'I know,' Stephanie responded.

'You do?'

'Not exactly. McGowan didn't give me the specifics. He just said you had something going on. So I decided to give you *some* grace for being a total prick.'

Devon snorted. 'Thanks. I appreciate it. It's not been easy, and some of it has spilled into my work through my actions and behaviour. I've lashed out, and that was wrong of me. I hope you can forgive me.'

'We're all struggling with something, Devon,' she said softly. 'It's okay if it spills into our work or careers. We're only human. We can't bottle everything up. If we did, we'd explode.'

Or pass out in front of fifty people, she thought.

The pressure on Devon's face eased. 'I also want to say thank you,' he continued. 'About earlier. With Clive. You... you could have thrown me under the bus and left me there for what I did at the vigil. You could have fed me directly to McGowan. But you didn't. Why?'

Steph inhaled sharply. 'Because I've always said I will fall on my sword to protect my team. The buck stops with me. Any mistakes you make, I make. Nobody else should get the blame for them except me, no matter how much they've done to convince me otherwise. That's just the way I like to lead, as long as it means you get some breathing space. God knows you didn't deserve it, though.'

He chuckled awkwardly. 'I know.'

'But it doesn't count for anything unless you learn from it,' she said, repositioning herself on the sofa into a more comfortable, open position. 'Tell me, what were you doing after Eve went missing?'

'What do you mean?'

'You disappeared. Giles and I tried to call you hundreds of times, but you didn't pick up.'

Devon began playing with his fingers, kneading his thumb into his palm. 'I panicked,' he started, his voice catching. 'I lost it. I... I tried calling Eve, tried finding her, looked everywhere, but when I couldn't find her, I knew something had happened. So I just... I just sat in my car for a couple of hours, having a panic attack. I couldn't face myself nor the thought that something had happened to her.'

Steph listened intently. Everything about his story suggested she shouldn't believe him. But she did. She doubted she would have felt or reacted any differently had she been in his position. The shock of it all, the rush, the fear.

'I blame myself for her death,' he continued, a catch forming in his throat. He tried to clear it, but was unsuccessful. 'If we hadn't gone to the vigil, she would still be with us. It's all my fault.'

Stephanie placed a hand on his back. His muscles were tense beneath his shirt. 'You shouldn't blame yourself. So far this killer has done everything for a reason. Part of me thinks Eve was going to be a victim one way or another.'

He glanced up at her, confused. 'How can you be so sure?'

'Intuition,' she replied with a wink.

'Well, I hope yours is better than mine.'

Devon rubbed away tears from his cheeks.

'You know,' Stephanie began, 'there was a time I thought you might have been our killer.'

The colour rushed from his face, eyes wide with panic.

'You didn't give me much reason to think otherwise,' she said jokingly. 'You were behaving like a twat. You were always close to the investigation. You opened the box at Paulina Potter's crime scene. You went missing at Priya's—'

'I had to pick up my son,' he answered.

'And obviously the incident with Eve. All the clues were there. The alarm bells were ringing.'

'Does anyone else think the same?'

She shook her head. 'I think your secret's safe with me. How did they get on today? What did I miss?'

Devon quickly brought her up to speed about Giles' interview with Tristan Penrose and how he'd thrown Martin Bell's name into the ring. The team had subsequently spent the afternoon looking for him, but to no avail.

'We'll get the team on it tomorrow,' she added. 'With any luck, one of their fingerprints will match the one we found in Claudia's room.'

'And there's also something else…' Devon jumped up and made

for his coat. He spoke to her while in the hallway. 'Noah spent hours at the crime scene with CSI this morning, looking through the woods. I'm not sure why, maybe it was intuition again, but it's a good thing they did. Because they found this…'

He returned a moment later with a plastic evidence bag in hand. Stephanie immediately spotted what was inside and felt her body tense.

'They found it in another box, around the corner from the first one,' he said, passing it to her. 'Now, I'm no expert, but that looks an awful lot like a baby voodoo doll to me…'

CHAPTER
SEVENTY-NINE

She held the coffee cup to her lips for a few moments after finishing it, savouring the taste and letting her tastebuds tingle. It was her third of the morning, and they were having absolutely no impact at all. Sleep, unsurprisingly, had evaded her. Not because she'd been thinking about the fact that the killer had also selected a baby as one of his next victims, but because Bart was missing. He had been taken from her, and she'd suffered as a result.

The only person to blame for that sleepless night was Kimberley, who, after multiple attempts, still wasn't answering her phone. Stephanie had resorted to sending her several explicit messages. It was, however, only just after seven am, so it was highly possible, if not probable, that her sister was still sleeping, hopefully in the comforting arms of her husband after a night of lovemaking.

Setting the mug down on the table, she made her way to the office exit. Despite the early hour, the office had filled up rapidly. She counted no fewer than thirty bodies moving about, many of whom were from the neighbouring counties, while from her team she only spotted Devon, Noah, and Giles. The rest would no doubt arrive soon.

While she waited, she hurried towards Giles' desk.

'How's the foot?'

'Don't even...' He spun round in his chair and raised his leg to reveal a set of hairy toes that were visible beneath a cast on his foot and ankle. 'Six hours in A&E last night,' he said. 'I haven't slept a wink, and I'm fairly sure I've caught AIDs or something, considering the amount of people coughing and spluttering in there.' Giles shuddered at the thought.

'Best night ever, by the sounds of it,' she replied. 'Why didn't you tell me? I would have said not to come in.'

'I need to find Martin Bell, ma'am. I'm doing it for Eve.'

'I get that, and it's very honourable, but if he sees you coming and runs away, you won't be much help. I'll get the rest of the team on it, and you can have the luxury of interviewing him. How does that sound?'

'Sounds delicious, ma'am.'

Stephanie chuckled, and for a moment she forgot about Eve and her sister. Her mood was dampened when she heard her name from the other side of the office.

McGowan was hovering outside his room, waiting expectantly for her like a doctor in a surgery.

She finished giving instructions to Giles, then hurried over, head bowed.

'Morning, Steph,' he said as she entered. 'I didn't expect to see you here this morning. Thought I told you to stay at home and rest.'

'You did, sir. I chose to ignore it.'

'We have plenty of support now, plenty of people working around the clock on this investigation.'

'And yet still no sign of the killer.'

McGowan let out a short puff of air. 'I suppose you have the magic wand that will help us find him?'

She shook her head, smiling proudly. 'Just hard work, determination, and a little bit of luck, sir. That's all you need in life.'

McGowan lifted his chin a few inches, looking down at her. 'Just… look after yourself. Take it easy. I don't want to have to deal with HR if something happens to you. I've got enough on my plate without you getting in the way.'

A thought occurred to her.

'Have you spoken to Eve's parents?' she asked.

'I have, and they want to get the funeral done as quickly as possible. They don't want us to keep the body any longer than necessary.'

'Understandable.' She lowered her gaze to the carpet in a moment of reflection.

'Don't blame yourself, Steph,' he said. 'I heard about what happened with your old sergeant. I know you blamed yourself for that. But you had nothing to do with Eve. It was nobody's fault.'

'Sometimes I feel like bad luck just has a way of following me around, you know? Like, sometimes, I'm not in as much control as I thought I was.'

Clive scoffed. 'Sadly, I don't think any of us are.'

CHAPTER
EIGHTY

Mercifully, the pain in his foot had subsided, but it still hurt like nothing else. Giles was no stranger to pain – playing amateur football with a bunch of hungover and overweight lads on a weekend did that to you – but he'd never experienced as much pain as this. And it was all thanks to a pinecone. He didn't know where it had come from or when it had got there, but all he remembered was looking down at the object on the floor after he'd collapsed. The cone had stared back, almost mocking him. Out of embarrassment, he'd kept that nugget of information to himself.

It was late morning, and the only real work he'd done had been getting himself from the office down to the interview room while everyone else was working hard around him. But now it was his time to shine. His time to show what he could do.

For Eve.

Between them, Noah and Devon had rounded up Martin Bell, the student welfare officer, from the university campus. Martin had been in the middle of making a second cup of coffee when the pair of sergeants had arrived, and he'd come willingly, though that somewhat amenable nature wasn't currently reflected in the man's expression.

'My name is Detective Constable Giles Swinger,' Giles began. 'Thank you for coming in this morning. I understand you're the student welfare officer at the University of Surrey, is that correct?'

'You already know it is.'

'How long have you been doing that?'

'Six years.'

'I imagine you must have come across a lot of students in your time.'

'A fair few. Just like everyone else at the university.'

'Do any names stick out to you?'

'I imagine you want me to say the victims' names, don't you?' Martin ran his finger across the length of the desk. 'Listen, I don't know what this is about, but I really don't think I should be here. I've never been in a police station in my life, and that's for good reason. I've never done anything wrong. What exactly have I been brought in for? Your colleagues weren't very forthcoming with information.'

Giles opened his notebook. 'Did you attend the vigil that took place the other night, Martin?'

As he asked the question, the pain in his ankle flared.

'A lot of people were there. And I think there were non-students present as well. I thought it was a lovely tribute for the victims… until it all went wrong, that is. But I still don't understand what that's got to do with anything?'

'Would you mind telling me your whereabouts that night?'

Martin's nostrils flared. 'I literally just told you. I was on campus.'

'When?'

'All day. I stayed after work.'

'What time did you leave?'

Martin thought for a moment. 'It must've been about nine-ish.'

An hour after the fireworks exploded.

'Can you remember where you were standing?'

'Sorry?' Martin leaned forward as if he hadn't heard the question properly.

'Standing. Where were you in relation to the fireworks?'

'I was on the field, where everyone else was…'

Martin's tone was becoming more abrupt, sharper.

Giles pulled out a map of the campus and slid it across the desk. 'Show me.'

'What is this? Honestly.'

'Please,' Giles said, his voice measured and calm. 'This will help our investigation.'

Martin let out a heavy sigh as he turned his attention to the map. 'This doesn't seem very "routine" to me.'

Giles said nothing as he waited. A moment later, Martin prodded his finger to a point on the map. It was to the east of the field, a short distance from Millennium House, the student accommodation. Within touching distance of where Eve had been stationed.

'Tell me what happened after the fireworks went off,' Giles continued, giving nothing away in his expression.

'I panicked, like everyone else. I got caught up in it all, so I retreated to a safe distance.'

'Where?'

'By Millennium House, along the main road.'

'Then what did you do? You were on campus for another hour. Why?'

'Because I was trying to calm down a couple of students. One of them had got hurt quite badly, a firework went off by her ankles so I stayed with her until she got proper medical attention. Understandably, she was in pieces.'

'How did you get home?'

Another flicker of confusion crossed his face. 'I drove. Same as I always do.'

Giles reached into his folder and pulled out a photo of Eve. 'Does this person look familiar to you?'

Martin dragged the sheet across the desk, lifted it, and inspected it for a moment. Giles noticed the man's eyes moving over every contour of Eve's young, beautiful face, lingering at the dimple in her cheek.

'I vaguely recognise her, though I couldn't say where from.' Martin dropped the sheet onto the table.

'Her name is Eve Hope. Does that ring a bell?'

'Is she a student?'

'No. She's a police officer. She was murdered on the night of the vigil.'

'And you think I had something to do with it?'

'We're just asking questions, looking for witnesses. Based on what you've said about your whereabouts on the night of the vigil, you were within touching distance of her.'

'That doesn't mean I had anything to do with what happened to her. I never saw her there. I didn't even know she was there. I saw *some* police officers, but they were all in uniform. None of you guys...'

Giles pulled the sheet back towards himself, glancing at Eve a moment too long before continuing. 'Did you see anything suspicious? Anyone perhaps manhandling a woman and placing her in the back of a car, or ushering her off campus at all? We're trying to piece together what happened to her.'

'Okay, good.' Martin said with a heavy sigh of relief. 'For a moment then, I thought you were assuming I'd done it. Because that would be ridiculous. You have no evidence against me, nothing to prove I've done anything to any of these girls.' He pulled the sheet back to him, as if they were playing tug of war with one of the last photos of Eve. 'Now, as for someone being ushered into a car, I mean... No. The place was bedlam. There were men and women, boys and girls, all holding onto one another, running away as fast as they possibly could. A couple of people moving together wouldn't have looked out of place, to be honest.'

That was what Giles had been afraid of.

'I'll ask around, see if anyone in my team saw anything, but I'm doubtful,' Martin continued. 'But the faces blurred into one, and I got this sort of tunnel vision. At that point, you're only focusing on yourself and nobody else.'

It was true. The same had happened to him. Lying there on the floor, dozens of faces had passed him, and yet he remembered none of them. They were a blur.

'Before we finish, would you be willing to give us some fingerprint samples so we can rule you out?'

Martin nodded. 'Absolutely. Whatever you need. I've got nothing to hide.' He held his hand up, in a gesture of willingness.

In the end, Giles thanked the man for his time, told him they would be in touch if necessary, and then sent him on his way to the exhibits officer before he took the long and painful walk back to the office.

CHAPTER
EIGHTY-ONE

Stephanie's knuckles rapped against the front door for the third time, sharp and insistent. The sound echoed along the quiet suburban street, but there was still no response. A light breeze rustled the hedges lining the driveway. Jason's car was parked in its usual spot on the gravel.

But there was no sign of movement behind the frosted glass panel. Nobody was home.

Steph crouched, pressing her face against the edge of the letterbox flap, and pushed it open with her fingertips. Daylight filled the hallway, but still no sign of life, no telltale patter of feet moving towards her.

She straightened slowly, her pulse racing, her throat constricting, blocking her air. Something was wrong.

Kim still wasn't answering her phone. Neither was Jason.

They had both vanished off the face of the earth.

Stepping back, she glanced up at the bedroom windows on the first floor. The curtains were closed. Then she surveyed the side of the house. On the left was a side gate. She hurried towards it and tugged.

Locked.

Backing up a pace, she quickly glanced up and down the street before looking at the high brick wall between their house and the neighbours'. At long last, it was time to put her climbing practice to use. She climbed awkwardly up the brick and then tiptoed along to the wooden fence. She grunted as she lowered herself down on the other side, landing with a jarring thud, her knees flaring.

The back garden was neat. A lot of time and care, Kimberley's time and care, had gone into maintaining it. But something was off. The glass of water on the garden table. The laundry that was still out on the washing line.

Overhead, a blackbird shot out from above the house before disappearing beyond another.

Stephanie moved to the rear patio doors and cupped her hands to the glass. The dining room and living room were spotless. No plates on the table. No leftover mugs. Still no sign of her sister.

She tried the handle. Also locked.

Frowning, she knelt beside the door and removed a flat hair clip from her pocket; she'd done this before, during a forced entry in her early days. A few jimmies of the lock, but nothing gave. So she stood and moved to the side window instead.

It was half open.

She eased her fingers under the latch, slid it up, and pushed gently. The hinges were stiff, but they gave. She wriggled her hand through first, then an arm, then angled her shoulder down and in, gritting her teeth as she hauled herself inside.

'Kimberley?' she called out. Nothing.

'Jason?'

Still nothing.

Stephanie moved from room to room: the kitchen, hallway, lounge. Nothing.

She climbed the stairs two at a time, her heart thudding. The bedroom was untouched. No sign of Kimberley's overnight bag or Bart the bear on the bed. No phone charging on the bedside table. The bathroom smelled faintly of bleach, the way it always did. No toothbrushes missing. No damp towels.

It felt like she'd just… vanished.

She pulled her phone from her pocket and quickly rang her sister again. Voicemail. *Again*.

With a sharp inhale, she tapped Fiona's name into her contacts.

'Steph?' Fiona answered, her voice muffled as if she were mid-bite.

'I need you to run something for me,' Stephanie said. 'Kimberley, my sister, and her husband, Jason. Surname: Taylor. I need contact details for employers, next of kin, anything. I'm at their house, but they're not.'

'You think something's happened?'

'I don't know. But I'm getting a bad feeling.'

'I'll get on it now.'

Stephanie ended the call and looked around the hallway one last time, spotting a family photo that filled her with chills. Stephanie, Kimberley, their mum, and their dad stood in the garden: Kimberley being held by their mum, and Stephanie standing in front of her father, his arms draped over her shoulders. All smiling happily at the camera.

Except there was nothing happy about that family.

Nor was there anything happy about Kimberley's current family situation.

Not if her worst fears were coming to fruition.

Stephanie ignored the photo as she left the house, her fingers trembling, and headed straight to the car.

She returned to the station twenty minutes later and made a beeline for Fiona's desk. The constable lowered a handset from her ear as she arrived.

'Got anything?' Stephanie asked.

Fiona prodded at a Post-It note on her desk. 'Contact details for Jason's and Kim's employers are there. I haven't called because I thought you'd want to.'

Stephanie thanked her quickly, then hurried to her office with the list in hand. She slammed the door shut and locked it behind her. She needed complete silence. Silence to calm the thoughts in her head. Silence to dampen her trembling.

She hurried over to her desk, then climbed beneath it, pressing her back against one of the wooden edges. Immediately she began to feel safe. Her breathing soothed, and her pulse slowed.

The drive from Kimberley's house to the station had given her a chance to think, to process. And it was then that something dawned on her. For the first time, she considered whether her brother-in-law was the one they'd been looking for.

From what she could remember, he had been away, out of town for work, on the nights of each of the victims' deaths. And that had been no more apparent to her than the night Eve had gone missing, the night Kimberley and Jason had their argument. Perhaps Jason had gone to the vigil, abducted Eve, and then taken her to the woods.

At that point, an image of the baby doll found at Eve's crime scene appeared in her mind, and her body flushed cold.

I'm pregnant. Her sister's words echoed in her head. *We didn't want to say anything until we had the all-clear from the doctor…*

What if Jason had taken his own wife to kill her. And her baby?

She daren't think about that any longer. She turned her attention to the Post-It note and began dialling Jason's employer. It was a switchboard number, and she spent the next ten minutes jumping through various hurdles, dealing with a handful of robots and humans, until eventually she got through to the right person.

'This is Lamar speaking.'

'Good afternoon,' she said. 'My name is Detective Inspector Stephanie Broadbent. I'm wondering if you could help me. I'm trying to get in contact with one of your employees, Jason Taylor. Could you—?'

'Jason?'

'Yes. I need to know where he is. It's urgent.'

'What's this regarding?'

'This is a police matter, sir. And I would appreciate your full cooperation.'

'I… I don't feel comfortable sharing this information over the phone.'

She sensed he was about to hang up, so she screamed at him to wait. 'Please,' she said, cooler this time. 'I wouldn't ask unless absolutely necessary. Jason is my brother-in-law, and I just need to know where he is or when was the last time you heard from him. If it helps, I can tell you that he is married to Kimberley, and they've been together for the past ten years. They're expecting their first child.'

'Are they?' There was genuine surprise in Lamar's voice.

'Yes. And that's what this is about. His wife, Kimberley, my sister, is in hospital, but we're struggling to get hold of him. Can you please help us?'

There was a pause. She could almost hear the indecision playing in the man's brain.

'He's in Edinburgh,' Lamar answered. 'On business.'

'Are you sure?'

'Yes,' he said. 'I've spoken with him this morning. We had a video call at nine o'clock.'

Stephanie's heart dropped, and she felt the entire weight of her body sink lower into the floor.

'He was complaining about having terrible signal and issues with his phone,' Lamar continued. 'Perhaps that might be why you've been unable to reach him.'

But Stephanie wasn't listening.

'I can get in contact with him and ask him to reach out to you, if that works?'

No response. She thought of her sister and the picture in the hallway. Of the happy family they'd never once been.

'Miss? Are you still there?'

Gradually, she came to. 'Yes... Sorry. Please... please get him to contact me as soon as he can. I need to speak with him.'

Stephanie hadn't moved since the call ended. She was trapped, thirty years in the past. Stuck inside the wardrobe. Her dad was holding onto the door so she couldn't move while he picked up Kimberley and began hitting her. His laughter was loud inside her head, echoing, drumming against the side of her skull. Stephanie screamed and kicked, thrashed her arms at the door and used all her weight to press it open, but it was no use. He was too strong for her.

And then her mobile vibrated. Unrecognised number.

She snatched at the device on the floor and answered the call.

'Steph? Steph, is that you?'

'Jason...' she said weakly.

'What's going on? I've just had a call from my boss, saying Kim's in hospital. Is she all right? Is everything okay with the baby? Do I need to come down?'

'You're really in Edinburgh, aren't you?' she said, rubbing her hand across her forehead, massaging the swelling pain.

'What? Yes. I had to get a last-minute flight the other night. Kim said she was staying at yours. What's going on, Steph? You're worrying me.'

Her breathing became shallow, panicked. Her body shook with fear. She didn't know what to say, nor how to say it.

In the end, she came out with: 'I don't know where she is. I've tried calling her, and I've gone to your home, but I don't know where she is. I think she's missing.'

'What're you talking about?'

Stephanie explained the situation as best she could.

'Why did you not tell me this earlier?'

'I tried…' Tears formed in Stephanie's eyes; she was moments away from collapsing. 'You didn't answer.'

'Jesus Christ. I'm coming back. I'll be on the first plane out of here. I'll be home as soon as I can. Please, please, please keep me updated.'

Stephanie nodded. 'I will.'

Jason swore as he hung up the phone. Silence fell in the room, but not inside her head, where a thousand different thoughts were flying off at thousands of different angles, colliding with one another, exploding, spiking her stress levels. Suddenly, the confines of her desk no longer worked, and the walls surrounding her began to close in, gradually enveloping her in darkness. Her breathing became shallower, and she started to hyperventilate. She rolled onto her side and tucked her knees into her chest.

You spiteful bitch! Don't talk to me like that again! You'll follow my rules while you're living inside my house.

As she lay there, tears trickling down the side of her face, her phone began ringing again.

Eyes blurred, she glanced at the screen.

Firstlings Care Home.

She answered the call. 'Hello?'

'Hi, is that Stephanie? It's Wayne from Firstlings. I'm just calling to let you know that your sister's here. She said she's having some issues with her phone and that you might have been trying to get hold of her. She didn't want you to worry.'

Stephanie shot up and clambered out from beneath the desk. 'She's with you?'

'Yes. She's been here a while actually. It's... it's your dad, you see...'

CHAPTER
EIGHTY-TWO

'He was perfectly fine in the evening,' Wayne began as he led her down the corridor towards her dad's room. 'He seemed his normal self. He was cracking jokes, giving us a couple of flashes of his cheeky smile, and then – boom. He just collapsed to the floor. If it wasn't for Meredith spotting him, I dread to think what might have happened.'

They rounded the corner and started down another corridor. Already, Stephanie could feel her body filling with dread, as if there were an evil presence, an evil bubble, surrounding her dad's room.

'So we got the local nurse down, and she suggested calling your sister,' Wayne continued. 'She's the only one we've got on record as an emergency contact, see.'

'That's for the best.'

Wayne made no gesture, nor offered her a dubious look. She imagined it wasn't the first time he'd heard it. Not every family was sunshine and rainbows.

'And did you say my sister's been here ever since?'

A nod. 'She arrived within the hour and hasn't left your dad's side since.'

That explained why she'd left the house, but it didn't explain why Kimberley hadn't messaged her or responded. Perhaps her phone had run out of charge; if she hadn't packed a charger for her overnight stay at Stephanie's, then the care home would have been the last place she'd find one.

'Where is she now? I didn't see her car in the car park.'

'I think she went out to get some bits. We've offered her food while she's been here, but between you and me, I don't blame her for wanting to go out.'

Before Stephanie could respond, they arrived at her dad's room. Everything was exactly as it had been during her last visit. Nothing had moved, and it looked as if the room had been staged. The photos sat neatly on the chest of drawers. The duvet cover remained the same. The shoes were in the same position on the floor. As was her dad, sitting upright in his chair.

In all honesty, Stephanie couldn't see a change in him. He looked the same as he always did. Well. Too well for a man filled with evil. A part of her had hoped that the news would be different; that Wayne would be telling her that her dad had passed. That he'd finally gone, left them for good. Sadly, that wasn't to be.

She grabbed her necklace as she crossed the threshold into the room.

He glanced up at her, his face lifting into a smile. 'Stephy! My darling! You've come to see your dear old dad?'

He seemed more lucid than before.

Stephanie said nothing as she lowered herself onto the end of the bed, unable to bring herself to look him in the eyes. He reached out a hand. She didn't move. Her body tensed, praying he wouldn't touch her. Mercifully, she was too far away, and his hand fell short of her knee.

'Well...' Wayne began, 'I'll leave you two to it. I'll see if I can get hold of your sister and let her know you're here.'

Please don't go, she thought. Please don't leave me here with him.

Before, she'd had the comfort blanket of Kimberley with her. Kimberley doing the talking, keeping the peace, maintaining the façade.

The room fell into an awkward silence. Out of the corner of her eye, she saw her dad staring at her, his arm still outstretched, willing her to make contact. She shuddered at the thought of his touch and shuffled uncomfortably on the bed. As she moved farther away from him, her gaze fell on something at the head of the bed. She froze. Stared at it.

Bart. Her beloved cuddly bear.

Her mouth fell open as she stared at it. Kimberley must have taken it from her bedroom and given it to him. She imagined her intentions had been pure and kind-hearted, but she doubted her sister had considered the psychological impact of it.

Then again, how could she? When she knew so little?

Colin noticed her attention was distracted and reached out for the teddy bear. He took the cuddly toy from the pillow, placed it on his lap, and began bouncing it up and down as if it were a child.

'Bart…' he said, traces of a memory lighting up his face.

'I… I have to go,' she said, and started out of the room. She didn't stop when she heard him calling her back. Frustration grew within her. She wanted to reach out and snatch the bear from him. She wanted to suffocate him with it. But she couldn't bring herself to be near the man longer than she had to be.

As she rounded the corner, Wayne appeared, carrying a trolley filled with cleaning materials. They came to a sudden stop.

'Sorry,' she said. 'I need to find my sister…'

Just as Wayne was about to respond, a harsh buzzing sound travelled up the corridor. An alarm. Coming from her dad's room.

'It's the emergency buzzer,' Wayne said. He left the trolley behind and sprinted towards the room. 'Your dad…'

Against her better instincts, she followed. Perhaps it was her innate desire to help people. Or perhaps it was morbid curiosity that made her follow. That he might actually be dead. Or at the very least, dying.

When she arrived at the room, she found him on the floor, collapsed, his finger pressing the emergency button on the side of the bed.

CHAPTER
EIGHTY-THREE

A fall. He'd had a fall.

From the chair onto the carpet. That was it. A distance of a few feet. But from the way the nurse and staff treated him, it was as if he'd fallen from a thirty-storey building.

To make matters worse, in Kimberley's continued absence, she'd been asked to stay.

Rather, forced. The staff had guilt-tripped her into it, convincing her it was the right thing to do. That right now he needed someone because, in Wayne's professional opinion, he didn't look like he had long left. That perhaps the end was near.

Reluctantly, feeling like she had no other choice, she'd obliged and spent the past hour perched on the edge of the bed, scrolling on her phone, replying to emails, catching up with the rest of the team, letting Jason know that she and her sister were at the care home. She did everything possible to avoid speaking to or even looking at her dad. She'd notified Fiona and the team of her whereabouts, apologised for the inconvenience at such a pivotal stage in the investigation, and then asked for an update.

Giles' interview with Martin Bell had been less than helpful. However, there was hope. One of the members of Kent Police had spoken with a witness from the night of the vigil, who'd reported seeing what they believed to be Eve and a man getting into the back of a car. Their descriptions of both the man and car had been fuzzy, but they'd been given enough to go on. As a result, the team was now trawling through what little CCTV there was on the campus and surrounding area, searching for a vehicle that loosely matched the witness's description. It was all systems go, and from the buzz in the background while she'd been on the phone to Fiona, Stephanie couldn't think of anywhere she'd want to be less.

To make matters worse, Kim still wasn't answering her phone.

The whole situation concerned her. But she had no idea where to go, nor what to do.

In the end, she decided to do something she'd been meaning to for a long time. For the past thirty years.

'Don't suppose you know where Kimberley's gone, do you, Colin?'

He grunted, shaking his head.

Stephanie pushed herself off the bed and began pacing the room. She was frustrated and furious. While she'd been sitting there, she'd been thinking about all the things he'd done in his life. How he'd ruined her childhood. Destroyed her mentally and physically. Thirty years she'd wanted to say something to him, to get revenge. But she'd never been able to.

Now was her time.

She began opening his chest of drawers, the same way he'd done when she was a child.

'You know, Kimberley and I turned out all right.' Her eyes fell on a pair of his underpants. 'No thanks to you. I looked after her, treated her like my baby. I stepped up, made sure she had everything she ever needed. And you were nowhere to be seen. I didn't miss you. But she did. And I live with the decision of not telling her the truth every single day.'

She pulled out another drawer. Froze.

'I know,' came the response.

Hands gripping the edge of the drawer, she spun round and looked at him. Her body flushed cold, and she was frozen with fear.

'I know why you don't come,' Colin began, his voice lucid, almost demonic. As if he'd travelled back in time. 'I'm not stupid, Stephy. I've never been stupid.'

She opened her mouth, but nothing came out.

Her mind was too busy thinking about what she'd seen in the drawer.

Thread.

Stuffing.

Buttons.

Another doll.

Before she could think to do anything, Wayne appeared at the door. In his hand, he held a rolling pin.

Stephanie stood rooted to the spot, her mind instantly making the connection.

She met his eyes. Gone was the quiet, obedient carer. His face was twisted with panic and rage, his mouth turning into a leering sneer.

He raised the pin, ready to bring it down on her. But she was too fast. Instinct kicked in. She ducked, dodging the blow. The rolling pin whooshed past and cracked against the chest of drawers, splintering wood into the air.

Stephanie grabbed the pin and tussled with him over it. For a small man, only a few inches taller and wider than her, he was surprisingly strong. Just as she was about to take it from him, he kicked her in the shin and pushed her backwards. She stumbled and fell onto the carpet, the back of her head knocking into the wardrobe.

As Wayne brought down the pin for a second time, she kicked him in the groin, grabbed his hand, and threw him over her shoulder and onto the ground. Jiujitsu style.

The man yelped as she bent his wrist backward. She reached for the rolling pin on the floor, but he was too quick. He grabbed it before her and sent it flying into her shoulder. The pain from her biking accident a few days earlier flared, and she released her grip on his wrist and fell backwards.

As she regained her footing, Wayne bolted for the door. Stephanie darted after him, sprinting down the corridor, pulling her phone from her pocket. Using Siri, she called through to the office.

Devon answered.

'Send help!' she said between gasps. 'Firstlings Care Home. Quickly!'

Wayne barrelled down the corridor, skipping around a cleaning trolley, then shouldered through a fire exit. The alarm shrieked to life, echoing down the hall. Cold afternoon air hit Stephanie in the face as she followed him out of the back of the building, her shoes hammering the gravel path.

Wayne was quick. She would give him that. But she was quicker.

A moment later, he reached the car park, veering between vehicles. Stephanie closed the gap, her breathing sharp but focused. He glanced back, just once, and that was all she needed. She launched forward.

Her shoulder drove into his side.

Wayne grunted, spun, and they both went down hard on the gravel. He lashed out wildly, catching her cheek with the back of his hand. She ignored the pain that flashed in her cheekbone and wrapped her arms around him, locking his arm and neck through her arm, anchoring the hold in position with her other arm.

'Don't move!' she snarled.

The man yelped in pain again, but she didn't let up. She kept her arms firmly in place. No matter how hard he thrashed and kicked above her, he was locked, trapped.

The only problem was keeping him there. She had no idea how far away backup was. No idea how long it would take to rescue her.

Within moments, other members of staff started to filter out of the building, talking amongst themselves, questioning what was going on.

'Stay back!' Steph called to them. 'Someone call the police.'

Mercifully, as she said it, the sound of sirens in the distance pierced the air.

A minute later, backup arrived. Her muscles screamed beneath Wayne's weight, but she paid them no heed. She was relieved.

Even more so when she saw Devon clambering out of his car and sprinting over.

He wasted no time in prying Stephanie's grip from the man's neck, flipping him on the ground, and pinning him there with his knee pressed into Wayne's back. The uniformed officers that arrived moments after Devon piled in and cuffed Wayne's hands behind his back.

As they hauled him off the ground, Devon came over and asked, 'Are you okay? Are you injured?'

She didn't respond.

'Steph? Are you there? Is everything all right? What about your dad?'

Her eyes darted towards Devon before she spun on the spot and sprinted back into the home. She tore through the crowd, skipped around the obstacles in the hallway, and raced towards his room.

When she got there, she found the room empty. He had gone. On the armchair, in his place, all that remained was another voodoo doll, staring back up at her.

CHAPTER
EIGHTY-FOUR

Her vision had become blurred and unfocused. Her mind was numb. She was only vaguely aware of the flurry of bodies moving quickly around her and the voices of her concerned colleagues trying to make contact.

It wasn't until Fiona forced a glass of water into her face that her vision cleared and she came to.

'Drink.'

It wasn't a question; it was an order.

Stephanie took the glass from her colleague and absentmindedly held it to her lips, as if she'd forgotten how to drink, how to even function. Fiona assisted by tipping the glass of water down her throat.

'Are you okay?' she asked. 'Do you need anything?'

Stephanie surveyed her surroundings. She was in her office, with four other people – far too many in such a small space. Outside, the sound of chatter, conversation, and telephones ringing filtered through. Beside her were McGowan, Fiona, Devon, and Olivia. She looked at each of them in turn.

'Where's my sister?' she asked.

'We're working on it,' McGowan replied. 'Wayne's being interviewed as we speak. We're hoping he might be able to tell us where she is.'

'Pointless,' she replied, lowering the glass to her lap.

'Why?'

She didn't answer. Inside, she knew the secret to her sister's whereabouts lay with her father, the man who had been intent on ruining her life since the very beginning. That he had been in control of everything from the start, the puppet master, with Wayne as the puppet.

'Has he said anything?' she asked, not looking at anyone in particular.

A moment of hesitation. 'It's been fairly straightforward so far. No comment all the way, as you'd expect.'

She smirked involuntarily. 'Of course. He's controlled and manipulated the man for so long. Of course he's not going to tell you what you want to know.'

That can only come from the man himself.

'Steph, what are you trying to say?' The question came from Fiona.

She wanted to answer her colleague, her friend, but she couldn't. She couldn't bring herself to share the truth with these people.

Not yet.

'I need some space,' she said, as pain suddenly welled inside her skull. She tilted forward, wincing. 'I just need time to think.'

'Are you sure?'

'*Please* leave me.' She ensured there was enough desperation in her tone for them to comply.

Within seconds, the team were out of the office, and the room fell silent.

Sitting in her desk chair, her eyes fell on her bag. Protruding from the top was the doll she'd found on her dad's chair. Something had compelled her to pick it up, to take it, to smuggle it with her. Also in her bag was Bart, her teddy bear. For obvious reasons, she had wanted to rescue him before the crime scene investigators began turning her dad's room over.

As she reached for the teddy bear, her phone vibrated in her pocket. The sensation sent shivers up and down her spine, filling her body with dread.

She removed the device and glanced at the screen.

Unknown number. But she knew exactly who was calling her.

She answered the call and carefully held the phone to her ear, holding her breath.

'Hello, Stephy,' came the voice that ignited a fire of fear and fury within her. 'I suppose you're wondering what the hell's going on. But then again, you were always a clever girl, too clever for your own good, so I suspect you've managed to piece some of it together.'

What do you think you're doing, you naughty girl? Come here, come here now!

'Would you like to see Kimberley?'

She clung to her necklace.

'She'd like you to come and say hello. I think there's a family discussion the three of us need to have.'

'Where?'

'You know where, Stephy. You've always known how this would end; the place it all began.'

CHAPTER
EIGHTY-FIVE

She hadn't been to her childhood home in over thirty years, ever since her mum died and she and Kimberley were moved into care. Since that night, the night everything changed, she had vowed never to return. Never to think about it. Never to set foot in it again.

That was all about to change.

She had grown up in Park Barn, in the north of Guildford, in a small two-bedroom terraced house. For years, she had wondered what the neighbours thought about the events that took place in her home. They must have heard the screaming, the banging, seen the bruises, and yet they'd done nothing about it. No tip-offs to the police. No visits to speak with her mum. Nothing. Complicity in the form of polite nods and averted eyes.

She doubted they were still there; the neighbours on either side had been in their fifties when she was growing up, so they had either passed away or moved on. A part of her wanted to ask them why they'd never sounded the alarm at the first sign of abuse.

If they had, perhaps her mum would still be alive.

Stephanie slowed the car to a stop outside the house that had made her. Broken her. It hadn't changed much. The driveway was cracked, with weeds growing through. The pebbledash façade was worn and decrepit, covered in brown stains from years' worth of grime and rainwater. The wooden window frames were chipped and rotted. The place had fallen to pieces over the years, its decline advancing since her dad went into the home. But what struck her most was the silence. A thick, expectant kind of silence. The kind she remembered from childhood, when footsteps in the hall meant danger, and the safest thing to do was breathe silently and make yourself invisible.

A gust of wind swept around her legs as she climbed out of the car and shut the door behind her. Despite the urgency of the situation, she was in no rush. She knew that, for the time being, while she was out of the house, her sister was very much alive. Her dad would cause Kimberley no harm. Not without her present.

The air smelled of rain, sharp and bitter. She clutched her coat tighter around her as she approached the house. Each step brought the past crashing in: the sound of a belt being ripped from a loop; the heat of a lighter flicked too close to her skin; her mother's screams as he forced himself onto her.

Stephanie took a deep breath as she reached the front door. To her surprise, it was open, left ajar just for her.

She gave it a gentle nudge and was immediately assailed by the smell of damp, accompanied by flashes of memories from her childhood. Coming home from school to find her mum at the bottom of the stairs, crying; Kimberley screaming upstairs; her dad shouting from the kitchen—

'Stephy!'

The call took her by surprise and filled her with dread. Almost as if he could read her mind, he appeared in the kitchen at the end of the hallway, his arm wrapped around Kimberley's neck, a kitchen knife pressed against her skin. Stephanie kept her gaze like steel. She wouldn't give him the satisfaction of seeing fear on her face. Not now. Not ever.

The man in the doorframe was completely different from the one she'd seen at the home. The slouched hulk of a man had given way to someone tall, taller than she remembered. And the washed-out, catatonic expression, the mask he'd worn for so long, was now replaced by someone lucid and calculating, who knew their next step and the step after that. Kimberley, by contrast, was a mess. She looked as though she hadn't slept in the time she'd been missing; her make-up was streaked down her face, her hair was dishevelled, and her eyes were red from crying.

'Give me your phone,' Colin began, pressing the knife deeper into Kimberley's throat. Stephanie kept one eye on the blade and one eye on her father. This wasn't about Kimberley. This was between the two of them. 'I know you've come alone,' he continued, 'but just to be safe.'

Colin gestured for her mobile. She pulled it out of her pocket and threw it over to him. He caught it in his hand and then switched the device off. No contact with the outside world. Just the three of them.

'Isn't this nice?' Colin continued. 'The family back together again.'

'Let Kimberley go,' she said. 'She has nothing to do with this.'

'Not unless you call me Dad.'

Stephanie's mouth went dry involuntarily.

'Steph, what's going on?' Kimberley asked, panting. 'Why is this happening?'

'Would you like to tell her, or shall I?' Colin said.

'Tell me what? Why are you doing this, Dad?'

Stephanie held her breath as the knife pressed deeper into Kimberley's neck. In that moment, as she feared for her sister's life, everything became clear.

'It was you…' Stephanie said, a catch in her voice. 'All along.'

Colin bared a set of yellow-stained teeth as he nodded cynically, a hint of glee creeping into every corner of his expression.

'But you couldn't do it alone,' she continued. 'You had help. Wayne…'

'He's not the sweet and innocent worker your sister makes him out to be.'

Stephanie said nothing. She waited for him to continue of his own volition, letting his ego fuel the conversation.

'We met in prison,' Colin began. 'He was one of the workers who helped offenders with their rehabilitation. I met him one afternoon and saw a darker side to him. He had a peculiar fascination with the people in there and the things they'd done. He particularly took a liking to me, and likewise. He was quiet, reserved, shy. I sensed there was a part of him that could be easily manipulated. Over the months and years, we saw a lot more of each other; I convinced him to smuggle some things through for me; we even exchanged phone numbers. And that was when I knew I could get him to do whatever I asked. Don't ask me why; perhaps he respected me in some way. Perhaps I reminded him of a father he never had. Then we got talking about what we'd done, about why I was in there. And then we came up with a plan.'

Colin removed the blade from Kimberley's neck and pointed it at Stephanie. In the low light, the blade shimmered ominously. 'Prison is a horrible place, but do you know what it's good for? Time. Time to think things through. Time to plan and perfect, time to sow the seeds that will later come to fruition. Time for me to get my revenge.'

'You should never have been let out of there,' Stephanie hissed, her voice cold.

'I should never have been in there in the *first place*.'

Stephanie's eyes flitted towards Kimberley's, whose were hopelessly fixed on her.

'How did you do it?' she asked.

Pride flashed across his face. 'Which bit?'

'All of it. The home. The murders. The dolls…'

His smile turned into a grin. 'The killings were easy. You can be anonymous on campus; you can be anyone, blend in. There are so many people, nobody's going to look at you, nobody's going to think of you any differently. So after a bit of undercover work – scouting out the different societies, monitoring the girls' movements – we knew when the time was right.'

'Wayne did it all while you just sat indoors. He took all the risks.'

Colin shrugged. 'He's an adult. He can make his own choices.'

'Except you manipulated him. You fed him lies. You *controlled* him.'

'I hear that's what I'm good at…'

Stephanie had no response. Her mind was racing, trying to keep up. But despite the noise in her head, she felt a sudden clarity, as if everything made sense.

'Wayne followed Claudia Bellini home on the night he killed her, saw she was legless, and then helped her into her flat. She had absolutely no idea what was going on. He could have done anything to her, and I mean anything, had it not been for my instructions. He took her to her room, messaged her friends, and then killed her. He was out of there before anyone returned.'

'How did he escape?'

'It's easy to slip out of campus if you know how,' he answered. 'Blind spots are everywhere.'

'And Paulina Potter?'

'Easy. She was alone in the room. That one didn't require much effort. He just had to slip away… blend back into his surroundings.'

'Maya…?'

His voice became animated, as if he were revelling in the retelling of their deaths. 'Ahh, now *she* was difficult. From what he'd told me, she was a monster, not to be messed with in a face-to-face contest. So we made the playing field uneven, unfair.'

'He hit her around the back of the head, then drowned her.'

'It wouldn't have happened if he hadn't thought on the spot, though,' Colin added. 'We hadn't accounted for her getting a lift to campus. Fortunately, Wayne's got some intelligence and followed on his bike.'

Of course, a bike. It had never occurred to her that the killer would flee the scene on a bike. She had assumed either on foot or by car. A pang of stupidity and guilt exploded in her stomach.

'Priya. How did he kill her?' she asked.

'He got lucky with that one,' Colin responded, his excitement growing. 'We had hoped to set her on fire in her room, but she presented us with a fantastic opportunity in her car. We weren't in a position to turn it down.'

Stephanie felt sick at the way he was describing the killings, the joy he was deriving from it, the sense of accomplishment.

'Now, when it came to Eve,' he continued, 'I knew we had to be careful. I knew we had to play our cards right.'

'How did you know she'd be at the vigil?'

'I didn't. I just figured you'd want people there to stop anything happening, and Wayne knew what she looked like after following you guys around the place, so it was a happy coincidence.'

You don't know me as well as you think you do, she thought.

'Were the fireworks your doing?' she asked.

Colin shook his head. 'Another happy coincidence. Wayne protected Eve, took her away from the fireworks, and then into the back of his car.' Colin's eyes fell on the carpet. 'He struggled with that one. Said she was heavier than he expected. It didn't help that it was pitch black in the woods as well.'

'How did he get away with this when he was meant to be working…'

'He only works part time. Though that doesn't mean to say he hasn't got into any problems with his employers. When he was working, he was always with me, creating the dolls and perfecting the plan. When he wasn't, he was on campus, just another student blending into reality. He even joined one of their runs – unofficially, anyway – running behind them at a distance.' He tilted his head to the side. 'Planning the murders was easy. What took the longest was laying down the groundwork, making it look like I was slowly losing my mind, convincing my family that I had dementia and needed to be put in a home.' He kissed Kimberley on the cheek. 'Sorry, Kimbo. All part of the plan. At first, it wasn't easy. There was a lot of trial and error, and I had to start it all the way back when I was inside. By the time I got out, there was only one option: send me to the home where Wayne would already be waiting for me.'

Confusion crept into Stephanie's expression.

'All part of the plan,' Colin said. 'He quit the rehab gig and got himself hired at the home first, then waited for me to arrive. We thought there would be an issue of me getting in, given my criminal record, but they didn't seem to care.'

Stephanie's eyes flickered towards her sister. She remembered the number of times Kimberley had approached her about which was the best home to put their dad in. Apparently, he'd started displaying signs of dementia and needed somewhere to go. Stephanie had neither cared nor wanted to know, so she'd left the decision to Kimberley, a decision they both now regretted.

'Why?' The question came from Kimberley and surprised them both. 'Why have you done this?'

By now, the tears on her sister's face had stopped, and the look of anguish had been replaced with a mixture of fear and desperation.

'Why have you done this?'

Colin chuckled demonically. 'Would you like to tell her, or shall I, Stephy?'

Stephanie tried to swallow, but her mouth was dry. She shuffled uncomfortably on her feet and began to feel hot beneath her jumper and coat.

This was it. The moment she had hoped would never come.

'It's time for you to learn the truth, Kim.' Steph looked deeply into her sister's eyes, and for a moment, it felt like it was just the two of them, hiding in the cupboard, holding onto each other's hands. 'Phillip never killed Mum,' she began, her voice almost a whisper. 'It was Dad. Years before it happened, even before you were born, he abused us; me and Mum. Physically, emotionally, mentally. Mum got the brunt of it. She was always the one leaving the house with more bruises than she had the day before. I got my fair share of it too, but Mum had it worse. The screaming, the shouting as he beat her and raped her. Some nights I couldn't cope, so I went in to defend her, but that only made it worse for me. And then you came along, and I knew I had to protect you, so that's why you and I used to hide in the wardrobe or under the bed. We used to sing songs so you wouldn't hear. We started to colour in to deal with the pain; that's why I took up painting. You were too young to remember any of this, though I think on some level you've probably repressed it, pushed it deep down where nobody, probably not even yourself, could find it. Nevertheless, I tried to protect you. And…' A tear formed in her eye and she felt a lump catch in her throat, which she swallowed down. 'And on that night, I knew something had to change. Because Mum was dead, and without her, he would have killed us next.'

'But you always said that Phillip killed her,' Kimberley said, her voice numb.

'To protect you. Dad strangled her on the sofa. I saw it all. I was the one who called the police. But to protect you from it, I lied and told you that someone else had done it and Dad had killed them in retaliation. Phillip was just a random person I made up. I don't know why I didn't tell you the truth. It would have been easier for both of us.'

'How could you?'

Steph broke eye contact and looked at the ground. 'I wanted to protect you.'

Kimberley tried to wipe away the tears streaming down her face, but Colin stopped her with a wave of his hand. 'Dad?' she asked. 'Please tell me this isn't true. Did you really kill Mum?'

Colin didn't reply. His expression turned dark, and his eyes narrowed on Stephanie.

'What did I tell you when the police took me away, Stephy?'

'That you would get your revenge.'

'That I would get my revenge,' he repeated. 'Yes. And how would you say it's gone so far?'

She didn't answer.

'I've done it. It may not be visible to everyone – after all, how is killing a load of random women revenge against the woman who put me in prison? – but *you* can see it, can't you, Stephy? Deep down, you know it's worked. Little by little, victim by victim, you've died inside. From what I hear from your wonderful sister here, the painter in you has vanished; you've stopped running, rock climbing, mountain biking, or attending jiujitsu class. Your entire life has become stale and stagnant. Everything about you, every part of your identity – your failed university education, your police career – it's all been chipped away until there's nothing left. Everything you've stood for has been killed. You are dead inside. And you know it. I can see it in your face.'

Stephanie felt numb. It was true. She was dead inside. He had killed her off, bit by bit. She now saw the relevance of each victim, the real connection behind them – *her*. She had been at the top of the tree, and each of their deaths had been another branch leading to her.

She had just never seen it.

The smirk returned to Colin's face. 'Impressive, isn't it? Now all I have to do to kill you entirely is take away the one last thing that keeps you whole – your family. Starting with your—'

Kimberley let out an ear-piercing scream that cut through the hallway. In the split second it took for the sound to register on Colin's face, she grabbed the blade with her hand, pushed it away from her neck, and ducked beneath it, freeing herself from his grasp. They began to tussle over the blade, screams filling the air, blood pouring from Kimberley's palm onto the steel. As Stephanie raced over, Colin pushed Kimberley away, kicking her in the stomach. Her sister collapsed to the ground, screaming in agony and clutching her belly.

In the scuffle, the blade fell to the carpet. Neither Stephanie nor Colin paid it any heed. They went for each other, grabbing whatever they could of one another's clothes. Stephanie tried to grapple with the man, putting her martial arts training to the test, but nothing worked. His hands clung to her face, fingers digging into her eyes. When she pulled away, she saw blood, Kimberley's blood, all over her arm and coat.

She lunged for him, bringing a fist down onto his cheek. He took a step back, dazed for an instant before he regained his composure. As Stephanie attempted to tackle him to the ground, he tripped her up and pinned her to the carpet. In an instant, his hands were wrapped around her throat, pressing on her windpipe and stealing the air from her body. Above her, she saw the demonic look in his eyes and the wicked, sinister grin on his face. It was the same expression he'd displayed whenever she had resisted him lifting her skirt and pulling down her underwear. Every time he had tried to force himself inside her.

Rapidly, she felt pressure begin to build in her head as she struggled to breathe. Colin growled and grimaced like a man possessed.

'You silly bitch!' he hissed, droplets of phlegm falling from his mouth. 'You were never strong enough to say no to me. Neither was your whore of a mother. Now it's time for you to die like her—'

He squealed like a pig as his body shuddered. Suddenly, he let go of Stephanie's throat and twisted his neck to look at the shiny metal object sticking out of his right shoulder blade. Behind him stood Kimberley, her face pale.

Stephanie gasped for breath, sucking in lungfuls of air. But it was too much. She coughed and spluttered as she crawled onto her elbows, then her hands and knees.

Meanwhile, Colin looked at the blade, at his daughter, and then back to the blade again. It was only a couple of inches deep. Not enough to seriously wound him or kill him.

He stumbled towards Kimberley, who had her back against the wall. As he neared, he pulled the blade from his shoulder like a rabid zombie in a horror movie and prepared to bring it down on her. Kimberley froze, rooted to the spot, her raised hands offering little protection.

Just as Colin brought the knife down, Stephanie grabbed it, stunning him. With her other hand, she prised it free from his grasp and took control.

The wound on his shoulder wasn't enough to stop him.

The wound on his shoulder wasn't enough to kill him.

But she would ensure the next one was.

So she plunged the blade into his stomach, inserting it deep into his abdomen. As soon as the knife penetrated his insides, Colin's eyes widened and his mouth fell open. He took a step back, the weapon sticking out of him like a cocktail stick, blood immediately spilling from the wound.

He collapsed to the floor, spluttering, convulsing, dying.

But it wasn't enough.

She had to make *sure*.

Pulling the blade out of his belly, she stabbed him again and again, repeatedly, slowly. Six times in all.

Once for each victim.

Savouring each incision.

'That's for Mum,' she said as she administered the final plunge of the knife.

She maintained eye contact with him as she leaned into the blade, pushing it farther into his body. He opened his mouth, but nothing came out. Then she reached into her pocket, pulling out the voodoo doll he'd left for her in the care home.

She placed it on his stomach, removed the blade, and then shoved it through the doll. 'This one's for you,' she said, her voice neutral, level.

Slowly, she watched the life leave his body until he gave one last gasp and his limbs fell limp by his side.

At that point, she rolled off him and rested against the wall, panting and catching her breath. Sitting on the opposite side, scrunched against the wall, was Kimberley, tears streaming down her face. They looked at one another and exchanged a glance.

Stephanie nodded. 'He's dead,' she said. 'He won't be in control of our lives anymore, Kim.'

Just as Kimberley was about to respond, a car pulled up outside, and a moment later, Devon appeared in the open front door. She hadn't realised, but she'd forgotten to shut it. The sergeant sprinted over, then skidded to a stop as he took in the scene.

'What the…?'

Stephanie glanced at the body, the knife, the blood. Then her eyes fell on her sister before turning to Devon.

'Are you okay?' he began.

'The situation's been dealt with,' she answered coolly. 'There won't be any more voodoo dolls appearing. What are you doing here?'

Devon let out a small chuckle. 'You won't believe it – intuition.'

She smirked.

'You left the office without telling anyone, so I figured something was wrong. A quick check on your phone signal showed you were last here, so I had a look. And then I found out why.'

'Are you alone?'

He nodded. 'But I'm going to need to call this in.'

As he spoke, the sound of police sirens approached in the distance.

'Looks like someone beat you to it,' she said, stretching her legs out.

Perhaps there were some good neighbours in the world after all.

CHAPTER
EIGHTY-SIX

The weak autumn sunlight beat down on them as they meandered along the lush green path, scuffing along the gravel. They were boxed in on either side by hedges and trees, thick with brambles, stinging nettles, and other unpleasant surprises. But along the way, through the gaps in the trees, glimpses of stunning fields stretched into the distance, delineated by rows of shrubs and trees.

Neither of them had spoken since they had started.

As they came to a small clearing in the hedge, DCI McGowan stopped. On the other side of the fence was a small group of police dog handlers and their canine friends, practising in the field. The dogs leapt over obstacles as their handlers barked orders, sprinting faster than Steph's eyes could follow.

Stephanie felt a smile creep onto her face, the first in the days since her suspension and the start of the IOPC's investigation into her conduct.

McGowan placed his hands behind his back. She felt the sun begin to warm her neck slightly.

A couple of moments passed before she spoke. 'You're not going to feed me to the dogs, are you, sir?'

McGowan gave her a sideways glance, a flicker of warmth behind his usually unreadable eyes. 'I think you've had enough chunks taken out of you the past few days, don't you?'

Stephanie let out a small breath of amusement.

'I've had a word with the IOPC and advised them you have a temporary suspension while everything goes on in the background.'

'Thanks, sir.' She watched one of the dogs chase after an evading suspect clad in protective clothing and leap onto him, pulling him to the ground. 'I wish I'd set one of those on my dad.'

'You still got the same end result,' McGowan replied slowly.

'He didn't suffer enough.'

At least, unofficially. Her official version of events had been that he had had a manic episode and, during a fit of rage, had attacked her and her sister with almost superhuman strength, leaving her with no choice but to defend herself the way she had.

Clive half-turned to her. 'Speaking of suffering…'

She let out a small sigh. 'I know what you're doing,' she murmured.

'Do you?'

'This is the part where you tell me I need a break.'

He didn't deny it.

'You've been through a lot. You lost a colleague, a friend. You almost lost your sister.'

She was grateful he didn't mention that she'd lost a father.

'I'm fine.'

'Steph…' McGowan studied her for a long time. A soft wind rustled through the hedge beside them. The barking and shouting in the field seemed to fade into the background. 'You need to grieve properly,' he said finally.

'No, I don't.'

'You do. You just won't let yourself.'

They stood in silence again, save for the distant thump of paws against soft grass.

McGowan stepped closer, his voice lower. 'You remind me of someone I used to know. A brilliant detective. Took on too much. Wouldn't share the weight with anyone.'

'What happened to them?'

He looked out across the field. 'They burned out. Just… flickered, then went dark. Never came back.'

Stephanie swallowed.

'I've been through enough to know my limits,' she responded. 'I… I'm in control. For the first time in my life, I feel like I'm finally in control.'

He looked deep into her eyes, sizing her up.

'It's funny, isn't it? He was out of my life for thirty years, maybe more. And yet it still felt like he had a hold over me, even though I never spoke about him, never saw him. It's just like he was there, you know. Lingering…'

'And now?'

'Gone.'

'I'm pleased to hear it. But I need you to promise me something, Steph.'

She turned to him.

'If it starts to feel too much, if you really start to feel it, then you come to me. No recrimination. Whatever you need.'

Steph's throat felt tight. But she nodded.

'Good.' He gave her shoulder the briefest squeeze. 'Now, come on. I hear Giles is finally taking his cast off today, and the team have got a wager on how bad it smells.'

CHAPTER
EIGHTY-SEVEN

Letting go of the wall was a welcome relief for her forearms.
Pop music filled the air as she gradually descended from the top of the climbing wall. A few moments later, with her feet safely on the ground, she unclipped herself from the harness and stared up at the route she had just conquered to achieve her personal best.

'Solid work,' said the instructor who had been guiding her. 'You ought to try bouldering next. No harness. Just you and the climb. It's a bit riskier, but you're the one in control.'

She was. Not just in rock climbing, but in every aspect of her life. She could feel it coming back – slowly.

There was, however, one area of her life in which she felt helpless.

'Maybe,' she said, then added, 'Excuse me,' as she padded across the mat to her bag. She crouched down, opened it, and pulled out her phone. Unlocking the device, she found Jason's number and dialled it.

The call connected after a few rings.

'Hey,' she said. 'It's me.'

A pause.

'Not right now, Steph. She's still not ready to talk.'

The words drenched her like cold water.

'I get it,' Stephanie replied. 'And the baby?'

Another pause. This time Jason spoke more quietly.

'Fine. The doctor said there's no lasting damage, but I'm worried about the mental side. She's not eating properly, not sleeping. She's struggling.'

'Can I come over and see her?'

'I don't think that's a good idea.'

'Please, Jason. She's my sister.'

'Now's just not the right time. You can see her when she's better.'

Stephanie let out a long sigh. 'At least tell her I called.'

'I will.'

Stephanie thanked him and then hung up. For a long moment, she just sat there, staring at the mat, surrounded by people laughing, chatting, climbing, and falling. Thinking about her sister, thinking about Colin. Two weeks had passed, and she had started to get her life back on track. She was eating properly again. She was running, exercising, and, more importantly, painting. She was beginning to feel like herself; a new version of herself, one that didn't have her dad's influence deep inside.

Except for her relationship with Kimberley. Her sister hadn't spoken to her since the night of the incident, and she there was no amount of convincing she could do to change that.

Even though he was dead, it felt as if her dad was in control of that aspect of their lives and had somehow convinced her sister to shut her out completely. For one desperate moment, she wondered if it would ever change. But then she remembered how much she had overcome, how much control she had taken back in such a short space of time, and how much more she had left to grow.

In time, she was sure their relationship would heal.

The future was bright, and she was determined to ensure everyone in her family was a part of it.

THE END

But not quite. The story continues with *The Bogeyman*, the next book in the series:

Sometimes to find the truth, you have to confront the nightmares of your past.
Thirty years ago, the people of Guildford were haunted by a figure who crept into children's bedrooms and watched them sleep.
When he escaped, he left behind a single party balloon.
And then he vanished. The visits stopped.
Now it's happening again.
Has The Bogeyman returned or is a copycat terrorising a new generation of victims?
With pressure mounting and panic rising, DI Stephanie Broadbent must untangle the past to stop a predator stalking the present.
But what she finds may bring her closer to home than she ever expected…

Coming August 30th
Click here to pre-order now

ALSO BY JACK PROBYN

The DI Stephanie Broadbent Surrey Hiller Crime Thriller Series:

BOOK 1: THE VOODOO KILLER

She returned home to start again. Instead, she woke the darkness she thought she'd buried. Before she's even settled in, a university student is found dead in her halls of residence after a night out. What first appears to be an open and shut case takes a darker turn when a voodoo doll is found near the body. Stephanie is forced to confront the ghosts of her past—while racing to stop a killer whose next move is already taking shape in thread and cloth.

Read The Voodoo Killer on Kindle and Kindle Unlimited

BOOK 2: THE BOGEYMAN

Thirty years ago, the people of Guildford were haunted by a figure who crept into children's bedrooms and watched them sleep. When he left, he left behind a single party balloon. And then he vanished. The visits stopped. Now it's happening again.

Read The Bogeyman on Kindle and Kindle Unlimited

BOOK 3: THE BURNING MAN

When the charred remains of a body are found in the quaint Surrey Hills, the trauma of DI Stephanie Broadbent's past is reignited. When another body appears, Stephanie uncovers a connection that threatens to set the world — and more bodies — alight.

Read The Burning Man on Kindle and Kindle Unlimited

ALSO BY JACK PROBYN

The DS Tomek Bowen Murder Mystery Series:

BOOK 1: DEATH'S JUSTICE

Southend-on-Sea, Essex: Detective Sergeant Tomek Bowen — driven, dogged, and haunted by the death of his brother — is called to one of the most shocking crime scenes he has ever seen. A man has been ritualistically murdered and dumped in an allotment near the local airport. Early investigations indicate this was a man with a past. A past that earned him many enemies.

Download Death's Justice

BOOK 2: DEATH'S GRIP

Annabelle Lake thought she recognised the Ford Fiesta waiting outside her school, and the driver in it. She was wrong. Her body is discovered some time later, dangling from a swing in a local playground on Canvey Island.

Download Death's Grip

BOOK 3: DEATH'S TOUCH

When the fog clears one December morning in Essex, the body of a teenage girl is discovered lying face down in a field. As a result, the case quickly lands on DS Tomek Bowen's desk who, while trying to juggle his newfound life as a single parent to a thirteen-year-old daughter, must unearth the deadly sequence of events and bring the truth to light.

Download Death's Touch

BOOK 4: DEATH'S KISS

The darkest secrets never stay secret for long…

When the body of a homeless man is discovered on Southend seafront, wedged between the beach huts of Thorpe Bay, the people of Essex don't raise an eyebrow.

But when the post-mortem reveals the identity to be that of local MP, Herbert Tucker, the town begins to sit up.

Download Death's Kiss

BOOK 5: DEATH'S TASTE

Some secrets never wash away…

On a windy and blistering cold morning, Morgana Usyk, owner of Morgana's Café, visits Mulberry Harbour a little over a mile out to sea. A short while later, her body is found in the shallows, floating beside the harbour.

Download Death's Taste

ACKNOWLEDGMENTS

No book is a solo project — and this one was no exception.

A massive thank you to my incredible beta readers for your insight, sharp eyes, and guidance. You helped me plug plot holes, catch the odd six-fingered character wandering off, and ensure the darker sides of Stephanie's personality were portrayed with authenticity.

Helen, Karina, Val, and Sharon — thank you. I'm so grateful for your time, your notes, and your belief in the story.

MAKE AN AUTHOR'S DAY

Here we are. The end.
 Well, I say "we"… I mean *you*. Thank you.
Thank you for getting this far and sticking with me as I conjure up these greatly wild and bizarre stories in my head, and then later translate them to paper (or rather, digital files).

Amazon is littered with millions of books (literally, and I don't use that term lightly), and so it's often difficult to find your next read. You just want to know which book to dive into next. But sometimes you don't have the time to sift through them all, so what do you do?

Look at the reviews, of course.

We use them in every aspect of our life. Restaurants. Films. Our next television set. Pair of headphones. Almost everything is governed by the thoughts of other people.

Crazy, isn't it?

But what happens when you come across a book with no reviews? You might shy away from it. It's difficult to trust the book.

Your time is precious. Your time is valuable. You don't want to be wasting it on disappointing stories. Nobody does. And I don't want that for you. Sometimes I worry the same thing might happen to this story. But there's a solution.

A review goes a long way. And it gives me the confidence to

continue crafting the crazy thoughts in my head — one day of turning this dream into a full-time career.

So, to help new readers discover the books, and to you reading more of the same, you can leave a review at the below links:

Amazon US
Amazon UK
Amazon CA
Amazon AU

Thank you.
Your Friendly Author,
Jack Probyn

IF YOU'VE BEEN AFFECTED

If you or someone you know is struggling with an eating disorder or the effects of abuse — support is available.

In the UK, you can contact:

- **Beat Eating Disorders** – beateatingdisorders.org.uk

- **Mind** – mind.org.uk

- **Samaritans** – samaritans.org

ABOUT THE AUTHOR

Jack Probyn is a British crime writer and the author of the Jake Tanner crime thriller series, set in London.

He currently lives in Surrey with his partner and cat, and is working on a new murder mystery series set in his hometown of Essex.

Don't want to sign up to yet another mailing list? Then you can keep up to date with Jack's new releases by following one of the below accounts. You'll get notified when I've got a new book coming out, without the hassle of having to join my mailing list.

Amazon Author Page "Follow":
   1. Click the link here: https://geni.us/AuthorProfile
   2. Beneath my profile picture is a button that says "Follow"
   3. Click that, and then Amazon will email you with new releases and promos.

BookBub Author Page "Follow":
   1. Similar to the Amazon one above, click the link here: https://www.bookbub.com/authors/jack-probyn
   2. Beside my profile picture is a button that says "Follow"
   3. Click that, and then BookBub will notify you when I have a new release

If you want more up to date information regarding new releases, my writing process, and everything else in between, the best place to be in the know is my Facebook Page. We've got a little community growing over there. Why not be a part of it?

Facebook: https://www.facebook.co.uk/jackprobynbooks

Printed in Dunstable, United Kingdom